UNSTITCH

ELODIE HART

Copyright © 2024 by Elodie Hart

All rights reserved.

No part of this book may be reproduced in any form or by any electronic or mechanical means, including information storage and retrieval systems, without written permission from the author, except for the use of brief quotations in a book review.

Cover image on ebook / special edition paperback is Mitchell Wick by Michelle Lancaster

For my readers.
Remember, you are worthy of love
exactly as you are.

CONTENT WARNING

This isn't a particularly dark book, but it contains adult themes and super high spice levels. If any of the below sounds like it's not for you, then please take care of yourself and walk away!

Unstitch is an MMF romance and contains graphic depictions of male-male sex and threesomes in various positions. It's set in a sex club and also contains some voyeurism. Max also does several things to Dex of a sexual nature without having had Dex's explicit consent first (biting and kissing mainly).

The main theme I'd like to draw your attention to is discussion of purity culture and religious beliefs (mainly Catholic) that range from conservative to downright radicalised. This results in graphic depictions of bigotry, homophobia, transphobia and hate speech. Dex, one of my MMCs, has internalised homophobia as a result of his upbringing.

There is no OW / OM drama and there is a great big HEA waiting for Dex, Darcy and Max at the end of the book.

PROLOGUE - DEX

Apparently, God is love.

Apparently, His love is boundless.

Call me crazy, but that sounds a lot like the *love is love* movement to me.

Except it's not.

It turns out, when God's love is filtered through endless rulemakers and gatekeepers and fearmongers, from those who penned the blood-curdling cautionary tales of the Old Testament to every fearful, dogmatic parish priest I've ever met, it emerges beyond recognition.

A love of bounds.

Of conditions.

Of expected conformity.

According to my parents, and to the priests and monks who taught me all through my formative years, God's love is straight and cisgendered and exclusionist. He may love a sinner, but our only chance of salvation, of basking in the unparalleled warmth of His love, is to repent. To promise not to sin.

Which comes to the crux of my problem.

The realest, most visceral, most pressing emotions, desires, I've ever experienced in my thirty years can all be classified as one neat category.

Sins.

So I suppress them. I deny them, even to myself, even knowing as a person of decent intelligence that there cannot truly be anything wicked about them.

And, every day of my existence, I attempt to make peace with knowing that this straight, bounded *thing*—the thing I've been taught exemplifies love—is as close as I'll come to the true experience of it.

But it's an uneasy peace, because this limited type of love cannot, surely, be the reason we've all been put on this earth.

1

DARCY

You know that part in *Pretty Woman* when Edward is taking in the sight of Vivian lying in his bed on that first morning, and her hideous blonde wig is nowhere to be seen, and her hair is the kind of gorgeous, glossy auburn that Julia Roberts pulls off so well, and it's *so much better* than the wig? Like, not even comparable?

Well, not to toot my own horn too much, but that's basically the level of transformation my sister Gen's genius hair stylist, Giorgio, has pulled off for me today in his swanky Chelsea salon.

It's weird. I was so morbidly obsessed with the prospect of skin damage when I was living in Australia that I wore sun cream obsessively. I literally slathered myself in the stuff. So my skin is actually pale and creamy and pretty fucking luscious, I would say.

Not so my hair.

Apparently, all those times I wore sun screen and a baseball cap did bugger all for my hair, which I totally neglected. The entire time, my poor hair was being nuked by good old Aussie sunlight and dried out by long days of surfing, which meant that the ponytail I left hanging out the back of my cap ended up nothing short of bleached and *stringy*.

Maybe it wasn't as helmet-y as Julia Roberts' blonde wig, but it was definitely as skanky. Let it be said, in a moment of humility, that until this afternoon, I had, as my sister put it, the hair of a skanky ho.

Nice.

This is where having an older sister who's not only obsessive about grooming and extremely generous but on the verge of marrying an actual billionaire comes in very handy indeed. Gen took one look at me after I turned up at her old flat last week and shuddered before speed-dialling her darling Giorgio and begging him to take me on.

I have to admit, he's as fun as he is talented. His initial judgy bitch face when he saw me has given way to some excellent gossip-sharing over the past two hours. Boy, does he have some famous clients. I could chat to him all day long. And now, as I gaze at myself in the mirror, I am fucking gobsmacked, which is no mean feat.

Given the way I began this story, it may not surprise you to hear that I've traded the skanky bleached blonde in for...

Red!

I know. Shocker, right?

Well, not red. I basically told him to give me *Pretty Woman* hair. And, given what he had to work with, I'd say the guy's a miracle worker. The hair in the mirror is three inches shorter than it was when I turned up—apparently the bottom three inches were way beyond salvageable—and sleek AF.

Giorgio explained to me that the semi-permanent vegetable colour and the gloss he put on afterwards would nourish my hair and add back shine, but this is a whole other level. I smile at myself in the mirror and shake my head, watching as my newly glorious mane swishes and bounces and settles around me like a soft chestnut cloud.

Sure, it's a tad Nineties Supermodel, but that's what you're gonna get when you ask for *Pretty Woman* hair. It doesn't matter, because I won't be able to pull off this level of blow-dry by myself, even with Gen's Dyson hairdryer.

Do you know what else it is?

Expensive.

That's right. I look expensive, which, aside from looking hot, was my number one objective when I turned up here today. Farewell, cheapo Gold Coast Darcy. Hello, expensive Mayfair Darcy.

This is an important thing to get right, because when I go up to dance on that stage at Alchemy Cannes, the seasonal French pop-up of the super-exclusive sex club my sister co-founded, I need to look classy.

It's not enough that my moves will be balletic. Mesmerising. Erotic beyond belief. My entire demeanour needs to scream *you can't afford me*, because nothing makes rich, entitled douches crazier than not being able to get what they want.

My sister, a woman not known for mincing her words, put it this way when she told me to *come the fuck home and stop fannying around on the other side of the world.*

'You don't touch them,' she said. 'And you definitely don't let them touch you. You're basically their fluffer. You're the one thing in that club they can't have, and it's going to piss them off. You'll be the shiniest jewel in there, just out of reach, and you'll fucking dazzle them. They're going to keep coming back, just to try to close the deal with you. And every time they fail, you'll send them a little crazier, and every time you do *that*, they'll stay longer and fuck harder and get more and more hooked.'

Let me tell you.

Red rag to a fucking *bull*.

I was booking my flight home even before she threw in the sweetest of all sweeteners: that I could live in her gorgeous, dreamy, magazine-worthy flat. For *free*. I suppose when your adoring fiancé has an enormous mansion in Holland Park and one in the South of France *and* the chalet version in Gstaad, you can afford to pay it forward to your penniless, pathetic little sister.

In case I haven't made it clear, Gen is probably my favourite person on the planet, and definitely my favourite person in our family. But I adore this mega-wealthy version of her even more.

And I can barely get my head around how much more amazing my London lifestyle will be thanks to her crazy generosity.

A job dancing at *the* most exclusive sex club in London —*and* its South of France outpost.

Check.

A beautiful, luxurious flat in South Kensington.

Check.

Now I just need the hot sex. If I know my sister, she'll cockblock as much as she needs to if it means keeping me away from her patrons. Keeping them ravenous and crazed with frustration.

I'm the juicy steak the club intends to dangle in front of the horniest, wealthiest men and women in Europe.

But none of them will be allowed to sink their teeth in.

2

MAX

Well, well, well.

Gen Carew's little sister is a fucking visual feast, that's for sure. And my excellent dinner at Hotel Eden Roc is long forgotten, because I am fucking *starving*.

The Carew women are something. I should know. I had the distinct pleasure of fucking Gen last year, when she and Anton—my best mate and boss—were playing mind games with each other. My colleague David and I may have got ourselves stuck in the middle of their screwed-up dynamic.

And by *stuck in the middle,* I mean Anton orchestrated a full-on group sex session in his office. I ended up fucking Gen on the floor while David, our in-house counsel, fucked her mouth. Anton managed every detail like a conductor coaxing the most intoxicating symphony out of an orchestra. And all the while, he was getting sucked off by his then executive assistant.

Ah, happy days.

Gen's a knockout. She's the full package, with her platinum hair and killer curves and even more killer *froideur*. I have never, in all the years I've known Anton, seen any of his ex-wives or girlfriends handle him like Gen can handle him.

It's no surprise she's turned the legendary Big Bad Wolff into a fucking Labrador puppy. A puppy so intent on freeing up more playtime with his favourite human that he's recently transitioned from CEO of Wolff Holdings, his extensive global web of corporations, to the far less onerous role of Non-Executive Chairman.

And who has he appointed to take the weighty reins as CEO, you ask?

Why, none other than his faithful Chief of Staff. Yours truly.

All of which gives me more reason to enjoy these aimless, halcyon nights under a vast, gold-shot sky before work kicks up a notch or ten. The fabulous pad just outside of Cannes that plays host to the hedonistic revellers in the summer months boasts an equally fabulous view. The Med sparkles in the distance of the ample grounds, and, in the foreground, the villa's smooth, well-irrigated lawns are dotted with white tents, as discreet as they are lavish.

Because there'll be far too much fucking tonight for one villa to accommodate.

I should know. Wolff Leisure, one of our subsidiaries, licensed the Alchemy name to test out the pop-up concept last summer, at this very location. It was a resounding success, to the point that we're rolling out two more European ones this summer in Ibiza and Mykonos, with a superyacht format in Monaco *and* a permanent Manhattan location set to open at Christmas.

Sex sells, and no one does it better than the Alchemy guys. I can personally attest to that.

Which brings me back to the delicious little bombshell in front of me.

Surely dancing is the single most effective leading indicator for how good someone will be in bed? If I'm right, Darcy Carew's undulations promise untold carnal pleasure.

I stand at the front of the throng of people and drink in the spectacle before me with the appreciation of a true connoisseur. This is the first time I've had the distinct pleasure of feasting my eyes on Darcy. She's been staying at Anton's pad with the rest of the Alchemy clan and their kids, so I've been slumming it at the Hôtel du Cap Eden Roc.

Gen told me her little sister was twenty-five—at least a decade younger than her. (She also told me to "keep my filthy paws off her", but I'm taking that with a pinch of salt.) She's young. Really fucking young, or so it seems to this forty-year-old guy.

She's also ravishing. *Ravishing.*

For this most carnal of celebrations, the Alchemy team has had an enormous gilded bird cage erected. One of the founders, Cal, masterminded this party. Previously, he's been the most fun of the lot of them—the others are far too loved up. He and I had an absolute blast out here last August.

But this year, he's wandering around with none other than the famous—and sexy as fuck—broadcast journalist Aida Russell on his arm, looking like he's been hit hard over the head with a love stick, so he's no fucking use to anyone.

Those Alchemy guys are dropping like flies.

Anyway. This contraption. It's fashioned like a huge, ornate Victorian bird cage, large enough for the mesmerising creature within to writhe sinuously, hypnotically. She's naked except for her high heels, an enormous pair of intricate wings, and a bodystocking dusted with tiny crystals. It's so sheer that the overall effect is one of shimmering nudity.

And let me tell you, this woman's brand of nudity is one I can get on board with.

Her sister has what I'd call a banging body. It's voluptuous and ultra feminine, with curves and dips enough to make a man weep. The kind of body that would make even the most seasoned sex maniac wish for a repeat performance, if said sex maniac wasn't so painfully aware of his boss' obsession with her.

She has the kind of body that even now brings an inner hit of triumph when I take her in and recall the delights hidden beneath her immaculate clothes.

(I will never admit that to Anton. Obviously.)

But I'll freely admit Darcy is on another fucking level. Yeah, she has tits and an arse, both of which are pretty damn important. But she's a dancer, and it fucking shows. She's strong and toned and compact, the sculpted planes of her upper arms and inner thighs as charming as the generous curves of those untethered tits.

Her hair is loose and glossily, gloriously chestnut. Her skin beneath that bodystocking is pale and creamy and flawless. Titian would have had a field day with this woman.

I'd have a field day with this woman.

The marks I could leave on that milky expanse of skin.
Teeth.
Lips.
Fingers.

The DJ we have here tonight has a hypnotic chillout tune going, with soaring vocals and a pulsing beat. The younger Ms Carew is going for it. Her movements are unhurried. Sensuous. She writhes and rolls and sways in her cage, gold-tipped wings flapping as she moves her arms, the setting sun casting her in a halcyon light so she appears to be made of gold and precious stones.

She's dancing to her own beat, seemingly oblivious to the crowd of partygoers around her. There, trapped in her gilded cage, she moves her glorious body, and I know every man watching wants to release her, if only to claim her immediately for himself.

Unfortunately for them, I suspect most of them don't have a tenth of the tenacity that I do. I adjust my trousers and sink my teeth into my lower lip as Darcy turns, and sways that impeccable arse, and spreads her legs, and bends all the way forward, wings fluttering behind her.

There's no diamanté between her legs. Nothing but the sheerest mesh to cover her. She's completely bare, and it strikes me that the sight of that glistening pussy is the most alluring jewel of all.

The roar of the crowd around me has nothing on the rush of blood in my ears.

3

DARCY

Being the designated fluffer at an event like this is decidedly un-fun.

I mean, come on. I'm in one of the most beautiful places on earth, at easily the most fabulous party I've ever attended, and I'm the star attraction.

Everyone wants me.

And no one can touch me.

What the actual fuck? I've been circulating for no more than half an hour since I finished my set and swapped out my bodystocking for a long, completely backless and fairly sheer black dress, and I could've got laid a hundred times over. Not just laid, but laid by guys who are so hot it is actually insane.

First, a good half of them are French or Italian. So there's that. Much as I appreciated the buff Aussie surfers, these European playboys with their sexy accents and dark hair and great tans and chic as fuck outfits are so outrageously hot that I'm sweating like a nun in a cucumber field.

It isn't bloody fair.

I only want one. Just one nice, fat, juicy dick as a reward for dancing so beautifully and working them all up.

Or maybe two.

This is an orgy, after all.

That's it. A lovely Euro dick or two and I'd be a happy girl. After all, I've never actually had more than one guy at a time, for all that I talk a good game, and it's a source of great misery to me. And now I'm here, and my sister doesn't want me to 'partake.'

A hot guy in all white saunters past and says something to me in French that sounds very, very dirty, and I swear my arousal starts to dribble down my inner thighs. Now that the sun has set, the real purpose of the party is becoming apparent. The rules are clear: the main outdoor space stays clothes-on. Nudity and fucking can be enjoyed inside the villa, which is fully set up for debauched kinkery, or in the white tents around the periphery of these beautiful gardens.

The night air is thick with the scent of citronella candles and the sultry bass of the music. Above the beat dance laughter and conversation in a dozen languages. Meanwhile, I feel like the sad little princess whom everyone came to see but whom no one's allowed to touch.

I amble over to the funky perspex bar to order myself a consolation cocktail. No point in going indoors—I may as well stay out here with the rest of the losers who aren't getting laid. I'm enjoying the arse of the sexy French barman as he mixes my mojito when I hear a deep voice say my name.

It's my future brother-in-law, and he's not with my sister. What a shocker. I thought they were joined at the hip. 'Hey,' I say. I give him a bright smile. He's ridiculously old, but I can still appreciate what an attractive guy he is. That Big

Dick Energy of his is undeniable. And he makes my sister deliriously happy, so I'm definitely a fan.

Besides, he's the most generous host *ever*. Staying at his villa this weekend is the highlight of my life—even without any sex.

'I heard your dance was fantastic,' he says. 'I didn't think it was appropriate to watch it. I stayed well away.'

That makes me laugh. 'Yeah. It probably would have been creepy to watch your future sister-in-law dance in the nude. *Especially* as I'm young enough to be your daughter.'

He swipes me playfully on my shoulder. 'Watch it, kiddo. I do have someone I'd like you to meet, though. Rather, he's desperate to meet you.'

'Desperate, you say?' I ask, arching an eyebrow at him as I accept my mojito from the smiling barman and turn around.

'*Ravenous*, more like,' Anton's friend says, and there's something about the way he drawls it in his posh accent that stops me in my tracks.

I take him in.

Holy fucking Christ.

There are a lot of hot, rich, confident guys here tonight, but this one takes the cake.

He stands perfectly still, one hand clutching a tumbler and the other slung casually in his pocket. But his eyes aren't still. No, sir. They're taking in every single *inch* of me like I'm the most sumptuous feast he's ever seen and he wants to gobble me up. The guy doesn't lie. He's *starving*.

As we stand there and eye fuck each other so hard I may actually get pregnant, I devote the same attention to him that he's lavishing on me. He's very, very good-looking in a way that's predictable enough to make me despise myself.

Light brown hair, slicked back. He's an inch or two

shorter than Anton, who's seriously tall, and has a leaner build. I bet he's athletic, though. Great posture. His eyes are blue and piercing, even in this dim light. He's hot and patrician and looks like he was brought up with yachts and ski chalets and vintage cars. He's every British fantasy Ralph Lauren ever had. Even his jaw looks well bred.

Ugh.

He's in much the same uniform as a lot of the guys here - beige chinos and a white linen shirt.

But it's none of that stuff that gives me pause, necessarily. It's his demeanour. If his face is that combination of pretty and chiselled that only the likes of Matt Bomer can usually get away with, everything about the way he's sizing me up tells me this guy is a fucking animal.

Some people exude sex, and this guy is one of them. So everything falls into place when Anton says, 'Darce, meet my good mate, Max.'

4

MAX

I watch her beautiful face brighten with the light of clarity when Anton says my name.

'*Max,*' she says, her mouth twisting in an amused smirk that tells me she's heard far too much about me. 'Got it.'

I don't take the bait.

'How do you do?' I ask as I lean in to kiss her on both cheeks, allowing my free hand to brush her upper arm as I do. She smells like fucking roses and her skin is velvety.

'I should caveat this entire introduction,' Anton says with a nervous glance over his shoulder, 'by saying Gen's already warned Max off you. And if she finds out I've facilitated your meeting, there'll be hell to pay.'

Darcy cocks her head as she openly surveys me once again. 'I bet she has.' I suspect she knows all about my previous encounters with her older sister, but even I have enough emotional intelligence not to rub Anton's nose in the fact that the love of his life has, in fact, shagged his best friend. Even if he was the Master of Ceremonies for that little party.

'Yeah.' He looks over his shoulder again. Bloody hell, Gen has truly pussy whipped this powerful man beyond all recognition. 'Unfortunately for me—and you—Max is very persuasive.'

'I am.' I grin at Darcy. 'And I always get what I want.'

'Is that a fact?' she asks before taking a sip of her drink through her straw. I watch her lips close around the paper and marvel at how seductive that little gesture is.

'Mate,' I say to Anton, suddenly impatient for an opportunity to work my charm on her. 'You can clear off now.'

'No.' He looks from me to Darcy and back. 'I—'

'Go,' I tell him. 'I'm sure Gen's wondering where you are.'

That does it. He begins to back away. 'Okay, well'—he waggles a finger at me—'behave yourself. All right? There's an entire garden full of women to fuck. But don't. Touch. Darcy.'

I roll my eyes at him and wait until he's disappeared off to find his paramour before turning my attention back to Darcy. I take a couple of steps closer, effectively caging her in at the bar.

Fuck, she's stunning. This little black dress is a fucking joke—I can see her pert nipples outlined in the centre of her perfectly round tits. The stretchy fabric showcases every spectacular curve, and her chestnut hair falls in soft waves over her shoulders. She has the same big blue eyes as her sister, but facially they're quite different. Darcy's face is more elfin.

'The problem with being told not to do something,' I muse aloud as I look down at her, 'is that it always, without exception, makes me want to do it even more badly.'

She releases her straw and gazes up at me through her lashes.

'Yeah, I get that. I have the same unfortunate wiring. And what is it you want to do?'

'Not what.' I trace a light, but deliberate, fingertip down her bare arm. Her ensuing shiver is gratifying. 'Who.'

'You're too old for me.' She sounds like she's trying to convince herself.

I scoff. 'I'm forty.'

'From where I'm standing, that's not exactly a great defence.'

'I'm not old,' I insist. 'I'm experienced. There's a difference.'

'Yeah. I bet you're just *crawling* with experience,' she says, and I have a sudden urge to dip my head and sink my teeth so deeply into the luscious skin of her shoulder that it knocks every brattish thought right out of her head.

'I'm not crawling with anything, you insolent girl.' I tell her sternly. 'I get tested once a fortnight.'

Her eyebrows fly up. 'Once a *fortnight*? You must be having a lot of sex.'

'I am. Your sister and her friends run an amazing outfit at Alchemy. I'd be stupid not to avail myself of it. My point is, you'd be safe with me. Actually, let me rephrase.' I close the last remaining foot between us and trail my fingertips back up her arm, up the creamy column of her neck, and along her jaw. 'You'd be completely safe with me where STDs are concerned, and very, very unsafe in every other way. Do you get my meaning?'

Her rose scent mingles with the scents of this beautiful Mediterranean evening, and it's heady beyond belief. Her breath is coming faster now, tits heaving.

Message received loud and clear.

She licks her lips. 'Sadly for me, I'm not supposed to

fraternise tonight. They just brought me in to get everyone hard.'

'I bet they did, you little tease. Well, you certainly did that. Every single man in this place wants to fuck you. And probably most of the women, too. How does that make you feel?'

'Pissed off beyond all belief,' she says with a pout, and I laugh. I suspect she's just like me.

Used to getting what she wants.

'Who imposed this little non-fraternisation policy?' I ask, and then I answer my own question. 'Genevieve, of course. And do you always do as you're told?'

'I do when she's given me a job and her very nice flat,' she says. 'For now, anyway. I don't want to fall at the first hurdle, you know? Anyway, I'm not interested in fucking you.'

What a bare-faced little liar.

'Bollocks,' I say, affording her pointed nipples an equally pointed glance.

'I'm not. When in France, you know? French guys are so hot. It'd be a shame to waste this evening on a crusty old Brit.'

I spit out a surprised laugh. She really is a piece of work. 'I'd like to put you over my knee and spank that insolence out of you. And I think you'd like that, too. But it'd be a waste of my time, because there are lots of gorgeous women here who want my cock tonight—and a good number of those hot French guys too, probably. Whereas it sounds like you're not getting any cock tonight. Of *any* nationality.'

She sets her jaw like a pissed-off teenager, and I lean in to her ear. 'It was an absolute pleasure to spar with you, Darcy. Enjoy your evening of enforced celibacy and excruciating frustration.'

I pull back enough to shoot her my dazzling signature smile before turning on my heel and heading out into the throngs of beautiful people.

I got the last word, naturally.

I always do.

5

DARCY

If I wasn't facing out onto one the most beautiful views I've ever seen, I'd be extraordinarily pissed off. As it is, I'm fairly pissed off. I stare out at the gorgeous vista from the fancy terrace in Anton's insane pad. The terrace leads onto an emerald green lawn—irrigation costs be damned—that in turn runs down to a spectacular pool area via a shallow flight of sandstone steps.

Beyond the pool? Pines. And then a drop to the Med itself, sparkling and glorious and its trademark azure on this perfect June day.

My sister told me she and Anton first got it on—after an extensive period of mind games on her part and ambushes on his—at this very table. That they first fucked down by the pool. That's kind of hot and kind of creepy, because, come on. She's my sister. And he's old. But it's still pretty cool.

I can definitely see the attraction of having a super hot, super eligible billionaire trick you into staying with him alone at his evil lair and then seducing you by the pool.

I'm just happy someone's getting some action, because

I'm definitely not. Last night's Alchemy opening night was the equivalent for me of dehydrating to death on a life raft in the middle of the ocean. Men, men, everywhere, and not a single one to fuck.

Just the thought of it fucks me off, and I may stab at a sliver of perfectly ripe cantaloupe a little harder than necessary. Two rounds with my rose vibe when I got home took the edge off, but wasn't the same. It was the equivalent of trying to fill yourself up with a protein shake when you really want a bar of chocolate.

The worst part was that it wasn't the endless array of hot Europeans that got me off in that dark room beneath my pristine white duvet, but the memory of that guy, Max, telling me he wanted to put me over his knee.

I bet he would have.

I bet he would have thrown me over his shoulder, and carted me off to some tent, and *fully* taken control.

Ugh. I suppress a full-body shiver, because I wasn't lying last night. I'm not interested in fucking him. There's the smorgasbord of gorgeous guys that Alchemy affords me (or at least affords people who are allowed to avail themselves of it), and then there are guys like him. Guys who are simply too much. Guys who could easily get under your skin.

I didn't come back to the UK for *that*.

Breakfast at Anton's villa is a family affair. His own kids aren't here. There wasn't enough room for them this weekend, but they'll be here, obviously, in a few weeks, when Anton and my sister tie the knot. I cannot *wait* to see her in stepmother mode. It will be fucking hilarious, especially since it sounds like his twins are mini versions of how I was at their age, but with presumably a tonne more entitlement than I had. It'll be priceless, and I intend to have a front-row seat.

Even without his kids, his huge villa is rammed. Two of my sister's three best mates from uni are here. Rafe and his new wife Belle, who I haven't met yet, are still away on their honeymoon. Zach's here with his two sweet little girls and fiancée Maddy, who I've already fallen madly in love with. And—be still my beating heart—Cal's here too with his girlfriend and her two boys.

Cal. Sigh. The crush I had on that guy when I was like eight or nine and Gen used to bring her mates home from uni for the weekend. Rafe was too cool for school, and I always remember Zach being handsome and sweet and pretty quiet, but Cal? He was so patient with me, and he looked like a model. He was better looking than any popstar.

I may or may not have named one of my Ken dolls Cal. The name lasted for a couple of years, but that is a secret I'll deny until my dying day.

Anyway, he may still be hot as fuck, but my hero worship of him has long faded. He's just a great looking, fun guy. Besides, he's revoltingly in love with Aida Russell, which kind of blows my mind. Should have known he'd end up with an actual celebrity, though I wouldn't have guessed he'd go for a strikingly sophisticated older woman.

If anything, Zach and Maddy are the biggest surprise. Obviously, I followed the tragedy of his late wife's horrifyingly fast demise from cancer from a distance. I was in Oz by then, but Gen kept me posted. It was so horrific.

So it's amazing to see him here with his daughters, having a blast, while being head over heels for Maddy. From what I've seen, she and I have a similar personality type, so seeing her with the Hot Nerd is all kinds of fun. I've heard her call him Spreadsheet once or twice, too, which cracks me up.

Of all the couples here, my sister and Anton are the most obvious fit. She tried to feed me some *opposites attract* bullshit about him, but it's clear these two belong together.

Naturally, a breakfast table that's as heaving with kids as it is with delicious food is not the place for a post mortem on last night's shenanigans. I console myself with the knowledge that no one around this table will have wild tales to share, given how coupled-up they all are. Instead, the conversation focuses on the plans for today. In a nutshell, Anton will take Zach, Cal and the kids out on his boat for a couple of hours, leaving the womenfolk to sunbathe and gossip.

Sounds just the ticket after last night.

6

DARCY

'So, you were definitely the star of the show last night,' Maddy tells me as she tops up my rosé. The boys and kids are blissfully absent and she, Aida, Gen and I are camped out on two of the huge daybeds. The pool is empty and tranquil, and the air is quiet. I swear, Cal makes more noise in the pool than any of the kids combined.

'Thanks, love,' I tell her, peering dolefully into my glass. 'Fat lot of good it did me, thanks to Cockblocker Carew here.' I jerk my head in my sister's direction.

Maddy belly laughs. 'I can't believe you dragged your sister home so you could pimp her out and you won't let her get any action,' she tells Gen.

I twist to face her. *'Thank you.* Exactly.'

'I'm trying to do precisely the opposite of pimping her out,' Gen protests. 'Fuck's sake. It's one thing giving her a dancing job, but I don't want every playboy at Alchemy crawling all over her. I'm trying to protect her.'

'Not just the guys,' Maddy says, wriggling on the day bed in her tiny white bikini. 'I was into it. You were *hot*.'

'Aww, thanks, hon.' I cock my head. 'Good to know.'

'You really were,' Aida says. 'Your dancing is fucking amazing. I wish I could move like that.'

I shrug modestly. 'Thanks. If it makes you feel better, I can't name any member of Parliament except the Prime Minister.'

Everyone laughs.

'I appreciate that—I'll take it as a tiny consolation,' Aida says.

'Know your strengths and limitations, right, Dots?' my sister asks.

'Don't call me that,' I growl.

'Want to tell the others why I call you that?' she asks with her trademark sly tone, and I want to punch her in the face.

'I hate you.'

'Dots is a cute name,' Maddy muses as I shoot daggers at my big sis.

'Darcy's not her birth name,' Gen says, and there is so much fucking glee in her voice. 'She changed it by deed poll when she turned eighteen. Right, *Dots?*'

I put down my rosé and crash face-forward into the mattress. 'I'm going to fuck every guy at Alchemy just to get back at you,' I mumble into the fabric.

'I'm sorry, I didn't hear a word you said,' my sister says airily. I hate her. 'She was born Dorothy—we called her Dots or Dottie when she was little—and she decided it wasn't sexy enough, so she changed it to Darcy.'

'It *wasn't* sexy,' I insist as Maddy's howls ring in my left ear. 'I mean, Dottie, for fuck's sake. You got Genevieve, which is an objectively stunning, elegant name, and I got fucking Dorothy.'

'Did your parents like *The Wizard of Oz?*' Aida asks.

I sigh and hoist myself up onto my elbows. 'No. They liked God.'

That sets Maddy off again. 'I'm sorry,' she gasps. 'For some reason I'm finding this hilarious.'

I roll my eyes. Maybe she's not the potential ally I thought she was. I turn to my sister, who's smirking like the cat who got the fucking cream. To be fair, she did. Perched on the daybed in a gorgeous coral one-piece, huge sunglasses on and her platinum hair swept back, she looks every inch the fabulous lady of the manor. Or villa. Or chateau, or whatever it is.

'I would think that if I was about to marry a smoking hot actual *billionaire*, then I'd be a little nicer to my poor, celibate, penniless sister,' I hiss at her now.

She doesn't look remotely sorry. 'You're not penniless. We're paying you through the nose, and I've basically handed my flat over to you. You can have all the sex you like —just stay away from the Alchemy guys, okay?'

That reminds me. 'Guess who I met last night?' I ask archly. I pause for effect and then say, *'Max.'*

'Oh, Lord,' Gen says as Maddy starts laughing again, so hard she has to clutch her stomach.

Aida frowns. 'Anton's friend, right? The super attractive one?'

'Right,' I say. 'The same guy who's taking over from Anton as CEO of his entire business. Because they like to *share*.' Now it's my turn to smirk at my sister.

'They didn't share me,' Gen protests, and Aida's perfectly groomed eyebrows wing up above her sunglass frames.

'What?'

'Uh oh,' Maddy singsongs. 'The journo can smell a story.'

'Gen and Max *know* each other,' I chime in. 'In the

Shakespearean sense. The Big Bad Wolff got his friends to, um, *service* my sister while she was rejecting his advances. And by *service* I mean *spit roast*. And Anton watched.'

As Gen groans audibly, Aida runs her tongue over her lower lip in a move she's internationally famous for. She's super sexy. I really, really love that Cal fell for her. She reminds me of my number one girl crush, Aubrey Plaza. Not that I'm really into women. But if I was, Aubrey would be it for me.

Anyway.

Back to humiliating my sister.

'That's pretty hot,' Aida says slowly. She takes a sip of her wine as she processes.

'Was it hot, Genevieve?' I ask innocently.

My sister clears her throat. 'It was very fucking hot, and we don't speak of it anymore. Max and I are fine now. Anton and Max are fine. Anton just doesn't need his nose rubbed in it. Okay? But honestly. Max is a great guy to be friends with, but he's at Alchemy every night of the week, fucking everything that moves. I don't want him going anywhere near you.'

'I dunno.' Maddy cocks her head. 'Max definitely has strong Daddy energy. I would, if I wasn't annoyingly in love with Zach. But is it icky if he fucks two sisters? I can't decide.'

'It's horrifying,' Gen says at the same time that I say, 'I think it's fine.'

Aida laughs and shakes her head. 'Oh, boy. I plead the Fifth on that one.'

'If you can get over the sister thing,' Maddy persists, 'then I think he could be a lot of fun for you. I mean, deep down, he's a decent guy, right? He seems to be. And Anton trusts him with absolutely everything. Plus, he's gorgeous and filthy and experienced. He could definitely show you the ropes, if you catch my drift. I bet he'd be fucking amazing in bed.'

Max's words from last night drift uncomfortably through my brain.

I'd like to put you over my knee and spank that insolence out of you.

And I think you'd like that, too.

Jesus Christ. I think I would, too.

I suspect deflection is the best strategy here. 'All I'm saying,' I tell my sister, 'is that you can't protect me forever. I get around. I'm not some innocent little flower. If I want a big bad man to do bad things to me, I'll let him. When I'm not at the club, my time's my own. Got it?'

I'll get on that stage.

I'll dance.

I'll fluff those guys at Alchemy till they're rock fucking hard.

But now I'm back in Europe, I'm going to make sure I have fun.

And if that fun includes a few harmless spanks from Anton's best man when the wedding comes around next month, so be it.

After all, I'm my sister's bridesmaid.

It would be rude not to.

7

DEX

It's slightly affronting that packing up to leave a country after an eight-year stint there should be so effortless. Plants without deep roots are far easier to transplant, I suppose.

It seems humans without deep roots are, too.

But when I look around my Upper East Side apartment, the neat pile of packing boxes strikes me as an equally neat metaphor for the complete lack of baggage that tethers me here. I can't imagine the emotional stress of moving home will be any greater than the logistical stress.

I shrug aside the fleeting thought that if you flee to a place for the wrong reasons, some well-meaning part of your subconscious will prevent you from ever getting too attached to said place.

Because at some point, you'll yield to the inevitable.

It's almost time to go home.

Instead, I focus on the very appealing view in front of me. My west-facing apartment is a few floors away from being a penthouse, but it's high enough that I'm blessed with the vista of a perfect June sunset. I love Manhattan at this time of year—it's warm, but not stifling.

London will doubtless be prettier—it's a far more graceful, elegant, *green* city than New York—but it won't have the energy that's kept me here this long. The energy that keeps me busy. Moving forward. Constantly in motion. I'm a great white shark, for whom movement is oxygen.

Even prettier than the sunset is the glossy, almost-naked brunette sitting on my kitchen island. Claudia is a gorgeous lawyer whose ambition matches mine and who puts in even longer hours than I do. That's the beauty of working in the equity markets. At four each day, when the closing bell rings, your day is done.

For a junior partner in asset finance law, it's pretty amazing that Claudia gets away from work as early as she does, but I have a feeling that has less to do with her commitment to proving herself at Clifford Chance and more to do with her attachment to me. While I don't share that attachment, the fact that she's crying pretty tears—she even cries prettily—at my impending departure enhances this evening, somehow.

It's as if the fact that at least one of us has some emotional skin in the game will elevate our last coupling and allow me to feel something, even by proxy, with absolutely none of the guilt I might feel at breaking her heart, because this move isn't on me.

It's on Loeb, the Swiss boutique bank who sought out a meeting with me when I was in London recently and offered to bring me on board as a partner. It's a far smaller outfit than my current employer, the mighty Goldman Sachs, but the latter is well known for dangling the carrot of partnership over its managing directors' noses for years to keep them on the hook. I made the call that going in as a big fish to a far smaller pond with the partnership thing done and dusted was the right thing for my career.

You only get to make the trade from Goldman to another bank once. The money Loeb is laying out to poach me tells me *this* is the trade. And the fact that they've made me head of the entire Equities division, rather than just the Cash Equities role Goldman was proposing in London, has sealed the deal for me. I might have waited years and years to get that opportunity if I'd stayed put and drunk the Kool Aid like a loyal little Goldmanite.

Claudia understands you don't leave something like this on the table. Still, I get that it sucks for her. I get that, over the month we've spent fooling around since our introduction by mutual friends at a charity gala, she's fallen for me. And if I feel guilt, it's that I didn't nip this arrangement in the bud as quickly as I usually do because I was conscious that we had a natural expiration date.

Somehow, despite my having been unequivocally clear from the outset, Claudia has failed to get that memo.

'I could come to London for the weekend,' she sniffs, her perfect little nose rosy red and her huge brown eyes clouded with tears.

I step between her legs and she widens them for me. With my thumbs, I wipe away the tracks of her tears. 'No, baby,' I tell her as gently and clearly as I can. 'There's no point in prolonging the inevitable. We'll both be working our arses off—I'll have to seriously prove myself when I get over there. And you'll finally be clear of unhelpful distractions.' I smile at her. 'Let's just call this what it was—a really great time—and enjoy this last night together.'

It's not a lie. I have had a great time with her. There's a reason I only fool around with professional women: they get it. The last thing I need is some little yoga queen pouting in my bed and teasing my cock at five-thirty in the morning when I have to go to work and she wants to go get juice together.

Women like Claudia are exactly like me. Hungry, relentless, and driven as fuck. The dinner dates are full of smart, witty conversation. The sex is hot. Uninhibited. And, most importantly, efficient. Claudia has never stayed over. We fuck, and she goes home to her apartment across the park and does a couple more hours of work before she retires.

Our arrangement has been perfect, as have my arrangements with other, similar women over the past eight years. If I can find something similarly mutually convenient in London, I'll absolutely take advantage.

If not, I'll put my head down and work.

She surveys me through her tears and nods sadly. 'Yeah. I just—I dunno. You're the whole package, you know? Those freaking eyes. *And* you have that whole fancy, well-mannered British thing going on... You're smart, as well as being super hot. And nice. I don't think you realise how rare that all is.'

I'm genuinely touched by her words, even if they don't quite hit me as hard as they should. 'I'll miss you,' I tell her with a sincerity I don't feel, because she's a beautiful, impressive woman, and if I can't give her a little morale boost before I walk away without a backwards glance, then what kind of a man am I?

She nods, like she needed to hear it, needed a breadcrumb of validation from me that she could shore up for when I've gone, and I see her visibly pull herself together, blinking away her tears.

'When you say *enjoy our last night*,' she says now, placing her hands on my chest over my button-down, 'what were you thinking, exactly?'

I grin and move my hands down her face. Down the sides of her neck. I brush the straps of her stunning, intricate bra off her shoulders, enjoying the smoothness of her skin under my palms as I let my eyes drop to her nipples, small and pinky-brown and hard as pebbles through the delicate lace of her bra. Claudia is queen of the lingerie game.

'I was thinking,' I murmur, my voice low, 'that we give each other a few memories to get off to when we're alone in our beds next week. What do you think?'

She takes in a shuddery breath. 'Yeah. That sounds good.'

'Excellent.' I drop my lips to her shoulder and kiss her there. 'Glad we're on the same page,' I murmur as I get to my knees in front of her.

8

DEX

I love this part. I really do. A beautiful, sophisticated, lingerie-clad woman, laid out on my kitchen island for me to sample. I fucking love eating pussy. And Claudia doesn't disappoint. I hook my thumb into the thin strip of lace that passes for her thong and tug it to one side, exposing her lovely, bare centre.

'Would you look at that,' I murmur. 'All nice and wet for me.'

She shudders and leans back, bracing herself on her palms. My viewpoint as I glance up at her is wonderful. Flat stomach. Smooth olive skin. Perfectly pert breasts encased in exquisite lace. Long, dark hair, flawlessly blown out, caressing her skin. I'm a lucky guy.

Fuck, she tastes like sin.

Depraved, carnal, *mortal* sin.

The kind of sin you don't come back from.

The kind of sin that makes you turn your back on those pearly gates quicker than you can say *damnation*.

Every single religious teaching that every single adult, from the Benedictine monks who taught me at Ampleforth to my own fucking father, has rammed down my throat swims through my aroused brain like a taunting, intoxicating sickness as I slice through her slick centre with my tongue. Back to front. *Jesus.*

I planned to go slow. To tease her, wind her higher.

Not happening.

Instead, I go for it. Maybe it's the knowledge that this is our last time together. The perverse monster in me wants to leave my mark on her. Give her something to remember me by.

I get stuck in. Licking her. Tongue-fucking her. Sucking on her clit. I pull away for a second and scramble to my feet so I can unhook her bra and lay her back on the island. Then I'm dragging her thong down her legs. She puts her feet on my shoulders but lets her knees drop open, affording me every single fucking millimetre of the delights she's offering.

Who am I kidding? I'll manage without Claudia, but I won't manage without this. I'll need to hook myself up with some top-notch pussy as soon as I get back.

At moments like this, when most of my blood is in my cock and I'm so brain-whipped with arousal that I can't think straight, it feels to me like my brand-new, annoyingly impressive brother-in-law and his mates might just be the smartest humans on the planet. An exclusive, sophisticated, decadent club created purely as a temple to sex?

For a guy who'll be pulling seventy-hour weeks when he gets back, it's looking like more and more of a compelling prospect. Even if I know that after I've come and my biochemistry has returned to normal, civilised levels, I'll find it morally repulsive again.

Claudia, bless her, doesn't stand a chance against my onslaught. She mewls and writhes and makes breathy little gasps, and she's fucking adorable. My zipper is biting into my straining cock, so I up the ante. I need to be balls deep inside her. *Now.*

She's there. She comes like the well-bred, well-educated girl she is, with just the right amount of ecstatic whimpering. Enough to make me feel like a porn star; not enough to disturb the neighbours. As soon as she's come down, I give a last, long lick—*delicious*—and help her up to sitting. She wraps her arms and legs around me and I carry her like that through to my bedroom and drop her on the bed.

I have to say, she makes a lovely sight against my crisp white sheets. Naked and long-limbed and bronzed, eyes still glassy and filled with appreciation as she watches me unbutton my shirt as quickly as my compromised fine motor skills will allow. I get the shirt off and make quick work of my trousers and boxer briefs, and then I'm tugging open the drawer of my bedside table and pulling out a little foil square.

Condom on, I crawl over her, enjoying the outright awe on her face at the sight of my cock, fully sheathed and ready for utter fucking oblivion inside the body of this beautiful, lithe woman. I lower myself so I can kiss her. Slowly. Indulgently. I want her to taste her own arousal on my mouth, taste how honey-sweet she is.

Then, with an arm wrapped firmly around her, I flip us over so she's sprawled perfectly on top of me. 'Give me one last show,' I whisper, and her face flickers with understanding and—possibly—the thrill of a challenge. There's no way this competitive little power player can resist picking up that baton: the challenge to make her own mark on my memory.

We're not dissimilar, Claudia and me.

She pushes herself up, treating me to the immensely

gratifying sight of her hovering right above my cock. How this woman holds down such rigorous workout and waxing and blow-drying schedules on top of Clifford fucking Chance, I have no earthly clue, but she's in spectacular shape. I'm sure she views every stray body hair and ounce of subcutaneous body fat as a personal affront to her self-discipline.

Whatever demons propel her forward, I'm here for the results, because she's wrapping her long, slim fingers reverently around my dick like it's a fucking Oscar and lowering that hot, primed pussy down, down, until my tip is in, and I groan-laugh because it feels so fucking good.

'Fuck, yes,' I hiss, running my hands up her toned thighs. The sight of her above me has me wondering how long I can hold off before I shoot my load. Her tits are small and so perfect. I want to sit up and take one pebbled little nipple between my teeth and roll my tongue around it, but a larger part wants to lie here and give her as much leverage as possible so she can drag those impeccable internal muscles up and down my poor, swollen, aching cock.

Happily for me, Claudia's as much of an overachiever in bed as she is at work, and she milks me perfectly. We find a rhythm, and I interlace my fingers behind my head and grit my teeth as I drive up as hard as I can with each thrust. She's into it; she's half lost in the chase of her own bliss. She reaches behind and cups my balls, and holy fucking Christ.

I'm close. Close enough to lose most remaining inhibitions. Most of my pride. Most of my decency. 'Do that thing, baby,' I say through gritted teeth. 'With your finger.' I screw my eyes closed for a second, because I hate asking for it as much as I love getting it.

I'd like to say at this point that it was she who started this. It wasn't my idea, but she did it off her own bat one night, and I practically shot off the fucking bed. It's an important distinction in my head.

I open my eyes, and she smiles like she's pleased I asked her for something. For this one last sexual favour. And then she releases my balls and sucks her finger into her mouth seductively before reaching back again and breaching that tight ring of muscle that guards what is always, or at least ninety-nine-point-nine percent of the time, strictly an exit hole for me. It's only in these brief moments of arousal so extreme I lose my fucking mind that it's an entrance hole. It's only in this fleeting abyss between sanity and insanity that I allow myself to acknowledge the deep, clawing hunger I feel to have this hole breached and filled and violated and—

As she works her finger in and out of my arse and my dick in and out of her pussy, the hazy form of my impending orgasm gathers mass. Takes shape. Burns brighter. Sharper. This time, I squeeze my eyes even more tightly closed. I don't see the beautiful woman undulating on top of me during a New York sunset as she rides my cock. I don't offer her the connection I know she must crave in these final moments together.

Instead, I'm somewhere else entirely.

I'm—God help me—in one of the shower cubicles at the Goldman gym. I'm standing facing the wall, palms flat on the cool tiles, the torrent of water like a baptism.

There's a guy there. At work. I don't know who he is, or where he works. Somewhere on the Macro trading floor, I think. Fixed Income, maybe? I've seen him get off the elevator on the forty-ninth floor a couple of times.

He's huge.

He's ripped.

And he gives me looks, sometimes.

Looks that—

Never mind.

But right now, as Claudia's finger crooks inside me and my cock bottoms out inside her, over and over again, Gym Guy is standing behind me. His skin is so fucking soaked, and his huge palm is an anchor across my stomach, and I can actually feel his chest muscles contracting against my shoulder blades, and it's the second best thing I've ever, ever felt, because the best thing is without a doubt the burning, excruciating epiphany that is his huge, hard cock, pumping into the most shameful, secret, filthy place in my body from behind, over and over and over until I'm in danger of screaming the whole fucking place down and his free hand clamps over my mouth.

When I come, deep within the body of the beautiful woman who's let me inside her, it's not her finger back there. And it's not her face emblazoned on my mind's eye.

Thank God I'll never have to see that guy again.

Because the stuff I've imagined with him, with others, makes the sin of fucking willing, available women look like the faintest of stains on my eternal soul.

I may have made uneasy peace with the knowledge that the purity culture I was brought up with is bullshit at best and dangerous at worst.

But *that*? That's a sin I will always, always rage against with every fibre of my self-control.

9

DARCY

When I say my sister's South of France wedding is an operation, I mean it's an Eras Tour-level operation. We're talking insane amounts of logistics and expense. But the weird thing is that neither Gen nor Anton have seemed particularly stressed by it.

I suppose Anton's tied the knot three times before, and while he's endlessly vocal about how he's never felt anything like how he feels about my sister, he's an old hand at this. And Gen's not exactly a flapper. She was never going to be bridezilla. *And* she does operations-type stuff for a living—she's Alchemy's Chief Operating Officer, after all. So this is her milieu.

Still. My real takeaway from watching the wedding and its three million related circuses take shape in the couple of weeks leading up to them is that when you have gazillions of pounds, you can make anything happen and make any problem go away.

Last-minute guest list additions or cancellations?

Pas de problème. The scary Parisian wedding planner will take care of those.

BA just cancelled an outbound flight that loads of the guests are booked on?

Whatever. Somebody will charter another private plane for those guys.

It's fascinating and brain melting and kind of horrifying, too, but it's certainly made my life as a bridesmaid very easy indeed.

The hardest part of my role in the celebrations, to be honest, has been dealing with my mum and dad. Though I have to hand it to my sister: there's nothing like marrying the country's most respected billionaire to placate the most obnoxious, judgemental parents.

They're not awful people. They're just... themselves. Which is Surrey born and bred, socially mobile middle-class people who care far too much about what their friends at the golf club think of them and, I'd say, far too little about their daughters stepping fully into their own potential as children of the universe.

(Yeah, they're a lot less woo-woo than I am.)

It's like this: Gen's always been the straight-A student, so they've basked—happily and loudly—in her reflected glory. When she worked at JP Morgan, they talked about it a *lot*. But when she left the City to start a sex club, she instantly became She Who Shall Not Be Mentioned. They won't talk about it with her, and they definitely don't talk about it with their social set.

A tiny part of me gets why they are the way they are—they're stuck in their own claustrophobic social bubble where everyone is white and ostensibly straight and works in some respectable, middle-class job. They and their friends are the exact result of everything they've worked so hard for, for decades now, and they're terrified of pushing boundaries and damaging optics.

But a far larger part of me can't fucking stand their ostrich mentality. That's the same part who moved to the other side of the world to get some freedom from their suffocating brand of affection.

It's all really unfair on Gen. Of the two of us, I'm the one who had it all handed to her on a platter. Gen had to be a star at absolutely everything she did, but when I turned up twelve years later, after multiple miscarriages for my poor mum, I was so desperately wanted—and so damn cute—that I was indulged and coddled beyond belief.

It was also suffocating beyond belief.

Suffice to say, we've both pissed our parents off no end, and, while it's their own fault that they hold us to some weird, outdated standard of what a successful and compliant daughter looks like, I get that their disappointment in us feels as real to them as our disappointment in them feels.

They worked hard so they could educate us privately, and we've never wanted for anything, so I think our lack of appropriate gratitude bewilders them. Just as their inability to accept us as beautiful, fully realised human beings living their truth bewilders us.

Ugh.

Sorry.

I tend to get on a roll when it comes to slagging off my parents.

Anyway, they're here. And they're ecstatic. They'll dine out on this match at the golf club for the rest of their lives. Anton, I have to say, has been so suave and sexy and attentive that they're pretty much constantly in a semi-orgasmic state. He definitely knows how to play them.

And when Anton Wolff tells them their daughter is

simply the most exquisite, talented, unique human to have ever graced the earth, they listen.

There's only one black sheep left in the family now.

IF I WASN'T ALREADY CRYING tears of happiness for my beautiful, amazing sister as she marries the man she loves, I'd be crying at how perfectly stunning this entire event is.

Because it really is.

It's flawless.

They legally tied the knot yesterday at the Hôtel de Ville, or town hall, in Nice, as French law dictates. But today's the big celebration. An enormous structure has been built on the main lawn around the side of the villa—kind of like a giant pergola—whose wooden struts are interwoven with jasmine and other unknown, but very pretty, white flowers. It provides the guests with some shade on a hot early July day in this glorious part of the world.

I follow Zach's daughters, Stella and Nancy, down the aisle as the strains of violin music from the string quartet fill the air. They're both wearing white broderie anglaise dresses and have little wicker baskets full of white rose petals, which they're scattering as they go. Everyone *oohs* and *ahhs* at them. They're so adorable, and so well behaved, it's ridiculous.

I'm aware I look seriously good in custom Givenchy, which is what the bride and groom are wearing too. Gen's not one of those brides who has to make sure she looks better than everyone else—she does that effortlessly. But it's a testament to her generosity that she let me pick the design of my dress.

I opted for palest sea-foam green, which works so well

with my auburn hair. My dress is crêpe-backed satin, but the satin side is next to my skin while the matte side provides the perfect lustre. It's long and flowing, with thin straps and almost no back.

My sister's behind me with our dad who, to be fair to him, has been a blubbering mess all day. He seems genuinely moved (and not a little relieved) to be handing off his eldest daughter to a guy who's basically a Mr Darcy-level catch.

Anton looks fucking good in his black tuxedo with satin lapels. That man has excellent posture. His eyes are trained behind me, and the quiet joy and disbelief on his face as he watches my sister have me choking up a little.

Not so his henchman—I mean best man—whose eyes don't leave me. Not for a second. Max looks as serious as I've seen him this weekend, and the expression on his face gives me shivers.

He's even more devastating when he's not smiling and joking and dropping innuendos.

I step off to the side at the top of the aisle and make way for the bride.

And fuck, is she fabulous.

She's not wearing a veil—a veil wouldn't be Gen's vibe at all. Instead, her platinum blonde hair is swept back in an immaculate up-do, with a couple of perfect camellias pinned into it. Apparently, the camellia thing is some sort of joke between her and Anton, and he had them flown down from Chanel's own hot house in Paris.

The up-do and lack of veil means there's nothing detracting from the dress itself, which is fucking *incredible* and which makes her look like a silver screen movie star. It's ivory duchesse satin, with lots of concealed corsetry going on that takes her hourglass figure to a whole new level, and the back of it cinches in under her fabulous arse before flaring out into a fishtail.

But my favourite part is the neckline. It has a high collar completely encrusted with pearls, and the dress' bodice cuts away at the front and back so it tapers into the collar, leaving her entire shoulder area bare. The waistband has the same pearl-encrusted belt going on.

Apart from the pearls, it's really simple, but the fabric is so rich, and the tailoring so impeccable, that she looks a million dollars (or a billion, I suppose). Gen's always had an excellent arm game, but she's been toning up for the wedding, so the strong but feminine curves of her delts are truly fabulous. And I give that compliment as someone who can work a pole for hours.

In a word, she takes my breath away. She's flawless, and radiant, and so fucking speechless with joy that I'm in actual awe.

Dad gives her a kiss on the cheek and winks tearily at me as he takes his seat behind where I'm standing. When I stop ogling my sister and let my gaze flicker over to Max, he's still staring straight at me like he wants to throw me over his shoulder and march me out of this wedding and back to his cave where he can ravage me and then, I dunno, make me a fire.

It's a lot.

I quickly avert my gaze and look out at the attendees. Some of our relatives are in the front row with my parents, and right behind them the bride's side is well represented by what I like to call the Alchemy Massive. Zach and Maddy each have a flower girl on their lap, and Maddy's smile is so wide it could split her face open. I know she shipped my sister and Anton right from the start.

Belle's sitting between Maddy and Rafe, looking tanned

and golden and insanely gorgeous. She has to be one of the most beautiful women I've ever seen. And on Rafe's other side are Cal and Aida with her boys, Pip and Kit. These guys have been more of a family to my sister than my parents have over the past decade, and I adore them for it.

I knew I'd feel emotional. Weddings always are, and this one is not only a stunner but features my favourite person in the world.

But nothing could really have prepared me for the awe and emotion I feel as I watch my beautiful sister recite the vows she wrote to the man she loves. It's like I'm in the presence of something greater than me. Greater than them. Greater than all of us. There's magic in the air today. This love they have for each other feels sacred and awe inspiring and marvellous.

And I doubt there's a single person here who isn't touched by it.

10

MAX

'The best man and the bridesmaid. Oldest cliché in the book. We should do it.'

I gaze down at the stunningly beautiful woman in my arms with what I like to call my Closing Smile, but this is one deal I appear to be struggling to close.

'*Oldest* being the operative word where you're concerned,' she retorts, and I grin, because, while her attempts at holding me off are tiresome, I'll admit they're also mildly amusing.

I'm pretty confident they're also verbal foreplay.

I've stood next to Anton at the top of the aisle three times now. We didn't know each other when he married his first wife. Never have I seen him this happy, and never have I been as fond of—or as *sure* of—any of his matches as I am of Gen.

(I've also never fucked any of his wives—before, during or after his relationship with them—but that's beside the point.)

So yeah, I've loved every bit of this weekend. Loved the rehearsal dinner they threw by the sea last night, down at the Eden Roc Hotel, where Anton took Gen on their first date. The jaunt to Nice's Hôtel de Ville to legally seal the deal was brief, thanks to the chopper, and this evening has been magical enough to soften even my unromantic heart.

As I glance around the space, I can admit Anton's money and Gen's impeccable taste are a pretty powerful combination. It's a relatively small wedding, which says less about the importance of this union in Anton's eyes and more about his total lack of interest in having business acquaintances and industry bores present to witness what he calls his forever match.

It's intimate. Everyone here is important to Gen or Anton. But low-key it is *not*. I eye the long trestle tables that sit under the pines and French oaks. They look less immaculate post our four-course dinner than they did when we sat down, but they're still beautiful. Their centrepieces of sculptural white flowers and thick candles in hurricane lanterns look stunning in the evening light.

Over Darcy's exquisite shoulder and beyond the guests in their silks and sequins and white tie, the swimming pool shimmers with the light of hundreds of floating candles. On the small stage behind me the world-famous tenor, Santiago Vale, croons.

He looks disgustingly debonair in his white tie, if a little too alpha for my tastes, but at least I don't need to worry about Darcy making a beeline for him. The whole world knows he's hopelessly smitten with his father's former chef.

When the happy couple swayed their way through their first dance to Santiago's sultry arrangement of *The Best is Yet to Come*, even I grew misty-eyed. Told you this entire setup was romantic.

Verbal foreplay may be my jam, but I'm not particularly in the mood for sparring tonight. Besides, I don't feel like giving Darcy the satisfaction. I'll let my body do the talking —let's see how she likes that. I tug her closer against me, my palm splayed across the soft skin of her bare lower back.

While her sister changed out of her wedding dress for the reception and into some gloriously sexy white beaded mini-dress reminiscent of the Roaring Twenties, Darcy's stayed in her bridesmaid gown, and I approve of it just as much as I did when I watched her slink down the aisle earlier.

I don't miss her slight shiver as I slide my palm slowly up her back. She sighs softly, resting her head on my shoulder in what feels gratifyingly like surrender, her arms staying loosely around my neck. One of the photographers for the event pads around us, stance crouched, seeking out the perfect shot, and I think to myself, *good*.

I'm glad this moment is being immortalised, and not only because having a photographic record that Darcy will undoubtedly see may help my case, but because I suspect we look pretty fucking good together. There's me in my shirt, top button open and white tie hanging loose and cuffs rolled up—because, come on, it's Antibes in July and it's still pretty fucking warm—and this sensual redhead swaying barefoot in my arms, her curves swathed in reams of the palest sea-foam silk.

I'd go so far as to wager that we look like a Gatsby still or a Vettriano painting: a fleeting moment, but a timeless image. Even if I suspect the reason she's slumped against me so willingly has more to do with the amount of Krug she's consumed and less to do with her willingness to submit to this "crusty old Brit".

Whatever her reason, I'll take it. And if the alcohol has tempered her suspicions of me slightly, I'm not above using that advantage. Although if she gets much more drunk than this, I'll obviously step away. I'm not a total monster. Even so, my fingertips are grazing the little bumps along her spinal column of their own accord.

'I'm not having sex with you tonight,' she mutters, shifting her head slightly on my shoulder. 'Although, why do you have to smell so fucking good?'

The unexpected compliment excites me less than her use of a qualifier. She's not having sex with me *tonight*.

Hmm.

Interesting.

'Le Labo,' I tell her. 'And, obviously, my own lethal sex hormones.'

She pokes me in the shoulder with a finger. 'You're so arrogant. That's one of the reasons I won't have sex with you. I won't give you the satisfaction.'

'But arrogance turns you on, yes?' I ask her, dipping my head so she can hear me above Santiago Vale's exuberant take on *Mack the Knife*. This is not the right song to slow-dance to, but I couldn't give a shit.

She groans into my shirt. 'Ugh, yes, and I despise myself.'

I laugh. 'Resistance is futile, darling. Just surrender to it.' My hand has found its way to the base of her spine, and I can't resist copping a little feel of the silk standing between me and that gloriously peachy arse of hers.

'Fuck me, your arse is spectacular,' I murmur into her hair. It really is. I slide my hand over its sleek curves. It is the arse of champions: toned and taut, but ample, you know? Grabbable.

I am most definitely taking this arse in the not-too-distant future. I bet she'd look so fucking perfect bent over for me. And I bet she'd love it, too. An image of her draped over the back of the very expensive sofa in my new flat comes to mind, her long limbs tensed in anticipation, and her red hair tumbling everywhere, and that tight little hole on full display, just waiting for my cock to breach it.

'You're imagining fucking it right now, aren't you?' she asks, and I bark out a shocked laugh in response, because she is a piece of fucking work.

'That's not an answer,' she points out.

'I am, as a matter of fact,' I tell her. Both my hands are all over her arse now, taking their fill on this dim dance floor. 'I'm imagining how tight you'd be, and how much you'd love it, and, of course, how utterly exquisite you'd look, naked and bent over for me. But the real question is, are *you* imagining it?'

She moves against my body like I've made her restless, her perfect tits brushing against my front as she does. 'I'm not *not* imagining it, if you catch my drift.'

'Jesus Christ,' I groan. I'm the finest sliver of self-control away from getting a full-on boner here. 'I have a very pleasant suite back at the hotel. Why don't we slip out of here and put each other out of our misery?' I reluctantly remove one hand from her arse and trail it up the length of her back before I burrow under all that gorgeous hair and clasp her neck. I kiss her hair, too. I'm definitely not the only one who smells indecently good this evening.

'Don't be ridiculous,' she huffs. 'I'm the fucking *bridesmaid*. I can't just disappear and then miss breakfast here tomorrow. Even if some very old but weirdly sexy guy is trying to coax me back to his insane suite to pop my anal cherry, Hôtel du Cap style.'

That gets a laugh out of me, despite my frustration. I'm well aware she's staying here with her parents. I'm well aware it would look dodgy as fuck if she did a no-show. And I'm also well aware that, all this being the case, I would have been far better off making a move on someone else tonight.

But, honestly, no one else here holds a fucking candle to Darcy.

I could get a cab over to Cannes for the Alchemy pop-up, which would still be going strong at this time of night, but that's a dick move after spending the evening at my best mate's wedding. Right now, though, I have a more pressing issue to deal with.

I subtly press my fingertips to the silk-covered cleft between her cheeks.

'No one's ever been in here?'

'No,' she mumbles, and I sense defensiveness. 'Anal might be, like, first base for sex obsessives like you, but it's not exactly a core offering on the menu for a lot of people.'

'You're not a virgin, are you?' I ask, mainly to piss her off.

And piss her off it does. She uses her hands on my shoulders to push herself away from me so she can give me a glare. 'Do I look like a fucking virgin to you? Seriously, Max.'

I smirk. 'No. You look like every male fantasy of female sexuality, and the female form, since the fucking Renaissance. You look like a woman Titian and Rubens and Botticelli would have ached to paint.' I dip my head so our lips are mere inches apart and whisper, 'And you look like you were created to take my cock in every single perfect hole in your spectacular body.'

She's staring at me, lips parted, her blue eyes with disbelief and, it seems, arousal. I get so close that our noses brush as I turn my head and whisper the most important words in her ear.

'And you will take my cock. Maybe not tonight, but you *will* take my cock in every one of them.'

11

DARCY

Alchemy still hits me every time I show up here. I have to hand it to my sister and her mates—they've walked the line between classy and debauched to perfection.

I've danced in dive bars on the Gold Coast, but when I walk up the immaculate sandstone steps of this stunning townhouse on a fancy street in Mayfair, and ring the bell on the glossy black front door, and step into the entrance hallway, with its shiny black-and-white tiled floors and discreet lighting, it feels nothing like walking into a sex club and a lot like entering a smart hotel or members' club.

No wonder they attract so many rich, powerful people here.

It's Maddy who answers the door. I haven't seen her since we got back from France a few days ago, and we both squeal as we hug each other in an excited little dance. I love this chick, and I adored getting some lounger time with her before and after the wedding.

'What are you still doing here?' I ask her. It's seven

o'clock, an hour before our doors open and two hours before I go onstage. She's usually long gone by the time I get here, but I'm glad she's around to let me in because the huge, scary-looking doormen haven't arrived yet.

'Shooting this one,' she says with a bright smile, stepping aside. 'Ta-da!'

This one is Natalie, one of the club's hosts. I've met her a few times, but we haven't chatted much. She's stunning and seems very sweet. It's her job to greet members when they arrive, and let me just say that she is every bit as expensive and classy-looking as every other first impression this establishment makes.

'Wow!' I say, my eyes wide. 'You look *amazing*. I mean, you always look great, but this is another level.'

'Thanks,' she says with a smile that's quietly assured. She's not the most obvious candidate to be a sex club host, but I'm sure that's precisely why my clever sister hired her. She's always beautifully dressed in all-black, her hair, which is a few shades darker brown than Maddy's, hanging in a sleek curtain. Her colouring is a bit darker than Maddy's all-round, actually. She has a perfect, even tan and big brown eyes and the kind of petite frame and fragile bone structure that I can't help but envy sometimes, even if I love my curves.

And never has she showcased any of it more than tonight. As she steps out from behind her host's lectern, I get the full effect.

Wow.

She's in a strapless black jumpsuit with a fitted bodice and flared trousers. The bodice is embroidered with a swirly pattern in gazillions of tiny jet beads, and the effect is beautiful. The outfit fits her like a glove.

She looks a million dollars.

I whistle. 'Holy cow, you are a smoke show, woman! This is so gorgeous.' I lean forward to admire the intricate beadwork. Alchemy must be paying her very well to keep her in threads like this.

'Guess what?' Maddy asks. 'She made it *herself*.'

'What the hell?' I ask in disbelief. 'There's no way, right?'

Natalie flushes. 'I have a fashion label—it's tiny, really. I just do private clients. It's demi-couture, so between couture and ready-to-wear. But I've been working on this one for months, and when Maddy asked to feature me on Alchemy's social channels, I figured I'd give it an outing.'

'Damn right,' I say, still taking her in. It's blowing my mind that sweet, quiet Natalie is a ninja with a needle and thread behind closed doors. 'So you're running a fashion brand by day and doing this by night? Hopefully you'll get lots of interest in your brand from the members.'

'It's more like building than running a brand at this point, and I really don't want to push my own agenda,' she protests, swiping a shiny sheet of hair over her shoulder. 'But your sister's been so encouraging, and she even says she wants to order a jacket, which is amazing. Even if I'm kind of terrified that I'll mess it up.'

'You won't,' Maddy says firmly. 'Honestly, I have a strong feeling this is your time, Nat. You're so talented it blows my mind.'

'This is super cute,' I say, pointing to the little black patch on her upper arm that I know, from being around plenty of health nuts, covers a blood glucose monitor. Except this one is fancy. It has a circle of tiny crystals around the edge, and the swirly Alchemy *A* picked out in crystals, too. 'Biohacking, Alchemy style.'

She laughs. 'Sadly it's not by choice. I have type 1 diabetes, but I figured I may as well try to glam my patch up. So I bedazzled a few of them for when my outfits are sleeveless.'

'Well, it looks amazing,' I tell her.

'Chic as fuck,' Maddy pronounces. 'And *look* at these photos.'

She puts her phone down on the lectern. I crane my neck so I can see as she swipes. Yeah, these are great. Natalie's standing beside the lectern, one elbow resting on it and the other hand on her hip.

'You look like a model,' I say. 'You're the perfect ambassador for your brand. I suspect your main issue tonight will be keeping the members' hands off you—they'll go crazy for you.'

'I don't fraternise, actually,' she tells me.

'Really? I didn't know that,' I say. 'That makes two of us. So you're there to fluff them, just like me?'

She goes bright red. For someone who comes over as poised and seemingly assured, clearly sex-talk is way outside her comfort zone. It makes her an even more interesting hire by my sister.

'Haha, definitely not like you,' she says, fiddling with the simple bangle on her wrist. 'I've heard your dancing is amazing. I'm here to greet, and welcome, and flirt gently, and cross absolutely no lines. I'm a totally different type of host from the hosts in the club. It's my choice—I honestly feel more comfortable that way.'

I get it. The hosts in the main bar and in The Playroom are salaried members, but they have carte blanche to have whatever fun they want to have with the members, if you get my meaning, and most of them go for it. Gladly. The female hosts wear white to help them stand out more easily among the patrons.

Meanwhile, the angel in black is untouchable, by her own choice.

Unlike yours truly.

12

MAX

Wanting something badly and not being able to have it is a new and deeply unpleasant experience for me.

If I'm completely honest, wanting something badly full stop is pretty rare. I suppose it makes me entitled beyond belief to conclude that I never *want for* anything sufficiently to actually *want* it.

Even the top job at Wolff Holdings came to me seemingly effortlessly, in the end. I've had my beady little eye on that glittering prize for the two decades that I've worked for Anton, and, sure, I wanted it like an aggressive little Jack Russell who's always nipping at his master's heels.

But did I think Anton would step aside and free up this most coveted of roles? Not on your life.

Not until a certain glacial blonde stepped into his life in those elegant heels of hers and blew every other ambition, every desire he'd ever had, right out of the water.

The job is mine: CEO of Wolff Holdings, the largest privately owned corporation in Europe in terms of enterprise value and turnover. Some might say timing has poisoned the chalice—I know Anton views it as such. Crystallising the value we've created in the form of an initial public offering is the next obvious step, and Anton feels like he's dodged a bullet there.

He's always adored the work itself. The nuts and bolts. The empire building. He's great at the limelight, but he doesn't need it. And, having found his true love later in life, he'd rather be off fucking his beautiful bride poolside than enduring what is undeniably the total and utter circus an IPO entails: endless roadshows and hoop-jumping and investor-courting.

That's why he's found the perfect successor. I'm that circus dog. Stick a plastic bow-tie on me and I'll cavort through every hoop there is. I love being the centre of attention. I fucking thrive on this stuff.

What I don't thrive on is being kept waiting. Nobody holds off on me—not in business, and definitely not in my sex life. Which is why the conundrum of the woman moving so beautifully on stage is making my head ache as much as my balls.

She's in a bodystocking again. It's similar to the one she wore in Cannes, adorned with strategically placed diamanté, only tonight's version is sheer black.

It conceals nothing.

The way they've lit her is perfection. A chrome pole is centre stage, and boy is she working it, but the way Darcy moves isn't like any pole dance I've seen before. It's almost like... she's edging it. She sways onstage, her body a sensual silhouette, backlit so it appears to glow, her loose hair a red halo.

She caresses the pole.

Abandons it.

Sways some more.

Hooks a knee around it and lets herself glide slowly, weightlessly, in a full turn to the hypnotic opera-techno mix playing before sinking to the floor.

Perhaps it's my extreme state of arousal that has me over-identifying with the pole. Poor fucker. It's like a giant cock, and *she will not get the fuck on it and ride it properly.* It's driving me insane.

Her body is beautiful. So beautiful. Strong and curvy and sensuous. The way she moves almost brings tears to my eyes. She's a free spirit, in thrall to the music and no one else, and it occurs to me that this is her secret. *This* is where her magic lies. The way she's engaging with the stage, the music, the pole, feels private. She is absolutely, one hundred percent, playing for the audience, but the way she's doing it makes me feel like a grubby little voyeur, watching a show that's intended for no one else's eyes but hers.

I don't know how she does it, but it's spellbinding.

This is no seedy strip club where the woman dancing is beholden to engage by the promise of tips, by the allure of potential tens and twenties and fifties if she pouts and winks and bites her lip and holds eye contact.

Oh, no.

She's above that. She's above *us*. She has no apparent interest in the roomful of men and women whose rapt attention she's garnered, whose gazes are devouring her almost-naked form as their hands and mouths devour their neighbours' bodies instead. The attraction, the arousal, only runs in one direction tonight, and she has all the power.

As soon as she takes her bow and exits the stage for the final time to rapturous applause, I push through the crowd, declining the advances of a very attractive blonde I'm pretty sure I've fucked in here before. I have the advantage, given the number of nights I've spent in here and Wolff's pop-up JV with Alchemy, of being something of an insider.

Which is to say I know where the dressing room is.

I head downstairs to the basement as quickly as my erection will allow. It houses not only another, more hardcore playing space—The Vault—but six additional private rooms and a small dressing room the performers use. Darcy's is the only performance scheduled for tonight, which means she should be alone.

I knock.

'Who is it?' she calls.

'It's Max.'

There's a pause, and I shove my hands in my pockets as I wait.

She opens the door and stands there, one hand on the doorframe and one on her hip. She's still in her bodystocking, obviously, since I gave her about a twenty-second head start before following her down here like a stalker.

And I look.

I take her in shamelessly.

Every curve, every tiny, glinting crystal on her body. The flush on her cheeks—from exertion and from the adulation she received, no doubt. The way the sheer black gauze turns her furled nipples darker while defining them perfectly and showcases the neat line of hair between her legs so light it's barely visible.

She told me in France she was a natural blonde. I suppose that's my evidence.

When I drag my eyes back up to her face, she's surveying me in amusement.

'Have you quite finished?'

Unstitch

'I could look all night,' I tell her. It's true.

'Clearly.' She nods at my stiff dick.

'You did that. Bending over like that at the end. You dirty, dirty girl.'

'What do you want, Max?'

I lean in and kiss her on both cheeks, noting the heat radiating off her body. Not surprising, given the feats of athleticism it's just performed. Her workouts would put my punishing gym regimen to shame.

'Can I come in?'

'Not a good idea.' She gazes at me as I pull back, and the hunger in her eyes tells me it's not because she doesn't want me to. Rather, she's upholding her sister's bullshit rules.

I let my gaze flicker south again, to those perfectly taut little buds. I could stoop and take one in my mouth right now. 'Do you get turned on doing that? Knowing every single guy in there wants to fuck you? Knowing that whichever poor woman they sink their dick inside now, they'll be imagining she's you?'

'Obviously,' she says, and I don't miss her shuddery exhale.

'Are you going to get yourself off now?' I crane my neck to see if she has any toys lined up in there to help her.

'Yep.' She pops the *p*. 'And I'm going to enjoy every second.'

Jesus Christ. 'Let me do it for you.' I glance around. The corridor's empty. 'No one has to know,' I plead. 'I'll put you on that table and make you come so hard with my tongue. Think how good I can make you feel, even through the fabric.'

'Max. No.' She tightens her grip on her waist.

'Fine.' I didn't expect her to give in, anyway. Not here. 'I want you to dance for me tomorrow. At my place.'

She widens her eyes. 'What the actual fuck? No.'

'Seriously. No one needs to know. You can do it off the books.' I pause. 'I'll give you twenty grand.'

Her face is a picture. If I didn't want this so badly, I'd laugh.

'What—that's ridiculous! You're insane. You can't pay twenty grand for a dance.'

'I can and I will. Give the money to charity if you don't want it.'

She rolls her eyes. 'Is this your fucked-up way of getting me to sleep with you?'

I sigh. Time to lay my cards on the table. It'll go better for me, anyway. 'Look. There's something between us. You might be in denial, for some unknown reason, but that's fine. I don't pressure unwilling women to let me fuck them.' I never have to pressure any woman to let me fuck her, if she must know. 'I want to fuck you, yes. I want to fuck every hole in your perfect body—I told you that already.

'But I also want you to get naked and dance just for me. I want to enjoy you without sharing the pleasure with anyone else. And if you want to fuck me afterwards, then great. If not, no problem. But I'm categorically not paying you for sex. You'd have to do it because you want to. Do you understand?'

13

DEX

My little sister is crying into my shoulder, her giant tears soaking through the cotton of my t-shirt. She's pregnant with her first child, though, so I won't mention that her waterworks feel a little excessive.

I'm not brave enough, or stupid enough, to do that.

'Eight years,' she howls. 'It's taken you *eight years* to come home to me.'

Guilt squeezes my heart tightly. 'I know, love. I missed you too. But I'm back for good now.'

'In theory,' she says with a sniff, lifting herself off my shoulder. 'God knows, they'll want their pound of flesh from you.'

I smile weakly, because it's true. I may have just landed this morning on a red-eye so short I got way too little sleep, but the reception I received at Loeb when I went in to show my face was exuberant enough to make me panic. It seems I'm their Great White Hope for turning the fortunes of their Equities division around, and I have a mountain to climb to prove that this budget-busting hire was worth it.

'They'll let me out occasionally,' I promise with more confidence than I feel, 'and you'll always be my first call.'

'Glad to hear it,' she says with a warning thump to my upper arm, and I grin at her.

Belle is objectively beautiful, inside and out, and it pains me that I wasn't around for more of her formative years. The force of my need to cut ties with my father and the toxic values of my upbringing was so great it obliterated all else. Even the desire to be around for my little sister.

That said, she's done okay for herself. The more I get to know Rafe, the more soundly I approve of him as a life partner for Belle. He seems a rock-solid guy, as do his mates, and I couldn't have asked for her to find a more adoring husband. It's clear he thinks she's the sun, moon and stars.

'The place is looking great,' I say, looking around. An all-white textured panel that must be six feet tall and three feet wide dominates the round hallway. The panel itself is curved. I guess it was commissioned for this exact space. 'Holy fuck, that piece is amazing.'

Our parents infused both of us with a keen aesthetic sense and an appreciation for good art. They've long invested in paintings and sculpture—our mum has a great eye—and Belle has picked up the family baton.

'Never marry an art dealer,' Rafe quips. 'The art budget is through the fucking roof.'

I laugh. 'I can well believe it.'

'He's worse than me,' my sister protests. 'He's such a pushover. He says yes to every piece I suggest.'

'That has nothing at all to do with the paintings,' Rafe says, and the way he looks at Belle as he says it, with love that's soft and fierce all at once, is really something.

'You've done a great job,' I tell her quietly as I stroll into their open-plan kitchen and living room. We're on the upper ground floor of their new townhouse, and it really is a beautiful space.

'Are you knackered?' she asks, putting a light hand on my shoulder as we cross over to the island.

'Fucking destroyed,' I say, pressing the heel of my palm to one of my bloodshot eyes.

'Well, we'll get you fed and you can have an early night,' she promises.

'That would be great,' I admit. I still have to get back across town. I've rented an apartment in the City, which is depressing but necessary. I'll be burning the candle at both ends this year, I have no doubt, and the last thing I need is to add a painful commute into the equation. Sure, I'd rather be over here in Holland Park on the weekends, but I'll have my head buried in my laptop most of the time, so what's the point?

'You still on for Sunday lunch?' Belle asks, following her question with a giggle when I roll my eyes, because the last thing I need this week is to play Happy Families with our parents.

'I guess so.'

'You guess. You're such an American.'

'I *suppose*. You being dragged along too, Rafe?'

'Wouldn't miss it for the world,' he says with a sarcastic cheeriness that has me sniggering.

'Poor fucker,' I observe, taking the bottle of cold beer he's handing me. 'Thanks. You definitely married into the wrong family.'

Long story short. Our dad's a religious nut and our mum never got the memo she was allowed her own beliefs. Neither did my sister, who was brought up even more strictly than me, with purity culture rammed down her throat at that convent school she went to.

That she took matters into her own hands and hooked up with a much older sex club owner was so out of character I still can't really believe it.

Our dad coming home early from a trip and walking in on Rafe butt-naked in his home one morning was the real scandal, though.

Suffice to say, it forced a lot of tough conversations between my sister and our parents, and it taught our dad that his days of patriarchal rule and brainwashing were firmly over.

I feel so guilty that I wasn't around for my sister, even if Rafe well and truly proved his mettle during the entire shitshow. I'm beyond proud of her for having the courage to lay down some boundaries and stand up for her own happiness, no matter how much that happiness was at odds with the values our parents had imposed upon us.

At least one of their kids has turned out not to be a giant fucking coward when it comes to accepting themselves for who they truly are.

'I can handle Ben,' he says, topping up Belle's sparkling water before cracking open his own beer. 'He knows not to push it with me. And your mum's come around, I think.'

'Definitely,' Belle echoes. 'She loves you.'

'Not sure she loves me. She loves the prospect of how many babies I'm gunning for,' he teases.

'Ugh,' I say jokingly, because while the thought of anyone impregnating my little sister leaves me cold, it massively takes the pressure off me to settle down with some nice, British version of Claudia and dutifully produce babies.

Wait. That leaves me even colder.

What warms my heart and feeds my soul, though, is breaking bread with my sister and her new husband in their beautiful, art-filled home. Even if our family unit is not what either of us would have hoped for, she's my person. She always will be. And it's not right that I've been apart from her for so long.

It's not right that the young woman sitting across from me, happy and carefree and loved up and secure in her own skin, should be a relatively unfamiliar version of the studious, blindly obedient girl I grew up next to. And I want to make amends. I want to be fully in her life again.

Just as I want her fully in mine.

She's the best person I know.

Which is why, when she pleads with me to accompany her and Rafe to Alchemy this weekend, "just for drinks in the bar", I don't have it in my heart to turn her down.

14

DARCY

Max is a smiling assassin.

I know better than to underestimate him.

The whole jocular Brunch Daddy vibe he has going on is hot—more than hot—but it's a persona. I know for sure that if he got a woman to himself, that smirk would vanish, and he'd be intense as fuck. It's there, that energy, thrumming right below the surface. I can feel it, and most likely it's the true source of my attraction to him.

Still, twenty grand for a dance feels indecent, even for a guy like that. Aggressive, somehow? The way he threw it out there was so cavalier, but that doesn't mean I should treat it the same way. Paying out that kind of money for a dance may be normal behaviour for him, but accepting it definitely isn't normal for me. I can't make head nor tail of it, if I'm honest, even if I've spent half the night turning it over in my head.

Nor can I ask my sister for advice. I wouldn't dare share such an indecent proposal with her, even if she wasn't currently pootling around the Greek islands on her brand new husband's yacht.

Unstitch

There's only one person I can ask.

Maddy.

I message her before she's even got into work to beg for a quick meeting.

> I had an indecent proposal last night and I'm not sure what to do about it. Fancy talking some sense into me? x

Telling Maddy you need advice on a weird sexy-ish proposal is probably worse than waving a big red cloak in front of a starving bull. Judging by the capitals and exclamation marks in her flurry of replies, she could not be keener to meet. So I drag myself out of bed, shower, and put on my workout gear before taking the tube a few stops to Green Park, the nearest tube station to Alchemy.

Maddy meets me at Pret, where we brave the throng to grab a coffee and a granola pot each before escaping into the park. It's a lovely morning, and London's self-appointed "green" park is showing the signs of this heatwave we're having. The trees are verdant but the lawns are getting scorched.

We give the scratchy grass a wide berth and sit down on a bench, because, even if I'm in Lululemon, she's in a seriously cute and seriously high-maintenance pink and white dress with straps that tie on the shoulders with huge bows. She looks like a doll. A very innocent doll. I bet Zach goes crazy for it.

'So, you can't just drop a text bomb about an indecent proposal and leave me hanging,' she complains, popping the lid on her granola pot. 'Shoot, motherfucker.'

'It's from Max,' I say with a pointed sideways look at her that's meant to communicate *need I say more?*

She widens her eyes, spoon frozen in front of her mouth. 'Max? God, he's such a dirty bastard. I love it. Go on.'

'He wants me to go to his place this evening. He's offered me twenty grand to dance practically naked for him in private.'

Maddy's a gratifying audience. She shoves her spoon straight back into her yoghurt and granola and sits up straight. 'You are *shitting* me.'

'Nope.' I take the opportunity for a quick mouthful of compote and yoghurt. Yummy.

'A "naked private dance".' She says it like we both know exactly what it's an innuendo for.

'Exactly.'

She smirks. 'Fuck, that's hot.'

I laugh. I wasn't expecting that—more a *how dare he?* or a *go for it*. 'What do you mean?'

'You know.' She narrows her eyes at me and flicks her perfectly blow-dried hair over her bare shoulder. 'Like, he's throwing his money around because he wants you so badly. It's seriously fucking hot on so many levels.'

'Yeah,' I say, because it really is, and it makes me feel better that Maddy thinks so, too. 'Doesn't make it okay, though.'

She cocks her head as she considers. 'Do you think he's doing it because it's the only way he'll get you to agree? Or is it, like, a kinky power play? He's doing it because he gets off on paying women to do that kind of thing. Because if you wouldn't do it for free, then don't feel you have to do it for the money. You're not hard up, are you? But if you're attracted to him, then seriously, babes, take it and run.'

I frown. 'I dunno. A bit of both, maybe? I mean, I definitely find him majorly attractive. He's such a...'

'Daddy,' Maddy finishes with a decisive nod. 'Yep. Totally. And overtly filthy, you know what I mean?'

She's not wrong there. 'So the thought of dancing for him definitely doesn't give me the ick.' Quite the opposite. 'The chemistry between us is crazy—I told you we danced at the wedding, right?'

'Right,' she says. 'So why haven't you two fucked yet?'

'Something's been holding me back,' I admit. 'It didn't feel right to hook up in France—I wanted to be there for Gen. But I suppose I like the chase. He's the kind of guy who'd be all over you till he got what he wanted, and then you'd never see him again.'

'Totally.' Maddy digs through her little pot to get to the compote at the bottom. 'But that's not a problem for you, is it?'

'God, no. He and I are probably quite similar in that respect. I suppose I'm just holding him off because it's fun, right? He's a cocky shit, so it's entertaining to be the thing he can't have.'

'Hence the five-figure sweetener,' she says, pointing her spoon at me.

I grimace. 'Exactly.'

'I'm assuming "private dance" is code for "fuck"?' She wiggles her eyebrows at me saucily.

'That's the thing,' I say, folding one leg under me. 'I asked just that and he categorically said it was a dance only. He said he'd pay me to dance, and if I wanted to fuck him after then even better, but he wasn't going to pay me to fuck him.'

'Hmm.' She deflates slightly. 'Interesting. So he's not doing it for "hooker kink" reasons. I think what you have here is a win-win, babes. I mean, come on. A hot guy you've been lusting after throws cash at you to dance for him, so you can really go for it, and then he can seduce you, or you can seduce him. Whatever.

'And he's super powerful now, which is even hotter. He's basically Baby Daddy Anton now that he's CEO. You know they're gearing up for an IPO? It's going to be the biggest IPO in Europe in, like, years. And apparently when he stepped up, he negotiated a fuck-tonne of pre-IPO stock, so when Wolff Holdings floats, he'll be worth mega-bucks. Not that he isn't already. There'll be lots of lock-ins, obviously. He won't be able to liquidate it for years, but still. It'll be raining cash over there.'

I narrow my eyes suspiciously. 'And you know this much about the whole thing because…?'

She sighs. 'Zach's talked about it. *A lot*. He's really excited about it.'

'That makes one of us,' I say.

'Right? Poor little nerd. But he's so fucking cute I don't mind at all. And it means you shouldn't feel guilty about taking Max's money. Now Anton's married and retired, Max is *the* catch.'

'Seriously?' That surprises me, for some reason. I know he's insanely sexy and, from the sounds of it, about to be insanely wealthy, but still. I hadn't thought about him having much of a profile.

She leans forward. 'Are you kidding me? *Tatler* just did a spread on him—he topped their list of non-aristocratic eligible bachelors in the UK. The women at Alchemy go crazy for him, and not just because he has a big dick and knows how to use it. Actually, it's probably great for him to have Alchemy. It means he doesn't have to go out and about looking for his next fuck. It's all on tap for him.'

I'd really, really like to ask her what else she knows

about the size and skill level of Max's dick, but I have a more pressing, if less fun, question.

'About the money. I honestly don't know. It feels really immoral.'

'Are you morally opposed to sex for money?' she bats back.

'No... I don't think so. No, I'm not. In real life I'm fine with it, and in fantasy life I'm all over it like a rash.'

She nods sagely. 'Same. I nagged Zach for *so long* to buy me at Slave Night. We weren't even together then. And he did, and it was the hottest night of my life.' She smiles fondly.

'I kind of love that I've fallen into this family of people who reminisce about Slave Night like most people would reminisce about their first dinner date together,' I say, and she howls with laughter.

'Right?! God, I love it. But why are you having issues with the money? I've been with Spreadsheet long enough to know that if you both have something the other wants, then you have a market. So what's the problem?'

I sigh. I can't articulate what the problem is, even to myself. I can't deny the money would come in handy. I'm in this weird position where I have a lovely quality of life, thanks to the dancing gig and Gen's amazing pad, but I'm not contributing much.

Even if she doesn't need the money, I'd rather pay her something. She could always give it to charity, or something. I may be a free spirit, but I'm not a freeloader. I've basically spent the past few years dancing, surfing, drinking, and living like a bum on a low budget. It would be nice if London was a fresh start. A chance to show I'm not the baby of the family anymore—I don't expect a permanent free ride.

So, obviously, twenty grand would come in handy. More than handy. It would last months. But I'd like to earn it, and doing one sexy, naked dance doesn't feel like the right exchange for twenty thousand crisp British pounds. It's too easy, and yet it's hard. It's morally questionable (something I have no problem with), and it's loaded with... what? Expectations?

'It feels weird,' is the only explanation I can come up with, which is lame as fuck, but Maddy seems to know what I mean.

'If you think about it,' she muses, mushing her granola and yoghurt and compote together into a big pinkish mess, 'twenty grand's not that much money. I mean, he's loaded. It's not like he offered you a million quid to have sex with him. Twenty grand for a dance is a bit stingy, if you ask me.'

She grins at me. I take her in, a vision in her pink and white sundress, her beautiful diamond solitaire glinting in the sunlight of this early July morning as she does disgusting things to her granola pot. I know exactly what she's doing. She's being deliberately flippant, underplaying the whole proposal so I stop overthinking it.

'That's pretty obnoxious,' I say. 'Twenty grand is more than what people on minimum wage earn in an entire year. God.' I drop my head and rub my free hand over my face. 'That makes me feel even more shitty. Some people earn that in a whole year of being a hospital porter, or a street sweeper, or whatever else godawful jobs pay minimum wage, and I'd get it for one dance. It gives me the ick.'

'I totally agree, it's utterly shit. Life's not fair. But skills have a value. Look at footballers—it's outrageous what they earn, but it makes financial sense for their club. *Because their skills have value.* You're a beautiful dancer. Truly. And a hot, powerful man is so smitten with you that he'll pay five figures to get you all to himself for one dance. So, for God's sake, don't feel bad about it. Take his money and give him what he wants.'

I'm not sure about Maddy's logic. I'm not sure about any of it, and I suspect I called her precisely because I knew she'd enable me. Which probably means I've subconsciously wanted to say yes to Max's proposal since the moment he made it.

15

DARCY

Max lives in One Hyde Park, which is a development so swanky that I'm pretty sure its closest food store is Harrods' food hall. It overlooks Hyde Park, oddly enough, and its next-door neighbour is The Mandarin Oriental. I thought you'd need to own a very large oil field to be able to afford a flat here, but apparently not.

I take the lift up to the fourth floor, feeling far more nervous than I thought I would and far more like a hooker than I thought I would, too. I'm in a long, floaty sundress, the bodystocking I took home from work last night folded carefully in my bag. It's still broad daylight, of course, a fact I overlooked and am now cursing. Maybe he'll draw the curtains? The prospect of dancing in the sunlight feels far more daring, more exposing, than being carefully lit on the stage of a dark club.

He's waiting when I get out of the lift, standing in the doorway to his flat. My Havaianas make an embarrassing flapping noise against the lobby's glossy white marble floor. By contrast, Max is still in his work clothes. Dark, perfectly fitted trousers and a white shirt, top couple of buttons undone. His light brown hair is combed casually off his forehead, and that white cotton shows off his tan far too well.

He really is ridiculously attractive. Not that he needs anyone to reassure him of that fact.

'Thanks for coming,' he says softly. His smile as he takes me in is sincere. Appreciative. He bends to kiss me on both cheeks, and I catch a vague whiff of his cologne. It's lovely but very faint, and I kind of like the fact that he hasn't reapplied it since he got home from work.

Although, why should he? This isn't a date. He hasn't showered, or changed out of his work clothes, or preened. He's paying me to be here—he doesn't have to make an effort or prove anything.

I wonder what it would be like to come to a place like this for an actual date with a man like this. To have him sweep me up in his arms and whisper a muffled *hello, darling* against the pulse at the side of my neck. I wonder if guys like Max are even capable of falling for anyone, or if they're too busy to focus on anything more than their next fuck or, failing that, a little post-work titillation in the form of a private dance.

His flat, when he ushers me inside, is vast, and light-filled, and impeccably, expensively decorated, and completely devoid of any kind of personality. The designer went for a Fifty Shades of Taupe vibe, it seems. But holy fuck, that view of the park is obscene.

'I just moved in,' he says behind me. 'It's a corporate flat —perk of the new job.'

I turn and raise my eyebrows in surprise. 'Wolff owns this?'

'Yeah. Anton didn't want to live here, so they used it to put up overseas management and clients.'

My new brother-in-law lives in an orgasmic white stucco wedding-cake villa in Holland Park whose interior is a cacophony of sumptuous furniture and colourful, jaw-dropping art. I'm not surprised he turned his nose up at this show home.

'Definitely not his vibe,' I observe.

'Not really mine, either, but I'm too busy right now to care,' Max says. 'Thank you for agreeing to my proposition and giving me an excellent reason to get out of the office. I would have changed, but I got back about ten minutes ago and I didn't want to run the risk of being in the shower when you turned up.'

I let my gaze roam over him, which is really no hardship. He looks a bit more dishevelled than his usually dapper state, but still positively edible.

'You're good,' I tell him, flashing him a smile, which he returns with a wolfish grin.

'Still. I'd like to unwind so I can enjoy this properly. I might jump in the shower while you're getting changed, but let me get you a drink to take through, eh? Champagne? Rosé? G&T?'

'Rosé would be lovely,' I tell him. I could do with something to take the edge off, but the last thing I need are champagne bubbles bloating my stomach when I need to get basically naked in front of this god.

'What kind of music do you want?' he asks as he hands me my drink. 'I'll get it going—it might help get you in the zone.'

I'm touched. It's a thoughtful suggestion, and he's right, of course. Hearing the music I dance to several nights a week will undoubtedly make this whole setup feel more natural.

'Pull up the Alchemy playlists on Spotify, and I'll show you,' I tell him.

TWENTY MINUTES LATER, I'm standing in my heels and bodystocking, admiring my reflection in his huge guest bathroom. The lighting in here is bloody fantastic. My sequins sparkle in a million directions, and I feel like a human disco ball. I've brushed my hair out but worn it loose—I know how much he likes my hair. My sister, God bless her, has been treating me to top-ups with Giorgio since I got back.

I let my hands sway high above my head and twirl for myself as I give myself a pep talk. This is what I do. I'm a dancer, and I'm bloody good at it. The shapes I make with my body speak of sex. My movements change my audience's brain chemistry, even when I've gone so deep inside myself I'm barely aware of who's watching.

That won't happen this evening.

When I down the rest of my rosé and exit the bathroom, the atmosphere has changed. The sexy music I instructed Max to put on is pulsing its hypnotic beats through the space. The blinds are lowered, blocking out the view of the park and almost all the sunlight. Now, the vast living area is lit mainly by floor spots in the kitchen area and a couple of table lamps.

And best of all? Max is standing in the middle of the room, hair damp and combed neatly back off his face, nursing what looks like scotch and wearing nothing but a white t-shirt and grey sweats. In true male form, he's failed to dry himself off completely, so there are some damp spots on the t-shirt, but it's soft and hugs his lean, muscular frame to perfection.

Don't even get me started on the sweatpants, because every fibre of self control I possess is now engaged in avoiding staring at his crotch area in an attempt to spot the outline of his cock. I don't doubt for a second that if I looked, I'd see it. I could try telling you I have an excellent BDR—Big Dick Radar—but the truth is, my naughty sister spilt the beans one night over too much red wine.

I have it on good authority that Max Hunter is not over-compensating for *anything*. And, while I've given him a hard time recently about being old and crusty, this guy is neither.

He is fucking perfection.

I'm so busy eye-fucking him without seeming like I'm eye-fucking him that it actually takes me by surprise when he gives me a once-over of his own and utters a low, quiet *wow*.

16

MAX

'You've seen me like this before,' she protests.

'Yeah.' I take a step towards her. 'Up on stage in a club full of people. And last night, in your dressing room, when you couldn't get rid of me fast enough.' I lick my lips. 'But it's not every day I have a stunningly beautiful woman in my home, almost naked and prepared to give me my own private show.'

'Glad to hear it,' she mutters. Her body language isn't self-conscious—she's far too comfortable in her own skin to feel anything like that—but her face is guarded. I shouldn't like it that she feels out of her depth here, alone with me, but honestly?

I fucking love it.

I suspect she's underestimated me until now, and I'd love nothing more than to teach her a lesson.

Be careful about strolling so nonchalantly into the lion's den, little girl.

This pathetic excuse for a costume is one half-hearted tug away from disintegrating in my hands. She's chosen to wear the nude version rather than last night's sheer black one. It's a bold move, because it's as see-through as the sheerest pair of stockings. She may as well have stuck those little crystals on her bare skin.

It ghosts over the heavy curves of her breasts and showcases every detail of her delights, from rosy nipples to golden landing strip. I can even see the outline of her pussy lips. The sight of her bared for me like this has my mouth watering.

I already know this is the best money I'll spend all year.

I jerk my head towards one of the small matching tables at either end of the sofa. 'I've set out a glass of water for you, in case you work up a thirst. But you're the boss. I'm ready when you are.'

I'm being disingenuous, obviously.

There's only one boss in this room, and it's not Darcy.

I glance down. 'Why don't you take off your heels? I want you comfortable.'

What I really mean is that I intend this dance to feel intimate. Don't get me wrong—a beautiful woman in nothing but a pair of heels is hot as fuck, but I want her unconstrained and unabashed, and if she's barefoot she can move more freely. Contort herself for me more fully.

'Whatever you want,' she says smoothly. She steps right up to me and puts a hand on my shoulder, dropping her head and going to bend one leg, but I stop her with a steadying hand on her waist.

'Wait. Allow me.'

I'm not some earnest, wholesome Prince Charming. I'm sweet little Cinders' worst fucking nightmare, so it feels perversely right that I perform this anti-Charming move of removing the glass slippers. Once she's righted herself, I sink to one knee before her. My face is six inches from her cunt, and I can smell the faintest musk of her scent.

This time, it's me who dips my head. I resist the temptation to trail my fingertips down her calf, because she hasn't agreed to my touching her tonight, and instead focus on the tiny, delicate buckle at her ankle. I undo it and its twin before sitting back on my heels and smiling up at her. She's staring down at me, lips parted, like she doesn't know what to make of this man who pays a woman to dance for him like a true cad and then stoops to unbuckle her shoes like a gent.

With a wink, I get to my feet, grab my tumbler of whisky from the table and take my seat in the middle of the sofa. It's situated to enjoy an uninterrupted view of the terrace, which means that I can now enjoy an uninterrupted view of this enchanting creature dancing just for me.

Let the show begin.

17

DARCY

I thought being bathed in radiant sunlight while I danced for a single man would be confronting, but maybe I misjudged. Between the heavy blinds and the thick glass that wipes out the thrum of the London traffic a few floors below us, Max's cavernous flat has transformed into a curiously intimate space.

It's just me, the music... and him.

He's manspread across the centre of the huge sofa, holding his crystal tumbler in place on his thigh with one hand, the other arm flung across the back of the cushions. A king in his castle, entitled and handsome and seeking entertainment. I'm the dancer in the music box, fated to dance and dance until the king has had enough—except the king is in here with me, and the air is thick with the weight of his expectation.

Twenty grand buys you high expectations indeed.

I close my eyes, and I begin to sway, and I take the feelings of vulnerability and exposure that having Max's attention on me provokes, and I bite down on them. I allow them to ramp up my heart rate, to scatter goosebumps along my skin.

This isn't defencelessness. *It's power.* This man wants me. Badly. He has eyes only for me. He's come home early from work so he can feast his eyes on the alchemy I conjure with nothing but my body. Those blue eyes of his glitter in the dim light; they stay trained on me as he raises his glass to his lips and drinks.

He doesn't want to miss a second.

The playlist segues into one of my favourite pieces, a sexy beat over soaring strings and the unmistakable whimpers of a woman's orgasm building. It charges the air further, charges *me*, because I know there's no way Max can hear this and see what I'm doing and not think only of sex, of how I might sound beneath him, of whether my whimpers would be just like that, throaty and achy and needy. Of whether my body would undulate around his cock in precisely the same way that it's undulating around thin air right now as I writhe and rock and twist.

The answer, of course, is that it would. I may be classically trained, but I left my ballet days behind many moons ago and happily pursued a kind of dancing that fitted my curves and sang to my soul. Now, the way I move is the way I have sex, and the music I move to is the soundtrack of that sex.

The poor guy doesn't stand a chance around me, just as I don't stand a chance around him. And for all I've acted coy over this evening's little 'proposition', I'm well aware there's only one way tonight will end.

It's impossible to imagine any other outcome, and I've made peace with that far more than I've made peace with the idea of taking Max's money.

I turn around and close my eyes, and despite both of those things, the heat of his gaze sears into my arse as it sways in front of him.

I don't know how long I dance for him like this. Ten minutes? Twenty? Thirty? It's soulful and unchoreographed. It's a precise combination of how I imagine he wants me to move and how he makes me feel. I haven't touched him—he didn't ask me to agree to a lap dance—but that makes no difference to him, because, when I turn around and look at him again, it's clear he's been growing more and more agitated.

He drains his drink and sets the tumbler on the cushion beside him. He spreads his legs further. Shifts forward and runs his fingers through his hair as he groans, low and male. The tent in those sexy grey sweatpants is quite the sight, but his eyes don't leave my body. Not for one second. And mine don't leave his face again.

Still the music pulses on.

Still I dance, lithe and barefoot and moving on instinct, the laser focus of his attention the headiest drug I've ever, ever experienced.

Finally, he breaks the silence between us. 'Darcy. Fuck.'

I smile, as mysteriously as I can, and hold my arms above my head, giving him the perfect view of my tits swaying.

'Fuck,' he says again. 'Turn around. Bend over.'

Yes. The command is another hit to my bloodstream.

'Yes, sir,' I say, spinning on my heel so I'm facing the wall of blinds. I spread my feet and hinge at the hips, lowering myself down, down, till I'm cuffing my ankles with my fingers and giving him the perfect view of my pussy. It's throbbing and wet, and the faint rub of the bodystocking against it is the most delicious form of torture.

His words from the wedding dance through my mind, over and over.

You look like you were created to take my cock in every single perfect hole in your spectacular body.

They were the best kind of menacing when he said them, but damn, if what's unspoken in that gaze of his isn't a million times more.

I truly believe Taylor Swift was staring deep into the abyss of the attention-seeking whore that is my soul when she wrote *Mirrorball*. Whatever version of myself someone wants up there on stage, they'll get. However far I have to contort myself, I'll do it.

And in this lavish, soulless apartment, I'm barefoot and stripped back and effectively naked for Max. I'm just me, with a sultry soundtrack and a few sparkles. No pole. No cage. No props. I may be the one folded over like a piece of paper, but I'm betting he topples like a fucking house of cards.

'God, that's good,' he says hoarsely. I open my eyes to see upside-down Max push himself off the sofa. He stops where he is, rooted to the spot.

'Tell me you're as turned on as I am,' he growls. 'Because, from over here, your cunt looks wet.'

'I'm turned on,' I pant, the blood rushing to my head in this position. His eyes on me are the only aphrodisiac I need. 'You've been looking at me like you can't decide whether to eat me or fuck me first.'

He lets out a humourless laugh. 'That's exactly right. And I don't know if you'll let me do either. But I want to do both. Over and over.'

I pause—because this is the point of no return—and sigh. The exhalation has me hinging forward even more.

Who am I kidding? The point of no return was when I texted him from Green Park this morning.

'You can do whatever you want to me,' I tell him. 'I want it all.'

18

MAX

I want it all.

My body is propelling itself towards her before she's even finished her sentence, bare feet pressing into the soft, thick tufts of the rug underfoot, hands outreached, my only coherent thoughts being that *she said I could touch her* and that I need to press my poor, aching cock against that sweet, warm space she has on full display for me.

Then I'm there. I come up flush behind her, sinking my fingertips into the flesh of her hips, my jersey-clad erection rutting against her cunt a couple of times of its own accord.

'Get up here,' I grit out, and she unfolds herself easily, gracefully, a flower unfurling its soft petals against my hard body. I'm under no illusions that Darcy is an angel, but she certainly feels like one in the context of Alchemy: that untouchable celestial being who dances but doesn't engage, the rules clear:

Look but don't touch.

I've spent far too much time these past weeks suffering

as this creature teases me, riles me, whether she's been backlit by a French sunset or spotlit on a London stage.

And now, every moment of agonising delectation reframes itself as foreplay. That yearning—if only in its basest, most physical form, because I don't do emotion—makes this instant where I unwrap my glittering prize all the sweeter for having been hard won.

As St. Paul, a man famously appreciative of the punch a good epiphany can pack, said, *this light momentary affliction is preparing for us an eternal weight of glory beyond all comparison.*

I'm not convinced the glory will be eternal—right now I'm merely hoping not to disgrace myself—but I *am* confident it'll be beyond all comparison.

Delayed gratification is as unfamiliar a concept to me as the self-control that must necessarily preempt it, but it's already selling itself, the pleasure of putting my hands on Darcy's body surely as welcome a relief as that surge of blood when a nipple clamp is removed.

Hmm. Nipple clamps. Now *there's* an idea.

Her shoulder blades hit my chest, her hair, when she shakes it out, brushing my face before she lets her head loll back against my shoulder.

'That's it,' I croon in her ear. I nip lightly at her hoop-laden earlobe as I allow my hands to skate up over her hips, to dip in at her waist, before I drag my palms up her body, my fingers splaying over her rib cage. 'Arms up, like a good girl.'

She floats them up, bending one so it caresses the back of my neck like she's closing the gap between us even further as she wiggles her delicious bottom against my angry cock. I suck in a sharp breath through my teeth and let my hands wander over the perfect swell of her tits until I finally encounter those nipples.

Jesus, my mouth starts watering at the mere feel of them, because they are the most deliciously taut little pieces of candy, and the mesh is no barrier at all. Yep, clamps would do very well for these indeed. I roll them, pinch them between my fingers, and she gives the breathiest whimper.

So sensitive.

So responsive.

But I suspect, like me, she's on a knife-edge of arousal. I'm not the only one here whose libido has suffered weeks of torment.

I play with them for a few moments as she mewls and squirms against me, arching into me, her hands clawing at my head and gripping my hair.

'Very, very nice,' I tell her. 'You know you should have let me touch you before, shouldn't you?'

'Yes,' she practically sobs, rubbing her arse against my dick again.

'Quite right,' I say. I release one nipple and drag my hand down her front, over the soft curve of her stomach so I can cup her pussy roughly. Fuck, she's so wet and hot. 'You wouldn't have had to wait so long to feel like this if you hadn't been such a little prick-tease, would you?'

Her *no* is a moan.

'That's right. And what happens to little prick-teases?'

'I dunno.' She slurs her words.

'They get teased right back. And *then* they get fucked.'

'Oh, God,' she says as I reach behind me, grabbing her wrists and pinning them behind her back so I can frog-march her over to where I want her.

'Bend over,' I order as we hit the back of the sofa. She does as I say, hinging forward. I release her wrists and lay them over her head so her hands touch the seat of the sofa. She may need to push back against me shortly, when I'm railing the living daylights out of her.

'So obedient,' I tell her as I drop to my knees behind her, my cock painting the inside of my jogging bottoms with precum. I yield for a moment to the temptation of being at eye-level with those very holes I vowed to violate, burying my mouth and nose in her heat and inhaling hard as I run my hands up the backs of her legs. By God, she smells other-worldly good. Arousal is pumping off her. She's an animal in heat.

I pull away. 'I hope Alchemy has more of these things,' I observe mildly before getting a grip of her bodystocking with both hands and tearing it. The pointless mesh rips right down the seam of her cunt, but I tug savagely until it's ripped the whole way up the back, too, and I can't resist a huff of satisfaction.

Because now her spectacular body is fully open to me, and I have free fucking rein. Her cunt is waxed bare underneath, and it's all glossy rose-pink gorgeousness and pretty petals that will look so perfect stretched around my cock.

And further up?

The darker, puckered skin protecting the hole so verboten as to be a fucking red rag to this twisted bull.

I yield to temptation.

I dip my head to her pussy.

19

DARCY

Max finally takes pity on me.

I can tell he's pissed off that I've made him wait this long, and I can also tell he's going to make me suffer for it. I don't care, because every second he spends teasing me, edging me, will make my climax more explosive when he grants it to me. There's only one way this evening will end.

His pity comes in the form of my cheeks spread wide by his hands and a soft kiss bestowed upon my pussy. I don't for a second mistake the softness for tenderness. It's a power play, pure and simple. A reminder that he's in charge, that he's setting the pace and the intensity.

'Fuck,' I whisper as his lips brush my flesh. How typical of Max that the first time he kisses me, it's on my pussy. I suspect that tells me all I need to know about him.

Straight for the fucking jugular, this guy.

He shifts behind me, tapping lightly at my entrance before tracing a line upwards. His fingertip brushes over my little ring of muscle, and it feels like a warning. An omen. Then it's trailing south again, and I shiver at the sensation.

It's so laughably short of what I need, but if I focus on what he's giving me, rather than what he's holding back, the pleasure is real.

'Did you enjoy dancing for me just now?' he murmurs, his hot breath dancing over my swollen flesh.

'So much.' I wiggle my bottom for emphasis.

'What did you like about it?' He puts two fingers on me and spreads me wide open.

I wait for his next touch.

He waits for my answer.

'I—uh—I liked how you were looking at me. It made me feel sexy.'

He laughs a little. 'There's no question about that. Is that why you like dancing for everyone at Alchemy? The attention?'

'Yes,' I confess. The slight discomfort I feel being bent over this sofa is nothing to the ache my poor pussy feels at being so near to and yet so far from euphoria. 'But this is better.'

'Good. Why?'

'Because it's just the two of us, so it's more intense. I like dancing for your eyes only.'

'Fuck, I like that too, sweetheart,' he moans, then rewards me with a single long, hard, heavenly lick. 'Having you dance for me when I've had to share you with all those fuckers these past few weeks... We can have a lot more fun when I get you all to myself, can't we?'

There's something seriously ominous about the way he says the last line, but the celebratory thumping of my pulse in my pussy drowns out the alarm bells, because I want *all* the fun with this twisted bastard. I want him to knock himself out on my body. To plunder and pillage and leave me reeling and useless.

He's still holding me open. He pushes two fingers inside, hard, and I let out a strangled cry of pleasure as he presses his mouth to my clit.

'And when you flaunt these holes at a man, over and over again for weeks, and don't let him touch you,' he growls against my needy flesh, 'it makes him very, very dangerous.'

'I want you dangerous,' I slur, and it's true. I want him unleashed. Animalistic. I've certainly pushed him far enough.

'*Good.* Because I'm going to push you hard tonight.'

With those magic words, he flicks his tongue over my clit, and I nearly lose my mind. But then he's muttering something unintelligible, and I'm not sure if it's appreciation for how I taste or an admonishment to himself, but my fears of being edged seem unfounded, because he lets me have it, fingers jamming inside me roughly as his taut, flat tongue laves me hard.

He adds a third finger before pulling away from my clit, but before I can protest, he's spitting right between my cheeks and then his other hand is there, one finger prodding and pressing and demanding entry as his tongue finds my clit again, and I can't. I just *can't*. He's too good.

Jesus *Christ*.

He was right about working me hard.

He hasn't even got his cock involved yet.

20

MAX

She comes so fast and so hard after I start working her properly that it's as if a dam has burst. I have a front-row seat to the show, my head bent so I can get to her around my hands, my nose and mouth buried in the exact fucking place they've wanted to be for weeks as her plush inner walls clamp around my fingers and my tongue laps up her arousal.

I dig deeper with my fingers, I lick harder with my tongue, and I drive every single drop of that spectacular orgasm from her before I hoist her upright and turn her in my arms. Her face is flushed. Eye makeup smudged. Hair everywhere. She's limp and sated and trying to catch her breath.

She's fucking perfect, and I don't miss the look she gives me. It's as if I'm the second coming of Christ: far beyond approving to the realms of worshipful.

That bodysuit is ripped from her pussy to her ribcage, so I wedge her between my hips—or my dick, more like—and the back of the sofa before giving the fabric a good tug. It splits in two down the front, and I slide it down her arms. I have her top half completely bare now, and it's a sight for sore eyes.

'Better,' I say, aiming a dirty grin at her tits before reaching for the hem of my t-shirt and tugging it up over my head, because I need to be balls-deep inside her *right now* and this position will do nicely. I make a tight fist in her hair and smash our faces together so I can take her mouth.

Mmm. Even her kisses are that perfect balance of pliant and hungry. I've taken the edge off, but now she needs me to fill her up just as much as I need it. She lets her hands slide over my bare shoulders, exploring my biceps and my shoulder blades as my pecs press up against the soft, plump tissue of her tits.

'*God,*' she moans into my mouth. She's all hot and squirming and greedy in my arms, and I need inside her *now*, so I fumble in the pocket of my sweats and pull out a foil square.

'Put it on me,' I grit out, holding it up, and she grabs it. I plant her arse on the sofa back and hold her in place, my fingers digging into her waist as she rips the packet open. We both look down, foreheads touching, as she frees my monster cock from the waistband of my sweats and proceeds to pinch the head of the condom and roll it on with every bit of the skill I'd expect from a little minx like her.

'Jesus,' she says, a hint of a giggle in her voice.

'Yep, time to start praying, sweetheart,' I tell her. I'm holding my cock in my hand, pointing it straight at her like a loaded gun. I'm half-crazy with need, but still I pause for a second to take her in: tits so round and creamy, her sexy little nipples hard as fuck and her legs spread, that warm, wet cunt primed and ready for me.

I bite down on my lower lip as I drag the head of my

cock through her slickness, and then I'm pushing in, banding one arm around her back and sinking the fingers of the other one into her hip as I drive home.

Fuck, she's tight and soft and so deliciously welcoming, and it will take every ounce of my self-control not to rut my hips into a blur of movement and make myself come in seconds. There's so much I want to do with her. To her. I want to lay her out on my bed and suck on those tits, and nip at her flawless skin, and flip her over, and pound into her from behind, and then flip her over again and cover her body with mine.

I want to spread her out and tie her up and clamp those nipples and paint her stomach with my cum, and I will. I'll do all that and more. I'll discipline her and control her and punish her and use her and edge her and break her. God knows, I'll command every vestige of my self-control to toy with my delectable new plaything for hours and hours and hours, until she doesn't know which way is up and has only one word in her vocabulary.

Max.

But for now, I just need to finish inside her. It's a potent combination, the physical need I have to come and the equally visceral desire I have to show her who's boss now after weeks of her running circles around me. I dip my head and bite down hard on her shoulder, licking the spot I marked as I drive savagely into her heat.

'Fuck,' she moans incoherently.

'You like me marking you while I fuck you?' I mutter against her skin, dragging my lips along the ridge of her shoulder to find her neck. I bury my nose in her soft, fragrant hair, but then she's tilting her head, giving me access, and I suck on her neck instead as I continue to pump steadily in and out.

'Too much,' she whispers. She clings to me as she rocks her hips as best she can in this precarious position, meeting my thrusts beat for beat.

'Good,' I hiss. 'Because I told you already, you're my little fucktoy now, and all your tight, greedy, teasing little holes are mine to fuck and fill and violate. Got it?'

I raise my head so I can swallow her moaned *yes* with a savage kiss, fucking her luscious mouth as intensely as I'm fucking her sweet little cunt.

'Fuck,' she says with a whimper. 'I knew you'd be filthy, but *fuck*. It's too good.'

I tighten my grip on her hair, my breath coming in harsh spurts from my attempts to kiss her and fuck her and talk dirty to her. I love this. I love that I'm undoing her with my words as much as my dick.

I *knew* we'd be compatible. I knew she'd want me to treat her like this.

'That's because you're a dirty little slut who needs a good fucking schooling from a real fucking man,' I growl. 'And you have no fucking clue what that looks like, because we're only getting started.'

I hold her hip more tightly, and she clings to me as I let rip, pistonning my poor, desperate cock until she's a sobbing, writhing mess around me and I find white-hot oblivion deep inside her body.

21

DEX

It's been a long week of fighting jet lag and settling into life at Loeb. And while the London outpost of a boutique Swiss bank has nothing on the intensity I've known at the New York headquarters of one of the most demanding banks in the world, it's still been full on.

I'm not some fresh-faced graduate who can arse around and take his time getting to know how things work. Nope. I'm Loeb's new Head of Equities, the gamble they've paid a pretty penny for, and I'm expected, to steal a phrase beloved by my former employer, to hit the ground running.

In the past five days, I've had not only a full day of training on Loeb culture and standards but sit-downs with the heads of our Investment Banking, Investment Research, Operations, and Fixed Income, Currency and Commodities —FICC—divisions. I've already been wheeled out to meet the Chief Investment Officers of some of our biggest institutional investors—including the likes of Legal & General and Fidelity—over lunch, dinner and drinks.

The brief is clear. I'm a big-name hire from a bulge-bracket bank, and I'm here to legitimise Loeb. I'm to transform it from a second-tier player in the equity capital markets to a first-tier player, an equity franchise that's a real contender for the all-too-thin flow of business the markets are seeing these days.

When there's a deal to be done, Loeb wants in on the action. In essence, there's very little business to be had out there. It's a total bun fight.

And Loeb wants a great deal more buns than it's been getting.

It hasn't taken me five days to work out that Loeb will be a far more pleasant place to work than Goldman. The bar is lower, the work ethic is healthier, the employees' ambition levels are less intense than they were where I came from.

All of which makes it both a delightful culture and far harder place to get anything done. The management at Loeb may be solid, but its staff are infinitely more complacent. At Goldman, there was a constant three-line whip to move forward, an ever-present expectation that you devoured potential business with all the cut-throat zeal of a *Grey's Anatomy* surgical intern or you'd be left high and dry by those who wanted it more badly.

There was a carrot dangling over one shoulder and a stick hanging over the other every single day.

Here, I suspect I may have to light a lot of fires under a lot of arses to get anyone to give enough of a shit to exert themselves.

All of which is to say that I'm fucking exhausted, I can recall the names of about five percent of the people I've met this week, I don't know which way is up, and I'd like to spend my Saturday evening rewatching *Succession* with a nice takeout and a glass of good red.

But it's not to be.

Because my little sister wants me here tonight, and that's more important.

Let me say that when your brain tends towards inappropriate fantasies about inappropriate people at inappropriate times, it feels really bloody great to see a woman and have an instant, visceral reaction to her. It's a warm bath after being battered by emotional hail storms. My blood heats in my veins, and I feel the purest sense of enjoyment as I take her in.

She's beautiful—the kind of beauty that stops traffic—and she looks vaguely familiar. When I enter Alchemy's bar with my sister and Rafe, she's the first person I see, and she's sitting next to Maddy, so it's entirely possible we've met before. But I'd remember her, surely? I flip through a mental who's who of Belle and Rafe's wedding but come up short. I was under the impression we were catching up with Maddy, Zach, Cal and Aida this evening, no one else.

I make my way through the greetings, bro-hugging Cal, kissing Aida, who looks incredible as always, on both cheeks, shaking Zach's hand with genuine pleasure—he's a great guy—and hugging Mads, of whom I'm genuinely fond. She may have been out of control when she was younger, but she's been a great friend to Belle, especially this past year. I'm glad my sis has a fearless female to cheerlead her and egg her on in the pursuit of her own happiness.

Then I'm in front of the Titian-haired beauty. Her creamy skin is on show in a slinky, low-cut black dress that looks as though it ties at the back of her neck and puts her spectacular breasts on full display. I'm genuinely trying to ignore them, but it's not easy. Her eyes are blue, and her smile is electric—far warmer, I suspect, than the tentative one I'm giving her.

'Hi!' she cries, opening her arms wide for a hug. 'I'm Darcy—Gen's sister.'

Gen's sister. *Darcy.* Of course. From the pea-soup fog of information Belle threw at me last weekend, I manage to retrieve the fact that Gen's sister is back in London, having been in... Australia, maybe? And that she's dancing at Alchemy.

Oh fuck. *She dances.* God help me.

'Of course you are,' I say slowly as I process. 'So lovely to meet you, Darcy.' I abandon all hope of a polite English double kiss and allow myself to be pulled into a hug and crushed against her soft breasts and enveloped in her heady scent as her laugh at my obvious confusion tinkles in my ear.

She's a veritable feast for the senses, this one.

She's all consuming.

I END up sitting between her and Mads, naturally. Everyone's in couples, and I seem to have been paired up with Darcy. Whether that's intentional or not is anyone's guess.

My plan for tonight involved zoning out this sex club as fully as possible while enjoying a pleasant catch up with Zach about the markets, or with Aida about current affairs. I need to get myself properly up to speed again on the European political landscape.

But no.

Instead, I'm on a low stool next to the most incandescent woman I've seen in a long, long time, as her scent invades my nostrils and her laugh rings through my ears. Her bare skin is far too close to my arm, and her energy is far too infectious. She makes Claudia's lean, groomed beauty look sterile. Forced. She's like happening upon a glorious, riotous tangle of wild roses in full bloom—natural. Irresistible.

And worst of all, when I turn my head to take her in under the auspices of good manners, that's when I spot it.

Her very own scarlet letter.

A huge, fresh love bite on the side of her neck.

22

DEX

Her hair is pinned loosely up, showcasing acres of silky skin and confirming from this angle that her dress could indeed be undone and her breasts untethered with a casual tug of the bow at the nape of her neck.

Someone's been with her, in the past night or two, it looks like. Someone's sucked and bitten on that neck; someone's marked her and claimed her, and it strikes me simultaneously as typically unfair that he got to her first and a very helpful reminder from the universe to stay the hell away from creatures like her.

Mostly, it's a confirmation that this woman, who screams carnality at twenty paces, *is* carnal. She's carnal, and she has someone she lets bite her and mark her and, let's be honest, most likely fuck her, too. Even so, the love bite is so blatant, and it feels tasteless that she should show it off like this, that she should wear her hair up and flaunt her sexuality instead of wearing her hair down, or at least putting some makeup on it.

I'm staring at her neck without meaning to when she turns to me and catches my eye and laughs, her hand going up to cover the mark. Her fingers are long and slender and covered in tiny gold rings, some of which only hit the second knuckle.

'Oh fuck, you're looking at my love bite, aren't you?' she asks with a laugh that suggests she's not remotely bothered.

I blink. 'No, not at—of course not. I would never.' My words come out rushed and garbled, and I despise myself.

'He's so polite,' she says to my sister, who's draped over her husband on the opposite side of the table. She pats my thigh in a way that feels patronising, like she's inwardly laughing at my awkwardness.

She probably is.

You don't dance in a place like Alchemy if you have the slightest inhibitions. Although, looking around, I have to admit it's far more sophisticated and far less terrifying than I feared. The room itself is staggering and feels like an uptown Manhattan bar, and the clientele is well-dressed and, thank fuck, fully clad.

But I'm not interested in the clientele's levels of nakedness, because Darcy doesn't remove her hand from my thigh. Instead she leaves it draped there, like I'm the arm of her chair. I stare down at her long fingers on the black wool of my trousers and feel a stirring of panic and something else.

'What love bite?' Maddy demands from my other side, and Darcy leans forward so she can see.

'Oh my God!' Maddy exclaims. 'Is that from who I think it is?'

I groan inwardly, because everyone around the table has now perked up at this clue that gossip is on the horizon, and

Unstitch

I have a feeling I'm about to be the ball in a Maddy-versus-Darcy game of Gossip Tennis.

'Fuck, yes,' Darcy tells her with a wink at me, like she's revelling in my discomfort.

'Tell us,' Cal demands. I know from having spent a weekend with Rafe's friends when he married my sister that Cal's FOMO is epic.

Maddy rolls her eyes at him. 'Who do you think?'

'I don't know,' he cries. He's getting agitated now.

Rafe sighs like Cal's obtuseness is personally affronting. 'Who's the one person Gen warned her to stay away from?'

Cal's face is a picture. 'Fucking hell. You fucked Max, didn't you? You dirty little minx. Your sister will have your guts for garters when she finds out.'

Everyone laughs, and Darcy squeals delightedly, and I instantly resolve to hunt down this Max character, whoever he is, and kill him with my bare hands.

'Oh, boy,' Belle says, but her eyes are shining. 'That's big.'

Maddy leans in towards me. 'So Max is Anton's mate, Max Hunter. He offered Darcy twenty grand if she'd go to his flat and give him a private dance, because not only did Gen tell her not to touch him with a barge pole, but she's not supposed to be fraternising with the patrons here, full stop.'

I clear my throat in a disapproving fashion. I don't want or need to know any of this, but Jesus fuck.

Max Hunter.

His reputation as a businessman and Anton Wolff's right-hand man precedes him, and he runs Wolff Holdings, whose imminent IPO should be the biggest we've seen on this side of the pond since Prosus listed in The Netherlands a few years ago.

Darcy's playing with the big boys, clearly, but *Max Hunter*. He's a coup by any measure, but the idea of this enchanting creature dancing for, and fucking, and being marked by one of the most ruthless corporate empire-builders out there rankles.

It really fucking rankles.

Don't get me started on the thought of him throwing money at her to ensnare her, because that's morally repugnant, no question about it.

It seems Rafe feels the same way. He leans forward, knees wide, elbows resting on them and hands steepled. 'He paid you to fuck him? Gen is going to fucking garrote him when she gets back.'

'No!' Darcy slaps my thigh, and I flinch. 'He paid me to dance for him. I fucked him for free, *and* I said no to the money afterwards, because even if some people around here have a hooker kink'—she glares at Maddy—'I'm not going to take his money if I've slept with him.'

I spot the dark look Rafe shoots Belle, and her ensuing blush, and decide that if my little sister has a hooker kink, I categorically don't want to know anything about it.

'So you fucked him,' Maddy says, shimmying excitedly on my other side. I meet Zach's gaze and see the quiet sympathy there.

Yeah, mate.

Being pinned in the vortex of a gossip session like this is a nightmare of epic proportions.

Maddy leans forward, resting her glass of champagne on my knee. Jesus Christ, what is it with these women and personal space? They're talking in low voices now, but, trapped where I am between them, I'm unfortunately privy to every word.

'Mmm-hmm,' Darcy says coyly. 'And it was fucking amazing.'

Of course it was. I'm sure Max Hunter lives up to his name and possesses a giant cock to go with the size his bank balance will be once Wolff floats on the London Stock Exchange. And of course he knows how to use it. I close my eyes in despair.

Maddy makes a little noise of happiness and pokes me. I open my eyes.

'So Gen fucked Max once, on Anton's orders,' she tells me, 'and she said it was amazing, but she thinks he's a total man whore. He's been sniffing around Darcy, so Gen warned him off, but clearly he got you while your sister was off shagging her hot new husband. Right?' she asks Darcy.

I would classify absolutely all of that as Too Much Information, but I suspect Mads doesn't care. I groan, and the girls giggle.

'We're traumatising Dex, I think,' Darcy says with an overly-familiar pat of my thigh.

My smile is polite but strained. 'Not at all. But I don't want to get in the way. Why don't I switch places with you, Mads, and you guys can catch up?'

'Not so fast, Mister,' Darcy says. 'Maddy, Zach looks lonely. I want to interrogate this one.'

Maddy winks at me, no doubt catching the trepidation on my face. 'Don't worry, babes. She doesn't bite. She prefers getting bitten, right, Darce?'

Darcy giggles.

I grimace.

It's going to be a long night.

'So.' Darcy twists her body towards me and finally releases my thigh, giving me that dazzling smile instead. 'How does it feel to be back in London?'

'Tiring,' I admit. 'It's actually been harder to adjust to working for a new company than being in a different timezone. It's honestly been a blur this week, between client stuff and trying to meet as many people internally as possible. I'm pretty shattered.'

She hums sympathetically. 'I can imagine. Where are you living?'

'I've rented a place on Poultry.'

'That's the City, right?' She screws up her sweet little nose. 'God, that's boring.'

'Yeah.' I give her a sheepish smile. I'm so fucking exhausted, and she's so fucking beautiful. I wish I could sit here and not talk and just stare at her. 'But it's a five-minute walk from the office, and I think I'll be pretty boring for the next few months while I get up to speed properly.'

'That's a shame,' she says seductively. It takes every ounce of self-control not to look down at her breasts. I wish I could lay my weary head on them. 'Do you have many friends here still?' she asks, and I tell myself to snap out of it.

'I've got all my uni mates, yeah. Fuck, more people I have to catch up with, and a lot more weddings to go to.' I give a little laugh and tug on the back of my neck with my hand. It's so stiff. 'Everyone's dropping like flies. But that's something you wouldn't know anything about—you're far too young.'

'I'm twenty-five, and, unlike your sister, I have no intention of getting married anytime soon.'

'Quite right.' *Twenty-five. Fuck.* 'What about you—how long were you away for?'

'Two years,' she says. 'I spent a year after uni trying to

find a permanent dancing job, but it was so hard, so I took out a credit card and bought a one-way flight to Australia, and danced in bars for a couple of years.'

'Is that so?' I ask, entranced. Granted, I studied Economics at Cambridge, but every single one of my uni mates got straight on the corporate ladder after graduating. I suspect a lot of us could take a page out of this free spirit's book. 'What made you come back?'

'The timing felt right. Gen offered me her flat when she got engaged, and it's gorgeous. She offered me a job here, too. And I was bored of bumming around. So I came home.'

'I'm going to regret this,' I say, passing my hand over my face, 'but what kind of dancing do you do?'

She giggles and encircles my wrist with her delicate fingers, tugging my hand away from my face. 'It's okay. Don't be scared. I'm classically trained, but I got too tall for ballet, so I stopped. I do all sorts, though. Street, salsa, contemporary. You name it.'

'But at the club...' I prompt. I'm grinning tiredly at her and I don't care. Her good mood is infectious, even if I don't want to consider what might have prompted it.

I'm glad she's holding my wrist, because there's a tendril of hair hanging down the side of her face, and I'm tired enough that I might feasibly forget all social etiquette and reach out to tuck it behind her ear.

'At the club,' she says, wiggling her eyebrows naughtily at me, 'I do *naked* dancing.'

'Sweet Jesus,' I mutter, attempting to free my hand so I can cover my face again, but she holds my wrist firm.

'I'm messing with you.'

'Thank God.' I let my shoulders sag.

'I wear a bodystocking. A *completely sheer* bodystocking, except for a few glittery bits.'

I shake my head in despair. 'You're a bad, bad girl.' It just comes out, but I don't miss the way her entire body goes still, alert, at my words.

Well, that's more data I categorically didn't need to gather.

23

DARCY

Because I'm off duty tonight, and I've maxed out Alchemy's strict two-drink limit (Max-ed out, haha-ha), and because I have a scorching hot booty call with a scorching hot man back at his icy cold flat, I decide to head over there when the others make a move to go next door.

'You're not tempted to check out The Playroom?' I ask as Dex ushers me out of the club, a light hand on my bare lower back. I glimpse the horror in his stunning eyes before he gives me the same fixed, polite smile he's been using all evening.

'Not tonight. I'm pretty tired after the week I've had. But it was lovely to catch up with everyone.'

I snigger as we walk down the steps and out onto the stylish Mayfair street. 'You're so polite. Translation: you'd rather run a mile.'

He looks down at me, weighing his words before he answers with a sigh. 'It's not really my bag, if I'm honest. I'm quite old-fashioned.'

We stand there in the street, and I take the opportunity

to drink him in head-on instead of via the furtive, sidelong glances I've been giving him all evening. Twenty-four hours later, I'm still in a sex coma from Max, still reeling from the crazy, animalistic sex we had in his living room and then in his bed before I insisted on taking myself off home.

There was no way I was going to be that girl who woke up, vulnerable and awkward, in the bed of London's most eligible, elusive playboy.

And the playing-hard-to-get worked. He's been texting me all afternoon from Lords, where he took some VIP clients to watch the cricket, and from The Dorchester, where he's been wining and dining them at China Tang, begging me to come over.

I'm so going over there for a replay.

Max is hot as fuck. More than that, he's a total daddy. He's threatened all manner of filthy things, and I can't wait to see him make good on them.

This guy, though.

Dex is so physically perfect it actually hurts to look at him. His hair is a lot darker than Belle's. It's a dark brown that's cut quite long on top, but he's wearing it combed lightly back, and it seriously does it for me.

Everything about him is finely drawn. The straight nose. The lean curve of his jawline. The perfect cupid's bow of his upper lip and the plump arc of his lower one. It's his eyes that are impossible to look away from, though. They're like Belle's—huge and green-gold, like exotic, mesmerising tiger eyes—and they are fucking hypnotic.

I wonder if he's as deep as his eyes make him look. It would be so disappointing if he had these mysterious windows to his soul and then his soul was just plain basic. Kind of like mine. But I suspect his isn't. He's been painfully polite and very sweet all night, but there's a stick rammed so far up this guy's arse that it would be almost impossible to pull it out.

He plays his cards close to his chest. I suspect he vaguely disapproves of us all. My sister and Maddy have filled me in on Belle's upbringing, and Maddy mentioned that Dex has stayed away so long precisely because his parents are so fucked up, but I wonder if he's still a little fucked up too.

There's only one thing I'm confident of: that he's attracted to me.

A girl can tell when a guy wants to get in her knickers (if she's wearing any, which I'm not), and the way Dex is looking at me is honestly like a shot of crack. He's drinking me in with those big, golden, soulful eyes like he's been on a fast for forty days and forty nights and I'm a Full English Breakfast.

I love the way Max looks at me. He holds nothing back, disguises nothing. He's all want, and it's so blatant as to be kind of intimidating (in a *really* good way). But Dex looks like he's struggling. As if he's trying to hold everything back and failing miserably, and that kind of repressed self-denial thing has me hot.

As if by telling me he's old-fashioned, he's actually trying to tell me a million other things about his desires and his fears and his demons.

But I don't do very well with subtext, because, like I said, I'm pretty basic. So I prefer to use my words.

I stare up into his face.

'Would you be willing to check The Playroom out if I was dancing? Because I'd really like it if you came to watch me.'

A muscle twitches in his jaw. His entire body stiffens.

He knows exactly what I'm asking.

I'm telling the truth. Having Dex's big, soulful, tortured

eyes on my almost naked body as I dance would be a religious experience, I have no doubt.

'The ninety-nine percent naked dancing, you mean?' he asks.

I treat him to my most coquettish smile. 'Got it in one.'

'Um,' he says. 'Well. Um. Possibly. I'm sure I could. That is...'

He's so uncomfortable it's painful to watch.

'Your call,' I tell him. 'Have a think about it.'

He's so deeply, unfairly handsome in his smart black shirt that enhances his gorgeous olive skin. I've always thought it was weird when men are called 'beautiful', but Dex really is. He's so beautiful.

'I will,' he assures me. 'I promise. Are you off to see *Max*? Can I hail you a cab?'

It's the unmistakable snark in his voice when he says the name of the man I'm heading off to fuck that makes me brave.

'Yeah.' I put my hand on his shoulder. 'But I can get myself a cab, thanks. Goodnight, then.'

I tilt my face up to his, and he bends and kisses me slowly, deliberately, respectfully, on both cheeks. We draw apart and stare at each other a moment longer. It seems to me we're both reluctant to walk away from each other.

I bite my lip and dig my fingernails into my little gold clutch. Here goes. 'I just wanted to say—I think you're the most beautiful man I've ever laid eyes on.'

I catch the wide-eyed shock on his face before I smile at him and walk away.

24

DARCY

'Take it off,' Max growls in the vicinity of my dress as soon as I cross the threshold of his flat. He's in another perfect white t-shirt that I bet cost more than my entire wardrobe and a pair of navy athletic shorts.

I give him my most coquettish smile and hand him my clutch so I can undo my halter neck. 'Whatever you say.'

'Wait,' he says. 'Have you eaten?'

I consider. 'I had a Snickers at five, maybe?'

'You had a Snickers at five?' He looks at me in horror and grabs one of my wrists, pulling it away from my neck. 'Bad, bad girl. You need to look after yourself.'

'I'm fine,' I protest, but I kind of love the way he puts my clutch on the console table and hooks an arm around my waist, drawing me right up against him. I smile happily up at him.

'You're not fine,' he says, but he's grinning down at me. 'You're a bad girl, like I said. You're a dancer, for fuck's sake. You should know how to look after your body.'

'Uh, dancers are the *worst* when it comes to looking after their bodies,' I scoff, but I don't argue my case further, because he's closing the distance between our faces, releasing my wrist so he can slide his hand into my up-do and angle my head just the way he wants.

'Well, that stops now,' he whispers before taking my mouth in a kiss that's simply fucking perfect. It's soft, but ardent, and hungry, and he tastes of scotch, and I adore it. I adore how his tongue seeks mine, how his body is so hard pressed against me, how he keeps hold of my head like he can't get enough.

But then he's pulling away and slapping me on the arse.

'Come on. I brought half of China Tang home with me. There was so much food left over.'

At the magic L-word I follow him obediently through to his enormous marble kitchen area. Bloody hell, he wasn't lying. In the middle of the big white island is a massive stack of fancy-looking plastic takeaway boxes.

'Oh my God,' I murmur reverently.

He busies himself pulling off the lids. 'You ever been to China Tang before?'

'Nope. Isn't it crazy expensive?'

'Obscene,' he mutters, pushing a box in my direction and handing me some chopsticks—not wooden takeaway ones, but fancy black lacquered ones with a delicate gold pattern winding its way down their length. 'That's why I couldn't bear the thought of leaving all this stuff there. What a waste. Do you want me to heat it up for you?'

'Are you kidding me?' I waste no time delving into the nearest box with my chopsticks. 'Cold Chinese is the dog's bollocks. Is this what I think it is?'

'If you think it's lobster noodles, then yep.'

I wind my chopsticks around a good chunk of my noodles and bend right over so I can feed as huge a portion in as possible. The mouth-gasm hits instantly. 'Oh my fucking God,' I moan with my mouth full, and Max laughs.

'Good, right? I'm stuffed, so knock yourself out. Let me open some wine.'

I take him at his word, shoving food in my mouth like I've never been fed as he slides various boxes over to me, each one containing tastier delicacies. Peking duck. Crispy tofu. Sesame-drenched pak choi. Even some cold and deliciously stodgy dim sum. I had no idea I was hungry, but I'm fucking starving.

Max puts two glasses on the table and comes to stand next to me with a bottle of white, which he uncorks with controlled efficiency. He pours us both a glass, slides mine over to me, and stoops to drop a kiss on my shoulder. It's intimate and sweet and not necessarily what I'd expect from a man like him. A man who devoured me last night and has summoned me here for a booty call.

'I need to slow down,' I mumble, 'or I'll be too full to have sex.'

He laughs. 'I overdid it, too. We can take our time—there's no rush. You're staying tonight.'

It's not a question. I sigh as I reach for my wine. 'Fine. How was your day with your clients?'

He runs a fingertip across my back, tracing my shoulder blades before coming to perch on the stool next to mine. 'It was fine. The cricket was excellent. The company was pretty dull.'

'What kind of clients were they?'

'They weren't clients, actually. They were investors. Permira and Sequoia—two massive private equity funds who together own thirty-four percent of Wolff and have a very keen interest in ensuring that the IPO process is on track. Here—try a prawn.'

He picks one off its bed of lettuce with his fingers and holds it to my lips.

'I thought Anton owned the whole thing,' I say before I close my teeth over the tasty morsel he's dangling with all the finesse and patience of a baby crocodile.

He laughs. 'No. He still has a majority stake, which is pretty mind-blowing. But we've brought private equity in over the years to help us grow. Like most companies, we use a mix of debt and equity capital to fund growth, scale, diversification. That kind of thing.'

I swallow my prawn. 'So will they sell when the company floats?'

'It's a good question. They'll sell down their stakes, yeah, because they've done very well indeed out of their investments, so it's time for them to crystallise that value.

'We're going public partly because it's the right time, and partly because our investors want an orderly exit, but also because we'll raise primary capital—that's fresh capital—in the public markets to fund even more growth in the future. Does that make sense?'

I smile at him as I swirl my delicious wine around my wineglass.

I like that he's feeding me. Spoiling me.

I like that he's not just behaving like I'm some random he's invited here to fuck, even if that's all I am.

I like that he's taking the time to explain his work stuff without talking down to me like I'm some total dumbass.

And I really like that he's so impressive, so clearly great at what he does. My competence kink is in overdrive, and it's giving me the horn.

'It makes perfect sense, thank you,' I tell him.

'Good.' He strokes a loose tendril of hair off my shoulder and then grazes his fingertip up my face, tucking the strand gently behind my ear. 'You really are extraordinarily beautiful, you know. I was hoping last night would get you out of my system, but if I'm honest, I knew it would just make me want more.'

We stare at each other. He has that hungry look on his face again, the one he always gets around me. But it feels deeper, more charged, somehow. Probably because we both know how good it is between us. I love the anticipation of fucking someone I've felt great chemistry with, but it's even more fun when you've consummated that chemistry.

This is the second time in less than an hour that I've stared deep into the eyes of a heavenly man, and his words have the added unfortunate effect of triggering the flurry of butterflies I felt when I told Dex he was beautiful.

This, right here, is great. Perfect. I'm thrilled to be here with Max, in his mausoleum of a flat, while he feeds me extortionate Chinese leftovers before sweeping me off to bed. I know what a catch he is. I know how good we are together, even if it's casual.

But I'm a greedy, greedy girl. I just spent a couple of hours sitting next to a guy whose sheer physical perfection would challenge even Max's. I know he wants me, even if I suspect he'd need a hell of a lot of cajoling to do anything about it. I suspect he's shy. Moral. Noble. And I suspect none of those personality traits, however impressive, will do my cause any favours.

But I'd like to have a crack at him, anyway.

And everything I know about Max tells me he's open-minded and kinky and up for anything. We're casual, and he won't have wanted to put any dibs on me yet. He shared my sister with Anton. Jesus, he shared Anton's *assistant* with Anton, according to Gen.

He's a naughty boy, and that's a huge part of his attraction for me. I love his debauched side. I want more of it. I came back here to work in a sex club but, last night aside, I've been as virtuous as a nun.

Maybe Max is the key to my letting loose.

I set down my chopsticks.

'Can I ask you a question?' I ask.

He grins adorably, putting his warm hand on my thigh and massaging it through the slinky silk jersey of my dress. 'You can ask me anything.'

Here goes.

'Would you be up for a threesome?'

25

MAX

I'm fucking gobsmacked.

I thought Darcy and I were having a moment. I told her how beautiful she was; I opened up about wanting more of her. I said all the things women love to hear. Not that they were insincere—I meant every word—but I was confident I could predict the effect they'd have on her.

Nope.

Would you be up for a threesome?

Who the actual fuck is this woman?

Because I think I'm in love.

I bark out a laugh. People don't shock me. Not in business. Not in bed. But I sure as hell didn't see that little proposition coming.

'That's a heck of a non sequitur,' I splutter, but I'm not affronted. I'm tickled as fuck.

'Yeah.' She smiles and takes a sip of her wine, her blue eyes wide above the rim of the glass as she waits for me to expound.

'Where did that come from?'

She puts her glass down and shrugs. 'Answer the question and then I'll tell you.'

Okay then. 'Why not? I'm sure you're well aware I'm more than fine with group activities. The more the merrier, I say.'

'That's what I thought.'

'What about you?'

'I've never had one.' She twirls her wineglass by the stem, avoiding my eyes. 'And it's really been bothering me. It was one of the main things on my bucket list for when I got back here, but my cockblocking sister won't let me loose in Alchemy.'

'Hmm.' I take a sip of my wine as I survey her thoughtfully. 'Well, as you know, I'm happy to fill up that greedy little bucket of yours whenever you like.'

We grin at each other.

'Any particular... catalyst for this admission?' I ask casually. 'Are you thinking a man or a woman? Because God knows I'm fine with both.'

Her mouth twists. I didn't think Darcy had a self-conscious bone in her body, but she looks almost bashful as she meets my eyes. 'A man.'

Isn't that interesting? 'So you want even more cock than I gave you last night, you greedy little slut? Would this "man" be someone you met tonight, by any chance?'

'Yeah,' she confesses. 'And I know this is—you and I are casual, but I also don't know how the hell something like this would come about unless we're in Alchemy and it's, like, a spontaneous free-for-all.'

'It's definitely easier at Alchemy,' I muse. 'So, who was this guy? Do you think he'd be game?'

She laughs then. 'No. Honestly, I think he'd be absolutely horrified. He'd run for the hills.'

I frown. 'So how come you've brought it up?'

'Because I know he wants me, even if he doesn't want to.' She covers my hand with hers on her thigh. 'And I'm definitely attracted to him. But then I thought, why not have both of you?'

A smile spreads slowly across my face. 'You little fucking beauty,' I drawl. 'Why not indeed? You want both our cocks at the same time, do you?' God, the mere thought of it has me hardening in my shorts.

'Well, I thought about it in the cab over here,' she confesses. 'And then I couldn't stop thinking about it. And I like to think I'm pretty liberated, but clearly I haven't messed around as much as I should have, and, honestly, the thought of both of you naked with me is so insanely hot that I can't even handle it.'

'You wouldn't be able to handle it, you little wench,' I mutter. 'You'd fucking combust with pleasure when we made you take our dicks.'

'Oh, God,' she groans, shifting on her chair, her hand clamped on mine so it stays securely on her thigh. Like I have any plans to move it away.

'You didn't tell me who he is,' I press. 'I might know him from Alchemy.'

She snorts. 'You definitely won't. He's an Alchemy virgin —tonight was his first night stepping foot in there, and he didn't even go into The Playroom. It's Belle's brother, Dex. He just moved back from New York.'

'Belle's brother, Dex,' I repeat. 'Don't know him. What's their surname?'

'I dunno,' she says, visibly wilting. 'Bugger.'

I reach for my phone. Let's take a look at this guy who has my little minx frothing between her legs. 'Was he at your sister's wedding?'

'No, but he would have been at Belle and Rafe's, obviously. Were you there?'

I shake my head. 'I don't know them well enough. But I do follow Belle on Instagram—she's been sourcing some art for me to liven this place up.'

Her feed is a mixture of professional and personal. Paintings from Liebermann's, the high-end gallery she works for, and beach shots. She and Rafe spend far too much time on holiday, from the looks of it. I hand my phone to Darcy. 'Here. Have a look through—see if you spot him.'

She bites down on her lip as she scrolls, and I take her in with pleasure. She's seriously fucking adorable: fun, and uninhibited, and sexy as fuck. Asking me to raise the kink factor is the icing on the cake.

'Ooh,' she says, staring at my phone. 'Group shots. Hang on—Yes! Bingo.'

She passes the phone to me, and I swear there's a flush on her face.

I roll my eyes. 'Let's see him, then.' I look down and freeze, because the guy on my phone screen with his arm around a radiant Belle isn't just attractive.

He's a Greek fucking god.

I take in the triangle of olive skin at the open neck of his shirt, white tie undone and hanging loose. The dark hair raked carelessly back. The easy, sexy smile that shows off his white teeth. His eyes, which are—I have no fucking clue what colour they are, but they're remarkable, that's for sure, and they're staring straight at me, and the way I would bend this guy over and fuck that smile right off his face is nothing short of—

'Jesus fucking *Christ*,' I manage, putting the phone reluctantly down between us on the island.

'Right?' Darcy asks. 'He's hot, isn't he?'

I laugh mirthlessly. 'He's hot, all right.' What a grotesquely inadequate term that is for such aesthetic splendour.

She cocks her head. 'Is he—do you...?'

'What is it you want to ask me, sweetheart?'

'Do you like men, I guess?'

'Yes.' I watch her face and see only curiosity and, I think, pleasure.

'Do you sleep with guys?'

'Yes. Not as often as I fuck women, but yes.'

'At Alchemy?'

'Mainly, yeah.'

'Huh.'

'Why the *huh*?' I ask her.

'No reason—it's just—the stuff my sister told me about you, it always sounded like the woman was the focal point in your, um, interactions with Anton.'

'She was.' I stride over to the fridge and yank the door open, pulling out the open bottle of white so I can refill us both. 'I've never laid a finger on Anton.'

'Do you find him attractive?' she presses.

'Obviously. It would be impossible not to find him so. He's objectively an incredibly impressive physical specimen. But he's far more interested in women, and anyway, we're both tops. It would never have worked with him.'

'Ahh,' she says, like this is a revelation for her. 'Of course you are. So if we—if I managed to convince Dex, somehow, would you be...?'

I laugh again, and once again there's an edge to it, because this conversation and this guy's photo have both got me hard, and there's zero point in even entertaining the idea of anything with him. 'Poor guy,' I tell her. 'Not only have you ensnared him in a threesome without him having any clue, but you're also conspiring to have me royally fuck him, too. Unlikely.'

'Oh.' She deflates, her shoulders dropping, and slumps on her bar stool.

'Did you get the impression that he likes men?' I ask.

'Not in the slightest,' she says, and it's my turn to slump. Inwardly, that is.

'Listen, sweetheart,' I say, filling her glass up, 'if you can find a way to get this guy over the threshold of The Playroom and into a private room, then I'm game.'

'Really?' She brightens. 'Because I asked him if he'd be up for coming to watch me dance, and he kind of looked like he wanted to run for the hills but also come in his pants.'

I throw my head back and laugh a genuine laugh. 'Poor fucker. I bet he didn't know what had hit him when he met you. But what man could say no to watching you dance?'

'I dunno,' she mutters. 'He's skittish, that one.'

'Get him to the club,' I order. 'I'll take it from there. If he wants to lay a finger on you, he'll have to do it in front of me.' I slide my hand around the back of her neck and caress the delicate skin there. 'And if you, my beautiful little thing, want both our cocks, I'll find a way to make it happen. I'm extremely good at ambushing people—I learnt from the best. You understand me?'

26

DEX

I think you're the most beautiful man I've ever laid eyes on.
Who even says that?
Who speaks those words aloud to someone they don't know, bestows them like a gift, then walks away?

It's not that the sentiment, coming from the mouth of a woman, is remotely new.

But the context was new.

And the woman was new, and unexpected, and enchanting, that's for sure. So hearing that sentiment, those words, from *her* mouth in particular was really quite something.

I've been mulling over them all night, just like I've been mulling over the way her scent hit me, and the playful way she grabbed my wrist, and how open she was about dancing practically naked for a living.

Unfortunately, every time I allow myself to dip my toe into that deep, warm well of pleasure, my brain reminds me that she bade me goodbye and walked straight into another man's arms.

The man who's had the extraordinary privilege of watching her dance naked for him.

Of sucking her neck.

Fucking her.

Max fucking Hunter, that's who.

'Easy there, tiger,' my sister says, gently removing the bottle of claret from my grip with one hand and the corkscrew with which I'm stabbing it with the other. 'What's up with you?'

'Nothing,' I say. 'Just tired.' I look over my shoulder towards the archway that separates my parents' kitchen from their vast open-plan living space and lower my voice. 'And already dreading this.'

'You and me both,' she says. 'But you've had eight years off. So suck it up.'

That makes me snort. I love it when Belle gets feisty. 'You were Mum and Dad's little bitch, so don't complain to me.'

'I was until Daddy walked in here and found Rafe pretty much exactly where you were standing, naked as the day he was born.'

'Don't.' I press my lips together to stop myself from losing it, because, the genuine horror of that episode aside, it seems really fucking funny today. 'The money I'd pay to have been a fly on the wall,' I say, shaking my head.

'You're so awful. You know it was the worst moment of my life.'

'I know, love,' I say quietly, nudging her with my elbow. It wasn't good. I do know that much. The day Dad came home early from a three-month-trip with Mum and discovered that his obedient, virginal daughter had hooked up with the upstairs neighbour was the cause of a huge rift between them.

But it was also the start of a new dawn for Belle, a new era where she put her own beliefs first without agonising about placating Dad and aligning with his incredibly fucked-up moral compass.

Fate forced her hand that day, but it was definitely for the best.

'Where is he, anyway?' I ask her, because Rafe is notably absent. 'I thought he'd be here?'

She sighs as she systematically winds the corkscrew into the cork. 'He decided to nip over to Windsor—there's a racehorse he's thinking of buying a stake in.'

'Which is code for...'

'He and Daddy get on best when they don't see each other too often.'

'Amen to that,' I mutter, because I very much get where Rafe is coming from. My relationship with my father was all the easier for eight years due to having an ocean between us.

'Yeah, well, he's really good about showing up when it's needed, but it's just more tense all around when they're in a room together.'

I get that even more.

Dad and Rafe can be civil to each other, but come on. Dad will never truly forgive Rafe for corrupting his previously compliant daughter by shagging her out of wedlock, and he'll definitely never recognise their marriage as legitimate in the eyes of the Church.

He didn't even come to their fucking wedding, for fuck's sake. He couldn't put his religious beliefs aside to fly to St Tropez and walk his only daughter down the aisle. Mum did it, in a move that was uncharacteristically independent-minded of her. She defied Dad, and she gave Belle away in a pitch-perfect humanist ceremony at a vineyard, and she hosted the wedding breakfast, too.

I'll never stop admiring Mum for standing up to the man

who's emotionally bullied everyone in this family for so many years, just like I'll never forgive Dad for choosing his church over his family.

And, given Rafe and Belle are still living in sin in Dad's eyes, I'm not sure which is more surprising: that Rafe is ever willing to cross the threshold of their home, or that Dad lets him.

AFTER DAD'S SAID GRACE, and we've marked its conclusion with a muttered *Amen*, we get stuck in. Mum's a bloody amazing cook, and I can count on one hand the number of proper English roasts I've had since I first moved to the US, so it's with genuine appreciation that I stuff an entire roast potato in my mouth.

'Wow,' I groan. It's orgasmic, that's what it is, though that's a descriptor my parents would *not* appreciate. 'So crispy,' I say once I've swallowed it. 'Did you use an entire jar of goose fat?'

'It's best you don't answer that, Lauren,' my dad interjects, 'for the sake of plausible deniability at my next medical.'

We all laugh. After the week I've had, a sit-down with my parents is the last thing I need, though I owe it to my mum to spend some time with her. I don't give a fuck about dad. Much as I've been dreading it, this feels nice, the four of us sitting in my parents' stunning apartment, enjoying Mum's excellent cooking and a spectacular bottle of Pauillac from Dad's cellar.

And I suspect what my sister left unsaid is that it's easier when it's just the four of us because no one is observing us, which means we don't need to suffer the excruciation of hearing Dad's bigotry through someone else's ears or sitting in silent fear that a guest will innocently raise a topic that's kindling to Dad's extremist rants.

Examples of things that spark him are varied. The slightest thing can set him off. Charities that fund or condone contraceptive education in the Third World. Anything on the subject of queerness or God forbid, transgender rights. It's a constant fucking minefield, and, in true Catholic style, our family likes to keep our secret shame under wraps.

It's why Mum and Dad still don't know Rafe owns a sex club, for God's sake. It's why they only know about Cerulean, the small hedge fund he runs with Zach, Cal, and some of their mates. Because, honestly, what is there to be gained by telling them?

Sure, in theory Belle should emancipate herself fully. She should be an open book, and then it's Dad's choice whether or not to accept her and her husband and their lifestyle, or to sacrifice his relationship with his daughter and future grandchildren to his beliefs.

But that's easier said than done, and life is far less black and white than we'd like, and I get it. I really do. There is something to be said for meeting in the middle, for keeping the peace, and for guarding those pieces of yourself others haven't earned the right to see. Those pieces of yourself you don't *trust* others to see and not to judge.

So my sister walks that tightrope, and Rafe walks it with her because he loves her. Belle has chosen to have a relationship with our father on some level. She's stood up for her rights and her morals and she's made it very clear to him that his reaction to her decisions is not her responsibility. But she hasn't pushed her agenda so far as to alienate him for good.

And rather than despair of that, I admire it. This is real life, and real life is messy, and while I ran off to hide in New York, my sister stayed here and stood up to Dad and built a life for herself in the meantime.

I really fucking admire that.

Because, God knows, there are shadowy aspects of my personality that I refuse to entertain myself.

And never, ever would I expose them to my father.

27

DEX

The way the sunlight hits the verdant wilderness of Hyde Park today is pretty spectacular, and my parents have a first-class view of its majesty from their lovely terrace. There's no doubt London is gentler, prettier, than Manhattan. It's less frenetic, and therefore less confronting.

I can almost breathe here.

'So, spill it,' Dad says as he sips his coffee across from me. 'How've you found the first week?'

Mum and Belle have disappeared into my parents' bedroom to examine Mum's latest shipment from her personal shopper. She and Dad have a black-tie gala to go to next week, and she wants my sister's opinion, so it's just us men on the terrace.

Work is always our go-to conversation topic. It's where we have common ground. Dad is the Chief Investment Officer of a large London-headquartered investment firm, and I genuinely enjoy discussing all things finance with him. He's a veteran in the industry with an impeccable track record.

He may have been disappointed to see me leave Goldman before achieving that elusive partnership status—*Loeb partner* doesn't have the same cachet as *Goldman Sachs partner* when he's dining out on his son's success—but he recognises the size of the opportunity I face.

I cross one ankle over the opposite knee. 'Fine. Challenging. The culture's a lot more relaxed than GS, which is a good and bad thing. But I've been seriously impressed by their research.'

All investment banks have Investment Research divisions, which conduct research on the thousands of companies whose stocks trade in the public markets. The research analysts look not only at the companies' fundamentals but at the valuations of their stocks, and usually issue Buy, Hold or Sell ratings accordingly. It's precisely this kind of service that the fund managers at investment firms like Dad's pay the banks for.

'Agreed. That's where they really punch above their weight,' Dad agrees. 'I assume they're desperate for a piece of the Wolff action?'

'Obviously. They've been pitching for months. Dunno what their chances are. Their research is their strongest card.'

God knows, everyone's desperate for a piece of the Wolff deal, but the bulge-bracket banks are all over it, too. I have no idea if Loeb will score a place on the ticket. And I really fucking resent the fact that the merest mention of Wolff makes me think of Max Hunter and then of Darcy.

I shrug off the mental image of her marked neck. Of her graceful fingers going to cover the bruising.

'What else?' Dad asks. 'I assume they've sorted out their culture over there.'

He's referring to the infamous City incident from a few

years ago, when Loeb's then Head of Equities, an Italian guy called Lorenzo Beneventi, was accused of sexual misconduct by multiple female employees and was fired. It was a scandal whose ripples were felt across the pond, and Loeb's been diligently cleaning up its culture and repairing its tarnished reputation ever since.

'They're squeaky clean,' I assure him. 'I spent a full day this week being briefed on cultural, diversity and inclusion issues. For a smaller bank, they do it well. I was impressed.'

In fact, I considered it a day very well spent. The sessions I and other new joiners from all parts of the firm underwent were fully thought out and perfectly executed. It seems the firm has a thriving, and extremely active, LGBTQ+ community for which it's become a City poster child, and the spectrum of support, dialogue and education around such issues is admirable.

Obviously, as the head of one of the bank's largest divisions, I'll do everything in my power to promote and celebrate and advocate for every single one of my subordinates, even if I am a cisgender, straight white male and therefore a less than ideal role model.

My father, however, is rolling his eyes. 'I can only imagine what they're force-feeding you. My advice, son, is to take it all with a pinch of salt.

'Clearly, they can't have weak-willed idiots like Beneventi running amok and indulging in the pleasures of the flesh when he's on the clock, but, quite honestly, the expectation these days that we should all pander to these deviants in the workplace is utterly ridiculous.'

I'm so appalled, so revolted, I almost drop my coffee cup. I return it to the low table between us and unfold my leg, planting my foot squarely on the floor.

For fuck's sake.

'Dad. That's a completely unacceptable thing to say,' I say. I don't miss how my barely controlled rage is making my voice shake.

He deliberately misses my point. 'It's just us. Relax. No one from HR is breathing down our necks.'

'That's not what I mean,' I grit out. 'You can't call people *deviants*. It's extremely offensive, even if there's no one but me to hear it.'

He raises his eyebrows in a *you can't be serious* way. 'I didn't realise you'd got so touchy. The Americans really did a number on you, didn't they?'

There's no point in having this conversation. Zero. At least, there's no point in trying to say or do anything that will change my dad's mind. His beliefs, always religiously devout and socially conservative, have moved so far right over the past decade or two that he's basically a Catholic Fascist these days, if that's a thing. He operates in a terrifying alternate universe of dogma and defensiveness and us-and-them, where diversity of thought or identity is a threat, plain and simple.

But not being able to change his mind doesn't mean staying quiet. I want it on record between the two of us that I'm not on board with his bigoted bullshit. Eight years of physical distance between us has given me the gift of emotional perspective. I'm not afraid of him, and I'm not afraid to call him out when he crosses the line.

If my little sister can put her foot down and live her life the way she wants, then I can damn well stand up to him in conversation.

'I'm not *touchy*,' I tell him now. 'I'm offended on behalf of the people you're insulting. Jesus, it never fails to astonish me how you can be so excessively pious and so goddamn prejudiced at the same time. It's unbelievably hypocritical.'

'Don't take the Lord's name in vain in front of me,' he snaps.

Seriously? *Jesus* is the only thing he got from what I just said to him?

'How about I don't blaspheme and you don't call our fellow children of God *deviants*, hmm?' I rest my elbows on my knees and clasp my hands so tightly my knuckles turn white, because there's something about this smug, narrow-minded prig that makes me fucking feral.

'It was a turn of phrase, son,' he says, and he looks almost amused at the state I'm working myself up into. I remind myself he's always done this: he's always turned things on their head to suggest it's the other party, not him, who's out of line.

Gaslighting bastard.

'Words have power,' I say quietly. 'Nothing is just a *turn of phrase*.'

He grows serious. 'Look. Our society is in decline. Rapid decline. Sacred foundational building blocks of our very civilisation, like faith, and gender, are being undermined. It's insidious, and it's dangerous, and it's everywhere.

'Do I think people who call themselves homosexual or transexual are evil? No, no I don't. I truly, in my heart, believe they're sick, and I pray for them every day and every night, I'll have you know. I pray they'll find strength in God's presence and comfort in His love and that the light of redemption will shine upon them.

'But I do think they're subversive. I think they're subverting our values, and the values of innocent children, and it's all gone too far. We're at a tipping point in society, make no mistake about it.

'So when I tell you, Dexter, not to over-immerse yourself in all of this toxicity, I mean it.'

I cannot get out of there quickly enough.

I need to shower.

I need to wash off the grime all that toxic hatred and bigotry masquerading as religious virtue has coated me with.

I need to scrub my skin *raw*.

28
DARCY

MAX

How's Project Ambush going, sweetheart?

> I haven't made a move yet

Do you even have his number?

> No. I'll get it off Maddy

What are you waiting for? That greedy pussy won't fill itself...

> You say that, but I have a fine selection of silicone at home

A poor imitation of the real thing(s) and you know it

> I'm growing quite partial to your thing, actually

Get over here and suck it then

> Hahaha

> I'M SERIOUS. GET OVER HERE AND SUCK IT.

Which is how I find myself, an hour later, freshly showered and trotting across the palatial marble lobby of Wolff Holdings' Mayfair headquarters. It's eleven on a Tuesday morning and all I can think is that I'm actually losing my marbles.

Or I'm just horny.

Why is it that the prospect of being summoned to Max's office to suck him off is so fucking hot? Because it really, really is.

It's the power thing, probably.

He's ordered me here to service him at his Big Dick desk in his Big Dick office where he works on Big Dick deals.

See what I mean?

Hot.

Although I probably wouldn't have agreed to come if I'd accepted that twenty grand from him. That would have been too close to being his actual whore. There was no way I was leaving with a cheque the other night after letting him fuck me senseless (if cheques still even exist. Though I bet Max is old enough to have a chequebook). Instead, I told him to give it to charity.

Yes, I deserve a fucking halo.

A scarily poised and elegant brunette who introduces herself as Rix collects me from reception and takes me upstairs, depositing me at Max's open door.

Well, well, well.

I was right.

The Big Dick-ness of this entire setup is truly epic.

He's standing behind a huge, old, expensive-looking desk, grinning at me. He has on a pale blue shirt and a navy tie. His hair is slicked back and he looks every inch the corporate legend he apparently is. I may be tall, but in my sundress and flat sandals I feel vulnerable and even a little gauche. Maybe not gauche, but I'm definitely not of this world.

He doesn't want me to be of this world, I remind myself. I bet Rix can't work a pole like I can. Max has invited me here precisely because he wants an *escape* from work.

'Well, hello there,' he says, still grinning as he rounds his desk and comes towards us, his hands in his pockets. 'Thank you, Rix. Miss Carew and I are not to be disturbed. We have some very important business to attend to, don't we, sweetheart?'

'Of course, Mr Hunter,' she replies smoothly as I flush. I'm not sure if it's the endearment or his allusion to why I'm here that's getting me flustered. It's definitely not for business—though I suppose I have an important *job* to do.

Still, it's all a bit intimidating. I've come here for a booty call at the behest of the CEO of Europe's biggest private company, and the old-school art on the walls and the thick white carpet on the floor and the deferential way Rix addresses Max all conspire to make me feel a little out of my depth.

He's on me as soon as the door clicks shut behind us, wrapping one hand around my neck and clamping the other to my bum so he can pin me against him. I look up at him, at the approval in his blue eyes and the arrogant smirk on his handsome face.

Yep. This is definitely a better plan than my original one

of arranging all my romance paperbacks on my sister's bookshelves.

'I enjoy it when you do as I say,' he murmurs against my mouth before kissing me. I decide responses are overrated and open for him instead, winding my arms around his neck and revelling in the decisive force of his tongue pushing into my mouth, and the possessive way the hand on my neck moves upwards to grab a fistful of my hair, and the hard press of his lean body against my curves.

It's not until he's released me that I retort, 'I only do what you say when it suits me.'

'Of that I have no doubt at all,' he says drily. 'Except I'm amazed it didn't suit you to take twenty grand off me.'

'It didn't suit me to take money for sex.'

'It wasn't for sex,' he says slowly and deliberately against my lips, as if I'm being deliberately obtuse. 'It was for the dance. The very, very sexy dance. You earned it.'

'Yeah,' I say, 'like I'm going to dance for you and fuck you and then walk off with your money. I don't think so.'

'Suit yourself.'

'I did. And I will, thank you very much.'

'So, today it "suits you" to take some cock, does it?'

'It's that or rearrange my bookshelves,' I deadpan, and he throws his head back and laughs.

'Un-fucking-believable.'

He manages to slap me on my arse before I wriggle out of his arms. I toe off my sandals and set about exploring his office. Oh wow, this carpet is like velvet. I could happily go to sleep on it. I could—

Oh, shit.

'Is this Anton's old office?' I ask suspiciously, whipping my head around to look at him.

'It is,' he says. He's crossed his arms and is watching me

with an expression of amused hunger, which seems to be his default when it comes to me. It's as if he can't decide whether to pounce or to leave me to my own devices a little longer for his entertainment.

I make a face. 'Ew. So my sister knows this carpet well, then?'

Another hearty laugh. 'Yep. And that boardroom table.'

'Oh, God.' I grimace, though I don't really blame her for rolling over in here. She was probably as powerless against this room's Big Dick Energy as she was against Anton's. I stand in front of a chic dark grey bookcase housing not only a terrifying amount of business books but tonnes of awards for Wolff. *Ethical Employer of the Year: Winner. B-Corp of Year: Finalist.*

Impressive.

For some reason, I didn't expect Wolff to be anything more than a big, fat, dirty conglomerate. I wonder if anyone on the marketing side ever dared suggest to Anton that a company name that sounded like a ravenous predator might not be the smartest branding decision, even if it is his surname.

Maybe it's just me. Maybe Anton's reputation precedes him in the business world.

I don't really care, because Max has walked up behind me and is sliding the straps of my sundress off my shoulders. It's one of those long, boho ones made from a kind of white cheesecloth that looks like a baby's muslin. It has elasticated smocking all across the chest and then flares out.

Basically, it's very easy access.

He buries his face in my neck and inhales sharply against my hair. 'Believe me, I didn't invite you here to reminisce about your sister.'

'No?' I manage.

'Nope.' He winds an arm around my waist, tugging my back against his front.

'If sending a young lady a text saying "Get over here and suck it", *in capital letters*, I might add, is your way of inviting her over, then you might want to work on your etiquette. Maybe watch some Bridgerton.'

He laughs softly against my hair. 'You're not a lady. Or you won't be by the time I've finished with you.'

'Rude,' I say with difficulty, because his hand has snaked up from my stomach to close over my right boob, and I really, really love the way he's touching me.

'I'll watch it if you come over and watch it with me,' he whispers. 'No fucking way am I sitting alone in that godforsaken flat and watching some period drama.'

'That's a good idea. You might need me there to take the edge off for you. It's very raunchy.'

He nips at my ear. 'Sounds like a date, *young lady*. And you look fucking beautiful, by the way.' His fingers flick at my nipple through the smocking, and I arch against him, but he removes his hand and backs away from me. I turn, pouting as he looks me up and down.

'You should have a crown of wild flowers in your hair,' he murmurs, reaching above me to grab the bookshelf and effectively caging me in as his gaze darts over my face. 'You're a beautiful, ethereal, untamed nymph. If I was a man of paint you'd be on every surface of every wall I own—I'd never get tired of trying to capture you.'

I stare up at him in astonishment. This man gives me whiplash. He orders me over to suck his dick and then spouts compliments Julia Quinn herself would swoon over. Who the hell does that? 'Um, thank you,' I say haltingly.

His grin turns wicked, and now I swoon, because *that's* the Max I know and, um, lust after.

'But I can't paint for toffee,' he drawls, pushing off the bookshelf and strolling over to his desk, 'so, instead I'll take a striptease and your very best blowjob, if you please.'

29

MAX

She goes slack-jawed with disbelief at my curveball and I mentally punch the air as I pull my heavy swivel chair away from my desk and take a seat. I make a show of settling into a comfortable position and shoot her a cocky grin.

'Go on. I'm waiting.'

'Such a twat,' she mouths, but I can tell by the heat in her glare that she wants this, too.

'What's your point?' I ask. 'Get on with it, for God's sake.'

She reaches for the top of her flimsy little sundress. I already know she's not wearing a bra—the weight of her tit, full and heavy through the fabric told me that. I could flip the top down in a second and have both tits untethered, but it's also deeply gratifying to have Darcy expose herself for me.

She doesn't flip it, instead tugging at the sides and dragging it down her body. She shimmies a little as she pulls it over her hips, and then it's falling to the ground in a soft white cloud that she neatly side-steps.

'What an obedient girl you are,' I drawl in a voice dripping with sarcasm, because we both know no one in their right mind would call Darcy obedient. 'Is that a thong? Give me a look.'

She smiles and twirls around slowly, her arms floating above her head in a way that recalls that wonderful dance she gave me, hips swaying slightly as she moves. I adore everything about this woman, but most of all I adore how utterly unselfconscious she is in her own skin. Her thong is white and flimsy, intersecting that creamy expanse of hip and arse in a way that makes me want to go over there and tug it in two.

But after I ruined her custom-made bodystocking, she made me promise not to ravage her clothes or I wouldn't get nice things. So I behave myself.

'Off,' I grunt. 'Then get over here.'

She spins back around to face me and shoots me a dazzling smile. I swear, I wasn't joking about that flowery headdress bullshit. She looks like a pre-Raphaelite nymph come to life, and I am powerless to resist her siren's song.

The powerlessness of my resistance is now manifesting as a rock-fucking-hard cock, so I lean back in my seat and unbuckle my belt. I need to stick it in some part of her glorious body without delay.

I take in her stupendous curves, those pale tits, the taut little furls of her nipples. I take in the strip of fair hair as she tugs her thong down and sashays towards me. The little beauty.

'Fuck me,' I groan, freeing my cock from my boxer briefs and fisting it as she comes around the desk to stand in front of me. I rake my gaze hungrily over her body.

It might come as a shock to everyone who knows me that I haven't christened this office yet, but I've had no fucking time. This IPO will be the death of me, and it hasn't even kicked off yet. But in this moment I'm in the office I fought tooth and nail for, behind the desk that stands for every ounce of influence I've won in this company.

In this corporate kingdom, I'm the king, and I both wield the power and bear the burden that goes with that poisoned chalice.

What I say goes.

And what I say is that it would be a crying shame not to bend this auburn-haired beauty over my desk and bury my face in her cunt before I let her loose on my desperate cock.

'Come here,' I say, slapping the desk with the hand that's not wrapped around the base of my cock. 'Sit up and let me see.'

She licks her lips and tosses her hair over her shoulders as she plants her very nice bottom on the edge of the desk.

'Let me see,' I repeat in a voice that brooks no argument, and she obliges, gripping the edge of the desk with her hands as she manoeuvres her legs wide. I keep my eyes on her face, my gaze boring into her as she positions herself. We both want this. Need it. We both crave that sacred exchange where she yields her power and I cradle it in my hands so I can deliver what she truly desires.

Only when she's in place do I let my eyes flicker to that rosy, hallowed spot. I sigh when I see it, because she's fucking perfection.

I scoot my chair forward so my knees are between her legs and allow myself a single upward stroke of my cock. It feels so good. So right. 'Hold yourself open for me,' I order her in my coldest voice, and she makes the tiniest noise at the back of her throat, as if she's been waiting and hoping for exactly that instruction.

Her long fingers with those gold rings part her delicate outer lips, and I lean right in. In towards that pretty pink cunt, its centre slick for me and its clever little bud already greedy and swollen and pulsing, this most private sanctum of her body betraying that Darcy is indeed mine to use as I like.

I slide a single finger inside her, two knuckles deep, her body sucking me in, her gasp audible. My thumb hovers over her clit. A glance up at her face shows me her head bent forward, lips parted, eyes fixed on the spot where I'm touching her.

'Legs on the arms,' sweetheart,' I tell her, and she grips the desk harder as she hikes her legs up gracefully, one on each arm of my chair, putting her in the same position she'd be in at a gynaecological exam.

Mmm. There's an idea for a role play.

I pull my fingers out and hold both her ankles in place so I can lean forward and dip my head for a taste. And as my tongue slices through her soaking flesh I observe that this is already the best lunch I've had since I took over this office.

30

DARCY

Max eating me in his office in the middle of the day is hotter than hell. I'm naked and trussed up on his Big Dick desk for him, legs spread and pussy on display while he's impeccably suited, and the power imbalance is so fucking skewed and such a turn on I can hardly bear it.

I plant my palms behind me and lean my weight back, giving him even more access. The appraising glance he gives me as he looks up at my naked body tells me he approves. I have a feeling, though, that the way he's tending to my pussy isn't for me. The licks, the sucks—they're decadent and ravenous and perfect, but they're *taking* licks and *taking* sucks.

Knowing he's using me for his own pleasure, his own reward, has arousal coursing through me even more than his skilful ministrations. I'm the entertaining little intermission in an otherwise busy day of wheeling and dealing and power playing and whatever other high-finance stuff he does, and I love it. I love serving him.

On which note, I want to service him. I want to be naked under that desk, sucking him off.

'I want a turn,' I tell him as articulately I can given the astonishing pleasure he's unleashing on my body.

He bestows one long lick upon me, from my entrance to my clit, and then glances up, his gorgeous face bright with desire. 'Fuck, yeah,' he says roughly. 'Get down here and earn the rest.'

He releases my ankles and helps me drop my feet to the floor, and then I'm clambering down, my knees hitting that velvety carpet. From this position, he cuts an even more imposing figure. His poor cock is still standing to attention, long and thick and so hard the skin around it is stretched satin-smooth. There's precum beading temptingly at the tip, but when I look up at him, he's smirking like he's not a man driven to the precipice by sexual frustration. He wraps his fingers around the edge of the armrests and shifts his arse—and dick—forward, leaning back as if he's settling in for a nice rest.

'You look even better at my feet like that,' he tells me from his lofty, Big Dick position. 'Show me what a good little whore you are, sucking me under my desk. If someone came in, they wouldn't even know you were here, would they?'

'No,' I say, launching myself forward. His words are a lit match to the petrol trail of desire he's laid. God knows, no one in their right mind would call me submissive, so why the fucking hell does the idea of being the *good little whore,* tucked away like this and existing solely for this powerful man's needs, make my primed, swollen pussy throb even harder?

I wrap my fingers around the base of his cock. I can't get to his balls like this with just his flies undone, so I use my other hand to grip the taut muscle of his thigh as I flick my tongue over the precum. It's salty and unctuous and just for me. He shudders and makes a noise that's half laugh, half groan, like even the tip of my tongue is too much to bear.

I know how you feel, mister.

It's time to go for it. I let myself lick and lave, swirling my tongue around the smooth heat of his crown, smearing the precum as I go. He smells clean and aroused and masculine, and I fucking love it. I lick him kind of like I dance: instinctively, naturally, with lavish sweeps of my tongue and sensual strokes of my lips.

I tease his frenulum, and he moans loudly. I lick along the big vein running down the underside of his dick, and he shudders. He's unabashed, losing himself in his own pleasure. And when I take as much of him as I can in my mouth, his entire body tenses beneath me and he claws at my hair, fisting handfuls of it. I expect him to grab my jaw and demand to set the pace as he fucks my mouth, but when I'm mid-deep-throat he hauls me off him and kisses me greedily, his tongue plundering my mouth with hungry strokes.

'You're too good,' he mutters against my lips when he comes up for air. 'I need to fuck you.'

And, with that, he spins me around and, with a decisive hand between my shoulder blades, hinges me forward until I'm bent over the desk, arms outstretched. He holds me in place like that, my pussy exposed and screaming, the antique dark-green leather surface cool against my cheek and far too smooth against my poor, needy nipples, as he rummages in a drawer. Then there's the telltale rip of foil and he removes his hand while he busies himself with the condom.

The rough dig of his fingertips into my left hip is the only warning I get before he's notching his tip at my entrance and shoving in, hard. It's rougher than I expected, and his is not the easiest dick to accommodate, but I'm so primed, so wet, that I take him. And then he's in, his hand going back to splay between my shoulder blades as he prepares to move.

It's indescribable, the sheer, overwhelming completeness that wipes every thought from my mind except how to survive the onslaught and how badly I need to come. His thighs are flush against mine, the wool of his half-undone trousers bunching against my skin. He withdraws slowly, and I swear I feel every single millimetre as he drags himself against my inner walls.

The fingers on my hip caress my arse as the hand on my back entangles itself in my hair. 'Fuck me,' he says softly. 'I don't even know which way I like you best. Straddling my chair; crouching under my desk; bent *over* my desk with all your holes on display for me... So. *Fucking. Beautiful.*'

As he utters the last word, he drives forward, burying himself up to the hilt inside me, slamming my hips into the jutting edge of the desk and knocking the breath right out of my lungs. I cry out because *Jesus Christ* it's perfect, and I need him to do this to me over and over and over, exactly like that, until he's forced every last morsel of frustration and need out of me.

'You want it rough, sweetheart?' he asks, satisfaction lancing through his tone.

'Yes,' I whimper, because I need it like this from him. I need him to use me and fuck me and unleash himself on me, and I'm willing to sport a straight line of bruises from hip to hip for the rest of the week if it means I can come the way I want so badly.

He sucks a harsh breath in through his teeth. '*Good.* Hang on.'

His body is shaking against mine, such is the effort of

holding himself off, but he stays bottomed out in me for a moment as he wedges his hands between me and the desk, and I push down with my palms and arch a little to give him the space he needs. He cups my boobs in both hands, squeezing and weighing before he pinches my nipples so viciously I practically come right here and now.

'Oh my God.' He can't get any deeper inside me, but that doesn't stop my hips from slamming back against him of their own accord.

'Needy little nipples,' he grits out. 'Needy, needy nipples from a needy little whore. God, I wish I had a roomful of guys right now so they could touch every perfect inch of you while I pound you into fucking oblivion.'

He twists them hard again, as if to underscore his point, before releasing them, and I collapse back across the desk. In this bright, shining moment of hyper-arousal, I wish everything he says could be true. God knows, I'd take it all. I'd take every lick and suck and touch from every single guy he put in front of me. I'd be the greediest girl in the world, lapping it up while a roomful of men wound me so high they could shoot me through the stratosphere.

'I want that,' I manage as he pulls out of me.

'You'll get it,' he promises darkly before he grabs a fistful of my hair so hard I yelp and really lets me have it.

31

MAX

It's not just the explosive, all-consuming sensation of shoving my cock into Darcy's cunt, over and over, with a whole lot of power and very little finesse.

It's the sight of it all that has me fighting for control.

My angry dick, disappearing between those plump, creamy arse cheeks.

The delicate curve of her spine as she attempts uselessly to arch under my unflinching palm.

Her beautiful face in profile, her usually angelic features contorted with her need to come as much as with the effort of withstanding the uncompromising pummelling I'm giving her. Her outstretched arms, hands clenched into fists, chestnut hair strewn prettily across the leather of my desk.

It really is a most gratifying picture.

I'm surrounded by art, accolades, by the trappings of wealth and power and having well and truly "made it" in the business world. But nothing says victory, nothing says the sweet spoils of war, nothing says *conquering hero* like having a beautiful woman strewn across one's desk to poke and fuck and defile.

Fuck me, if she's not the ultimate prize. It feels right to be christening this office, and this desk, by coming deep inside Darcy's beautiful body.

She wants more, greedy, wanton, delicious little slut that she is; she wants more cock from this Dex guy, but I'll be damned if she doesn't hobble out of here knowing that my cock alone is quite enough.

I flare my nostrils, breathing heavily as I force myself to keep my moves rhythmical. Every thrust must be a turn of the screw that'll wind her tighter. Drive her higher.

She's close. Those long, elegant fingers are clawing ineffectively at my desk's surface, her eyes squeezing closed as she pushes her hips back to meet me every single time. Every time I ram home, her entire torso shunts up the desk. It must be sore, but the breathy, desperate whimpers she's making are so fucking intoxicating they spur me on like a madman. I can't hold back, so I hope to fuck she comes before I do.

Her orgasm rips through her, and I grab both her hips so I can piston through it as hard as I can. She's a writhing, crying mess of hair and skin, bucking beneath my hands as those wonderfully toned internal muscles clamp down on my dick over and over.

I fuck her through it, the hot, pure glow of pleasure coursing through my veins and dancing across my nerve endings as I follow her over the edge with strangled curses and jagged thrusts. Then I'm stilling as deep as I can inside her as I shudder through my own spectacular climax, a tsunami that subsumes me, leaving my body limp and my head clear.

As it ebbs away, I bend and gather her up in my arms, pulling her sated body flush against mine.

'I THINK we've worked up a sufficient appetite,' I tell her as she emerges from my office's ensuite bathroom, swinging her oversized bag. She's back in her dress, having brushed her glorious just-fucked mane of hair into submission and wiped the mascara smudges from under her eyes.

She's glowing and beautiful.

'For what?' she asks.

'Lunch.'

She looks at me like I've just grown an extra head.

'You didn't think I'd make you come over here for sex and then turf you out, did you?' I ask.

'That's exactly what I thought.' She tugs the handbag onto one shoulder.

'Well, that's hurtful,' I say chidingly, moving closer so I can tug her against me. 'One, I'd like to think I've been brought up better than that. Two, and far more importantly, you've been the unmitigated bright spot in my day so far and I'm not in a hurry to get back to work.'

'I'd be pretty offended if it wasn't, and I'm not sure eating lunch with me will live up to what we just did,' she retorts.

'Of course it will. Your conversational skills aren't *that* bad. Come on.'

I take her around the corner to Nobu in Berkeley Square, my hand firmly in hers. I haven't booked, but that's never an issue.

'A sandwich will be fine,' she gasps as I usher her through their heavy doors. 'We could just go to Pret.'

'I don't do *fine*,' I tell her. 'Nor do I do bread, especially processed bread. This is healthy if you order sensibly, and it's delicious.' I lean in and whisper in her ear as we approach the front desk. 'That was a Nobu-level fuck, not a Pret-level fuck. Don't sell yourself short.'

The maître d' greets me by name and promptly shows us to my favourite table. I follow Darcy up the shallow staircase, my hand light on the small of her back. It's the usual business lunch crowd—fewer gold diggers and more dealmakers. Anonymous guys in the Mayfair hedge fund uniform of open-necked shirt, no tie, and suit trousers.

I consult with Darcy on her preferences—my experience watching her devour China Tang's best tells me she eats everything—and order a selection for us to share, going heavy on the veg and sashimi. I don't need to be in a food coma for the afternoon—I'm still sex drunk as it is. While I love nothing more than a good fuck, it takes the edge off my... edge. Which is not ideal when you're at the helm of a business the size of the fucking Titanic.

Bad analogy. Wolff Holdings is in excellent health.

Anyway, I'll take this lunch for what it is—an hour to enjoy myself in all my post-sex mellow bliss with the enchanting woman responsible before I reengage Corporate Mode.

Said enchanting woman is currently fiddling with the strap of her sundress. I wave our server away and pour out our bottle of Pellegrino myself. 'You okay?' I ask her.

'If I'd known I was coming here, I would've dressed up,' she says, wriggling in her seat.

'You're the most beautiful woman in this room,' I tell her sternly, 'so it's good that you're dressed down. Showing the rest of them up any more would have been plain rude.'

She smiles at me and I grin back at her with genuine pleasure.

'If you say so,' she says.

'I do. You have precisely as much right to be here as

everyone else. More, because you're with me. Okay?' I take a sip of my water.

'Okay. But you'll be sorry at the end of the meal, because I'm getting so stuck in it's not funny.' She wiggles her shoulders happily, and I cock my head as I survey her.

'What?'

'You're very... refreshing.'

She rolls her eyes. 'Refreshing like a wet wipe?'

'A lot more. You're a bit of a novelty for me, you know.'

'Uh-oh. That's not good.'

'Why not?'

'Because novelties by definition are only novel when they're new. Then they stop being fun.'

'I can't imagine you ever not being fun,' I say.

She looks at me over the top of her water glass. 'I try.'

'Do you?'

'What?'

'Try. Is it a conscious thing? Because it certainly doesn't seem conscious. Do you purposefully try to be fun?'

'I dunno.' She screws up her pretty little nose. 'It's part of who I am, I suppose. I'm the fun one, and Gen's the sensible one. It's always been that way.'

That sounds a lot less to me about *who she is* and far more about *who she's been pigeonholed as.*

The fun one.

The bright, beautiful spark who dazzles and amuses and entertains.

She's all of those qualities, of course—they're clearly intrinsic to her—but I hope she doesn't ascribe her value to them. But I suspect Darcy isn't a woman who welcomes unsolicited psychoanalysis.

'I see,' is all I say. 'Is that why you dance? Because it's fun?'

'No,' she says, 'definitely not.'

'Really? You don't find it enjoyable?'

'I do, of course, but not because it's *fun*.' She scans the room, seemingly trying to articulate something. 'I suppose it's like—I've never been the smart one, right? That's always been Gen.'

There she goes again, pigeonholing herself, allowing herself to be neatly indexed by someone else's fucked-up version of Dewey Decimal.

'You're smart, and you're socially agile, and you're emotionally intelligent,' I say firmly. 'I can tell. So don't say things like that in my presence, because it won't wash. And, by the way, it doesn't have to be binary. Gen and you can both be smart, and you are, so if your parents didn't make that clear then I'm sorry.'

'Thank you,' she says softly. 'That's really nice of you to say. But what I mean is, I wasn't academic. When I was at prep school, I wasn't studious.'

'Being studious or academic and being smart are totally different things,' I argue. I categorically can't let this lie. 'Take Richard Branson. Take me. I was a fucking nightmare at school—undiagnosed dyslexia and ADHD. I didn't get either diagnosed till I went off to Eton and my housemaster worked it out in days. Fuck knows how I got through the Common Entrance, but they let me in, and I'll always be grateful to him.'

She's staring at me in astonishment. 'You're dyslexic?'

'Yes. But this isn't about me. My point is, you say you weren't studious at school. So what? Doesn't mean you're not intelligent.'

'Okay, but I think what I'm trying to say is that there are different types of intelligence, right, and they're more like intuition. So you mentioned emotional intelligence—

that's one. But physical intelligence seems to be another. Basically, my body feels smarter than my mind, if that makes sense? It's like my brains are literally in my muscles.

'My body understands things without my brain even processing them, and it's instinctive and intuitive. I can hear music, even in my head, and just *know* how I should move to it. It's kind of like speaking a language and having no clue how you learnt it. All I know is, the music speaks to my soul, and my soul speaks to my body, and my body speaks back. Does that sound crazy?'

I take her hand across the table and squeeze it, but I don't let go. Because what she says moves me, for some reason.

'No,' I say. 'It doesn't sound crazy in the slightest. It not only sounds very sane, but very enviable, too, because I would say that kind of intelligence is a rare and beautiful gift to have.' I pause. 'And you've just articulated—with beautiful poignancy, I might add—one of the many reasons I find you so mesmerising. Is that a better word than *refreshing*?'

She rests her chin on her spare hand and smiles at me. 'It's much better, and I can spare a few minutes if you want to list all the other reasons.'

I throw back my head and laugh. 'Well, obviously, your shy and self-effacing nature is the main one. No, seriously. You make me laugh, when a lot of people bore the ever-loving fuck out of me.'

'As long as you're laughing with me and not at me.'

'Always with you. Always. And'—I lower my voice—'we've fucked, what, on three occasions, now? You're the first woman in a long, long time who hasn't tried to put a ring on my finger or at least get a new Birkin out of me.'

She makes a face. 'That's uncool. I just want you for your big dick. That and all this really good food.'

I laugh again. 'I'll keep feeding you, don't you worry. But I had to practically tie you to the bed the other night to get you to stay over. Most women would be freeing up drawers and trying to move their stuff in by now.'

'Maybe that works for women who like old, crusty guys, but not for me,' she deadpans, and I grin, remembering her words to me that first night in France. If I recall correctly, she called me a *crusty old Brit*. Cheeky little wench.

'We're back to that, are we?'

She smirks. 'Seems so.'

'I didn't notice you complaining when you were coming all over my cock just now.'

She doesn't look around to see if anyone can overhear. She doesn't bat an eyelid, which I fucking love. She merely pulls her hand away and picks up her water glass.

'What can I say? It must be that you're still a *novelty* to me.'

She's unbelievable. I raise my glass to her. 'Well played. I'll need to keep things fresh then, won't I?'

She clinks. 'Absolutely. You don't want me getting bored, do you?'

'Definitely not.' I grind my jaw. 'So let's mix things up. Did you get Dex's number off Maddy?'

Her eyes dart evasively around the buzzing restaurant. 'Not yet.'

'Lucky for you, some of us are doers. I DM'ed Belle on Instagram and asked her for it.' I slide my phone onto the table and pull up the exchange.

'Here you go. Send him a message.'

She looks at me, eyes wide. 'Now?'

I smile wolfishly. 'No time like the present.'

32

DARCY AND DEX

DARCY

> Hi Dex

> It's Darcy

> From the other night

> Gen's sister

DEX

Hi there

[Long silence]

> Chatty, aren't you?

Sorry, I'm just in a meeting

> Ah

> No worries

> Have fun!

I can guarantee I won't, but my fellow division heads will definitely wonder why I'm smiling in a budgetary meeting

> *Bats lashes*

Did you need me for something?

> I was wondering if you'd like to come and watch me dance this week?

At the club?

> Yes

It's not a matter of liking. I'd like to, very much. But I'm not a member and I'm not sure it's a good idea…

> You're the owner's brother-in-law

> It wouldn't be a problem

> And it's a GREAT idea

> Anyway

> Max said he'll sign you in as his guest

Did he, now?

> Yup

Still hanging around, is he?

> Very much so

The head of the Investment Banking
Division just asked me what was wrong
because I sighed so loudly

> So come and have some fun

> Wednesday???

> I promise I'll put on a good show…

That's what I'm afraid of.

33

DEX

If my little sister was brave enough to put her virginity in the hands of this club, then I can handle a single evening here.

That's what I tell myself, anyway, as the strikingly attractive brunette on the front desk signs me in. She hands me a clipboard to which is clipped a longwinded waiver. A quick scan of it tells me I'm signing a comprehensive NDA and an acknowledgement that I understand the code of conduct here at Alchemy and that any breach of those rules could jeopardise the member whose guest I am tonight.

Max Hunter has already signed it.

I sign with a flourish and head down the wide, elegant corridor like a sacrificial lamb to the slaughter, because it's eight-fifty on a Wednesday night and I have a five-thirty alarm call. I should be at the gym, or catching up on some of the giant equity research reports mocking me from my kitchen table.

I categorically should *not* be going to see some alluring woman whose scent still haunts my olfactory system and whose kind-of *boyfriend* has sponsored me tonight in a move that surely has kink or power games at its core.

Neither of those options bode well for me, and I can't believe I've allowed Darcy to talk me into this. Nothing good can come from watching her dance.

Nothing good at all.

When I open the next set of heavy doors and step into the bar area, it's buzzing in a low-key, genteel way not at all reminiscent of a sex club. I wonder if people come here to do deals and then go next door to fuck all that adrenalin out of their system once they've closed them.

Of course they do.

We're in the heart of Mayfair, at a club whose price-point would make Annabel's or Maison Estelle weep and which is populated by the great and good of British finance, industry and politics.

They can get up to whatever they want away from prying eyes.

I've only scanned a third of the room when my gaze meets his.

Max fucking Hunter.

He's sitting alone at a small table off to one side of the room, his eyes on the door as if he's been watching for me. He raises his hand in a small and totally unnecessary salute of acknowledgement, because his handsome mug is plastered on the front page of *The Economist* this week above the apt title: *Hungry Like the Wolff: The Next Era*.

Everyone in the City of London not only knows what Hunter looks like but wants right now to get into bed with him.

Figuratively speaking.

As I head in his direction, he unfolds himself from the

low velvet bench he's been sitting on and stands to greet me. Once again I have that *what the fuck am I doing* feeling.

I'm here because Darcy asked me to come, and she seems sweet, and she's very attractive, so watching her dance will be no hardship at all. Plus, she's kind of like a distant cousin by marriage, really, if you consider the Alchemy founders to be a family, which they pretty much are.

That's all well and good. But why the hell I've agreed to let the guy she's fucking sign me in and watch as I, some random guy, perv freely at his sort-of girlfriend, I have no clue. This feels like some awkward blind date, at a *sex club*, for Christ's sake.

God. I hope none of these people think he and I are here to…

Surely not.

He's lean. Tall. He has maybe an inch on me. Like me, he's in his summer work uniform of suit trousers and a shirt with the top couple of buttons undone. No jacket. No tie. My shirt is pale blue and his is white. But it's his eyes that get me. Deep-set and blue and piercing.

Alarmingly piercing.

His face is—I don't know—classically good-looking, I suppose. He sports an even, golden tan, a fact that only enhances his eyes. His smile, when he bestows it on me, verges on smug, but this guy has everything he wants, so the fact that he's a smug, self-satisfied bastard comes as no surprise at all.

He sticks out his hand, and we shake. 'Max,' he says. 'Dex, I assume?'

'Good to see you,' I say. God knows how he recognised me, but I know better than to ask him, because you never get a straight answer from guys as slippery as him.

I thank Christ my colleagues don't know I have any form

of personal intro to Max Hunter lined up for tonight, because they'd be relentless if they thought we had any tiny edge on the Wolff deal.

'Thanks for coming,' he says. 'Darcy's excited to have you here.'

I don't like that. He sounds like her pimp or her agent, and what the fuck is wrong with him, anyway? If I was with her in any form I'd go feral at the thought of her exposing her body to anyone else, let alone a club full of sex addicts.

But some people are weird like that. Maybe he gets off on knowing that everyone else wants her and he gets to have her to himself when she's got off stage. I couldn't begin to guess what kind of kinks a guy like Max Hunter would have.

I make some polite, ineffectual murmur of acknowledgement like *of course* or something equally banal, and we take our seats.

'She'll be on in ten minutes,' he says, 'so I grabbed us both a G&T.'

He slides a tall glass over to me, and we clink. A nice long, quenching gin and tonic is perfect, actually. I take a sip, and he laughs at my expression.

'It's practically all tonic. There's no way you're getting drunk in this place.'

'Makes sense,' I say, recalling the strict two-drink limit here the other night. While I'd like a little more hard liquor to take the edge off, it makes me marginally less uneasy to think none of the animals leering at Darcy next door will be drunk.

He crosses one ankle easily over its opposite knee and lolls back on the sofa. Not for Max that particularly British faux pas of exposing an inch of hairy leg above the top of his socks. No, he's wearing the longer, fine merino kind that my European colleagues wear and which were probably hand-knitted by wholesome young virgins. 'I heard you've moved back to join Loeb? Head of Equities, is that right?'

'It is,' I say.

'Congratulations. That's impressive. You're seriously young—you must be one of their youngest ever partners.'

I am in fact their youngest ever partner, singular, but I'm not one to toot my own horn. 'I am, yeah. I'm thirty.'

'Wow. And you've been back how long?'

'A week and a half, but it feels like a year already,' I confess, and he chuckles.

'I'll bet. I assume they've put you to work? You must be busy.'

'Not as busy as you,' I deadpan, and he rolls his eyes, amused.

'You've got that right. If I have to read one more RFP I'll shoot myself in the head.'

I can only imagine. The RFPs, or requests for proposal, that every bank submits as part of its pitch to win an IPO are as tedious as they are girthy.

'I don't envy you,' I tell him. 'So tonight's about a little light relief from the grind, is it?'

Something about the way his eyebrows wing up and the hand holding his drink freezes halfway to his mouth has me regretting my use of the word *grind*. I meant it as the epitome of relentless toil, but I suspect he's homed in on its possible double meaning, a hunch that has me flustered. He's probably the kind of dirty bastard who'll wring an innuendo out of the most innocent throwaway comments and manage to make them filthy in their raw physicality.

'Light relief, definitely,' he muses. 'And who knows what else, eh? The night is young.'

'Not if you have my wake-up call,' I say in a feeble attempt at a joke. 'It's nearly my bedtime.'

He surveys me, and for a second I have the most discomfiting feeling that he can see through every thread of the bullshit I wear like an ineffectual cloak.

'You're thirty,' is all he says. 'Live a little. Walk in there tomorrow when you like and don't even think of explaining yourself. You're a fucking partner. It's none of their fucking business how you structure your time.'

He's correct, absolutely, but I don't particularly care for this avuncular, fireside-chat style he's adopting.

'I'm sure you're right,' I mumble.

'Besides.' He leans forward. 'Sex is far more restorative than sleep. And you can have as much of it as you want next door—they'll go crazy for you. Guys. Girls. The lot. Take your pick.'

I stiffen. 'I don't—I mean—'

But he's not listening. He's draining his drink and looking around the bar. 'Let's go through, shall we?' he asks. 'And for God's sake, relax and enjoy yourself. Even good boys come first here, if they play their cards right.'

And with that he stands, slaps me far too hard on my shoulder, and strides off through the throng.

34

DEX

The Playroom is a masterclass in sensory overwhelm and disorientation, which I suspect is exactly the point. The music is seriously loud—some kind of house with sexy, moaning vocals overlaid—and this space I've been so nervous about stepping foot in is the oddest mix of classy and carnal.

It has high ceilings and huge white pillars from which billow gauzy white drapes. It's pretty full, and maybe it's because of the time of night, but the, er, coupling isn't as in your face as I was worried it would be. There are plenty of sofas dotted around, and I definitely spot some horizontal action on one of the near ones, but most people seem to be dancing and mingling and making out rather than hardcore going at it.

Thank fuck.

Darcy told me the other night that she was the patrons' fluffer, and it looks like she was bang on, because if everyone in here isn't desperate to hump each other after the show she puts on, then there's something physiologically wrong with them.

The stage runs down the right-hand side of the room. I stand beside Max towards the front of the dancing, writhing mass of bodies. We're almost shoulder to shoulder, which is far too close for my liking, and both nursing a pitifully small scotch that he procured from the bar across the room as soon as we came through.

His proximity, the heat pumping off his body through that beautifully tailored shirt, is bothering me, but it would bother me more if less of my brain function (and blood flow) was redirecting itself to the woman undulating on stage like every fantasy my teenage self wasn't inventive enough to conjure. I'm growing hard, and I despise myself for it.

QUESTION: how can a woman who looks like Jessica Chastain, all achingly delicate facial bone structure and russet waves and huge doe eyes, move like sin personified?

Because there's no doubt that everything about this situation is sinful. I quickly push away the thought that this must be my baby sister's second home. If I never talk to Belle about sex for the rest of our lives, I'll be happy. But I recall one thing she said to me, when she'd had it out with Dad and was happy and loved-up.

She told me that there was something about submitting to the sinfulness of it all that was downright delightful.

Maybe she's onto something.

Because this club and what it stands for contradict every last binary number of the moral framework encoded into my Catholic-shaped soul. And I'm standing here, clutching my pearls and trying my damnedest not to look and not to perv and not to desire, especially when faced with the woman on stage. I'm acting like I'm here against my will, which I sort of am. But nobody made me come.

I'm a grown man, for fuck's sake.

Maybe Max here is right.

Maybe I should take my fill tonight—visually, I mean—and strut into the office tomorrow at whatever time suits me, and stop railing against everything. Stop denying everything, just for an hour.

Everyone else is enjoying themselves. No one else looks to be beating themselves over the head with anything from a metaphorical Bible to a figurative Debrett's. In a room full of consenting adults, I can at least try not to be a total killjoy.

Besides.

Just look at her.

I'd be certifiably insane if I didn't drink in the sight in front of me with every fibre that makes me human.

She was dangerous the other night, I knew it then, with her perfect, perky breasts and disarming friendliness and her total lack of filter when spouting compliments that could fell a man.

But at least she had some fucking clothes on.

Now, though, she's dancing in a gilded cage onstage, naked except for her wings, some sheer mesh, and a few crystals that do nothing to conceal *anything*. Instead, they make her shimmer like some kind of mirage. They enhance her otherworldliness.

To be honest, when she told me she was a dancer here, I imagined a pole and a thong and some nipple tassels. Right? I didn't imagine an erotic *Cirque de Soleil*.

Her body is mesmerising. Exquisite. She's a bona fide bombshell, with curves in all the right places and a defined waist. Her legs are strong and shapely. The sight of her breasts has me wanting simultaneously to lay my head on them and to suck those taut little nipples until she's screaming to have my hand between her legs.

Speaking of... nothing down there is concealed at all. So help me God, I find my gaze flitting from the light strip of hair above her pussy to her breasts and back, hoping and wishing that she'll do something crass like bend over and show us everything.

What the hell is happening to me?

If the lines of her figure are perfection, the way she commands her body is sublime. Even if that bodystocking were fully opaque, I wouldn't be able to look away. She moves like water. She floats and she ripples and she morphs.

And when she performs a kind of vertical split, I swear my heart stops and my lungs empty. She flings one leg up high, foot resting on one of the front bars of the cage as she grips two of the neighbouring bars and arches back into a perfect crescent.

Her hair cascades down. Her upturned breasts fill the mesh perfectly. Her throat is white, her legs sinewed.

And her pussy is on full display, even if the scissored legs twist what I would rather see open.

The crowd roars and whistles and claps. The music's relentless beat throbs on. And Max leans in, right in, his lips going almost to the shell of my ear. His breath on my skin is warm, and it sends a smattering of goosebumps down my spine.

'She's quite something, isn't she?'

I turn my head to look at him and instantly realise my mistake, because our faces are far too close for comfort, and that grin on his face is smug and proprietorial, and I don't like it. I don't like it one bit.

The descriptor we used for the ruthless head of Equity Capital Markets at Goldman flits into my head.

Smiling assassin.

This guy does affable and debonair like he's got a Masters in the subjects. But I bet he'd slit your throat with a straight razor while grinning right at you, just like he is now.

I'd love to cut him down to size, but it seems far too churlish to give Darcy anything but the compliment she deserves in the process, so I tell him the truth.

'She might just be the most beautiful creature I've ever seen.'

His smile fades. He surveys me thoughtfully.

'You know, she said something very similar about you, too.'

She said something very similar *to* me, too, but I'm not inclined to tell him that. He's got enough of her already.

Instead, I avert my gaze from his piercing one and turn my attention back to Darcy.

35

MAX

The woman I'm involved with is onstage, pouring her body into shapes a more religious man would take as proof that there is a God. She has that look on her face that she gets when she dances.

Dreamy.

She's pulled a veil down between her and the crowd.

We can watch her, but we can't reach her.

She's communing with the music, letting it speak through her soul like she described at lunch. It's as awe-inspiring as it is arousing, and it elevates what should be something base to a level I find almost unbearably erotic.

Darcy Carew is the real fucking deal, and the thrill of possession courses through me, heady and strong. Because she's mine. For now, at least.

All of which makes it irksome that she's only occupying about three-quarters of my mental capacity.

The other quarter is taken up by the man standing next to me.

I shoot him a furtive sideways glance and twist my

mouth in what I suppose is a mix of amusement and rue. Amusement because every instinct I had when I saw his photo has proven to be right, and rue because I have no fucking proof that he's queer, no matter what my gut tells me.

If I'm right, and he is queer, I can find a way to claim him, that's for sure. But something else is certain: he's straight as a die. And I don't mean *straight* in the sexual sense; I mean he's a rule follower. I saw his WhatsApp exchange with Darce. He has impeccable manners. I bet he wouldn't put a foot wrong.

Unfortunately for him, not only is he the kind of handsome up close to which no photo could do justice, but I have a particular penchant for uptight good boys who are perpetually in denial and need a firm hand and a hard dick to show them what they're missing. Those astonishing dark-lashed eyes of his are trained fixedly on Darcy, so I take the opportunity to surreptitiously devour him with my gaze.

He's clean-shaven, like me. He's got a decent tan, but I can tell his skin is the kind of olive that still holds through the winter. His lips are full, his jaw as tense as the grip on his whisky tumbler. Still, the line of it is alluring. I'd lick along it before sucking hard on his neck to remind him who he belongs to. My nostrils flare just thinking about it, and if my dick could get any harder, it would.

He hasn't taken the bait of my last comment. Perhaps the most unfortunate thing of all for poor little Dex is that he's dealing with a man who will blithely turn anyone's greatest attribute into their greatest vulnerability before you can say *Achilles.* And in Dex's case, those attributes are most likely his impeccable manners and his hankering after our girl Darcy.

I lean in again, admiring how pretty his tanned neck looks bracketed by the curls of his dark hair and the crisp blue cotton of his shirt.

'You know what else Darcy said about you?' I murmur. The music's so loud that I don't need to keep my voice down. Neither do I wait for a response before delivering my killer blow. 'She said,'—my lips are so deliciously close to his jawline and he smells like shampoo—'she wants you to fuck her.'

That's got his attention.

He turns sharply, taking an immediate step back to reduce our proximity. 'What the hell?' he snaps.

Isn't he pretty when he's angry? Or discomfited. All I know is Confronted Dex is a treat.

'It's true,' I continue smoothly. 'She came straight back to mine last Saturday after she met you here. You made quite the impression. Imagine my surprise when she not only asked me for a threesome but said she'd found the exact man for the job.'

I watch his face. I'd hazard a guess it's far more expressive than someone as buttoned-up as him would want. That's quite the melange of emotions he has going on so close to the surface.

'Hang on,' he says. 'She wants a *threesome*?' He screws his face up at the last word, like it's one too offensive to have ever crossed his lips before, and I almost laugh.

'You didn't think I'd let you touch her without my being there to chaperone, did you?'

'Chaperone,' he repeats. I think I may have broken his brain. I turn to face him properly.

'Don't overthink this,' I tell him. I've built a career of sweet-talking and hand-holding and silkily, gently coercing people to do every single thing I want, and I have no intention of stopping now. 'She wants you. She was incredibly taken with you. And look at her.'

We both take a moment to turn our heads to the stage, where Darcy's dancing, an angel beating her wings inside her gilded cage. As we turn back, I risk a glance south, but it's too dark in here to see if he's hard.

When I have his attention again, I press on, making my voice softer, more cajoling. 'You know, she gets so aroused on stage, bless her. Do you blame her? Everyone's watching her. Everyone wants to fuck her. But none of them can. She's untouchable, except for me.' I pause. 'And for you.' I raise my eyebrows meaningfully. 'And you know what? She's never had a threesome—can you believe it? It's all she wants, and she wants her first time to be with you and me.'

I inject into my pitch all the emotion of Bob Cratchit advocating for Tiny Tim, and my acting skills are rewarded with a flicker of doubt in Dex's strange and perfect eyes as the twisted form of chivalry I'm pitching no doubt wars for dominance in his conservative little heart with what he considers to be seemly.

He's actually asking himself if he can do this.

Let's reel him in.

'Imagine touching her. Her skin is softer than you could ever dream. She feels so fucking good.' My tone is low. Confiding. He'd be a moron not to take this recommendation from the horse's mouth, as it were. 'Tastes amazing, too. Like nectar. I bet she wants your mouth on her cunt. I bet she'd let you fuck her with your tongue before you fuck her properly. Imagine it.

'And she's so fucking responsive. I know she comes across as feisty as hell, but in bed she's a submissive little doll. You'd get to lay her out and feast on her.' Time to close. 'This is the only way you get to be with her, mate.'

'Fucking hell,' he mutters, and if I wasn't so intent on winning this round, I'd almost feel sorry for the guy. I'm here to broker the deal I promised Darcy I'd swing, and if I have my own reasons for wanting to ensnare this hot little fly in my web long enough to forge my own inroads with him, then that's an added bonus.

That's what I tell myself, anyway.

'What are your concerns?' I ask him, sounding horribly like a salesman trying to close a buyer on a top-of-the-range mattress, but I don't think it's my selling style that has him barking out an unamused laugh.

'My *concerns*? I came here to watch her dance. That's it. No offence, but this isn't my scene. I'm not comfortable being here at all, and now you're trying to strong-arm me into some kind of kinky ménage—I don't think so.'

'Look, I get that,' I tell him. I don't, obviously. This place is Disneyland. 'She's nearly done, and I've got a private room booked. It doesn't have to be...' I choose my words. 'It's her first time. No DP, nothing like that. Remember, this is just about taking care of Darcy, making her feel good. If all you want to do is go in there and tell her what a great job she did and maybe give her a kiss, that's totally fine. Just come say hi. She'll be really hurt if you leave without swinging by backstage.'

And still he wavers. Honestly, if he can't handle that then the guy clearly has no fucking backbone at all, and she and I should cut him loose. He can run off with his tail between his legs and sign up for Hinge and hopefully find some nice, safe, lights-out, missionary action. Fuck's sake.

'Get a load of this,' I tell him with a jerk of my head.

He turns his attention to the stage again, but I keep my gaze on him. I've seen this routine a few times now, so I know she's gearing up for the big reveal, the money shot that might just achieve what my smooth talking can't.

And I know when she does it, because watching Dex watch Darcy spread her legs and bend over and expose herself fully to the crowd is my new favourite show.

I watch as his brow creases and his eyes narrow and he snags that plump bottom lip, digging his teeth in so hard that I have the novel and unwelcome sensation of being jealous of someone's *teeth*. If he could stop being an overthinking, jumpy little bitch for a few moments, I'd show him exactly how that lip should be bitten.

But then the miraculous happens.

'No guy-on-guy stuff, right?' he asks, inclining his head towards me but keeping his eyes fixed on Darcy's magical cunt. 'Because that's not my bag at all.'

I swallow a smirk. Sure it's not. 'Of course not,' I say, sounding shocked. *Where is my Golden Globe?* 'It's all about Darcy. Think of it like we're servicing her. She deserves a good servicing after dancing so beautifully up there, doesn't she? She's turned everyone in this room on, and she's aching to be touched all over her beautiful body, and I know you and I can do a good job of that together. Just think of how very, very good we can make it for her.'

'Yeah,' he says, his voice dreamy, and I know he's imagining gorging himself on her.

She's bowing, giving the audience a smile and a wave and a cheeky little shimmy of her hips, and I wedge my tumbler between my forearm and my abdomen so I can clap with the rest of them and then wolf whistle.

And as she turns to go, sauntering off stage with those

arse cheeks gliding against each other invitingly, I move in for the kill with a decisive hand on what is a very toned shoulder.

'Come on. Let's go and make a fuss of her, mate.'

36

DEX

Every part of my nervous system should be screaming *DANGER* at me right now. Instead, it's too busy whipping up the hormonal equivalent of crack to have any regard for my survival.

I stand clear of the doorway leading from The Playroom to a wide, dimly lit corridor to allow a laughing, semi-naked couple through. She's a petite blonde in a red latex bra and leggings, and he has her by the neck. It seems we're not the only ones ready for a little privacy thanks to Darcy's inimitable charms.

I should be watching them—her arse looks incredible in those leggings—but then they turn into the second room and Max strides in front of me, and for some reason I find my gaze glued to his arse instead, admiring from a purely aesthetic perspective how perfectly the supple weave of his wool trousers skims the curvature of his glutes. How well the tucks in the back of his pristine shirt follow the tapered small of his back to his narrow waist.

His tailor is a true artist, and I almost definitely couldn't afford him.

This corridor is like that of a trendy hotel instead of a sex club, its deep grey walls and limestone floor lustrous, thanks to the myriad dancing church candles that flank us in their hurricane lanterns. It strikes me once again that the vibe is intimate and decadent, but not seedy which, given what transpires in here, is a noteworthy achievement.

Max strides ahead of me like he owns the place, which he probably does, before stopping and knocking softly at the very last door. I catch him up in time to hear Darcy's chirpy *come in*.

The room is dimly lit and dominated by a huge bed. The walls are lacquered in a rich petrol blue, and chunky candles with flickering flames punctuate the space. It's just as stylish, as carefully tasteful as the hallway. But my attention goes straight to *her*.

She's still in her bodystocking, leaning against the wall beside the bed, one arm raised and crooked so she can use the other to stretch out her tricep. Her face is flushed and her big blue eyes are glittering almost feverishly, which I take to mean she's still very much high on the adrenalin of her performance—and possibly the arousal of it, too.

She pushes off the wall, a huge smile on her face. 'You came!' she says to me before padding over to Max, seemingly unbothered about the fact that she's pretty much naked in front of two men. 'I can't believe you got him to come,' she tells him, throwing her arms around his neck.

'I told you I'd get you anything you wanted,' he says, tugging her into his arms.

I watch in a tumult of emotions as he slides one hand over her bottom and one through the untidy waves of her hair. Their mouths crash together in a kiss that's urgent and open-mouthed and unselfconscious, and the sight of their lips sliding, of his hard jaw working and his hands gliding over her body and the wet-looking sliver of tongue as he tilts his head further, might be one of the most purely erotic things I've ever seen.

I'm still semi-hard from her performance, still dizzy over the potential minefield I may have just stepped foot into, but the jack-hammering of my heart is all from this.

I bet I could come just from this, without even touching them, without letting them touch me. I bet I could come just from the sheer beauty of watching as this pair of humans couple.

But I don't get to test that theory, because Max breaks free of the kiss and murmurs hoarsely to her, 'If my superstar asks, I fetch.' And then, with a thumb dragging along her jaw, he adds, 'Why don't you give our guest a proper welcome?'

That has me stiffening in anticipation and her smiling, and she reaches on tiptoes to peck him on the lips before coming to stand in front of me.

I look down at her, at this dazzling, radiant ball of energy before me, with awe and not a little shyness. I'm not sure where I fit in here. I'm not sure *if* I fit in. Apparently, there've been machinations between the two of them to get me here, but their kiss just now has me feeling like a gauche outsider.

'You were absolutely amazing up there,' I tell her earnestly, because it's important to me that she knows. 'You were... transcendent, really.'

Her smile intensifies, and I focus on what a wonderful, generous smile she has, and on the sweet, faint sprinkling of freckles across her nose, while actively forbidding my peripheral vision to focus on her breasts. It's easy to fixate on her mouth, which is still wet from Max's kiss.

'Thank you,' she says. 'I'm so, so happy you came.'

There's a moment where we both halt, and I wonder

what on earth I'm supposed to do next in this sex room with this couple, when Max fractures it.

'Kiss her, for God's sake,' he snaps. 'Show her how amazing she is. God knows, she earned it up there.'

I widen my eyes in a silent question to Darcy, but she's still smiling at me, her lower lip still bearing a trace of Max's saliva, and my body knows what to do. I slide a hand through her auburn tresses and around the back of her neck to tug her gently to me, just like I watched Max do, and I lean down and kiss her mouth.

Softness.

Her lips, plush and willing and kiss-dampened.

Her breasts, squished against my pecs, their warmth seeping through the cotton of my shirt.

Her touch, her long fingers going to my shoulders.

And—fuck me—the inside of her mouth, her tongue wet and willing and entangling with my own.

This isn't a natural, *done it before* kiss like the one she and Max just shared in front of me.

This is a first kiss, dreamy and wondrous and sensual and exploratory, the shiny newness of every single step like a wake-up call to my body. Because while it's not familiar, it feels like it should be, my soul recognising the utter *rightness* of each discovery.

Of course that's exactly how pillowy her lower lip should feel when I suck it between mine.

Of course that's how she should taste, the faintest hint of sweat slicing through her honeyed sweetness.

Of course my hips should shunt forward, exactly like this, seeking to align our bodies from head to toe.

I'm vaguely aware that my hands are taking their exploratory mission deathly seriously, my palms, my fingers mapping the gentle planes of her body as they roam, cataloguing her delights from the sweet indent between her shoulder blades to the totally fucking sinful handful of her bottom. This is total immersion, and I'm powerless to resist her.

I was by no means oblivious next door to the fact that the rainmaker who famously helped Wolff build his empire had me on the receiving end of the mother of all sales pitches. But his smooth, serpentine, cajoling words had nothing on this part of the pitch: the part where they let me take lovely, lovely Darcy for a test run.

And I'm so fucking in. My rational mind has harrumphed and stepped aside, clearing the way for my chimp brain to take the wheel.

And all the latter wants is *more*.

37

DARCY

Kissing Dex is a balm, a walk in the rain, a sensory bubble of self-indulgence. Max is all agenda, all the time, and it's the thing that gets me hottest: knowing he wants to use and abuse me; knowing he's taking and taking. It makes me crazy in the best way.

But if Max is happiest when everyone is kneeling at his feet in worshipful submission, I suspect Dex is happiest when worshipping. That's not to say he's submissive. The way he's kissing me isn't an act of submission. He's consuming me, devouring me.

It's just my way of suggesting that his agenda in this moment is me. This isn't a power play for him (unlike other people I know). It's an act of veneration. He's treasuring this kiss, this opportunity to learn me.

I sometimes wonder if part of the attraction for Max is knowing everyone out there wants me and he can have me. I don't mind if it is, because the same part of me that gets off on being used also gets off on being his sparkly little trophy. The pretty doll in the music box who spins at his command

and is his to defile. That dynamic does it for me every single time.

That distance I put between me and the audience is powerful and heady and addictive, and I'm a shameless little whore for all the praise Max lavishes on me after those performances, but the way Dex is touching me grounds me, because it makes me feel seen—seen as a flesh-and-blood woman and not some kind of toy.

And that sensation of being cherished is something I didn't know I needed until now.

Also:

I can't believe they're both here!

When they showed up at the door in their twin work uniforms, they looked so staggeringly hot I nearly died. I'm genuinely gobsmacked that Max managed to get Dex in here. I'm even more amazed that Dex is going for it with me.

Judging by the heat in those amazing eyes of his when he walked into the room and saw me in just my costume, I suppose I shouldn't be surprised. Even if this is just a one-time thing for the three of us, I intend to take every single second of everything these guys are willing to give me. I've wanted a threesome for so long, but a threesome with Max and Dex is like *insane*.

And now Dex's tongue is in my mouth, and his hands are everywhere on my body, and he's actually trembling as his erection pushes against my pubic bone, and oh my God, he might actually be aroused enough, immersed enough, to give us what we want from him tonight.

Max is clattering around somewhere behind me. 'In your own time,' he says drily, and we pull apart like guilty teenagers. My nipples are so hard they might tear through my fifteen-denier body suit, and I'm already soaked between my legs.

Dex's dark-lashed eyes flicker over my face, glassy with need. He looks slightly shell-shocked, and it almost makes me laugh. If that's how he feels after a kiss, all I can say is, dude better brace himself.

'You're amazing,' he murmurs, hesitantly releasing me, and I smile dreamily at him.

'Well, that was fucking hot,' Max announces breezily as he pops a champagne cork. 'Let's drink to playing very, very nicely together.'

I spin around. He's holding a bottle of Taittinger, and on the lacquered cabinet stands a full-on silver champagne bucket loaded with ice and three glasses.

'Where the hell did you get that?' I ask with a laugh.

'Stashed it earlier. Made it worth the server's time.'

I gasp. 'You're lucky my sister isn't here. She'd kill you.'

'Your sister is far too busy fucking my best mate right now to care. And you're the one entertaining not one, but two verboten gentleman callers in a private room.'

I snort. 'Way to make me feel like a lady of the night.'

He pours a glass and hands it to me. 'You are a lady of the night. You're my absolute favourite whore. And you'll be this one's favourite whore by the time the night is through, too.' He hands Dex a glass.

Dex frowns and opens his mouth to presumably defend my honour from such politically incorrect slurs, but Max beats him to it. 'Relax. She loves it. It makes her come like a freight train when I talk to her like that. You'll see. Doesn't it, sweetheart?'

'It does,' I confirm with a mischievous grin at Dex, and he gives me a watery smile back, like he can't believe I'm real. I don't miss the way his eyes scan my body as I slink closer to the both of them until we're standing in a cosy little triangle, flutes in hand.

Max raises his. 'To Darcy,' he murmurs, and Dex echoes his toast while I smile coyly. Jesus. I've always been an attention whore, but come on. Having these two gods direct all their focus on me is the best feeling in the world.

Maybe not *all* their focus. I've seen Max cast a few sidelong glances at Dex already. Still, it's more than enough for one girl. I eye them both up idly as I sip my cold champagne. They're both tall and lean, broad shoulders counterbalanced with flat stomachs and narrow waists. They look like they should be in an ad campaign together for some fancy label like Brioni or Tom Ford. Max is in fantastic shape, and my brief grope of Dex just now tells me he's similar.

Max lifts his flute and cocks his head, examining his champagne. 'You know,' he drawls in that manner I've come to know as studied insouciance, 'I bet this would taste even better if we sucked it off Darcy's tits.'

Dex chokes a little on his mouthful, launching a coughing attack, and Max slaps him manfully on the back as I try not to laugh.

Poor little lamb.

He's well and truly in the lion's den now.

'Only one way to find out,' I say, which is all the encouragement Max needs to spring into Dom mode. He sets his flute down on the cabinet and actually clicks his fingers.

'Dex, help me.'

Wolford makes my body suits in a single piece, which is apparently some feat of circular knitting that I don't begin to understand. They have no closures, only a neckline that's slashed shoulder to shoulder. This nude-coloured version is so sheer you can't really see the neckline from a distance. It requires shimmying carefully into it, and having help to take it off is always appreciated.

I've definitely never appreciated it *this* much, though.

'Tug it down from the shoulders,' I say as Dex puts his flute down and rounds me.

'You sure about this?' he asks, hunger and concern warring in his eyes. Just as it's Max's total animalism that attracts me to him, it's the whole repressed self-denial thing that has me crazy for Dex. They both want me, but Max is all in and Dex is doing battle with his baser instincts.

I cannot *wait* to see him come undone, hopefully inside my body.

'I've never been so sure of anything, believe me,' I say with a shudder.

'And if you need any proof...' Max interjects. He slips his hand between my legs, casual as you like, and swipes two fingers through the slick mess I've made of my bodystocking before holding them out to Dex.

Dex stands there, stunned, eyes darting from Max's face to his outstretched fingers.

'Go on,' I tell him. 'You can taste. I trust Max completely. Anything he tells you to do to me tonight, you can do it.'

'Tell him your safeword, sweetheart,' Max says.

The other night, things got pretty heated after our threesome chat and Max had me come up with a safe word.

I chose *folklore*.

No explanation needed, right?

But, as I say it to Dex and he repeats it slowly, I can tell the cultural reference is absolutely not hitting home.

'Come on,' Max says impatiently. He puts his fingers to Dex's mouth, pushing down on his lower lip slightly, and who can blame him? It's probably the closest he'll get to Dex tonight.

Dex opens, and he doesn't exactly suck, but he lets Max put his fingers on his tongue just like someone would take their Communion wafer, and his eyes drift closed in bliss for a second. I stare at his heavy lids, the dark, feathered arcs of his lashes above his cheekbones. It should be illegal for a man to be this beautiful. Max presses down before withdrawing his fingers on a long, reluctant pull.

Then Dex opens his eyes and turns them on me, but his entire demeanour is different now. More predatory, his hunger at the fore, his luscious mouth in a grim line. It's like that split second of alone time within the orange-hued respite of his lowered lids has shifted something in him.

'You taste like you really fucking want it,' he says, and even his voice is different. Harsher.

'That's what I've been telling you.' I hold out my arms and try to keep my voice steady. 'I want you to do everything you feel comfortable with.'

His capitulation comes in the form of action. With the ragged sigh of a man who knows he's crossing some line he can't un-cross, he hooks a finger under the edge of my slashed neckline. Max does the same, and together they peel my bodystocking down my arms until my boobs and stomach are exposed and the fabric is gathered at my wrists.

They kneel, as if by some unspoken agreement, pulling it off my wrists. Over my hips. Down my thighs. Max presses a kiss to my waist. The fabric's almost completely sheer, but as I look down at them, this Great Unveiling feels significant. They're quiet, gentle, their movements almost reverent. I use their shoulders for support as I step out of the suit, one leg at a time, the guys tugging the mesh over my feet in the same way a woman pulls off her stockings.

Then Max speaks, and I can tell from his tone that this is the last time they'll treat me with kid gloves this evening.

38

MAX

I get to my feet and Dex follows. Darcy's fully naked for us now, and the power hits my bloodstream with the burn of the most potent whisky. My long-term game plan to have this man submit to me with every beautiful bone in his martyred, self-righteous body will have to wait, shelved in favour of a more pressing, more attainable, and highly alluring goal.

And that's to press home the advantage of two against one, to use every weapon in my and Dex's combined arsenal to tease and plunder and defile this stunning woman so thoroughly, so expertly, that we'll take her sweet, nebulous wish for "a threesome" and decimate it as we launch her heavenward.

'Remember, her safeword is *folklore*,' I tell Dex now. 'That is the *only* thing you need to know. She says that, everything stops. Otherwise, she's fair game. Remember, she asked for this. Begged me to set it up. Got it?'

'Yes,' he says, like he wants to say *no*. His Adam's apple works as he swallows hard.

I trail my hand upward over the soft, soft skin of Darcy's stomach to cup her breast and flick my fingertip carelessly, casually over her nipple. She gasps, but I ignore her, keeping my eyes on Dex's face. It's imperative that he understands what I'm saying so he can help me give Darcy exactly what she needs.

'Have a go,' I tell him. 'Remember, you can do whatever you like to her.' The candlelight in here is intimate, but I have a far better view of him than I did next door, and he is rock fucking hard.

I keep my fingertip flicking, earning myself some lovely little whimpers from Darcy, and my eyes fixed on Dex. He glances at my hand, then at her face, then back at me. Finally, he reaches silently for his flute and, tipping it up, pours a stream of champagne over her left tit.

That's my boy.

I knew he had it in him somewhere.

Darcy moans as he bends and licks upwards from the underside of her tit over her nipple, the musculature of his jaw working as he does. And then he's fastening his mouth to her nipple and sucking hard. I follow suit, dribbling champagne over her right side and bending to suck, because I know how insanely sensitive this woman's nipples are. Having both of us tease them should send her through the roof.

Besides, it'll warm her up nicely for taking the surprise clamps I've got tucked away in my trouser pocket.

I wrap an arm around her back so she doesn't have to strain against us too hard to stay upright. We'll get her on a bed shortly, but this is pretty hot. Her champagne-soaked skin is fucking delicious, her nipple furling beautifully within the light vice of my teeth as I flick my tongue over it.

Not that I need confirmation of the effect we're having on her.

The rapture in the sounds she's making is evidence enough.

'What a lucky, lucky girl you are,' I hum against her flesh, trying to block out the extreme proximity of Dex's face to mine. We're both standing off to the side, but still. I open my eyes slightly to find his closed in blissful concentration, eyelashes fanned so seductively it's downright dangerous.

'Don't touch her cunt yet,' I warn Dex. 'Actually, do. Swipe a finger through and tell me just how much she's enjoying this.'

They groan in unison.

This is a puppet show.

Expertise level: basic.

Both so delicious. So malleable. So responsive.

Dex sighs and obliges, sliding a hand between her legs. 'Jesus fuck,' he rasps. I know he must have touched her clit because she practically shoots through the ceiling, and I band my arm harder around her before releasing her nipple and straightening myself. Her hands wind tightly around our necks, more to spur us on than for balance, I suspect.

'That's enough,' I bark. 'We don't want her blowing just yet.'

He straightens up and dips his head to kiss the side of her jawline, brushing her hair worshipfully off her shoulder.

I turn to her and grin. 'Look at this. You've got two fully-dressed men fucking dying to go to town on you. How does that feel?'

She's already dazed. There's an enchanting flush on her cheeks, and it's mirrored where we've been sucking on the pale skin of her tits. Her nipples are hard, needy little peaks glistening with our saliva.

'Like I already want to die from happiness,' she whispers, and I grin.

'That's my greedy little slut. Dex, mate, let's get her on the bed.'

39

DEX

The supreme assurance with which Max executes every little thing—commanding, acting, orchestrating—has my head dizzying and my confidence shattering. I've always held my own in bed. I'm a generous, capable lover. I'd even say I have a certain gravitas. Women respond to me.

But as I attempt to assist him in tying Darcy to this enormous bed, I feel like little more than a toddler whose preschool teacher is letting him help with tidying away the wooden blocks in a kindly attempt to build his confidence. Granted, this situation is a very big first for me. Still, it's obvious this comes as naturally to Max as breathing.

He has Darcy spread out on the bed with little more than a word and a nod. While I stand there, feasting my eyes on the impossibly perfect contrast of her creamy skin against the black bedlinen, he digs into the drawer in the lacquered cabinet, tugging out length after length of silky white sashes like a magician pulling endless silks out of a top hat.

'Wrists,' he says, lobbing a sash across the bed at me. It's so light, it flutters in the air and descends midway through its journey, coming to lie over Darcy's hip. I grab it and watch Max for instruction, noting that he ties one end around her wrist before fastening the other end to a chrome hoop hanging from the headboard, pulling her arms over her head.

As I tie my own sash, far less swiftly and skilfully, I allow myself to take Darcy in. She's smiling up at me, limbs languid and eyes hazy with acquiescence.

The generous gift of her submission astonishes me. She's allowing two men to tie her to a bed and physically overpower her. To take all manner of liberties with that milky skin and lithe body. To lick and bite and fuck her as we want, her only defence in the face of our animalistic urges a single, simple word whose connotations speak less of sex and more of legend.

Maybe there is something to her safe word, after all.

Maybe this evening will be the stuff of fairytales, of lore.

Improbable.

Magical.

Transcendent.

I return her smile with genuine joy before letting my eyes flick over to Max, who's tugging imperiously to test her silken bond, and I have a fleeting jolt of clarity so clear it steals the breath from my lungs as though it's the icy air of a New York January.

As strong as my desire is to crawl up this woman's body and take every sinful, perverted liberty I can, the desire to have an autocrat like Max tie me the fuck down and shut me the fuck up is enough to make my blood molten. I'm the predator and the prey in this situation, my urges baffling me as much as they stir me.

'Watch this,' he orders me, his command slicing through

the fog this unfamiliar three-way dynamic has whipped up inside me. Because I can do this. I can watch, and listen, and be his little sidekick as he demonstrates the art of kink to me with the kindly tolerance of a benign Dom.

He wraps his fingers around Darcy's ankle and pushes so her leg folds, knee rising up and her foot dragging along the sheets. 'Stay there,' he tells her. 'Dex, there's a hoop at the side of the bed.'

I look down. There is indeed another chrome hoop halfway down the bed. Max wraps another length of silk around her ankle and knots it before tugging the fabric taut. 'Foot towards me,' he barks, and she slides her foot across the bed, effectively making her spread her legs. 'Try to pull your foot in,' he says when he's secured the length to his hoop.

She attempts to close her legs, to no effect.

'Good,' he says, pleased. 'And try to stretch it out.'

Darcy tries to slide her foot down the bed, but the fabric is too taut. Jesus. She's got no leeway. She's held in place, leg bent and open. Once I get the other leg secured, she'll be spread out for us like a feast to do what we like with. I can instantly see that this position is far more exposed, more effective, than a regular spreadeagle.

'I'll do the other leg,' Max says, abandoning all pretence of collaboration and striding around to my side of the bed with the final tie. 'Dex, you get down the end and start thinking about all the things you want to do to her.'

Now *that's* an order I can get behind.

He has her other leg up in the same position, her ankle cuffed in his fist. She's open so wide it looks painful, but she's a dancer, so I suppose she's pretty flexible. I *know* she's flexible—that vertical split thing she did against the cage defied normal human ranges of motion. Max's movements as he bends over her, shirt straining against his powerful-looking shoulders, are efficient but not brusque. Even so, there's something imperious in his demeanour that stops me and, I think, Darcy, from speaking.

He's setting a scene here, the atmosphere growing more potent with possibility as he preps her. More sanctified, if that's not a ridiculous thing to think.

I look my fill.

I put my hands in my pockets, taking in the scene. Standing by while another man ties a naked woman up so he can present her pussy for both of us pushes the envelope far beyond the bounds of decency for me, but I cannot look away.

Darcy's head is resting on a big scatter pillow, her gaze fixed on me. I give her a little smile, but I can no longer withstand the temptation of her pussy. I watched in horrified hunger as she flashed on stage. I tasted her when Max slid his fingers into my mouth, and now it's fully on display for me, so pink and soft and wet—three utterly unremarkable words that depict a remarkable sight.

Max straightens up, satisfied he's secured her.

'She's all yours,' he says carelessly as he passes around the bed behind me. 'You know you want to.'

'What are you going to do?' I ask without taking my eyes off Darcy's body. She's outstretched and open, a truly wondrous thing. Her nipples are rosy pebbles pointing heavenward. The skin on her inner thighs is so pale, so satiny, a contrast to the glistening nirvana between her legs.

I step forward and put a knee on the bed.

'I'm going to clamp her nipples,' he says cheerily, and she gasps. I'm not surprised. It sounds aggressive.

'I'm not sure—' she begins.

Unstitch

'Unless you say your safeword, I'm not interested,' he barks. 'Do you have something to say?'

They exchange a heated look, and she shakes her head.

'Good girl.' He produces a pair of hot pink clips from his pocket. They look like silicone—not what I was expecting. 'Dex, start getting her worked up. I'll put these on for a few minutes. When she's getting ready to blow, I'll take them off.'

'Okay,' I say stupidly, but I stay frozen, one knee on the bed as he pinches and rolls each nipple before fastening the tiny Barbie-pink clips to them. They look ridiculous and outlandish and *sore*, but Darcy's little whimpers and sharp intakes of breath tell me she can handle the sensation.

'Come the fuck on,' Max says exasperatedly, and I put my second knee on the bed, lowering my head to the glossy pink haven between her legs.

40

DARCY

Even before Dex touches me, my body is thrumming like a tuning fork. I'm pure sensation. Arousal rolls over me in waves, the sharp pinch of my clamps dialling down as the blood flow halts and my nipples grow numb. But with my legs like this, the throb of my clit is so acute even the air is too much teasing to bear.

Dex already looks dishevelled from my kisses. When he crouches down on the bed, a thick lock of dark hair falls over his forehead. There's a grim set to his mouth as he surveys me through his lashes that spells trouble for me. And if that wasn't ominous enough, Max is pacing, hands in his pockets, like a panther who's been on a lentil diet and is out for blood.

'Remember who's boss,' he tells Dex roughly, pausing right by him. '*You are.* Make her take it. Whatever you like.'

Why the fuck this has me practically coming into thin air I don't know, but I'm pumped so full of anticipation I'm trembling in my restraints.

Dex closes his eyes for a second. 'Fucking amen to that,'

he mutters, and, his own blasphemous brand of grace said, lowers his head.

I'm expecting—I don't know—kisses and licks, soft and teasing, exploratory and beguiling. I'm *not* expecting the bite as his teeth close sharply around the skin of my inner thigh. It smarts, and I yelp, but then he's licking the same spot before he turns, his nose and mouth millimetres from my pussy.

He stares at me, eyes dark, and splays his hands over my thighs before he licks me, long and hard, his tongue taut and decisive, from back to front.

It's so perfect and gorgeous and wonderful and *everything* that I practically shoot off the bed, mewling my appreciation.

'How does she taste?' Max demands, resuming his pacing.

'Fucking unbelievable,' Dex mutters against my skin. His hands are still pushing my legs apart, his fingertips digging into my thighs, his breaths fast and hot and infuriating.

'Good,' Max says brusquely. 'Show her—go on.' He comes to the side of the bed and kneels, checking the clamps, kneading my breasts, stroking my stomach, brushing my hair off my face. His movements aren't tender, though. They're possessive. Like he's bought me and he's checking me over.

Dex clearly decides not to go so easy on me, because his next touches are far more teasing. He circles my clit like he's getting to know it. He removes a hand from my thigh and uses two fingers to part my lips, holding me wide open for him before blowing on my poor flesh and then licking along, between, every fold like he's learning me—which is romantic as hell and torturous as fuck.

I give myself over to the intense physical yearning. Every

lick, every movement of his fingertips against me, elicits a moan from me. And when he slowly slides a single finger all the way in and then all the way out of me, I almost scream the club down. He's not doing it to be gentle; he's doing it to drive me crazy.

'So fucking greedy,' Max observes to Dex.

'Mmm,' Dex murmurs. 'But so sensitive, too.'

'She's very amenable when you're playing with her cunt,' Max tells him. 'Less so the rest of the time, unfortunately.' And he promptly sticks two fingers in my mouth, flattening my tongue. I taste myself on them faintly. 'Suck,' he orders, 'hard,' and I obey. I can't move my tongue, but I employ all the suction in my cheeks.

'Fuck,' Max groans. 'I'll have to give her my cock in a sec. She sucks so well.'

Dex's face jerks up between my legs for a moment, like he hadn't quite thought through the full implications of agreeing to a threesome, but I'm too far gone to care. I'll do anything Max tells me to do. And if that means putting on a show and choking on his dick while Dex licks me, I'll do it.

'I've got to,' Max says, shuddering at the thought of it as he slides his fingers out of my mouth. He toes off his loafers and gets up on the bed, facing away from Dex and straddling me. I'm in the middle of the bed, arms outstretched above my head, and his knees land either side of my armpits.

I can't see Dex anymore, but all I care about is that he's started touching me again with slow, decadent swirls of his tongue and drags of his fingers in and out of my sensitive pussy. It seems he likes what he tastes, his low, male groans cutting through me almost as forcefully as the skill of his tongue.

Instead, I look up at Max looming over me, huge and

powerful from this angle, his jaw clenched as he rips his belt buckle open and tugs down his zip. He reaches into his black boxer briefs and frees his cock, letting it slap me on the cheek, his precum painting a wet stripe across my face. I turn my head and stick out my tongue, trying to catch it, and he laughs.

'She's so fucking eager,' he throws over his shoulder to Dex. 'I hope you're working her up. I want her so full at both ends she won't know what to do with herself.'

And with that he fists his cock and smears its wetness across my lips before jamming it inside my mouth. The male, musky smell and taste of him hit me right in my core, his sheer size and this angle confronting as hell. I struggle to adjust to him—my tongue can barely move around him. But the predatory gleam in his eyes as he readies himself to fuck my mouth has me growing even wetter, as does the fact that Dex has apparently decided to take him at his word, obliging Max's command to "fill me up at both ends" by sticking three fingers inside me, just as hard as Max has stuck his dick in my mouth.

I'm only vaguely aware of the strangled sounds I'm making around Max, but Dex's strained *Jesus fuck* suggests they're pretty carnal. I blink, trying to keep my eyes open through a veil of tears, because the sight of Max, bearing down on me, riding my mouth while his hands grip my jaw and, out of sight, Dex goes to town on my pussy, is quite simply the best thing ever, and the idea that I've previously opted for one man at a time when I could have been doing *this* feels nothing short of deranged.

'Fuck, she's taking me so well,' Max tells Dex, turning his head to the side.

'She's bucking like crazy,' Dex returns, and I moan around Max's cock at the loss of Dex's tongue.

'Okay—hold her off,' Max begs. 'I just need a minute more in her wet little mouth.'

Dex's licks turn soft and teasing and totally fucking inadequate, and the two-against-one thing suddenly feels less hot and more inequitable. But I can't really complain, not deep down, because my greedy pussy adores the teasing, it really does, and his gentle exploration is nothing to the onslaught of the face-fucking that has me foaming at the mouth and streaming from my eyes and fighting my gag reflex over and over.

'Fuck,' Max curses harshly, and then he's pulling out of me and climbing off me, dick proud and erect as he stands beside the bed.

'Let her have it,' he tells Dex, and through my hyper-aroused state, I don't miss the fleeting look of disbelief Dex gives his cock before he crouches down further and sucks my clit into his mouth.

'Oh my God!' I cry. If it wasn't for these ties, I'd shoot off the bed. My pussy is awash with warmth as my climax builds and builds.

'Clamps coming off,' Max warns me before pinching and removing them. There's a tingling sensation and then the feeling of my nipples flooding with heat as the blood flow returns. His hands are on me, kneading my breasts, flicking my nipples, rolling and pinching them harder as they fill up and grow rosy red, and I squeeze my eyes closed in an attempt to withstand this barrage of pleasure.

Dex fucks me with three fingers, driving them in hard and crooking them each time as he laves my clit as harshly as he can. Max is rubbing and pinching the shit out of my boobs, and, if I felt alive before, I now feel like molten treacle is being injected into every erogenous zone in my body. I may be tethered to this bed, but my soul is soaring.

'Fuck me, she's loving this,' Max says over my cries, his voice tinged with desperation. 'How wet is she?'

'Fucking *soaking*,' Dex says between licks.

It's true. I can feel my body sucking in his fingers with ease, can feel the slipperiness of his tongue against my clit. My entire being is fire and air. Max gets to his knees and leans over, sucking hard on one nipple as he works the other between his fingers, and it finishes me off.

The blessed heat rips through me, coursing through my veins and detonating me as I crest and crest and crest and crest with convulsions and shouts and huge, searing waves of pleasure that go on and on and on. As I come down from my crazy, unthinkable peak, Dex's licks gentle. When he's sure I've finished, he pulls his fingers out gently and drops his head, rubbing his forehead over my pubic bone as Max strokes my breasts, my stomach.

'What a good fucking girl,' he says. 'You came so hard for us.'

I turn my head and smile dazedly at him as, in my periphery, Dex staggers to his feet.

'Jesus fucking Christ,' he says.

Max turns to him with a strained grin.

'Now you get to decide which way you want to fuck her.'

41

DEX

I look at Max as I use my thumb to wipe Darcy's arousal off my lower lip before sucking it into my mouth. His eyes flare with *something* at the sight. I suspect he's pretty happy with the treatment we just gave his girlfriend.

'Um.' I look back down at Darcy. She's so unimaginably beautiful, cheeks and breasts flushed red, her huge blue eyes still glassy, her body still trussed up for us to do what we like with. The thought of it has the teeth of my zip straining against my dick. What I am categorically *not* doing is looking at Max's dick, which is standing to attention like some fucking truncheon.

The mandate was clear.

He and I convene to give Darcy a good seeing-to. We don't get all up in each other's business. I'm glad he straddled her like that when he fucked her mouth. The mere idea of having to watch that is confronting beyond anything I'm comfortable with.

'What would you like?' I ask Darcy, but Max tuts before she can reply.

'Nope. She owes you an orgasm, and she's going to give

her sweet little cunt to you however you like. I can untie her so you can bend her over and take her from behind, if you want? Or you can fuck her like this, or make her do all the work on top. Anything. Believe me, this body can take anything you give it.'

I don't doubt it. The woman is a human pretzel. My poor, tortured dick throbs at the thought of taking Darcy any which way as Max undoubtedly barks orders at us both. I don't know why the idea of him fucking her by proxy through me is so hot. Maybe it's that the sheer force of our combined power is so much greater than hers.

I'd love to flip her over and pound into that willing pink pussy from behind, but something tells me Max will go for her mouth in that scenario, and while it's clear he needs to come, and soon, I'm not sure I can volunteer myself for prime position to watch her suck him off. That would be more raw than I'm ready for. Again: more confronting.

Not that everything about this evening hasn't already been confronting as fuck.

Besides.

She's so gorgeous like this. She was the untouchable butterfly in the gilded cage, our erotic floor show, and now she's tied up in Max's finest spider web to be fucked. I'd like those legs wrapped around my waist, though.

'I want her like this, but her legs untied,' I tell him, my voice lower and rougher than I anticipated, and he nods, pleased.

'Good.' He turns and makes quick work of one ankle tie and then the other, his efficient movements at odds with the baseball bat sticking out of his trousers. 'Anything hurt?' he asks Darcy as he rubs her ankle briskly.

'No,' she says with a happy sigh, looking from Max to me. 'I'm dandy.'

'Good,' he says again, but he's already turning away from her, his voice more clipped, his brief flash of affection towards her subsumed by his Dom persona. 'Get a condom on.'

I follow the jerk of his head, turning to find a large ornamental bowl swimming with little foil squares. There's a moment where I falter, wrapped condom in hand. Max and I are both still fully dressed—aside from that monstrous cock of his, obviously—but my blood-deficient brain is slowly stumbling upon the fact that *I'll need to get my dick out.*

In front of Max.

Why I haven't thought of this until now is unclear. I knew, of course, we'd both be doing filthy things to her. I knew there would be licking and kissing and fucking and coming. But for some reason, unwrapping myself in this very specific way in front of him feels like a significant step, far more so than it would be if it were just me and Darcy.

If it was just the two of us I'd be balls-deep in her already.

As is becoming a pattern, Max's voice intersects my indecision as easily, as smoothly, as a hot knife cuts through butter. 'Let her see you get your cock ready for her.'

He's right, of course. I'm fucking Darcy. She'll want to see me. This is all for *her*, and I'd do well not to forget that. Neither Max or I have stripped for her. She'll presumably want an eyeful of my dick if nothing else.

I turn and stand back at the base of the bed, the vista of her still-swollen pussy leading up over flat stomach and perky, stained nipples to her face. Her eyes are fixed on me, and I keep mine fixed on her, sticking the foil square between my teeth as I unbuckle my belt with quick, efficient movements. I steadfastly ignore Max standing next to the bed, although I know his stare is trained on me, avid and without mercy.

Belt open, I release the hook of my suit trousers and pull down my flies just enough that I can push my shirt tails aside, reaching below the waistband of my boxers and releasing my poor, rabid cock from its prison. It's hot and hard in my hand, the skin stretched taut over my shaft. I make a strangled, involuntary noise at the relief of having my palm around it.

'Hear that?' Max drawls to Darcy. 'You've got him so worked up—he really is going to split you in two with that big dick of his.'

'I hope so,' she groans, and I give a pained little laugh as I rip the foil with my teeth and prepare to gingerly sheathe my sensitive flesh. Unlike Horse Cock beside me, I couldn't inseminate mares if I wanted to, but I do alright for myself. Women generally leave my bed feeling pretty happy, it seems.

'Fuck, I want this so badly,' I tell her as I crawl onto the bed, the dick in my hand a torpedo focused on a single target—Darcy's pussy. Max may be treating her like a plaything for us, talking about her to me like she's not there, but I can't do it.

I can't fuck her and not stare into her eyes and not tell her how insanely, completely, disgustingly aroused I am by seeing her like this, arms overhead and breasts on a platter and legs spread and pretty pink pussy on show for me. I'm here for her—I agreed to this whole charade for her—but it's giving me unspeakable pleasure to know I'll be inside her in seconds, so I'll do this my way, thank you very much.

I range my body over her, bracing on one elbow and keeping the root of my cock in a chokehold. She looks up at me, pliant and expectant and heavy-lidded, and I smile as I dip my mouth to hers, because she is heaven. Our tongues slide together like lovers separated too long, our lips dragging.

'I want to fuck you so fucking badly,' I grit out, pulling away enough to see her face and tracing the latex-covered tip of my cock through her wetness. 'I've wanted it since the second I saw you at Alchemy in that fucking dress with your tits on display.'

She smiles up at me. 'I wanted you too. I ran straight home and told Max I wanted to fuck you. *Both* of you.'

As if he's been cued in, Max speaks. 'Keep up this performance, sweetheart, and you'll be full of both our dicks next time.' He keeps talking as I dip my head to sample Darcy's perfect breasts for the first time. Her nipples are so fucking hard as I roll them around with my tongue.

'Remember how crazy she made you in The Playroom?' Max continues. 'Remember how she danced, how she showed that greedy cunt to everyone? Remember how fucking frustrated you were, and now *it's right there*, waiting for you to plough into it. So I don't know what the fuck you're waiting for.'

My face is buried in Darcy's breast, but I'm pretty sure he's moved closer. He's somewhere between a Disney serpent, slithering and hissing, goading and enabling, and an actual devil on my shoulder. He's every wicked and depraved corner of me personified, and it's as if his sibilant instructions are a carte blanche for me to do whatever I like to Darcy.

Because he's right.

What the fuck am I waiting for?

42

DEX

I fist my cock harder and lift my head so I can see her face when I enter her. Her eyelashes flutter, teeth dragging at her lower lip as she struggles to accommodate me. But she doesn't look away from my eyes, and I push, push, push.

The dam is open, the restraint and manners and innate sense of decency and all that bullshit—all gone. I wanted her last week; I wanted her tonight when she was moving and stretching and crafting languid, achingly beautiful shapes with her body; I wanted her while I was tonguing her and finger fucking her, and now it's *my fucking turn.*

She lets out a low, guttural cry when I bottom out in her and I get it, because I feel the same. Our eyes are locked, our faces inches apart, her body taking me in, welcoming me home. 'So beautiful,' I grit out, which is uncreative but the simple truth. I'm need and sensation, and her unctuous inner walls have my dick in a chokehold the likes of which I've never known—the happy bonus of fucking a world-class dancer, it seems.

'Isn't she stunning?' Max murmurs from beside the bed. 'And she can take it so hard. Have a go and see for yourself.'

One half of me wants to slap him and tell him to fuck off, but the other half wants the edge, the uncomfortable awareness his presence brings. I'm performing for both of them, and I find myself wanting to impress Max with my moves and stamina and technique as much as I want to wow Darcy with the things my cock can do to her body.

Besides, I need to let rip.

I need it so badly.

I begin to move properly, muscles firing as I brace above her, my hips rolling so I can drive my dick into her welcome heat over and over. She winds her long, supple legs around my waist, her chest rising and falling as she takes what I'm giving her. She feels astonishing, and yet I'm not sure she'll be able to come like this.

'Hang on,' I tell her, bracing my weight on one arm so I can reach behind her for a scatter pillow. I keep hold of the condom and pull out of her, Max jumping in to help. He wedges a couple of pillows under her bum as I get on my knees. This way, the angle's better for her, and I get a fucking fantastic view of her naked body, arms outstretched still.

I position myself between her legs, sitting almost back on my heels, and slide my cock through her folds again, wishing I was naked with her. But as I grip her hips hard and push hungrily back inside her, the quality of her moan tells me this is far, far better for her.

And for me.

Until Max puts a knee on the side of the bed, that is, and grips his weapon like he's planning to fire it. Those blue eyes, which seemed so cold earlier, are fire as they stare at the exact place where my dick is pushing into Darcy's body.

She's writhing beneath me, arching away from the pillows each time I hit home, so obliging and beautiful and perfect.

'Look at our little whore,' Max croons, stroking his cock. 'So exquisite, and so *needy*. She's already come once, but she needs to come again around your cock, doesn't she?'

'She does,' I grit out, hastily averting my eyes towards Darcy, because there's something deeply disturbing and quite entrancing about the firm, steady strokes he's administering to the monstrous purple-headed beast in his hands, the beast whose anger is so at odds with the deceptive calm of his tone.

He leans forward, using the tip of his dick to rub her nearest nipple, lacquering it with precum as he fondles her other breast with his fingers. She moans loudly, incredulously, bucking harder against my next thrust, and I automatically put my hand to her clit, because I'm damned if Max is the only one allowed to stoke her flames.

Fuck, she's wet. Her clit is a glossy little button, thanks to her arousal, and I watch with awe and fascination and not a little emotion at the miracle that is Darcy submitting to, responding to, our joint efforts.

To my dick, my fingers.

To *Max's* dick, Max's fingers.

It's a symphony of rubbing and dragging and pinching and stroking as we play Darcy's body like the most delectable instrument. She's growing more and more fevered, her sounds and movements growing more desperate as, together, Max and I wind her higher and higher. I'm falling into an altered state myself, a state where my world has shrunk to the tight, hot shunts of my dick.

Then Max is straightening and standing, his hands leaving her nipples as he instead starts to stroke himself properly with sharp, firm tugs.

'I'm going to come all over her while you come inside her,' he says, and Darcy whimpers an anguished *oh God*. I don't blame her, or him. In fact, I increase the savagery of my drives, because the idea of the two of us marking her, branding her, in our different ways while we have her at our mercy is too much.

I can't stop my eyes from darting between him and her. Her face, her eyes, her cries as she takes the epic fucking pummelling I'm giving her. His increasingly violent masturbation, the contrast between his still-immaculate work clothes and that angry, primal dick, the monster whose thirst can't be easily slaked. His handsome face is contorted, writhen with lust, and I'm aware of thinking *I knew it. I fucking knew that's who he was under the Italian shirts and the lethal, practiced smile.*

We're all making noises, too far gone and too turned on to be self-conscious. Darcy's whimpers go straight to my cock, an unspoken plea for *more, harder*. Max's low, rough grunts echo through my balls, their undeniable maleness reminding me she's outnumbered. Overpowered.

And then he roars a single, strangled *fuck* before he's ejaculating, pumping his seed all over her and the bed. It hits her stomach, her tits, her jaw, in perfect, creamy splatters so satisfying, their smacks against her skin so audibly wet, that it has every primal cell in my body celebrating. I'm about to come inside her, but if I could, I'd come everywhere. In and out. All fucking over her.

The sheer filth of having one man come all over her while another fucks the living daylights out of her must hit Darcy anew, because her cries go from shock at Max's wet onslaught to a whole new level of desperation.

Her hips are off the pillow, meeting me thrust for thrust as my balls slam against her. She's so fucking close, and while sweat is pouring off me and my impending orgasm is knocking on the door, I'm damned if I'll leave her anything less than wholly wrung out.

Max's exhale is long and shuddery before he releases his dick and puts a knee on the bed again, smearing his cum over her breasts and using it to rub and pinch and tweak her nipples, and Darcy pretty much screams the club down as she shatters around me. I pump and pump as her muscles milk my dick dry and the sight of her, tied up and screaming and covered in another man's cum while she climaxes on my cock, short-circuits what was left of my brain.

I am *so fucking close*. I am—

Darcy's cries are growing subdued, her convulsions are easing, and I'm only vaguely aware of Max bounding off the bed as my balls tighten. I squeeze my eyes closed, blocking out everything for a moment that isn't the sensation of heat flooding through my lower body, the impossible rising, tightening, readying of my balls.

But the mattress dips behind me, and there's even more heat—*body* heat—right up against my back, and Max is gripping my biceps, his breath warm against my neck, his voice so urgent and confiding and intoxicating that it drains my brain of any residual blood flow.

'You're doing so well,' he tells me. 'Fuck, look how hard you've made her come with your big, beautiful dick. Now take what you need. Fuck that greedy little cunt of hers and take something for yourself.'

I nod to myself. I'm delirious. Yeah. I'm going to take—I need to—I'm—

Right as my body releases its orgasm with all the violence of a catapult, Max lowers his face to my shoulder and bites me *hard* through the fabric of my shirt, so hard his teeth may well have found naked flesh. The pain is shocking and excruciating and intrusive, and it's fucking petrol on the flames of my orgasm.

It's less that I *come* than that my orgasm *happens to me*, like an explosion that rips through everything in its path, sparing nothing and leaving in its wake total oblivion.

That's how I feel as my climax subsumes me, annihilating time and space and sending me spinning through a vacuum as my physical being empties itself shudderingly into the condom, leaving an exhausted, stupified shell of a man.

43

MAX

It seems mine is the only brain in the room capable of adulting.

Dex slumps forward, head drooping, as soon as I release his shoulder from my teeth and his arms from my grip. Darcy's lying on the bed, trying to catch her breath, looking for all the world like stars are spinning around her head like a cartoon halo.

That's what I call a thoroughly fucking successful threesome.

I tuck my dick up hastily, stuffing my shirt tails back into my trousers but leaving my belt undone, and walk around to the head of the bed so I can untie Darcy's wrists. I release one hand and rub it between mine, but it's nice and warm, which is excellent. A knee on the bed and a bit of a stretch and I've got the second one loosened, too.

She raises them in the air and instantly makes a grab for the back of Dex's head.

'That was fucking unbelievable,' he murmurs to her, his voice soft and adoring and still slurred with the aftermath of his violent orgasm. She whispers something laughingly back, and he crouches as far as he can over her without getting the front of his shirt covered in my cum, kissing her with what a less cynical man would call ardour.

'Wait there—I'll get a cloth,' I order them both, striding through to the ensuite bathroom and cranking up the mixer above the washbasin.

I was definitely Billy No Mates in that scenario just then, but that was the idea. Tonight was about getting Dex to sample Darcy's delights, getting him so hooked on her that he won't be capable of declining next time we offer.

And, while it may also have been about acclimatising him to my presence, to having the three of us fool around together, it most certainly wasn't about making a move on him, or suggesting he should succumb to me in more ways than simply fulfilling my instructions for how he should touch Darcy, or doing the remotest thing that might scare him off.

All of which means there is no room in the slightest for the pleasing effect the lingering taste of laundered cotton in my mouth has on me.

And there certainly wasn't any room for that bite.

I wonder what he thought of it. I wonder if he's telling himself it was uncalled-for. Unfair. *Unwanted*. I wonder if he has any clue, any clue at all, how much pent-up desire, how much utter *savagery*, I left on the table.

I wonder if he has the slightest inkling of how lightly he got away, because that bite was a fucking drop in the endless ocean of the things I wanted to do to him in there. The things I wanted to show him. Teach him.

Make him fucking feel.

He gives me nothing. He gives me so little, in fact, that I'm absolutely certain his disinterest is studied. Most of the group sex I've had has yielded a certain level of camaraderie, if you like, among the men involved, even if there's no guy-on-guy action. I know he's uptight and conservative, but the only encouraging reactions he had to me were the involuntary ones.

The way my teeth sinking into his flesh had him hurtling towards an even stronger orgasm.

The looks he gave my cock, especially when I was coming over Darcy. I didn't miss them, and I didn't miss their meaning. Disbelief. Longing. But more like a longing he didn't permit himself.

As if it was a weakness he was ashamed of.

I would bet every pound I have that his reaction to me is far more than that of a first-timer in a threesome. Because, even if he's a spineless little liar, those beautiful tiger eyes of his don't lie.

They don't lie at all.

I rinse the washcloth under the hot water and wring it out more viciously than necessary before composing myself, grabbing a dry hand towel too and returning to the lovebirds. A man less kinky and less open-minded than me would have a fit if he saw his girlfriend like this with another man.

I'm less jealous than wistful, because Dex is a closed book with me, and an open one with her, and I wonder, I just wonder, how it feels to be Darcy in this moment. To have him still inside you, to have come together, to have him gaze at you through his lashes like that, as if your mere existence and ability to deliver a pretty orgasm is worthy of great wonderment.

And yet I can't look away, because Dex's orgasm wasn't endgame for me tonight—it was merely a turning point. Because where he was first suspicious and conflicted, and then needy and hungry, he's now relaxed and smiling and unguarded, and an unguarded Dex is a specimen I wish to study, to feast on, very much indeed.

'Here,' I say, sitting down on the bed. Dex raises himself up and eases out of Darcy as I prepare to clean my cum off her tits. I don't miss the flash of his cock as he gets up, almost entirely flaccid now but still long, still breathtaking, as is the lean jut of his jaw and the softness of the dark hair falling over his forehead.

He turns away from us to deal with the condom, but not before a tug of yearning pulls deep inside me at the thought of getting him to plaster his palms to a wall as I stroke that cock, tug at his balls, my body pressed against his, the hair on his calves tickling my shins and my dick teasing the enticing valley of his crack, his voice growing thin and reedy as he begs me and begs me and fucking begs me for release, and—

'You're such a good girl,' I tell Darcy, because she's all that matters now. 'You did so very well.'

This evening was for her, and this next part of the proceedings is for her, because she must be exhausted after her performances, both in The Playroom and on this bed.

So my queer, delicious fantasies about this exquisite, confused man can take a running jump for now.

She smiles dreamily at me, and I enjoy a moment of quiet, uncomplicated joy that we made her so happy this evening.

'Really?' she asks.

'Really.' I place the washcloth gently on her chest and begin to wipe my fluids off her. 'You submitted so beautifully for both of us. You let Dex fuck you so hard. Was it everything you wanted?'

She laughs a little at that, just as Dex turns around,

buckling his belt, and comes to sit on the other side of the bed. 'It was a million times better than I could have hoped for,' she says, looking from me to him and back again, her hips twisting, inner thighs sliding against each other. 'It was the most amazing experience of my life.'

'Good,' I say. I glance over at Dex to find him rubbing at the exact place on his shoulder where I bit him. Our eyes meet, and he presses his mouth into a grim line before turning his attention back to Darcy.

'You're so amazing,' he tells her, stooping to kiss her on the mouth. When he straightens up, he keeps his hand in her hair, smoothing it away from her face. 'You blow my mind.'

She smiles happily and shimmies a little on the bed. 'Oh my God. I could die happy. You two are amazing. Is it wrong that I just want to lie here all night and let you praise me?'

I chuckle as I wipe the last spatters of my cum from her stomach. 'I'll pander to your praise kink all night long, sweetheart. But we need to get you in the shower and clean you up properly.'

At my mention of *we*, Dex jerks his head up harshly. I respond in kind with an arched eyebrow. *Don't even think about letting her down now,* my expression says.

Darcy reaches up to touch the hand stroking her hair. 'It's okay if you don't want to.'

He hesitates, and I clutch the washcloth harder. I tell myself it's anger that he might bail on her, that he might have the fucking cheek to walk away without giving her the full breadth of aftercare she needs and deserves after she let him inside her. After she took a momentous step and let two men loose on her body.

But I suspect it's less anger than the singular agony of being on tenterhooks. I also suspect the discomfort of being an eighteenth-century piece of fabric stretched taut on its tenter by *actual* tenterhooks would be less disagreeable than this trepidation.

Because in five minutes time, I will either be naked under a torrent of hot water with Dexter Scott, or I won't.

44

DEX

I'm doing this for her.
Not for him.

'Of course I'll help you shower,' I say, smiling down at her. It seems miraculous to me that she can lie there between us, naked and unselfconscious in her skin, looking thoroughly fucked.

I did this.

I gave her both her orgasms with my mouth and my cock —though I suppose Max and his pink silicone friends helped. So I can finish the job. Show my appreciation. I'll get in and get out. I won't look at him. It'll be just like the showers at the gym: there's an etiquette.

Besides, this will never—can never—happen again, so I'll take a few minutes longer in this intimate, fucked-up bubble before I trudge back across town and pretend I didn't see the face of God tonight.

Her smile of genuine delight is almost painful to watch. She really didn't think I'd say yes. I stroke the delicate skin at her temple, letting my fingers drift through her beautiful hair like a man hypnotised.

I could get seriously attached to this woman, if the circumstances were different. She's the total opposite of my well-trodden path of bankers and lawyers. Sex with Darcy was fucking unhinged, and I'm appropriately discombobulated.

'I'm so happy you're staying,' she says, stretching luxuriously on the bed.

I give her body a slow once-over before saying, 'It's no hardship. Believe me.'

'It's past Dex's bedtime,' Max drawls, dropping a kiss on Darcy's nipple before climbing off the bed. 'I'll get the shower on.' He's tugging his shirt out from his trousers, unbuttoning it carelessly before he turns away, and it strikes me that for a guy who appears so perennially entitled, he's been pretty selfless tonight. He allowed me both of Darcy's orgasms. All he's had is a few minutes in her mouth and a wank.

Surely that's not nearly enough for someone like him. I just hope he waits till he gets her home before unleashing himself. The mere thought of them going back to his place —or hers—together is a rough hand in my abdomen, fisting my intestines, squeezing them between cruel fingers.

But it's better this way.

'Let me undress you,' Darcy says, pulling herself up to sitting, and I smile despite myself, because that would be nice.

'Very kind of you,' I say, drinking in the adorable smattering of freckles across her nose and upper cheeks as she makes quick work of my shirt buttons.

'Not kind at all.' She tugs impatiently at the bottom of my shirt. 'Totally selfish.'

I laugh and give her my hand, helping her off the bed. 'Knock yourself out.'

'I will,' she retorts. 'It's about time. You've seen everything I've got.'

The whole club has seen everything she has, but I don't remind her of that. 'I certainly have. And how gorgeous it is.'

She gets my shirt off, leaning up to kiss me as she undoes my belt buckle, and the wet slide of her tongue against mine is the purest form of happiness. Her nipples brushing against the fine hairs on my chest feel pretty fucking spectacular, too.

'I'm going to perv so hard at you in the shower,' she tells me, breaking away so she can shove my trousers down. I step out of them and tug my black boxer briefs down, too, getting rid of my socks while I'm crouched down.

When I straighten up, she's staring at my body with huge, hungry eyes. I'm already semi-hard again, which is fucking ridiculous after the life-changing orgasm I just produced.

'Jesus fucking Christ, Dex,' she says, her voice breaking. 'I can't—you are *so gorgeous*. You should stay naked the whole time.'

'Bit of a breach of my company's dress code,' I say, pulling her against me, because there's nothing like wrapping yourself around a naked woman. It's like our skins can speak, just by touching.

'Shower's ready,' Max shouts from the bathroom.

For fuck's sake.

I disentangle myself from Darcy.

'Come on,' she says, grinning at me. Excitement is etched all over her beautiful face. She's already turning towards his voice. I guess she has far more reasons to look forward to this than I do.

I grab her hips as I follow her through, because I'm not

above using her as a human shield if the situation demands it.

45

DARCY

I can't keep the smirk off my face as Dex and I walk through to the bathroom. He's so hot. He's so insanely, perfectly gorgeous that I want to lie him down and kiss every single inch of his body.

He swipes his abandoned champagne flute from the cabinet as we pass it and chugs it back in a single gulp.

Interesting.

Maybe the poor guy is less comfortable with the prospect of him and Max both getting naked than I am. I know Max had his own reasons for wanting this threesome tonight, but I have no idea if Dex is remotely interested in him, or actively appalled, or somewhere in between.

He's a hard guy to read, which made the way he looked at me and kissed me after coming inside me all the more magical.

'You sure you're okay with this?' I whisper. 'You can change your mind.'

The smile he gives me is tired but kind, and the little spank he bestows on my bottom is casual. Cheeky. 'I'm all good. But thanks, angel.'

I'm Dex's angel.

I practically skip through to the bathroom, which is the standard you'd find in a luxury hotel. It's masculine and vaguely Art Deco in style, the walls a matte black marble slashed through with thick grey veins. The shower boasts two massive raindance shower heads, and Max has them on full pelt.

He's already under the water, naked and glorious, his clothes dumped in a pile in the corner. Dude must have been in a hurry. His body twists this way and that under the spray. He's a Greek god, lithe and muscular, with broad shoulders and narrow hips, and I can't help but see him through Dex's eyes. But when I glance behind me, Dex is studiously avoiding looking anywhere near Max.

He enters the shower behind me, Max pulling me instantly into his arms and pressing me up against the tiles so he can kiss me hungrily. His hands are all over my body, the hot water cascading over us both, and I think I might be in bad-girl heaven.

When I break off our kiss to check in on Dex, he's already soaping himself up under the other shower head, his body (and dick) angled slightly away from us, face upturned to the torrent, hands slicking his hair back, and Mary, Joseph and sweet Baby Jesus, I cannot handle the combined hotness of these two men.

I just can't.

They're both *ridiculous.* The kind of handsome you rarely ever see in real-life guys. Dex is doing his very best to pretend Max doesn't exist, and Max is making no effort at all to hide the thirst in his stare as he takes Dex in, but no matter. I've got them both here. Naked. In the shower with me.

It's no wonder that washing myself just dropped straight to the bottom of my priority list.

I smile so widely it almost breaks my face in two and put my hands on my hips. 'Okay, Dex. Get over here.'

He finds the courage to look in our direction, tilting his head from one side to another as water cascades over him, slicking his hair back further and pouring down his neck in rivulets. This guy gives insanely good shampoo ad.

'Where?' he asks with all the confidence of a man being asked to streak across an actual minefield.

'Here,' I demand. 'This evening is for me, right?' I turn to Max. 'You said so.'

'Course it is,' Max assures me smoothly, stepping up behind me and winding his arms around my stomach. I lean my head back against his chest as I observe Dex. Conflicted isn't even the word. The sight of Max wrapped around me has his lips pressing together, but he still seems to think he's being ambushed.

On that point, he'd be right. But I'm a greedy girl, and he told me he was "all good".

So I'm making this shower count.

'What do you need, sweetheart?' Max asks.

'I need a full-on Darcy sandwich,' I tell them, laying my hands over Max's. 'I want you behind me'—I pat his hand—'and Dex in front of me, kissing me, and I want to feel squished. I want to feel every single one of your muscles, because I can't look at you both and not get that. I need it. I want all your hands on me. I want *all* the attention.'

I narrowly avoid stomping my foot like Veruca Salt.

Narrowly.

'And if you'd like to make me come with your hands, then I will absolutely be on board with that. And then,' I continue before either of them can say anything, 'I want you both over there'—I point to the wall of marble—'so I can serve you both, and play with you, and maybe jerk you both off at the same time, and *maybe* I'll get on my knees and take it in turns to suck you both, too, just because I can.'

The shocked silence from both of them is as deafening as the thunder of water all around us. I swear Dex might pass out from shock. Max's cock thickens against my lower back, and I shimmy happily against it.

And then: 'You heard the lady,' Max says smoothly. He should honestly win awards for his ability to sound more sexily calm and controlled the more aroused he gets. He keeps one arm banded tightly around my stomach, but his other hand comes down and cups my pussy. Hard. If that's not a provocation to Dex, I don't know what is.

Dex turns then, and he's hard, too. He doesn't say a word.

But he closes the gap with us.

46

MAX

He won't look at me.
I may as well be fucking Medusa for all the effort he's putting into avoiding my stare.

Smart boy.

If he looked, what he'd see in my eyes would burn into his soul, obliterating every memory of Darcy's beautiful body as he lies alone tonight with only his fist for company.

I'm staring enough for both of us, believe me. I'm staring the way a man does when he finally understands what compelled Zeus to carry off the young Ganymede so he could anoint his flawless body with nectar.

Dex's physical beauty is stark. Astonishing. Domed, broad shoulders and a collarbone made for licking. Flat nipples marking the curves of his pecs, adorning his torso like twin proud medallions. The perfect way the water draws the hair down his stomach into a perfect line. Crisp tan lines that denote precisely the length of swim shorts he's worn all summer and underscore that this section of his body is private.

Sacred.

That his cock, thick and long and straight, its crown flared and ruddy, isn't even the most spectacular part of him is a revelation in itself.

I want that cock in my grip, leaking and pulsing and straining, but I also want his nipples under my tongue.

I want the contours of his arse nestled just so against my dick as he settles in my lap.

I want to tug with my teeth at the delicate crease of skin where his arm bends.

I want to rub arnica into the mottled bruise that *my teeth have left* on his shoulder.

He comes right up to us, toe to toe with Darcy, and I reluctantly unwind my arm from her waist and release her cunt, because this is her fantasy, not mine, and the thought of leaving a woman's fantasy hanging is positively offensive.

He's close. So close that if I were to rest my chin on her shoulder, I could kiss the side of his neck. And that will have to be enough.

For now.

There's a wall of marble to my right. A wall of glass to my left. The whispers of our breaths mingle with the thud-thud of the water. The woman wedged between Dex and me is beautiful and sexy, and I can already tell that she'll need us to hold her up, so tired and aroused is she. I press forward, my dick snug between the cleft of her cheeks, her head lolling back against my shoulder.

I may not be able to touch him, but I can mastermind this situation. He's already shown me what a compliant little puppet he can be when I command him. My view is limited: the top of his head as he dips it to Darcy's mouth, the angry teeth marks I left on his skin, the muscles working below it. He tilts her head to the side and my view improves: their lips sliding. Noses rubbing. Tongues dancing.

Trying to unwind this guy is akin to the fable about the wind and sun competing to strip a man of his overcoat. I'm definitely the wind. I believe in brute force. I believe that when someone is fannying around on the precipice, a well-timed push is the best way to get them moving.

But Darcy is the sun, and she's shone her light on both of us, and it's so warm, so radiant, and so irresistible that she has Mr I-Don't-do-Threesomes stripping off and cavorting naked with us—her—*us* in the shower.

'How does she feel?' I murmur, acceptance yielding to FOMO as I brush my hands up her arms. 'Nice and slippery? Are her nipples hard?'

He breaks their kiss, breathing roughly, bringing his hands up to palm her tits. To squeeze them.

'Yeah,' he grits out. 'So fucking hard.' And he dives back in for a kiss she clearly likes, given the way she grinds against my cock.

'And her clit?' I persist. 'Rub it. I'll take her cunt.'

What she really needs is my dick buried deep inside her, but I know the filth of this scenario will get her there with just our fingers. I waste no time in squeezing my hand between our bodies, my fingertips tracing a line between her cheeks, past the ring of muscle I really need to work on, to where she's slippery and open for me.

If I have my way, Dex and I will both take Darcy with our cocks at the same time, and I really, really need to work her up to that. It's never too early to start stretching her.

Meanwhile, my fingers are slipping and twisting inside her. My knuckles brush Dex's fingers, and it sends an impossible frisson of arousal through me to think he's touching her so intimately at the same time that I am. I brush my thumb over her other hole again.

'I'm going to take you here soon, sweetheart,' I mutter in

her ear. 'I'm going to fuck your arse while Dex fucks your cunt, and you're going to let us. Imagine how full it'll feel having our dicks everywhere.'

'Oh my God,' she moans into his mouth. They're still kissing, messily and hungrily and unabashedly as he works her clit and kneads one tit. I reach my free hand around and massage her other tit with all the urgency of a man who knows what he's missing out on. I want this "Darcy sandwich", as she calls it, to be as filthy and full-on as it can be. I want her overwhelmed to the point of obliteration, wedged between two hard male bodies as we ravage her from the front and the back.

The water streams over us, the air thick with steam and sex. I'm rutting against her, and from the strangled, rhythmic grunts Dex is making, I'm pretty sure her elegant little fingers are wrapped firmly around his dick. She squeezes a hand behind her, little beauty, and grabs my dick, too. Her leverage is non-existent in this position—I'm far too close for her to really have a go—but the knowledge that our delicious little plaything is working us as we work her has my head spinning.

And I'm not the only one, because she comes like this, bucking and mewling and rubbing her arse against me and her tits against him like the dazzling little champ she is.

47

DEX

My dick is granite and my brain is vapour.

It's all too much: kissing her wet mouth and petting her soaking skin; stroking her tongue and teasing her nipple; fondling her clit as she pumps my dick; knowing her other hand is around *him*; knowing *his* fingers are inside her; brushing against them as we stoke the fire of her orgasm together.

And when she combusts and sags back against him, my haze of pride and desire and adoration has me forgetting to make space. It has me leaning in and kissing her, telling her how clever and wonderful and perfect she is. It has my knuckles brushing at the hollow above Max's collarbone as I slide my hand around her head so I can grip her hair. Kiss her harder.

Darcy's the one to break this improbable throupling, laughingly, breathlessly sliding out from between us, a palm on my chest to push me away.

'My turn now,' she says, and we protest in unison. *No, absolutely not. Rest up. Let us wash you.* But our words fall on the deaf ears of a woman with all the second wind of a kid who's trapped in a sweet shop and won't stop gorging herself until her body makes the decision for her.

'Up against the wall,' she says bossily, still wearing the ear-to-ear grin of a thoroughly satisfied woman. 'Both of you.'

I exchange a look with Max, uneasy at my end and amused at his, before we submit and collapse against the still-cool slab of marble. I tilt my head back and take this opportunity out of the spray for a full inhale and exhale.

'Holy fucking Christ,' Darcy says, face flushed and wet hair plastered to her shoulders and breasts, eyes dancing between us. 'I just found my new screensaver.'

That elicits an appalled laugh from me, Max guffawing far more heartily.

'Don't even think about it unless you want a good spanking,' he says.

She raises her eyebrows. 'And that's supposed to be a deterrent? Just *look* at you both. I could spend all evening on my knees—I'm not kidding.'

I groan at that and risk a glance at Max. His head is back, Adam's apple jumping as he watches Darcy, all wet, starry lashes and dark, predatory gaze. He and I are almost shoulder to shoulder, and though he has an inch or two on me—in height, I mean—we're not dissimilar.

I'm darker skinned than him, even with his golden playboy tan in full effect, but we're both long and lean. Athletic builds. Our arms hang loose, our dicks at full mast.

We're all aesthetes. I can appreciate the objective physical beauty of the male form as much as the next person. And Max is a man in fine shape. But more marked than that is his enviable demeanour. He saunters and swaggers, he dominates and demands. The man doesn't have a self-conscious bone in his body. That much is obvious, and it's magnetic.

Darcy steps between us, a mischievous smile on her face. 'I've suddenly stopped caring that my parents never took us to Disneyland.'

'Instead you're in Dickneyland,' Max quips, and I shake my head because that is lame as fuck. But Darcy's laughing like he's Michael fucking McIntyre.

'Dickneyland. Oh my God!'

'Come and sit on Uncle Mickey's lap like a good girl,' he says, and I snort. Creepy twat.

'It's not your *lap* I want to sit on,' she retorts, and then she's pumping the shower gel dispenser next to Max, and wrapping her warm, soaped-up hands around each of our dicks, and we both shut up and groan in unison, because if she wants to make us both come again, we're not stupid enough to stop her.

I watch in horrified fascination as she pumps us both with slow, deliberate strokes. Our soapy, swollen crowns disappear and reappear over and over, and I've given up all pretence of not watching. With every skilful stroke, helpless arousal roils through me.

'Fuck, this is hot,' she says. I couldn't agree more, but the heat of the situation comes not from her deft handiwork or her undeniable beauty but the fact that we're both using her, both fucking her fists, our hips moving in sync as we arch away from the tiles to rut into her hands.

'Let Dex finish in your mouth like a good little whore,' Max tells her through gritted teeth, the audible effort of forming words not detracting from the command in his voice. 'He's only fucked one of your holes tonight.'

I'm opening my mouth to protest—*no, no way; she's done enough tonight; she's not a whore*—when Darcy shivers.

'Oh my God, yes,' she says with a groan. 'Will you pull my hair and make him fuck my mouth?'

'Fuck, yeah,' he shudders out. 'Get on your knees.'

I step forward under the spray so I can wash the soap off my cock, dizzy with want, because she's going to suck it and he's going to watch and pull the strings, *both* of our strings, and Jesus Christ, this is every level of depraved and I don't know what these two are doing to me and I couldn't fucking stop it if I tried.

Darcy gets to her knees right under the jet of water, and it's pouring over her head and bouncing off her shoulders, and she looks so exquisite with her blue eyes closed and her wet mouth open and her hands on my quads and her small, pink tongue darting out to catch my dick, to flicker over my crown and then try again when it jerks like a puppy on a leash.

And while her handjob was world class, her mouth is a lavish, sensory feast against my poor, swollen flesh, all heat and silk. Max steps right up behind her, nudging her knees apart so he can stand between them, his hands raking her hair back into a sodden, coppery bridle that he wraps around one hand, and suddenly I'm no longer looking at Darcy.

His face is no more than a foot from mine, and I'm staring straight into his implausibly, absurdly blue eyes as he winds her hair tighter. He uses his rein to impale her mouth further onto my cock, her *mmph* muffled and her hands coming around to grip my arse tight as my sensitive tip hits the back of her sweet mouth.

And I know, I just *know,* that when he clenches his jaw and flares his nostrils in frustrated fury, it's a direct result of the anguish, the ecstasy, he sees written on my face. I jerk my gaze downwards, at the beautiful, amazing woman giving me this pleasure and away from the man presuming to be her puppeteer.

'It's so amazing, angel,' I croon, caressing her temple, her jaw, her shoulders. 'You're incredible.'

But fuck. He has his monstrous cock in his other hand, right beside her head, and he's jerking himself off with jagged, impatient strokes, and I freeze at the sight of it, of the water sluicing over it. At the *size* of it. The power.

'Look at me,' he barks, and I can only blame the alchemy Darcy's wreaking on my brain chemistry for the fact that I obey without a moment's delay.

'Keep going like that, sweetheart,' he tells her without taking his eyes off me. 'You're letting him fuck your mouth so well.'

So well is an understatement. Her magical mouth is swirling and whirling my cock into hyper-arousal so tormented my soul is on the verge of leaving my body. My hips are rutting against her of their own accord. And it's in this precarious state that I stare into Max's hypnotic eyes as he puts his thumb to my bottom lip and presses down on its very centre.

'Just as I thought,' he murmurs, his hand in my peripheral vision still moving over his length. 'Just as perfect as I thought.'

I don't know how or why it happens, but his thumb is sliding into my mouth then, tasting cleanly and tartly of soap, dragging against my teeth, and it seems the only rational course of action available to me is to close my lips around it and suck, my tongue swirling around its tip, mimicking Darcy's wonderful, extraordinary ministrations on my dick.

And I swear, my senses are so heightened that I can read the whorls of his thumbprint with my tongue. I can hear the violence of the desires reflected in his pupils as clearly as if he was screaming their savagery into my ear.

We're frozen in place, it seems, only Darcy's mouth and his hand and my tongue still in motion. Every other part of me is outwardly stiff and inwardly reeling. Without Max's strict guidance to steady her, Darcy pops off my cock, and she must look up at us, for she chuckles quietly.

'Oh, boy,' is all she says before she wraps her hand around my root and licks at my frenulum with the skill of an angel before taking me deep in her mouth again.

My only outlet?

To suck harder on Max's thumb with deep, hungry pulls that hollow out my cheeks.

And then he's yanking his thumb out, and gripping the back of my neck in a chokehold, and smashing our faces together with the sole purpose of biting down hard on my lower lip.

His teeth on my skin have the exact same effect that they had next door. The pain is a sharp, bright halo around my pleasure, sending me hurtling through worlds I've never seen. It's too much, this double-ended intoxication of Darcy's mouth and Max's teeth.

I sink one hand tightly into Darcy's shoulder and raise the other in what's intended as self-defence but becomes a pathetic fucking attempt to claw at his hair. To get him closer.

He releases my lip but keeps hold of my jaw, fucking my mouth with his tongue in a way that's angry and selfish and unleashed and *vocal*, because we're both moaning into the kiss as I tug his hair and he grips my neck.

He's relentless. She's relentless. And I'm gone, I'm useless, I'm practically weeping with the unutterable pleasure of the filthy, filthy pulses of his tongue, so when Darcy deep-throats me and holds me there, I spill and I spill as white-hot sensation wracks my body in a violent crescendo.

She pulls off me gently, sweetly, and I'm vaguely aware of her slipping out from between us, but Max has my neck in a *don't you fucking dare go anywhere* death grip as he plunders my mouth and brings himself savagely to a climax whose projectile proof the skin of my thigh feels even through the torrent of water.

48

DARCY

'Are you sure you're okay?' I ask Max. I can just about form words—my body and soul are wrung-out, bled dry by orgasm—but this is important.

He tightens his arm around me, and I snuggle a little closer to his chest. He was extremely clear that he expected me to spend the night at his after what went down, but it's not me I'm worried about.

It's him.

And Dex.

'I'm good, sweetheart,' he tells me for the millionth time. 'It was all just fun and games.'

Beneath the know-it-all drawl there's a forced bravado that tugs at my heart. While I'm confident Max couldn't list all the people he's slept with if you tied him to his desk for a year, I know he was invested in this evening on a level way beyond simply overseeing the execution of one of my fantasies.

I know he was invested in *Dex*.

Even so, he must have been surprised that Dex capitulated to him so quickly. I know I was, when I heard the low, male grunts above me and paused sucking Dex's gorgeous cock, only to look up and find him simulating the exact same thing *on Max's thumb.*

Holy fucking Christ, that was hot. Even hotter was feeling the force of Dex's climax in my mouth, of swallowing the proof that, between us, we'd aroused him that much. So to find them both kissing as I slipped out from below the vaulted chapel of their bodies blew my actual mind.

None of that changes, or helps, the fact that Dex pulled away as soon as Max had finished shooting his load.

Or that, after he stammered out some sort of choked apology and bolted into the bedroom to dress himself and flee what he probably considered the scene of a crime, Max was actually shaking when he pulled me into his arms under the spray.

He clung to me, and told me how proud he was of me, but I couldn't shake the feeling that it wasn't me he wanted in his arms just then. Maybe that was a stupid reaction—I don't doubt that Max's desire for me is real—but given what transpired between him and Dex, I wouldn't blame him for wanting a little closure.

'It was a lot of fun,' I agree now, 'but I'm sure kissing you was way, way out of Dex's comfort zone. He probably just freaked out.'

He laughs mirthlessly. 'You think?'

'You know what I mean. Don't take it as a sign that he didn't like it.' I mentally scrape the recesses of my exhausted, orgasm-addled brain for everything I know about Belle and Dex's family. 'If anything, it was a sign he liked it all far too much.'

'It doesn't make it okay that he bailed on you,' he huffs.

'It's inexcusable. He came in your fucking mouth and then buggered right off. Fucking rude, that's what it is.'

I'm quiet for a moment as I lie cradled in his arms, my fingertips brushing over the light hairs on his chest. His heart is beating way too fast for a guy who came twice tonight, even if both times were in his own fist. Dex came in my pussy *and* my mouth and Max didn't get anything—except a fleeting blow job from me and the fevered, glorious kiss that Dex immediately threw in his face.

I'm not sure how conscious Max is that he's being disingenuous, but I have to say it. 'I'm pretty confident it wasn't *me* he bailed on.' I snag my lips between my teeth and wait for his response.

'Doesn't matter.' His voice is brusque. 'He shouldn't have got in the shower with us if he wasn't comfortable. He's thirty, for fuck's sake. If he's labouring under some misapprehension that he's only into chicks, I have news for him. The way he sucked my thumb'—he sucks in a sharp inhale—'was like he couldn't get enough. He fucking *loved* it. Pity he couldn't look me in the eye afterwards.'

That reminds me of something Belle said in France, the morning after my sister's wedding.

'Belle had a freakout after her first time with Rafe. She told me he came all over her'—Max doesn't need to know the full, fabulous details of what she divulged around their hot priest and nun role play—'and she'd been having the most amazing time, but when he went to clean her up she had this, like, meltdown, because she felt so dirty and perverted for enjoying it. He had to give her lots of aftercare and reassurance.'

Max snorts rudely. 'That may be, but if you think I'm going to sit a thirty-year-old guy down and sing Kum Ba Yah with him while he agonises over the clear truth that he secretly likes dick, you can think again.'

This man. So impatient. Intolerant. Demanding. So black and white. No wonder Dex ran for the hills. If Max is right, and Dex got off on that kiss—which he absolutely seemed to—then I can only imagine the depths to which he's is spiralling right now.

And that hurts my heart, because I want Max to be okay, and I want Dex to be okay. I want everyone to have walked away from tonight with the same amount of joy and amazement that I have, because it was incredible. I'm sorry it if hurts Dex to accept this, but the three of us were fire together. Still, I feel the need to defend him, because I don't want Max thinking badly of him and I also don't want Max, somewhere deep down, blaming himself for coming on too strong and scaring Dex away.

'That's a bit harsh,' I say now. 'You presumably had a lot of navel-gazing to do when you came out. Dex hasn't worked through any of that.'

He shrugs his trademark impatient shrug beneath me. 'Not really. I found girls attractive. I found guys attractive—I wanted to fuck anything with a pulse, basically. My parents were cool with it. It was a non-issue.'

'Well, you're very lucky,' I tell him. 'Most people don't have that experience, or that kind of support. This is probably all very new and confusing for Dex.'

He laughs at that, tightening his grip on me and kissing my forehead. 'You're sweet,' he says. 'But that's utter bullshit. I'm sorry, but again—he's thirty. Even I'm not arrogant enough to believe that five minutes in the shower with me can turn someone.

'Nope, no matter how much denial he's been in his entire life, I'm telling you, he's thought about this before.

He's just never had the guts to admit it, to himself or to anyone else.'

He huffs against my temple. 'I get it, I suppose. It's fucking savage out there. I know it can be... hard. But that doesn't make it fun to watch a grown man run for the hills because he can't bear to admit to himself that he actually felt something.'

It's a fleeting concession, I suppose—a moment of grace from a man who's clearly frustrated and, I suspect, a teeny bit hurt. And I'll take it. I'll take it on Dex's behalf.

49

DEX

DARCY

Hiii

Thanks so much for coming last night

(Whoops I didn't mean that as a pun)

I had the most amazing time xxx

Hope you are ok… x

∽

DARCY

Hey - you ok? I just wanted to check in bc I know it was a lot

∽

DARCY

Dex?

Hi again… let me know how you're doing x

~

DARCY

Well this is embarrassing [sad face]

~

MAX

If you want to avoid me, fine. But for fuck's sake have the decency not to ghost Darcy, you spineless little cunt.

~

Jesus.

I feel like shit. I'm a horrible, horrible person. Max is right—I've ghosted the most beautiful, incredible woman for the past five days. She let me run rampant on her body. I took her pussy and her mouth. I took her trust, and I fucking torched it because I am indeed a spineless little cunt who can't look her boyfriend in the eye.

And therein lies the problem. God knows, I want to reply to Darcy. I want to tell her I haven't stopped thinking about her, that her lips and her breasts and her eyes and her pussy and her hair and her skin are imprinted indelibly on my mind, that I want more—*crave* more.

But I can't.

Because Max's eyes are etched even more permanently, as are the seams of his thumbprint and the short, sharp slice of his thumbnail as I ran my tongue along its edge. My lower lip still bears the bruising of his bite, his dental records committed in the form of tiny, painful cysts along my gum.

And if Darcy's body is a celestial delight from start to finish, Max's is an evil, evil thing, so depraved and violent and dangerous it could send a man crazy from wanting more of it.

So I've floated in a useless holding pattern of anguished stalemate, sleepwalking through the week at work and spending most of the weekend in the gym, denying and resisting and gritting my teeth in frustration as flashes of skin and slivers of tongue continue to haunt my waking and my sleeping.

Not to mention, the announcement of which banks are on the ticket for the Wolff IPO is expected in the next few weeks, and work is a fever pitch of excitement and pointless, endless speculation. If I hear Max's name one more time from my colleagues, I might take a leaf out of his book and bite someone, just to shut them up.

I'm staring into space in my office, my productivity void hidden from the trading floor by a bank of monitors that Bloomberg's black screens dominate. The FTSE and the Eurostoxx are more green than red today, which I'm sure I'd find encouraging if I could summon the energy to find anything encouraging at all.

My phone console rings, showing the name of my ultimate boss, Jochen Thum, head of Loeb's London office. I sit up guiltily. He can't tell I've been sinning by night and slacking by day, can he?

I pick up the phone. 'Jochen. Hey.'

'Dex.' His soft Swiss-German voice is friendly. 'Last-minute meeting. Moira Davenport has called and asked if their leadership team can come by our offices today for a quick chat.'

'A quick chat?' I repeat dumbly. What the actual fuck? Moira Davenport is Wolff Holdings' CFO and undoubtedly one of the most influential women in British industry.

'I know.' He laughs. 'Crazy, right? She emphasised that it's very informal and we shouldn't prepare anything. They want to have one more conversation before they allocate the banks for the IPO.'

'They want to see our bankers?' I guess, screwing up my face.

'Actually, they'd like a meeting with our Equities and research guys. It's a good sign, I think.'

Huh. It is a good sign. We're a small outfit compared to the bulge-bracket banks, who will absolutely expect a big role on the ticket. Our strength, though, lies in the breadth of our research. Wolff Holdings won't be a straightforward stock for any investor to analyse. It straddles so many sectors, from chemicals and consumer to hospitality and leisure.

That not only means that the banks' sector-specific research teams who advise fund managers on their investments will need to collaborate across sectors, but that the performance of the stock, when it starts trading publicly, can be affected by goings-on in multiple sectors. Bottom line —it's complex.

Jochen and I discuss the people we'll need to get in the room for this 'casual' chat before he drops his bombshell.

'Good. That all sounds workable. She said this has come straight from Hunter. He'll be coming along, so we want to put our best foot forward.'

I manage to wait until he's ended the call before I let my forehead drop to my desk with a loud thump.

Fucking seriously?

50

MAX

I've been to Loeb a couple of times before, for some industry events.

Never been this... wound up, I suppose.

If the little shit thinks he can hide from me—if he thinks I'll stand by and take no action while he disrespects Darcy—then I'm about to demonstrate to him how wretchedly mistaken he is.

I accept that commandeering an entire meeting around our imminent IPO may be overstretching, but this isn't just an excuse to see him. If I wanted to see him I'd show up here and demand a meeting.

No. This is a power play. This is a chance to show him who's boss.

I want to watch the arsehole squirm.

I'm all benevolence and easy charm as I stride into the large meeting room on Loeb's corporate entertaining floor. It's on the tenth floor of their offices, decked out with thick white carpets and linen-covered walls, its floor-to-ceiling windows affording the space plenty of daylight and an impressive view over the City.

There's a dozen or so people in the room when Moira and I enter with our Head of Strategy and a handful of others from our Strategy and Finance team. Good to see they've rallied the troops. But I'm not interested in numbers. I'm interested in—

Ahh.

There he is.

And he's lovely. Achingly lovely, in fact, to an extent I could well do without. In my mind, this past few days, he's been all petulance and spinelessness, but here, standing in sunlight so glaring the air around him is a swirl of dust mites, he is, in fact, quite something. I take him in at a glance. His suit is navy, his tie—probably plucked from his desk drawer in light of this unexpected meeting—is a pale pink one that looks like classic Hermes and works perfectly against the blue of his shirt and the olive of his skin. His hair's brushed neatly back, and he looks far better than a man who should have spent the past five days stewing in the shit-tip of his own poor decision-making has any right to look.

Those eyes, though. I swear they widen when he spots me from across the room, and I shoot him a neutral smile that's really more a purse of my lips, because I'm not giving this guy an inch.

If he hasn't been stewing already, let him stew now.

Jochen Thum, the CEO here in London and an all-round decent chap, approaches with his arms outstretched. He kisses Moira on both cheeks before shaking me heartily by the hand.

'It's wonderful to have you here,' he says, all jocular welcome. I bet it is. Truth is, Loeb punches far above its weight with the quality of its research, and we'd be naïve not to factor that into our decision making. We'll probably end up in the top five companies in the FTSE 100 by market capitalisation, which means everyone will have to hold our stock. They'll need as much decent equity research as possible to help them with their investments.

'Thanks for accommodating us at such short notice,' I tell him. 'I hope it hasn't been too much of an inconvenience.'

'Not at all, not at all,' he says, hands flapping. 'Come and meet our team.'

I shake hands with two women and a handful of men from the various equity research and trading teams before we come to a halt in front of Dex. I stand there, left hand in my pocket, and watch him closely. He's too professionally assured to show his discomfort, but the panicked darts of his eyes between me and Thum tell me he's trying his best to read the situation and act accordingly.

'Now, this is our new Head of Equities, Dex Scott,' Thum says, slapping him fondly on the shoulder. 'He's come to us from Goldman in New York, and we're very excited to be investing in our Equities business through experienced hires like him.'

There's a second, just a second, where he opens his mouth like a suffocating fish, and I can tell he's deciding whether or not to divulge that we know each other, and it's so fucking tempting to leave him hanging.

But I don't.

'Actually,' I interject before he can say anything, 'Dex and I have met each other socially. Haven't we, mate?' I stick out my hand, and he takes it, and his grip is firm, and his lethal fucking eyes are fixed on mine, and he's not smiling, and I can't help but squeeze a little tighter.

Haven't we, mate?

'Uh, that's right,' he says.

Thum chuckles delightedly. 'Well, you kept that quiet,' he tells Dex. 'I had no idea!'

'It's a very recent introduction,' I say smoothly. 'We just met last week. We have a… friend in common. Don't we?'

'Exactly,' Dex manages. He extricates his hand from my grip and directs it at Moira, bestowing on her the blinding smile that he seems to save only for women, the same smile that had me wishing I was Darcy after he'd finished shooting his load inside her. 'Dex,' he tells her, 'It's a pleasure.'

I can only stand politely and pretend I'm not drinking in every fucking second of our proximity.

'How do you do?' Moira asks, and she may be fifty-five if she's a day, but I swear she preens at Dex's panty-melting grin. Who fucking wouldn't?

'Let's get you all a coffee,' he says, stepping back and ushering us over to the long console bearing the cafetières and china cups.

I incline my head as I saunter past him.

The game is only just beginning.

51

DEX

I end up running the meeting, which is unplanned and unhelpful. I fumble my way through it with reasonable success, mainly because I'm MC and my colleagues all deliver what we require during their sections. The Wolff team seems genuinely impressed with the breadth and depth of our research capabilities and with the teamwork between the traders who trade the various sectors adjacent with Wolff's individual businesses.

As the Head of Equities, my role here is to underscore Loeb's expertise in the secondary market. Getting a place on this deal isn't just about being a bank known for deals—the bigger banks own that status. It's about convincing the Wolff team that investors will look to *us* for advice once the stock is trading publicly.

I have no way of knowing if this meeting is remotely necessary or whether Max has set it up to fuck with me. All I know is that the timing is fishy as fuck, and that everything I say during the fifty minutes we're at the table is a blur, because every vestige of strength I possess is spent trying not to look at him.

Trying not to remember how hard his tongue fucked my mouth.

Trying not to rub my own tongue over my lacerated gum, like I've been doing all week.

Trying not to think about the fact that he probably had Darcy in his bed this morning.

Darcy, Darcy, Darcy.

Fuuuuck.

He's sitting across from me, all slick hair and sharp eyes and perfectly cut suit, jacket hanging on his chair back and muscles straining under his shirt. He's fully engaged, as far as I can see, asking incisive questions of everybody. Articulating his vision for Wolff's future. Reeling every person at the table in. Casting his spell. And I'm supposed to sit here and watch him and listen and pretend I don't know how fucking angry and potent that cock of his was when he fucked his fist and came all over my fucking thigh?

Nope.

It's impossible.

So when the meeting draws to a close and everyone is standing and shaking hands and thanking each other for their time, I'm weak with relief and fading adrenalin, psyching myself up to shake him by the hand once more and send him firmly on his way.

Until he stands right in front of me and looks me in the eye and asks me for a word in private.

In my office.

WE TAKE the lift down with everyone else and get off on the third floor with the traders and the Head of Equity Sales. 'It's this way,' I tell Max curtly, leading him across the trading floor and waiting with a mix of impatience and curiosity and nausea as he shakes their hands and thanks them charmingly for their time. *Again.*

The smile, the charm, fade as soon as we get into my small office.

'Lock the door,' he snaps, throwing his jacket over the back of the nearest chair and letting the research tome we presented him with fall to the table with a bang. I throw him a look I hope tells him I'm not remotely on board with any of this before doing exactly as he says and hitting a switch that makes the windows opaque for good measure. If he wants to bawl me out, as I suspect he does, then I'll take all the privacy I can get.

'Have a seat,' I say wearily, but before I can sit he's got his hands on my shoulders, gripping hard and frogmarching me backwards until I hit the wall.

'She cried on Saturday night, you know that?' he asks, spitting each word out through clenched teeth. 'She was pretty sanguine about it all after you walked out, but this weekend she was just really fucking sad and humiliated, and I want to wring your fucking neck for hurting her like that.'

Fuck.

I made her cry.

He's right—I'm despicable. Loathsome. If you take Max out of the equation, the way I've treated Darcy is abhorrent. I open my mouth to defend myself, but he ploughs on, fingertips digging into my shoulders and blue eyes cold as fucking ice.

'Alchemy may be a sex club, but you came and messed around with us privately, at her invitation, and you fucking know it. Shooting in her mouth and then fucking off is so fucking out of order that if you don't understand what you did wrong then I can't begin to explain it to you.'

The smooth-talking, jocular Max is gone. This version of him is as intense, as emotion-fuelled as he was in that shower when he took what he wanted from me. He's vibrating with fury, possessed by it, and it's devastating, because there's something about his careless, entitled ease that draws you in, but there's something about seeing him when he *does* care, when he *is* riled, that's simply catastrophic.

I won't have him thinking badly of me. I can't bear it. Just as I can't bear Darcy thinking badly of me, either.

Impossibly, the truth is the least gut-wrenching option right now.

So I spit it out.

'I know exactly what I've done, and I despise myself. But it has nothing to do with Darcy, and you know it.'

His face slackens with disbelief, like he can't quite believe I have the guts to come clean.

'Go on.'

I flare my nostrils. 'I haven't stopped thinking about her. I told you, she's the most beautiful woman I've ever seen. I adored every single second of being with her the other night. And you're right.' I swallow. 'I should message her and tell her just that. But I can't.'

'Because...'

'Because you guys are a package deal.' Nausea rolls through me and I regret that black coffee I drank on an empty stomach.

He releases my shoulders, instead planting his palms on the wall either side of me with a smack that makes me jump. He's got me caged in now.

Excellent.

52

DEX

This is worse, somehow, than him touching me. It's claustrophobic and stressful and the oddest kind of exciting. It's no surprise he's risen to the top of Europe's largest privately-owned company, because I bet this man gets every single thing he wants.

So to be captive within the frame of his body, to have every ounce of his attention on me, is shocking in the most literal sense of the word. It's as if a current is running through my entire body.

He surveys me for a moment through blue eyes that are heat and ice all at once. Then: 'You didn't have a problem with us being a package deal the other night.'

'I was so turned on,' I stammer. 'You have to understand, I was so far gone when you—I—Darcy was doing such an amazing job. I was in this state of extreme... arousal, and—'

My hands are flapping and I'm as disgusted with myself for the frailty of my argument as Max seems to be. But it's true. He could have done anything in that moment, and I would have found it arousing. Someone could have pissed all over my leg and I probably would still have come.

He took advantage of me during a moment of weakness, and, while I don't necessarily blame him, I don't wish to remember or ever, ever repeat the circumstances of our... moment together.

He leaves me to trail off ineffectually, pathetically. Those blue eyes stray to my mouth, and he licks his lips.

'Finished gaslighting yourself?' he asks finally. 'Please don't stop on my account. It's fascinating to watch, honestly.'

I scowl at him. 'I'm not gaslighting myself,' I spit.

He laughs. When he does that, he's impossible to look away from. 'I don't think I've ever seen someone narrate their own life quite so unreliably.'

That's just rude. 'I don't *narrate unreliably*. I'm telling you my experience of the other night.'

'Right.' He braces on one hand and uses the other to stroke along his jawline like he's assessing his stubble growth. 'Let me get this straight. You've been avoiding Darcy because you feel uncomfortable that I kissed you when you were in a vulnerable, aroused state.'

I nod, though I don't appreciate the sarcastic undertones I'm picking up. 'Exactly,' I say, staring at the long, capable fingers moving over his jawline.

'Because you're *straight*,' he continues, and I swear his face moves closer at the same time that he drops his hand and full-on *cups* my entire scrotum through my trousers, and I am as incapable of forming words as the day I was born, opening my mouth in a silent scream as my palms claw uselessly at the wall behind me.

All there is his face, so close and so strikingly symmetrical, and his eyes, which I now realise see right through my spineless, jellyfish soul, and his hand, so warm and firm and vicious, closing in harder, rubbing against my cock with his palm, and that's all it takes for the blood to vacate my brain and my heart and every fucking organ except my greedy dick, which swells immediately, impossibly, in his grip.

'So you don't like it when a man touches you,' he insists, and *like?* What does *like* even mean, because it has nothing in common with this dizzying, all-consuming ache as the heel of his palm locates and grinds against my crown with the cruelest precision.

'I'—*fuck*—'I...'

'Thought not,' he agrees, and for a hideous, infinitesimal moment I think he'll withdraw that blessed pressure, that he'll call my bluff and deny me, which would be even more humiliating than him busting me in the first place.

But he doesn't. He leans right in so his breath whispers along my jawline and teases my earlobe, and his entire hand, heel and palm and fingers working in sync, rubs at my once delusional and now, *so swiftly*, traitorous cock.

'You didn't like it when you sucked my thumb like a fucking rent boy, did you?' he croons. I wouldn't be capable of answering him even if I wanted to, which I absolutely do not. Thankfully, and also mortifyingly, my body seems to be giving him all the answer he needs.

My head hits the wall with a thwack, and my eyes roll back in my head, and I want him to rub me, abrade me, like this forever with the seam of my boxer briefs chafing against the tender flesh of my crown and my own humiliation roaring in my ears.

His words roll on, callous and dismissive, and I know they'll haunt me for the rest of my days. 'You didn't like it when you watched me stroking my cock, did you, or when I bit your lip, and you didn't like it when I fucked your mouth with my tongue, and you definitely didn't think about what it would feel like if I stuck my dick in there instead, did you?'

I groan at that, thrusting my hips into his grip, desperate

for as much friction as he'll give me. 'Please,' I moan brokenly, not knowing what I'm begging for. *'Please.'*

He pauses at that, stops rubbing, stops talking. He lifts his head and looks at me, and I stare back at a face I already know I'll never be capable of erasing from my mind, no matter how hard I try.

'*Please* what?' he asks, and his voice is softer, more openly curious, stripped of its acerbity, its mercilessness.

I freeze.

He waits.

This is it. This is fucking it. There's no going back from here. I'm rewriting my future with four words, and I don't care, because I don't care about anything in the world right now except making this ache go away.

I open my mouth. 'Please make me come.'

53

DEX

Time stops, but I'm not even embarrassed, because I'm too fixated on calculating the odds that he'll do as I ask. There's a twenty percent chance he pulls down my flies and jerks me off with ruthless, angry strokes, I estimate, and an eighty percent chance he laughs in my face.

After all, it would be the perfect revenge. Arouse me into confessing that I'm a cowardly little bullshitter and then walk off and leave me, hard and leaking, humbled and mortified, in my place of work.

His face clears, and he looks for all the world like a proud parent whose kid has *finally* figured how to pee in the fucking potty. 'All you had to do was ask,' he says softly, before releasing my cock and sliding my zip down slowly, carefully over my swollen dick.

The sound I make when his fingers find my bare, taut skin through the flap in my boxer briefs is shuddering and shameful and fragile and raw, and I'm powerless to stop it, because *Max has my dick in his hand* and I'm trembling with the beautiful, wondrous, disbelief of it all.

'I don't make a habit of doing this,' he says. His tone is conversational, but he's watching my face closely, and for a moment I think he'll kiss me. 'I don't make a habit of it *at all*, in fact, so you'd better appreciate it.'

I don't quite understand what he's getting at until he proceeds to drop elegantly to one knee, and then to both, his hand still a warm seal around my shaft.

'Oh my God,' I say. 'Oh my God. You don't—I didn't—'

'I know,' he says, and I cannot describe the experience of having him look up at me through his lashes, his lips a couple of inches from my tip. I know it's all wrong, that I should be the one kneeling at his feet right now and begging his forgiveness and showing him how laughably deluded I was, but his tongue slices through my slit, reaping my precum as it does, and my dick is flooded, literally *flooded*, with searing heat of the most amazing kind.

I groan again, deeply, the sound rolling up from my belly, as involuntary as breathing and the only outlet I have for this overwhelm. In response, he grips me tightly, far more tightly than Darcy did or would, I suspect, have dared. Women have a healthy respect for the fragility of this most critical of organs, I've found, but it seems men don't share that.

Max certainly doesn't, manhandling my dick in a manner that could charitably be called *robust* and uncharitably *vicious*. He squeezes; he rifles between my dick and my zip for my balls, and I swear some fabric rips.

He jerks my dick upwards, pinning it against the cold of my belt buckle as he buries his nose in the underside, sniffing hard and murmuring something unintelligible that I understand to be the basest sort of compliment. Then he licks long and hard along my vein before grazing his teeth over my crown so harshly I break out in full-body goosebumps.

And all the while I'm in survival mode, gasping and thrashing and riding out this wet, hot, carnal onslaught, taking every lick of his tongue, every drag of his teeth, every perfect slide of his lips, and, finally, every deep suck he sees fit to bestow upon me.

My world is blanketed in a man's warm, relentless mouth, and the rest of the universe can implode into subatomic matter, for all I care. I can't not touch him. I grab at his face with both hands, palms closing over his ears, my fingers clawing at his short, silky hair and earning a pleased, muffled grunt.

It seems inconceivable and yet inevitable that his mouth is as soft, as velvety, as yielding as Darcy's, even if his technique is anything but. Even less comprehensible, more wondrous, is that *the mere fact of it being him* has me deranged with arousal.

Forget that the man knows how to wield his mouth like a weapon.

It's just him.

Having him here.

Having him do this.

Having him *want* to do this.

It's the best porn I've ever, ever seen.

I'm rutting into his mouth, my orgasm building from my feet upwards, spreading like I'm walking into a sea of molten lava. I release his head—there is no place in this time-space continuum where Max Hunter swallows—and tilt my head back, squeezing my eyes closed and interlacing my fingers behind my neck as I brace for what I know will be total fucking annihilation.

'I'm close,' I pant. 'I'm so close. Jesus, you've got to—you can move—'

But he harrumphs his displeasure at that idea and keeps sucking, his soft, strong lips a perfect seal around my shaft, his tongue laving me with indecent gusto.

Behind my tightly shut eyes, the black turns purple and orange and red. Angry colours. Violent colours. My toes curl in their sensible loafers. The trembling of my entire body could register on the Richter scale. My fingernails threaten to draw blood on the back of my neck, and I rupture one of my nearly-healed blisters with my teeth. The sour tang of blood is nothing, though, because my body ignites as though Max has doused me in petrol and tossed a lit match at me, and if this is how Hell feels, count me in.

Count me *fucking* in.

He works me through my orgasm with the ruthlessness of one who will be personally affronted if he doesn't wring me human jerky-levels of dry. And when I'm softening and pulsing in his mouth, he cleans me with his tongue. I stare down at him, shattered and reborn, as he sits back on his heels and carefully tucks me in.

It's only when he's zipped me up and got to his feet that he looks me in the eye. 'How do you feel?' he asks with the detached concern of a drill sergeant who's watched you puke your guts up from exertion and wants to make sure you've got it all out of your system before he sends you on your way.

I laugh a little, because it's impossible to articulate how I feel, physically or emotionally. 'I don't know. Devastated. Euphoric. Fuck knows.'

He's hard, though. I know that much. Really, really hard, like he's got a rolling pin stuck down those impeccably tailored trousers.

'Do you...' I ask, gesturing feebly at his crotch. I don't know what I'm asking, and I certainly don't know if I'm remotely capable of following up on any implied favour I may propose.

Amusement flashes across his otherwise deadpan face. No one knows better than Max how pathetically ill-prepared I'd be to deliver on that vaguest of offers. 'The only thing I want you to do is process,' he tells my mouth, and I find myself wishing he would kiss me, even once. I want him to brush his dick-swollen lips over mine. I want to taste myself on him.

'Process,' I repeat stupidly.

'Process.' He taps my temple. 'Tell yourself some hard facts. Meanwhile, you're going to go and splash some cold water on your face, and I'll sit here and have a gander at this research—if my gut is right, it should cure me of any residual hard-on by around page five.'

I laugh a little. 'I'm confident it'll deliver,' I say shakily.

'Good. Take your time. I'll be gone when you get back—I can see myself out.'

I nod, deflating more quickly than an unknotted balloon. I feel needy and squirmy and flayed wide open.

'Oh, and Dex.' He smooths an errant lock of hair away from his face, and I find myself wishing I had thought to do that for him. 'I'll tell Darcy you're recovering from your little hissy fit. Come and have dinner with us on Friday night at mine. I'll send you the details.' He turns and picks up the weighty research report, pulling out the chair his jacket is strewn over.

I hesitate, watching him sit gingerly down and cover his erection with the report.

He looks up, eyebrow arched, and sighs. 'It's not a request.'

54

DARCY

DEX

I am so unutterably sorry for not replying to your lovely messages. It had nothing to do with you, but it makes me feel sick that I caused you doubt. I hope you can forgive me. For what it's worth, I haven't stopped thinking about you all week. You are incredible and I feel so honoured to have had that experience with you. I can't wait to see you on Friday xox

Thank you. I needed to hear that. Roll on Fri xx

It feels like my sister has been away for years, when it's only been a month. I've been excited to see her, obviously, mainly to catch up and hear all the goss from the honeymoon. But this past week I've felt as though my

world has been crumbling to pieces and I just need a hug from my big sis, dammit.

Dex's text yesterday made me tear up with relief, which is a bit pathetic, but honestly. That guy put me through the wringer. Max had already called me to tell me he'd "made him see sense", so the text wasn't completely out of the blue, but when Max came over to my place last night I couldn't believe the story that came out of his mouth.

"Made him see sense" isn't code for "gave him a blowjob at his place of work" in any reality I know, but it's given me real hope for the first time since Dex left me on read last Thursday—and all the days after. Because Max and I may not have admitted it to each other in so many words, but we're both insanely attracted to him, and I feel something for him, too.

Don't ask me what, but he tugs at my heartstrings (and my lady parts). It's probably stupid to say, because I'm sure every single human who crosses paths with him falls hard, but after what we did last week, I can't stop thinking about him. Can't stop remembering how it felt to have him lie on top of me and move inside me. The way his dark hair fell over his eyes. The shadows on his face as he came, like he was learning something new about himself.

I definitely didn't realise quite how many new things he'd learnt about himself that night, and I have to admit, I'm really fucking glad Max called him out on everything. That could have gone horribly wrong—Max is so impatient, and so intolerant. His riding roughshod all over poor Dex's Big, Scary Feelings could have been an absolute disaster.

I guess he found a better way of using his mouth to, erm, persuade Dex than by bawling him out.

Fuck, I wish I'd been a fly on the wall to see him undoing Dex. It must have been crazy levels of hot.

So, yeah, I'm feeling a bit more hopeful now that Dex has sent me that lovely text. I've only read it about fifty times. (Maybe sixty.) Still, the balance has now swung away from my worries that Gen will kill me—and Max—when she hears what I've been up to and in favour of getting some sisterly advice.

She and Anton got back last night, and I'm sure she'll have a tonne of work to catch up on, but I bet I can persuade her to grab a bite to eat. I'll rope Maddy into my plans too, and she can help coerce Gen if need be.

My sister looks revoltingly, stunningly tanned. Her skin is a dark, even gold and her hair is platinum and, in her ice-pink linen sheath dress, she's easily the most gorgeous and elegant woman in the Dover Street Arts Club today.

I suspect she's also the happiest. You could see her glow from space.

Maddy's dressed down in skintight grey Varley yoga pants and a cute pink cropped t-shirt. I'm pretty sure she's flouting the dress code, but I don't see any of the businessmen around us complaining. And I'm in an easy sherbet-yellow maxi dress that I've totally failed to iron, but no one is looking at the creases, because it's my boobs' best friend.

Yep. We're definitely the most interesting people in here.

Gen has given us the rundown of her honeymoon (to recap: sex, food, sailing, sex, food, sailing, rinse and repeat). It sounds like it was incredible.

'It's really nice to know Anton's stepped down, though, isn't it?' I muse. 'He'll have loads more time to spend with you now—maybe that'll make being back a bit easier.'

'You say that,' my sister scoffs, breaking open a bread roll, 'but he's gone into the office this morning. He's got serious IPO FOMO—the man's incorrigible.'

Maddy laughs while I freeze. If Anton's seeing Max today then it's another reason to come clean. No way will Max be able to keep his mouth shut, and my sister needs to hear this from me.

The conversation veers towards Maddy and Zach's wedding, which is happening in Puglia in a month's time. 'It feels so awful not inviting you,' she pouts in my direction, 'but Zach's being really strict about the guest list. I'm so sorry.'

'Don't be ridiculous,' I tell her. 'You've only known me a couple of months. I'd never expect an invitation.' I smile coyly. 'Besides, I've got some stuff going on that's keeping London interesting for me right now.'

Maddy shoots me an excited grin. She thinks she knows what I'm going to say, but she's not remotely up to speed.

'Go on,' Gen says in her best headmistress voice as she cuts a wafer-thin slice of beef carpaccio. The subtext is clear: *think very carefully before you get yourself into trouble.*

I shoot a panicked look at Maddy, who nods encouragingly, and take a deep breath. 'I've been seeing Max.'

Gen's head jerks up. 'Seeing as in...'

'Seeing.' He did take me for lunch that time, after all. Even if I fucked him in his office beforehand.

She frowns. 'I'm going to fucking kill him. I told him to stay away from you.'

'Well, he didn't,' I say. I won't mention his attempt to pay me to dance for him. 'And we're happy.'

That gets her attention. 'Really?' she asks, her voice softer. 'I get it, believe me. He's a ridiculously attractive, charismatic guy. But he's *Max,* you know? Variety is the spice of life for him. Anton says he despairs of him ever settling down. I just don't want him hurting you.'

'I know,' I say. I feel a bit emotional for some reason. 'For what it's worth, I don't think he will.'

'He's really into her,' Maddy volunteers. 'They've seen each other almost every night since he asked—since they got it on. Isn't that right, babes?'

I'm seriously relieved Maddy just didn't throw me under the bus with an accidental mention of his indecent proposal. 'Yeah. He's been really sweet. And... protective.' I think of how angry he's been with Dex for ghosting me. I could never have imagined Max getting so incensed that someone didn't follow through after sex, especially because he's probably done it to a million poor men and women himself.

'Well, that's lovely to hear,' Gen says, cutting into her watercress salad. She says it with feeling, but I suspect she's not totally convinced. Not yet, anyway.

'There's something else,' I say, my gaze flitting between the two of them. 'It's pretty crazy, and I don't know what to make of it, but it's driving me absolutely insane, and I need some advice.'

That gets their attention. They both set their cutlery down on their plates and stare at me expectantly. Maddy's grinning—she's the biggest gossip I know.

'This is really, really confidential,' I tell her specifically. 'You can't tell Belle—I mean it.'

She screws up her pretty little nose. 'Belle? What the heck does Belle have to do with it?'

'Do you promise or not?' I demand, pointing my knife at her.

She puts both hands up in surrender. 'Promise.'

My sister is watching me with a look of mild terror.

'Okay.' Here goes. 'I had sex with Dex last week. Belle's brother,' I add, in case my sister's unclear, though I'm assuming she met him at Belle and Rafe's wedding.

Gen's eyes go wide. Maddy's reaction is less circumspect —she gasps theatrically enough that a few people at the surrounding tables look around.

'You are fucking kidding me,' she hisses, pressing her hand to her chest. 'Does Max know? Oh my God, was it amazing? Was he good? And again—does Max know?'

I grimace. 'Max may have been... there.'

My sister's face is a picture. Maddy pretends to swoon, then pushes her chair back so hard it almost falls over and rounds the table, engulfing me in a massive hug. She pulls away and squeals, 'Oh my God! Oh my God! You had a threesome—'

'Shh!' Gen interjects, because we really don't need any more attention on our table right now. 'Keep it down.'

Maddy backs away from me, giggling as she returns to her chair. 'You had a threesome with Max and Dex?' she asks in a stage whisper. 'You fucked the two hottest guys in London, basically—you lucky, lucky bitch!'

I may, at this point, allow myself a smug little giggle, because it's honestly a ridiculous situation and I am indeed the luckiest little bitch-whore who ever lived—as long as Dex doesn't freak out and run for the hills again.

'Right?' I say to her, and then I point my finger at my sister. 'And before you say anything, Genevieve, I'd like to remind you that people in glasshouses shouldn't throw stones.'

Her mouth twists. 'I absolutely agree. But are you okay? That's all I care about.'

I sigh and put my elbows on the table. 'I'm not gonna lie. It's been a whole thing. But yeah, I'm okay. I think.'

'Tell us every disgusting detail,' Maddy demands. 'Because I can't work out how the fuck you pulled that off. I'm sorry—*Dex Scott in a threesome?* There's no fucking way.'

And so I tell them. I tell them how crazily attracted I was to Dex when I met him that night at drinks with Maddy and the gang. How I came clean to Max, and the look on his face when I showed him Dex's photo. How I begged Dex via text to come and watch me dance, and how Max agreed to help me lure him backstage afterwards (my sister definitely isn't happy when she hears that, but I know what I confess next will blow her no-fraternisation rules out of the window).

I tell them, in broad strokes, how the evening went down, that Dex seemed pretty happy with me and not at all comfortable with Max... until I caught them kissing as I finished Dex off in the shower.

By this point, Maddy has her face in her hands and is drumming her feet on the shiny floor. 'I can't bear it. I think you've broken my brain. Could you not have had the decency to sell tickets? I can't *believe* I missed it!'

'It wasn't exactly an open invitation,' I point out, but I get it, because Max and Dex naked and wet and kissing... it was pretty fucking special. I stand by my not-a-joke screensaver comment from the other night.

My sister is frowning. 'So Dex is bi? I hadn't realised.'

I laugh, but there's no mirth in it. 'Funny you should mention that. So, no, according to him, he's not, and he basically had an almighty freakout right after and ran off. He's given me the cold shoulder all week, and I got upset...' I trail off at the pissed-off purse of Gen's lips, because I really don't want her to hunt Dex *or* Max down and bollock either of them.

'Fuck,' Maddy says. 'He must have been going crazy, though. I mean, he's a lovely guy, but he's pretty square, you know? He looked seriously uncomfortable the other night at drinks, so I can't even imagine what must've been going through his head when Max grabbed him and kissed him.'

'Believe me, he was into it at the time,' I say. 'I was right there. But I'm sure when his orgasm wore off he got pretty stressed.'

Maddy grimaces. 'Yeah, that's a lot of reality to be hit over the head with. So he's MIA, is he?'

I glance at my sister. 'Not anymore. Max went and... had it out with him yesterday at work.'

'And by *had it out*...' Gen murmurs.

I look around quickly before miming a blowjob using my fist, my tongue and my cheek. Classy, nope, but it gets the message across. Their jaws drop open.

'Fuck,' Gen says, sitting back in her chair.

'I'm dying.' Maddy picks up the cocktail menu and proceeds to fan herself. '*Dying*, do you hear me? Dex, Dex, Dex. What would Daddy say? Well, I think that answers your question about whether he's bi, Gen. This is going to make their dad shit a fucking brick.'

'That's why you need to keep it quiet,' I hiss. 'He needs to tell Belle himself in his own time, if at all, okay? This isn't my secret to tell. And, from what Max says, he's got a hell of a lot of stuff to figure out before he even thinks about coming out.'

'Where does that leave the three of you?' Maddy wonders.

'Not sure. But Max has basically summoned him for dinner on Friday at his place.'

'Dinner.' She laughs. 'Nice euphemism.'

'Here's hoping,' I say, shimmying my shoulders, because the idea of getting those two guys to myself again without an epic meltdown from Dex has me all kinds of hot and bothered. 'Oh, and he sent me this yesterday. After Max—you know—sorted him out.'

I unlock my phone and show them my message from Dex.

Gen gives a little smile. 'Well, that's lovely.'

'Lovely?' Maddy demands. 'You should frame it. If only he'd sent it a few days ago, he'd be perfect.'

He would.

But he's not far off.

55

DEX

How is a man to reconcile himself with a lifetime of subterfuge in four short days? To sift through the layers of denial and misrepresentation, prevarication and obfuscation, like an archaeologist searching for a rumoured needle in a historically priceless haystack?

Cataloguing feels a far too rigorous science for the countless ephemeral feelings and fleeting desires I've experienced and disavowed over the years. Attempting to analyse, let alone label, the messy, sometimes sickening instincts that have skittered sinfully over the edge of my consciousness would be as efficient, as helpful, as trying to catch a ghost with a net and a jar.

I suspect labelling is overrated.

Because, among all the half-truths I force myself to confront in the hours and days that follow my unthinkable coupling with Max, one truth stands proud and inviolable when I gaze at my exhausted reflection in the mirror:

I came in the perfect mouth of an exacting, magnetic man, and it was the realest moment of my life.

By Wednesday, I break and call my sister. God knows, if anyone has taught themselves to navigate the perilous waters that lie between the lands of objective truth and subjective morality, it's Belle.

'I really need your advice on something,' I say, fully and guiltily aware that she'll drop any plans she has for me. 'Any chance you're free tonight?'

'Oh,' she says, and there's a pause. 'There's—could you come to the club? It's Diamond Night. Darcy's dancing. It'll be amazing.'

The only part of that sentence I care about is that Darcy's dancing. That works, as long as Max isn't there.

Will he be there?

Shit.

'We could have a drink in the bar first,' she says. 'Would that suit?'

A heart-to-heart with my sister and a chance to see Darcy. To say hi, to make amends, no matter how fleetingly, before Friday.

'Yeah,' I say. 'Thanks. That suits.'

It turns out Diamond Night at Alchemy is an excuse for the patrons to bedazzle themselves in crystals and as little fabric as possible. My sister has her shapely bump encased in a long, cream dress with diamond-encrusted straps and a slash so far up her thigh I'm amazed Rafe has let her out of his sight. In fact, I'm sure I'm the only guy in the entire club he'd let lead his pregnant wife away to a relatively quiet corner of the bar.

Which is exactly what I do once I've said hello to everyone. The women look sensational, I have to admit, and the amount of bling on show has me almost blinded, and Aida has persuaded Cal to wear a stretchy, sparkly headband in his floppy hair, making him look like a brunette Jack Grealish.

Maddy greets me with a huge hug and a wink as she asks if I've come to see Darcy, so I guess the sooner I fill Belle in, the better. I don't want to keep my sister away from her friends or the fun, but fuck if this isn't a big conversation to wrap up in twenty minutes.

'Is everything okay?' she asks as she sinks down next to me on the velvet sofa.

'I don't know,' I say. 'Look no one's dying, but I need relationship advice—more like life advice, really.'

She visibly brightens, flicking her sheet of dark blonde hair over her shoulder. 'Ooh, exciting! And you've only been back a few weeks. Nice work.'

'Don't congratulate me yet,' I say drily. 'I've got myself into a bit of a situation. But you should know, between you and me, that I'm kind of... something happened with Darcy, and I like her. A lot.'

'Ohmygod,' she says in a rush, gripping my forearm. 'That's so amazing! I'm so happy for you both—she's so nice! And so, so gorgeous.'

'Yeah.' I laugh weakly. 'She's both of those, and more.'

'So what's the problem?' she asks. 'You're keeping it in the Alchemy family. I love it.'

You have no idea.

'The situation is... complicated,' I say, watching her face carefully. 'Because of Max.'

Her face falls. 'Oh, shit. Of course. Woah—so Darcy's sleeping with both of you? That's not good.'

'It's not quite that simple.' I take a deep breath. *Fuuuu-*

uck. 'Something may have happened between him and me, too.'

It takes a moment to sink in, and when it does she claps both hands over her face and inhales sharply. 'Wait—the three of you are...'

'Kind of.' I say. 'I don't know. It's very early days.'

I fill her in with broad brushstrokes that are as asexual as is humanly possible when narrating a threesome, sticking to the events and my main emotional reactions (horror, all-consuming desire, horror, in a nutshell).

I tell her that I dodged Darcy's messages, which has her screwing her face up with the effort of not bawling me out.

And then I tell her about Max. How he ambushed me with a full-on meeting before insisting on coming back to my office.

I tell her something happened.

Broad brushstrokes, right?

I don't tell her how I folded like a cheap deckchair as soon as he cupped my dick in that infuriatingly entitled, know-it-all style of his.

Nor do I tell her how I abandoned all decorum, all pretence, and begged him to make me come.

I don't describe how it felt to have him take me in his mouth—like the earth had shifted on its axis.

I suspect I don't need to. I suspect it's as clearly visible on my face as it is audible in my halting prose. And I have my answer in her wide eyes and in the way she reaches for my hand and holds it tightly.

'Holy crap,' she whispers. She doesn't demand salacious details. She just asks, 'And how are you feeling?'

'Fuck knows.' I rest my elbows on my knees and drag my hands over my face before looking at her. 'That's what I'm trying to figure out.'

'And that's why you wanted to chat?'

'Yeah.'

'Wow.' She gazes around the room of happy, laughing people who are most likely secure in their sexuality and then back at me, tucking her hair carefully behind her ear and seemingly choosing her words. 'Can I ask you a question?'

'Sure.'

'Was this your first time... with a guy?'

'Apart from the other night with him and Darcy, yeah.' Even referring to him has my stomach flip-flopping.

She squeezes my hand tighter. 'Was it out of the blue? Or have you wanted to—you know—in the past?'

I sigh. 'He told me to go home and process, said I needed to tell myself some hard facts. So that's what I've been doing—or trying to do. And by far the hardest fact of all is that no, it wasn't out of the blue. I've had thoughts, I suppose, for years.'

I've never admitted that to a living soul before. Not even to myself, really, before this week. And my admission is the blow that fells my sister, because she releases my hand and instead wraps me in a huge, sideways hug.

'I can't bear it for you,' she mumbles into my neck.

'Hey.' I gently disentangle myself. 'Why not? I'm fine.'

Her eyes, when she pulls away, are huge. We've always been told our eyes are similar—we get them from Mum—and hers are limpid with compassion. 'Well you shouldn't be fine. You've had feelings for guys, and God knows how long you've been bottling them up, and it doesn't take a genius to work out why. I'm so fucking gutted for you.'

My sister hardly ever swears—or at least she didn't before she met Rafe—so her F-bomb reflects the full force of her emotion.

'Don't be gutted,' I urge her. 'I've been perfectly happy. That's why I'm so freaked out. I don't need this. It doesn't—'

'It doesn't what?'

'It doesn't fit with what I want for my life,' I confess in a rush.

As the words spill out, I realise they're true.

Unlike the way I've been taught by every adult in my life, from my parents to my priests and teachers at my super-conservative Catholic boarding school, I don't believe homosexuality is a sin or an illness or any of those other despicable, invalidating words they use to scare formative minds away from any kind of sexual or moral exploration.

I have nothing at all against gay people. But clearly I *do* have something against the idea that I might be in any way queer, because I *do* tell myself I'm sinful, shameful, when I have feelings for or reactions to or fantasies about other men.

Homosexuality is fine for other people, but it's not for me. That's the line I've always stuck to. I won't perpetuate hate or bigotry, but I won't colour outside those same lines I've always been taught represent the boundaries of what is good and decent and wholesome.

It's a matter of personal preference.

Belle frowns. 'What do you mean—you mean you want a nice, heteronormative wife-and-kids-type life?'

She doesn't intend it, but I can hear the gentle judgement in her voice. My sister has certainly come a long way in the years I've been gone.

'Well, yeah. What's wrong with that?' It's exactly what she's opted for, at the end of the day.

'Nothing's wrong with that. You'll make a great dad.'

She lays her head on my shoulder, and comfort flares deep within me. There's something about confessing to the person who grew up in the same fucked-up environment as you that's soothing. I don't have to explain my starting points to her. She gets it. It may be a case of the blind leading the blind, but we're together on this voyage of sifting through all the shit we've been told to believe and assessing which of it is real and valid and which of it is utter fucking bullshit.

So her next sentence hits me like a bolt of lightning.

'The thing is, when you say things like that, it kind of sounds like Max, or any other guy, doesn't fit in with what you've been *taught* you should want for your life. And no surprise there, because he'll never make a decent wife.' She clasps my hand again. 'But maybe, just maybe, if you give yourself permission to spend some time thinking about what actually makes you happy rather than what you think you should serve up for Mum and Dad, you'll be surprised at the answers.'

'That sounds complicated,' I manage.

'Really, it's the opposite. Forget about all the theory. What do you want, at the most basic level? What does your heart want? What does your *body* want?'

I make a noncommittal noise, because I'm not sure I trust myself to speak.

'Look,' she says. 'I'm the last person you have to explain yourself to. But I think one of the things that helped me break free from all that crap was that it just felt so good with Rafe, you know? And it got me wondering how something that felt so good, and made me so happy, could be bad.

'There is no institution on earth as capable of overcomplicating things and making them feel ominous and depraved and wrong as the Catholic Church is, or of making up all these endless, ridiculous, godforsaken *rules*. Honestly! It's so crazy.'

'It really is,' I murmur, and she lifts her head from my shoulder. She's grinning, and it's mischievous and charming and sweet as fuck.

'Okay, so I don't want details, because *ew*, but tell me this. When you were with Max, did it give you the ick? Is that why you're spinning out? Or are you spinning out because it blew your mind so amazingly that it was fucking terrifying?'

'Which do you think?' I ask her drily.

Her grin intensifies, and she nudges my shoulder. 'I knew it! Look. You're a smart guy. Just go and have some fun with this, okay? It's all good. Go get all the orgasms. Orgasms are good! Don't discriminate against who's giving them to you.'

I cover my face and pretend to groan. 'Okay, okay. I'm done with this conversation.'

'I'm proud of you.' She plants a light kiss on my cheek before standing up. 'Go have some fun and be outrageous. It's your turn to be the family black sheep for a while.'

56

DARCY

The curtain has well and truly been lifted tonight.

The veil I usually erect between me and the audience, for reasons to do with both technique and mystique is shot to hell, because when I emerge onto the stage for Diamond Night, the first person I lay eyes on is Dex. He's standing by himself at the front of the crowd, all in black, tumbler in hand.

He's grinning right at me, and even in the dim light I can tell his grin carries none of the circumspection from our first meeting or the anguished uncertainty from our hookup the other night.

It's a really great grin—though it might have something to do with the fact that I'm wearing a diamanté thong and what's basically a Victoria's Secret Fantasy Bra gone porno.

No bodystocking tonight.

Just barely-there, glittering underwear, heels and an enormous white feather boa made from the most lavish plumes. (Note to my sister: this is what you get when you give Cal too much creative licence with his events.)

I shoot him as big a smile as I can without ruining my

carefully crafted aura of mystique for the rest of the crowd, and I let myself go to the music. It's more upbeat tonight. Diamond Night should be called Diamond Disco, if the music is anything to go by.

I let rip to an epic remix that goes from *Atomic* to *I Feel Love* to *Young Hearts Run Free*, and I can tell you right now, my moves put Mercutio's to shame. The audience goes crazy, and it's impossible not to get swept up in the infectious atmosphere. I play up to the adulation like the queen that I am, the strobe lights slicing my movements, my poses, into a series of fleeting tableaux and lending the room, with its pulsing, grooving audience, a trippy feel.

Even better, I get enough glimpses of Dex to know he's a seriously good dancer. Bro's got moves. Not that I didn't know that—the memory of him moving inside me with gorgeous, rolling thrusts flashes through my mind—but he looks seriously sexy down there with the top few buttons of his black shirt unbuttoned and his sleeves rolled up.

He's going for it with Cal and Aida, who've materialised next to him. But *he's here for* me. *He's smiling at* me. And I hope to God he's waiting for me to finish.

I wrap my set up to wolf whistles and cat calls and applause, treating the audience to a little wink and a shimmy of my thong-clad bottom before chucking the feather boa straight at Cal. He catches it and gleefully wraps it around himself, earning an eye roll from Aida. And when I wave goodbye to the crowd, my skin slick with sweat and my legs trembling from my exertions, Dex is already rounding the stage.

I FALL on the door of my dressing room as soon as I hear the knock.

It's him, and by God he looks dishevelled and good enough to eat, that dark hair hanging over one eye and a light dusting of chest hair visible in the V of his shirt. The grin he gives me is a lot less confident than the one he shot me out in The Playroom. I suppose he's not sure how warm a reception he'll get given his ghosting stunt.

'Hey,' I say, resisting the urge to climb him like a tree.

'Hi,' he says. 'Can I come in?'

'Sure.' I stand back and close the door behind him. This room is small enough that his presence fills it, and the intimacy only increases when he looks my practically naked body up and down with a hunger that's frankly astounding, because I've had it in my head since Monday that Dex's brain would be full of Max, Max, Max and not much else.

'You look fucking incredible,' he says, dragging his orgasm-inducing eyes up from my boobs to my face with visible effort.

I smile coyly, never one to resist a compliment. 'Thanks.'

He takes a step closer. 'I want to say sorry, but—do you think I can hold you while I do?'

'Okay,' I say. I'm really sweaty, but it looks like he is, too. Besides, I'm wearing a fucking diamond-studded demi-cup with my nipples sitting prettily on top of it, so I figure he wins out, sweat or no sweat.

He hooks both arms around my waist and tugs me against him, running his fingertips up the groove in my spine. I look up at him—I've kicked my heels off so I need to crane my neck. His eyes are hooded. Haunted.

'Leaving you hanging like that after the other night was despicable,' he whispers. 'I'm a complete twat, and I've been beating myself up so much. I just—I was so busy getting my knickers in a twist about the whole thing that my solution was to bury my head in the sand and pretend it never happened.'

My eyes widen, because it physically hurts to hear that statement, but he backtracks.

'Fuck—I didn't mean... *Jesus*. Okay, let me start again.' His hands are still moving over my damp skin. I need to put a robe on or get in the shower before I get cold, but I don't want to move. 'Every single second with you was incredible,' he says. 'All of it. The bed. The shower. The things you let me do to you. It's no exaggeration to say it was the most incredible night of my life by a million miles. Do you understand?'

I nod, relief coursing through me. He wraps me up tighter, dipping his head lower till it feels like he might kiss me, and I wind my arms around his neck. It feels so, so good to be this close to him. My nipples are pressing against his shirt, his heat a balm to my rapidly chilling body.

'But the stuff with, um, Max was'—he chokes out a laugh—'a fucking can of worms the like of which I've never had to deal with, and when I tell you it sent me into a shit-spiral all week... I was far too busy freaking out and being in denial that I didn't take care of your needs, and I'm so, so sorry. I know that night was a big deal for you, too, and you handled the whole thing so much better than I did, and I'm thoroughly ashamed of myself.'

I consider my response. 'I know you were freaking out. It was pretty obvious from the way you left, and that's why I wanted to check in. But I needed some reassurance, too, that you didn't hate me for my part in it.'

Because no girl wants to be a part of someone's memory from hell, no matter how liberated they are, and no matter how much of a confident, sassy front they put on on stage.

So when a guy comes inside your body twice and then leaves you on read for days and days, it's hard not to take it personally and it's *really* hard not to feel stupid and clingy.

'I could never hate you, and I could never have asked for you to be more perfect than you are. You did nothing wrong. I'm a grown man, and my reaction to Max wasn't anything to do with you. I'm still kicking myself for walking out and not looking after your needs properly, and he quite rightly had a go at me for that.'

I twist my mouth at his reference to Monday, because all the spiralling I've done over his perceived rejection of me morphed into pretty full-on obsessing over his and Max's dynamic once I heard what had happened between them. And get this—I haven't even had major details from Max.

It's almost like what went down is too sacred for him to divulge, even with me. And while I'm pleasantly surprised that Max has that much respect for Dex, and for whatever dynamic is between them, it scares the shit out of me, too.

Because Max and I are great together.

Dex and I are great together.

But I can't compete with the kind of forbidden fruit Max may well represent to Dex or with the extreme challenge Dex clearly is to Max.

Dex is *that guy.* I don't have to have known him long to understand that. It's so obvious he's the one everyone would have fallen for at school. At uni. In New York. He's so staggeringly beautiful, so anguished and soulful and mysterious.

He's the guy you lose your heart to.

And while I accept his apology, and I truly believe he didn't mean to hurt me, I know exactly how capable he would be of unconsciously hurting anyone who got close to him if they let him.

Because he's quite simply devastating, even if he has no fucking clue.

Especially because he has no fucking clue.

So I stand here, and I gaze at him, my heart hurting, and I wonder how someone as sweet and genuine as him can be potentially so lethal.

'Say something,' he pleads, and I shake my head like I'm scared to let it all out.

'Where does all this leave me?' I ask, which is the bottom line, really. I could ask him how he feels about getting seriously intimate with Max. I could ask him if he's any closer to figuring out his sexuality or admitting truths about himself. But I'm wrung out from my performance, and I'm wrung out just from seeing him, to be honest, and I don't have the energy to be anything other than self-serving right now.

'That depends on you,' he says, releasing me so he can reach over and grab my big fluffy robe. 'Here, you're getting cold. Put this on.' He drapes the robe around me and ties it for me, and says, 'You being warm is more important than me getting an eyeful,' and his grin as he says it is so damn sweet.

I love that he noticed I was cold, and I like that he's put my robe on me, because it makes me feel less vulnerable.

'What do you mean, it depends on me?'

'I mean the ball's in your court. I know it might not be clear from my abysmal behaviour, but I am very, very into you. I didn't walk in here last week thinking I had the remotest chance with you—I thought Max well and truly had his claws into you. But I was all in as soon as he told me you were interested.' He gives a little laugh. 'I'm honestly not sure I've ever wanted anyone as much as I wanted you the other night, or as much as I want you right now.'

I suspect that's a half-truth. I suspect he hasn't wanted any other *women* as much as me. There's no way I can compete with Max in this moment, but maybe it's not a competition. Maybe Dex isn't thinking about choosing right now. To be honest, I don't want to raise it. I don't want to force his hand. I just want him to kiss me.

'I want you just as much,' I whisper, and he dips his face to mine and brushes his perfect, perfect mouth over my lips.

'Is it okay to kiss you?' he asks. 'Without Max here, I mean?'

Is he for fucking real? 'I don't recall him speed-dialling me before he wrapped his mouth around your dick,' I retort a little more feistily than I mean to, and he recoils.

'Fuck. I never thought about that. Not for one second. He was so—it was so intense, and I was so busy obsessing over how I was betraying myself that it never occurred to me we were betraying you.'

Well, that's wrong on so many levels I barely know where to start.

'Max and I aren't like that,' I tell him. 'We're not super formal. We're just... fucking.'

He frowns. 'But you've spent every night with him recently, haven't you?'

Yeah. I suppose I have. I shrug. 'What I mean is we haven't had that conversation. So it's fine. He can blow you and I can kiss you. It's all good. But it makes me sad when you say you felt you were betraying yourself. That's awful, Dex. Did you not enjoy it?'

He does that unhappy little laugh again, rubbing my back through my robe. 'I enjoyed it so much my soul left my body.'

'Well then,' I say softly, 'maybe that means you were finally honouring yourself. What do you think?'

He groans. 'I think I have so much work to do on myself it terrifies me.'

'You know what I think? I think I should come over later on Friday. I think you and Max need some time alone together to figure stuff out when he's not blindsiding you in the shower or ambushing you in your office. Hmm?'

His face falls. 'But I want you there. I'm scared of seeing him—I was counting on you being there.'

'I'll be there,' I say. 'Later. I promise. But if you're scared of seeing him then I can't be some kind of buffer. You need to spend some time together when you're not feeling vulnerable and defensive. Give him a chance. He's so amazing.'

'If you promise you'll turn up at some point,' he says, feathering my jaw with kisses. 'I want it to be the three of us.'

'I promise,' I say again. I really want this talk to be done so he can kiss me, dammit. But I have one more thing I have to get out, because Dex is damaged and scared, and he's on the defensive. He's already given me ample proof that he's not thinking about how his actions might go over with us. 'But listen to me, okay?'

'What is it?' he murmurs against my neck.

'Just give us both a chance,' I say. 'Don't armour up too much. This all works both ways—you're not the only one with skin in the game, you know?'

He lifts his head so he can look me in the eye. 'Oh, God. I know. And I'm so fucking sorry, angel. I'm still kicking myself. I won't hurt you again if you give me another chance, I promise.'

I cup his dear, beautiful face in my hands so I can make sure he's paying attention. 'I wasn't just talking about me,' I say, and I catch the flare of shock and, I think pleasure, in his astonishing eyes when my words hit home.

57

MAX

The yoghurt, salted last night and left to leak through a muslin for the past twenty-four hours, is now labneh, rich and delicious and adorned with lemon zest and crushed pistachios and torn mint leaves.

The aubergine, charred to within an inch of its life over the industrial-grade hob in this fancy kitchen until it was a pulpy, smoky mess, is now shot through with tahini and crushed garlic to form the most delectable moutabel.

The tabbouleh is prepped and heavy with fragrant herbs. I'd forgotten how conducive the dicing of endless vegetables is to a quiet mind.

The excellent Lebanese red is aerating in its decanter. The tiny roast potatoes are crisp and thyme-encrusted. The fish won't need more than five minutes under the grill to render it tender and flaking.

Everything looks to be in order as I glance around the kitchen. Which is good, because I want this evening to be perfect. I've been at home since five, taste-testing and tweaking garnishes and faffing endlessly. So when the intercom finally sounds, it's a rush of relief and a burst of adrenalin all at once.

'Send him up,' I tell the doorman, and then he's knocking, and I'm walking—striding—to the door, and he's here.

And he's flawless, even with the violet shadows that sully the fine skin under his eyes and hint at the toll I may have taken on him. Even then, he's faultless.

There's no obvious way to greet someone like him when your last encounter was like ours was. I mean to approach him like I would a skittish, traumatised rescue puppy. No sudden movements. Don't invade his personal space. Show him he's safe with you.

Easier said than done, given my past form with him.

'Good to see you, mate,' is what I go with, accepting the bottle of champagne he's brought and resisting the urge to touch him.

Mate.

So laughably inadequate.

I lead the way through to the main living area, trying not to look at him. Trying not to take my fill of those eyes and that hair and his fucking ramrod straight posture and the easy, athletic way he moves his body.

'Bloody hell,' he says, stopping and staring at my flat. 'This is insane.'

'Yeah,' I agree. 'Perk of the new job.'

'Did you just move in?'

'Few weeks ago. It's bland as fuck—I'm well aware.'

'But the views are incredible.' He stands and takes in the vista of Hyde Park on a hazy summer's evening, and I stand behind him and take him in.

He's all the view I need, and I'm nervous as hell.

'So, Darcy's coming later, is she?' he asks, hands in

pockets as he turns away from the view, reluctantly, it seems. I'll take him out to the terrace for our aperitifs.

I'll do anything he wants.

'She is. She wants to give us some time to chat first.' *She wants me to have some time to sink my claws in and, ideally, for you to locate your backbone.* 'Beer? Champagne?'

'Beer, please,' he says, following me at a safe distance to the bank of sleek black cabinets housing the fridge, freezer, and any number of cupboards.

I grab a couple of bottles of Peroni from the fridge and, having cracked them open, hand him one. We clink. 'Shall we go outside?' I suggest.

He's already chugging his beer down. I stand and gape helplessly at the fine, fine sight of his head cast back, throat working, of the slender, stubbled column expanding and contracting as it does. At the way his upper lip purses around the mouth of the bottle while his lower lip cradles it.

His jeans are faded. His polo shirt may be the kind of white that's worthy of a detergent ad, but I love that he hasn't shaved for me. It's a realer, rawer Dex than the buttoned-up version he presents to the world.

He lowers his beer and bows his head. 'Wait.'

I wait.

When he looks up at me, it's through downcast lashes, and while I know he's not doing it to be coquettish, I wish he fucking wouldn't do it at all.

'I wanted to say, up front that'—he rubs at one of the purple-hued shadows under his eyes and sighs—'I've come here in the spirit of, I don't know, trying. The past couple of times, I've been on the back foot a bit.'

He raises his head and looks me in the eye properly, and I see an unspoken accusation there.

Fair enough.

I nod to show him I understand.

'Anyway, I assumed tonight was a chance for us all to... talk it out, but then Darcy said she'd leave us to it for a bit, and so...' He clears his throat. 'What I mean is, this is... a date, right? I haven't misunderstood?'

I stay very, very still, not really sure how much of a flight risk he is tonight. 'I'd like it to be a date,' I say carefully. 'Very much so. But I'm just glad you're here. And if you'd rather it was a chance to clear the air instead of anything more, that's fine, too.'

Only, if it wasn't a date, I wouldn't have strained the yoghurt for twenty-four hours or risked setting the smoke alarm off by charring aubergine over a naked flame. I would have ordered in from my excellent local Persian restaurant, you twitchy, perfect thing.

'Okay then,' he says, which is the least helpful response ever, because what the fuck does *okay then* mean? *Okay then, you can go ahead and fuck me now we're on the same page*, or *okay then, it's a relief to know my options are wide open.*

But, because I'm me and because someone leaving the tiniest chink of possibility is akin to them throwing the door fully open, I take the pitiful advantage and press it home.

'Have you thought about how you'd like this evening to go?' I enquire. I take a step towards him, putting my beer bottle to my mouth.

He scoffs. 'Do you honestly think I've thought about anything else all week *except* how I'd like this evening to go?'

Who is this forthright guy with his clear, tired eyes and his unforced admissions? What's happened to the slippery little fibber from Monday who couldn't admit a single truth until I clamped a persuasive hand to his dick?

'Is that a fact?' I murmur.

'I'm so tied up in knots I can barely remember a single thing I've done at work this week.'

The realisation of what he's said hits him at the same time as my laughter.

I take another step forward. 'That's very disappointing to hear.'

'I didn't mean *that*.' To his credit, he doesn't back away as I close the space between us. 'Obviously, that's the *only* thing I remember from this week.'

'Which brings me back to my question: how would you like this evening to pan out?'

I stop a couple of steps away from him.

I have no intention of blindsiding him this time.

Everything has to come from him.

I won't have him blaming me for muddying his brain.

'Fuck,' he whispers. He sets down his beer bottle with a trembling hand, its base clattering a little on the marble.

'*Dex.*'

His eyes are wild and huge and troubled and ravenous. It's just me and him in the middle of my kitchen in broad daylight. No shower. No locked office door. No Darcy.

'I haven't worked out what I *ought to* want,' he stammers. 'I have no fucking clue, in fact.' He falters, and I wait. 'But I know what I *do* want.'

I'd call that progress. 'Go on.'

'The other day, after you'd left.' He takes a hurried gulp of his beer and sets the bottle down again, licking his lips. 'I couldn't stop thinking about how your hair had got messed up when you... And I wished I'd had the guts to rake it back into place for you.' He lowers his voice to almost a whisper. 'And I wished I'd had the guts to ask you to kiss me, too, because it was all I could think about afterwards.'

Something tightens in my chest, a physical memento of

how painful it was to keep my emotional distance that day. Having taken something so intimate from him, it felt prudent to stay dispassionate. Stern, almost. He may not be aware of this, but he needed, in that office, to be able to fall apart and know that I had my shit together.

The way he's looking at me, though.

It's as though he might die if I touch him, but he'll definitely die if I don't. He's a droplet of water trembling on a wind-teased leaf, so contained, so impossibly pure and undefiled, yet so fragile. So vulnerable.

It seems to me he's no less conflicted than he's been any other time I've seen him, but there's a courage there, a sort of moral fortitude that's determined to seek out the answers he owes himself rather than defaulting to well-trodden lies and endless prevarication.

I'm the cause of all these troubles—of that I have no doubt—and I want so very much not to be. I want to be a channel for them. I want him to unstitch this toxic cloak of godawful religious bullshit and false virtue and throw it to the ground and let me see him. Let me really, truly *see him*.

Even more than I want to shove him face-down and fuck him into the limestone floor, I want him to lay every last trouble at my feet and let me take them from him, because God knows, I won't let them weigh me down for a second. Sins lie as weightless as feather-down on me.

I'm a selfish man. I take and I push, without thought or remorse, but he makes me want to be selfless, because in this moment I neither want to take nor push him.

I simply want to free him.

I want him soaring and shameless and unleashed.

It works best for him, it seems, when I tell him exactly what to do. He may not know he likes it, but it's what he needs. It removes all the doubt, all the responsibility.

It absolves him.

I gaze at his mouth, at the slick of moisture the beer has left on his bottom lip, at the faintest arc its bottle has impressed above his Cupid's bow, and I marvel that he's met me in the middle of his own accord. Confessed aloud the kinds of desires he would rather have died than admitted to before now.

'Well, you'd better get over here, then,' is all I say.

58

DEX

He's so still. So entirely sure of himself. So commanding, without raising his voice or a finger. And it makes me want to put myself in his hands. Literally. Metaphorically. Emotionally. *Spiritually*, because I will give him my fucking soul if he wants it.

There's a smudge of colour high on his cheekbones, like the sun kissed him very recently, and I wonder how he managed to sunbathe during the work-week.

His forearms are taut, so taut, beneath the rolled-up sleeves of his slubbed linen shirt, and I can't stop myself from wondering how it would feel to have one of them banded around my throat as he tugged on my cock, laughingly and tauntingly and mercilessly.

His eyes are so blue they terrify me, because they possess none of the molasses-soft subterfuge of dark eyes. There's nowhere to hide when those eyes are on you.

And they're on me now, and that stillness is quite extraordinary. I made my move, and he's made his, and now he's waiting for me to raise or fold.

Whether walking straight into his arms is raising or folding, I'm unclear, which seems unwise, reckless even, with the stakes this high.

But walk I do, and I take all of one step before he's rushing forward to meet me, to yank me close, to band that arm around me and plaster me against his hard body, to grip my hair so brutally my eyes prick, and to finally, finally kiss me.

Our kiss in the shower was very specifically that of two people about to shoot their load. This is less angry but by no means less urgent. It's not a slow getting-to-know-you kiss; it's a pressing kiss with lips dragging and teeth clashing and tongues invading and breath coming in hurried gasps and hot, uneven pants.

I'm dizzy with relief at getting my hands on him, because I couldn't remember, *I couldn't fucking remember,* exactly how it had felt when he destroyed my mouth with his tongue or bitten down on my lip.

But this is so much better, because I'm not paralysed with horror or self-loathing or real-time denial. I'm an active participant, giving as good as I get, frantic with need and no fucking clue where to start.

He chuckles into my needy mouth, against my lapping tongue, before breaking our kiss so he can wrench my head to one side, his lever a fistful of my hair. 'You certainly did a one-eighty,' he observes tauntingly, his teeth dragging against my neck as he cups my arse and grinds our dicks together through our trousers, and it is so unspeakably, gloriously arousing that I might come in my boxers like a fucking fifteen year old.

'Can't help it,' I gasp, clawing at his shoulders, wriggling in his arms. 'When you touch me, I nearly pass out.'

It's true. I'm unmoored like this; I am absolutely not in control of my emotions or responsible for my actions. He's frying my brain with his clean-smelling skin and his greedy kisses, and when he puts his capable, confident hands on me, I am dead.

Dead.

I want them to never, ever leave my body.

My own hands are equally desperate. I get one under his shirt and press my palm flush against the arc of his lower back. Of all the things I've mourned this week, one was certainly the wasted opportunity last Wednesday represented. I was naked in a fucking *shower* with him, for God's sake, and I was so busy clutching my pearls that I barely did anything.

I've spent the past few days cataloging those memories, attempting to stuff what's far too ephemeral into a mental treasure chest. But mostly, I just remember fleeting moments.

That astonishing sideways view of his wet body as we stood almost shoulder to shoulder against the tiles, Darcy's hands moving our dicks in tandem and our hips rutting into her touch. The anchor of his thumb on my lip. Inside my mouth. The devastation of his praise. *Just as perfect as I thought.* That's something I know will never leave me.

But none of it was enough, none of it touched the sides of this yawning chasm of need he's conjured within me. So I'll take skin on skin however I can. Wet or dry, I don't care, though *God,* if he was to drag me into a shower, I know I'd never fucking leave.

Happily, he seems to be on the same page. 'Strip,' he orders, pushing away from me and running quick fingers over his shirt, sliding buttons through their buttonholes with elegant efficiency. 'I want to see you strip for me.'

I'm less elegant, less efficient, my motor skills as pathetically compromised as the rest of my brain function, but I cross my arms and pull my polo shirt over my head just as Max slides his shirt off his shoulders. And then it's a flurry of movements, of yanking belt buckles open and tugging at zippers and pushing trousers and boxer briefs down and, in my case, getting my socks off, until we're standing, naked and erect and breathing hard, in the middle of this light-filled room.

I've never wanted anyone like this, where I want every single thing all at once. I want my tongue, his tongue, in every conceivable nook, I want his hands around my dick and pulling my hair and squeezing my arse and pinching my nipples, and I want to do the same to him. It's all-consuming and a little paralysing, this blind fucking hunger, so it's a relief when he, predictably, takes charge.

'Don't move,' he orders. He turns and strides, godlike, across the kitchen, pulling one of the tall cabinets open so hard the bottles stacked on the door shudder and clink. Then he's returning with a large jar in his hand and unscrewing the lid as I gape at lines of muscle that would make Da Vinci ache.

'Coconut oil,' I say faintly. Of course.

'Extra virgin, naturally,' he says with a wink, and I grin despite myself. Evil bastard. But my grin fades when he scoops a load out and smears it between his hands. A step forward has him toe-to-toe with me, so he can reach for my dick with one richly oiled palm and his dick with the other, daubing them with firm, sure strokes that have me instantly making throaty sounds I have no business making as he chuckles at what a total fucking pushover I am.

And then impossibly, wonderfully, he nestles my dick next to his in his palm and I marvel at the heat of him before he closes his hand around us and grabs at the back of my neck. I'm opening for him before he even pushes his tongue into my mouth. I will open up everything, everywhere, for this man, if it means feeling like this and calling his oil-coated hand and cock home.

His hand is as brutal as it was the other day in my office, but his dick is pulsing next to mine and it's all so unctuous, the oil softening the impact of his grip, and I want to die from the sensory sublimity of it all.

He allows me a few strokes like that, indulging my agonised morse-code groans of *ahh-ahh-ahh* into his mouth, and I think he might let me come like this, in the silken grip of his hand with our crowns pressing up against each other's pelvic bones and my fingers clawing at his shoulders, his back, his hair, but instead he releases my mouth and our dicks and I'm hauled across the kitchen with one hand on my shoulder and the other around the jar of coconut oil.

'Brace your hands on the fridge,' he commands, and I want to weep at the joy of it all, because how many times, when I'm close to orgasm and fantasy bleeds into my consciousness, have I wished and prayed for someone to order me to do this so they can use me and defile me and render me utterly fucking useless for anything that's not this?

59

DEX

I shudder as I clap my palms against the black lacquered cabinet hiding the fridge, and it only intensifies when he steps in behind me, *right* in, his chest plastered to my back and his dick rigid between my cheeks and his thighs immovable behind mine. The warmth of his body is spellbinding, and I allow my eyes to drift closed, if only to absorb through my pores all the delights I can't see.

He wraps his arms around me, one a vice around my chest, the other with fingers splayed tight across my lower stomach, and rests his chin on my shoulder, face tilted inwards so his breath skitters across my jawline as his heartbeat thumps against my shoulder blade.

'The things I want to do to you,' he whispers, and it's more confiding than threatening. 'Everything—I want to do everything. I don't know where to fucking start.'

'Do it all,' I tell him. I'm not giving him permission—I'm pleading. I need him to do unto me whatever the fuck he wants, things that are so wicked, so depraved I can't even conceive of them, even while they exist as part of his vernacular.

I want him to show me, and do me, and take my hand, and walk me over the bridge, and let me *see*.

Let me see what I've been denying myself.

He laughs, low and musical, in my ear. 'Brave, foolhardy boy. What if I told you I want to fuck you so hard in that tight little arse I'll split you in fucking two?'

'I'd say,' I begin recklessly, and then recalibrate my risk profile to levels more appropriate for the future wellbeing of my digestive system, 'I'd say, work me up to that, please.'

He laughs again, like his brand-new fuck toy has delighted him, and I laugh with him, mainly from relief that not being able to have his way with me here and now doesn't seem to be a dealbreaker for him.

'How does the idea of my fucking you there make you feel?' he asks, the greased palm on my stomach sliding slickly down to tug lightly on my cock. It jerks in his hand.

'Ahhh.' I let out another groan, as shuddery as it is involuntary. 'I want it—I want it so badly.'

'Has anyone been back there?'

'Only a woman,' I confess shamefully, the gulf between my lived experience and Max's feeling infinite in this moment. 'Her, uh, finger.'

'Okay,' he says, hand burrowing beneath my cock to cup and fondle my balls, and I turn my head closer to his face, because I cannot. I cannot. 'I can work with that. Hang on.'

He pulls away slightly, taking another two-fingered scoop of coconut oil from the jar on the counter, and I mentally remind myself to run for the hills if I ever catch him cooking with that shit. But then those two fingers find the cleft of my arse, and he's rubbing oil the entire way down my crease, all the way to my perineum, and holy fucking Christ, the sensual slide of his fingers as he rubs *that place* has me moaning again and arching back against him, and he laughs like I'm the most amusing plaything on the planet.

Better amusing than pathetic, I suppose.

When his body presses right up against mine, though, I stand straight, my arms braced in front of me. He adopts his previous position: arm around my chest, hand around my cock, and begins to jerk me off as his own cock lies thickly, snugly, in my cleft. I stand there and take it, drinking in every miraculous second of his ministrations, and it's only when I'm shuddering so hard I can barely stand that he pauses.

'Step back. Bend over further.'

Jesus Christ.

I do as he says and he drags his fingertip through my crease until he finds the opening he's looking for, pressing in and breaching it as he finds my cock again with his other hand and begins to pump.

'Holy fucking hell,' he groans. 'You are fucking sinful, you know that? How the fuck can you be this perfect? I'm going to sodomise you every fucking way I know, make no mistake about it.'

His words roll over me like the sickest, most sacred oath I've ever, ever been privy to. The oil is making everything slick and easy and wonderful, but his finger inside me, thicker and stronger and more ruthless than Claudia's, still feels like the filthiest kind of invasion. And when he crooks it and pushes down on my prostate as he makes the strokes of my dick impossibly more vicious, I feel my balls tighten into fucking walnuts as the heat rips through my abdomen like a fire in an oxygen tank.

There's nowhere to go, no way to escape, and I'm writhing beneath his touch, my palms sweating and sliding against the front of the fridge.

'Use your abs like a good fucking boy,' he growls. He sounds as out of control as I feel. His hand is a blur as I stare down at it, that jabbing finger is ruining me from the inside out. And then I'm soaring and cresting and emptying myself all over the immaculate black lacquer of his pretentious new kitchen as he pumps and pumps and pumps.

He catches me once he's happy I'm fully spent, hauling me upwards and spinning me around and pressing me up against the fridge so my arse cheeks meet my ejaculate. And there he captures my mouth in a frenzy of lips and teeth and tongue.

I don't hesitate. I close my eyes against the lightheadedness that comes from shooting my load and straightening up, and I wrap my hand around his beautiful, monstrous cock. The cock I couldn't look away from last week.

It shouldn't feel that different from holding mine, but it does. It's bigger. *Hotter*. Its latent power is more palpable. I wrap my fist around it and look down in awe at the wonderfully raw, ruddy crown, at the way it pulses when I squeeze. My hand finds a rhythm, and my fevered mind reels, and my head hits the cabinet as he leans in to pinch my jaw between his thumb and forefinger, forcing my mouth open, his tongue jabbing inside as it keeps time with his cock.

I'm pleasing him. More than pleasing him, I'm unspooling him, it seems, and pure, sweet pleasure courses anew through my body. I have no idea how, but he's as much putty in my hands as I am in his.

He comes, his tongue in my mouth, his cum painting my stomach, my dick, my thigh, branding me just as he did in the shower that night.

Only this time it's *my* hand around his cock as he shatters.

60

MAX

'Can I interest you in a tea towel?' I ask, watching his face for a reaction, and he laughs. It's a gem of a laugh—genuine, unguarded—and it's a delight to see him like this. He's a man who's had the courage to follow his heart (or his dick, if you prefer), and it's a fucking revelation. He's not pinched or aghast or conflicted or any of the other go-to reactions he holds close.

He allowed himself to come, and he allowed himself to make me come, and he looks all the better for it.

'I'll take a tea towel,' he says, and his sheepishness has me glancing down again at my handiwork with all the pride of a three-year-old who's nailed Jackson Pollock week at nursery. And as he peels his backside off the front of the fridge, his skin separates from the cupboard with an audibly wet noise that has both of us cracking up.

'Was that your cum?' I ask, my hand flexing around the area where his neck meets his shoulder and he nods, biting down on his lip.

'Fucking hilarious,' I say, reluctantly backing away so I can grab the tea-towels hanging off the front of the oven.

'This is what happens when Darcy leaves us to our own devices. We turn into animals.'

I wipe my cum off his front before turning him around and looking after his sticky arse. The mere sight of his taut cheeks and the shadow of his cleft has my dick twitching again. I swipe at it with the tea towel. 'Move.'

His arse has left two nice wet imprints on the cabinet. I rub at them before wiping down the splatters further down and on the floor. Both surfaces are horribly smeared, but I couldn't give a shit.

'Come on,' I tell him, sauntering past and grabbing our beers. 'Shower.'

'I'll just grab a washcloth if that's easier,' he says, traipsing behind me.

'Who said anything about washing?' I ask over my shoulder.

His answering laugh is music to my ears.

So this is how it can be when he's relaxed.

Half-empty beer bottles on the shower's built-in shelf, and me, soaping Dex up, and him leaning against the tiles, surveying me openly, wantonly. Drinking me in. Eye-fucking me, even.

Time is on our side this evening. Darcy's not due for another hour at least and, thanks to the lack of time we wasted in getting each other off, our shower can be leisurely.

'What shall we do with her when she gets here?' I ask him, glossing his delts with suds and musing on the probable cost of having someone's likeness cast in bronze.

He pouts when he's thinking.

I wonder if he knows that.

'Mmm,' he hums luxuriously, letting those golden eyes flicker closed as he considers. 'Fuck her as many times as she'll let us.'

I laugh at the insouciance of a thirty-year-old with all the rounds of ammo a man could need. 'Good start. I need to work on her arse a bit more. I've started warming her up, but... I need to work on both your arses, to be honest. Seriously, if we're going to do this properly, I need inside you both, as soon as possible.'

'Put us both through buttcamp,' he deadpans, and I laugh aloud, throwing my head back, because now that he's done being an uptight little prick, he's pretty fucking funny.

'I'd be extremely careful what I joke about, if I were you,' I say, reaching around him so I can run a couple of menacing fingers between his cheeks. He's still lubed up with coconut oil back there.

'I'm not actually joking,' he says with a cocky little smirk that makes me want to wipe it right off.

'Just be thankful I'm playing a long game here.' I mean it lightly, but he jolts. Turns out, that's enough for him to lose his smirk.

'Does that freak you out?' I ask him.

'No.' He whispers it. 'I'd be freaking out a lot more if I thought this was a one-off.'

The very fact of his chest rising and falling with his breaths is a miracle to me. I need to get a grip. God, the idea of cutting him loose after this is unthinkable, that's what it is. But we've come a long way this evening. Not everything that could be said should be said.

'Your longevity,' I say, swiping my thumb over the wetness of that lower lip that haunts me, 'depends on how skilful your mouth is.'

I've thrown down the gauntlet.

We stare at each other, unblinking.

'You know I'll do anything,' he says, 'but...'

I frown. 'But what?'

'But I want you to make me do it,' he whispers.

I've purposely gone easy on him, because come on. Nothing about his reactions to me before this evening has been straightforward. So it would be gratifying to be sure he wants all this without my pushing him. But I've been too lust-fogged to see the precious gift he's handing to me.

The little beauty *wants me to push him.*

I grab at his hair, at the longer ends that curl over his neck, and yank hard enough to turn us both so I'm leaning against the tiles. I release him and cross my arms below my pecs as I eye him. We're both hard again.

'What the fuck are you waiting for, then?' I jerk my head. 'Go on. Get down there and suck me off, and get yourself off while you're at it. I want you to know how it feels to come when you're choking on my cock.'

I stand there, lips pressed tightly together in a mask of impatient exasperation I do not feel, but when his face contorts I know I've given him his first breadcrumb.

He rakes back his hair with both hands and gets to his knees in front of me, and I swear on all that is holy that my knees nearly buckle with the raw eroticism of having Dex naked and soaking and on his knees for me, ready to do my bidding.

His eyes articulate it all: the want; the anticipation; the apprehension, too. But then he's leaning forward and wrapping his hand around me and sticking out his tongue a little uncertainly, like it's the first time he's taking Holy Communion and he's not entirely sure how the mechanics work.

Little does he know that the mere sight of it—of his pink

tongue and huge eyes and earnest expression—is almost enough to have me shooting my load.

As he licks me, swirling the sluicing shower water over my cock, I put my hands to his head and follow the path he's raked through his hair. He's a beautiful, Mediterranean creature. A Greek god made man. A Renaissance prince, perhaps. He's timeless and exquisite and so fucking obliging once he gets the fuck over himself, and I allow my head to fall back against the tiles once more and my hands to claw deeper, to grip his jaw harder, to control the speed, the depth, with which his clever, supple mouth takes me in.

One particularly energetic tug on my part has him testing his gag reflex, and as the spongy tissues of his throat contract around me, I have to tense up not to come.

'You're a natural,' I grit out, caressing his jaw, allowing him a moment of latitude, and glancing down in time to see those blessed eyelashes flicker as he hums happily around my dick. His left hand stays clamped around me, his right arm working hard as he strokes himself, and I resolve to hang on tight.

'Tell me when you're about to come,' I manage a few minutes later, when his licks, his sucks, have grown messier and more desperate, and I fucking love that sucking my dick has him writhing and shuddering around my cock.

'Now,' he gasps out, popping off me for a quick second before sucking me back in.

Thank fuck.

'Good,' I say through clenched teeth, and I grip his jaw again and let him have it, my hips volleying, my dick fucking his mouth and my hands holding him relentlessly in place as he flails and bucks and gives me such wonderful, strangled whimpers.

'Rub yourself so hard,' I hiss. 'I want you to feel how

filthy this is, what a dirty little slut you are for getting on your knees for me so soon. And look at you. You fucking love it, don't you?'

I know how heartily he disapproves of the s-word, so I take enormous pleasure in throwing it at him when he's teetering on the brink of sanity. Let him take all that shame and humiliation and fucking bathe in it; let it light him up from within.

He comes so prettily, my beautiful, brave boy on his knees for me in my shower with my dick down his throat and his cock in his fist. He takes my cum, he tries, swallowing around me as cum and shower water and saliva drip from his mouth.

And when we've both quite finished, I haul him up by his armpits, and I fold his wet, tired body in my arms, and I revel in the righteous weight of his head against my shoulder, and I tell him how very, very proud of him I am.

61

DARCY

I have no earthly idea what to expect when I show up at Max's flat. I've second-guessed my decision to let Dex go over there alone so many times over the past forty-eight hours. I'm the buffer: Dex feels more comfortable around me, and Max feels compelled to act like some vaguely civilised creature and not a total fucking beast when I'm around.

I hope I haven't done the wrong thing by letting him wander into the lion's den.

What I'm categorically *not* expecting is to get up to Max's floor and find Dex lolling against the door frame with damp hair, wearing nothing but a pair of red athletic shorts that I suspect aren't his and a smile so wide it could split his face in two.

'Hi, gorgeous,' he says, hooking an arm around my waist and tugging me against his bare chest, which is frankly an excellent way to be greeted. 'You look fucking ravishing.'

'Who are you and what have you done with Dex?' I demand, planting my palms on his shoulders and dropping a kiss on his lips. 'What the fuck did you two get up to—are you drunk?'

'Not on booze,' he replies with a cheeky wink, releasing me and ushering me inside.

'He's drunk on dick,' Max calls from the living area, and I giggle.

'Nice. Started without me, did you?'

'And then some,' Dex mutters over his shoulder, and I marvel at his personality transformation.

'You jealous?' Max asks, climbing off his barstool as I enter the kitchen area and coming towards me. He's wearing similar shorts to Dex's, only in navy.

Matchy-matchy.

Cute.

'Nah. If you've got each other out of your systems, you can make it all about me now,' I say, eyeing him up appreciatively. Honestly, what a welcome. Two hot as hell, half-naked gods waiting for me. A girl could get used to this.

'Exactly right,' Max says with a grin before stooping to give me a very thorough, very X-rated kiss. He tastes of red wine and smells of shower gel and, I dunno, pheromones, probably.

'You wore that dress I love,' Dex says when we come up for air, pouring out a glass of red for me.

I give him a little shoulder shimmy. I'm wearing the black halter-neck dress from the night we met, and I'm tickled he noticed. 'I did indeed. You told me you liked my boobs in it, so I thought you could take it off me later.'

'You look very fuckable,' Max adds with a downright lascivious smirk, and I bask in his affection like a cat in the afternoon sun.

'Just the look I was going for.' I reach over and swipe my

finger through what looks like moutabel or babaganoush—I never know the difference. 'Fuck me, this is amazing. Did you make it?'

'I thought you were going to eat before you came over,' he says.

'I did. And your point is?'

He laughs. 'Told you Little Miss Leftovers would be all over it,' he says to Dex. To me he adds, 'Dex was worried about not getting through all the food.'

'Never fear, Darcy's here,' I say cheerily, pulling the bowl of aubergine towards me and nabbing a wedge of pita to better shovel up this smoky, gloopy goodness. 'Now, tell me everything. I want a blow-by-blow account.'

'Actually,' Max leans over and hooks a couple of fingers over the rim of the bowl, watching my face as he does, 'I wouldn't eat too much more if I were you. You won't want a full stomach for what we've got planned for you.'

His voice is careful, and gentle, and ominous as fuck. Nerves hit me with blunt, immediate force, turning the pita and aubergine to gluey mush in my mouth. I stare at him with wide, scared eyes as I chew.

Fuck fuck fuck.

I've known, and I suppose I hoped, this was coming, but I'm honestly not sure I'll ever be ready, and, more importantly, I'm not sure I'll ever believe it's anatomically possible to take these two. There's a massive difference in my head between the theory of being entangled with and filled up by them and actually, physically accommodating two very large dicks.

'Both of you?' I croak through a mouthful of food, looking from Max to Dex and back again.

'Only if you want to,' Dex says, brushing his lips over my

bare shoulder as he slides my wineglass towards me. 'Only if you're ready.'

I pick up my glass and gulp as I push the bowl of dip towards Max with my fingertips as if it's radioactive.

62

DARCY

It's later now, and I'm nicely buzzed from the wine. Through the French doors, the park is all muted indigo shadows beneath a lavender sky. We've talked, and laughed, and kissed, and I've watched with amazement how the guys are together. How comfortable, how easily affectionate. How often their gazes turn to each other. It's truly amazing to see.

I really should have turned up an hour earlier than I did and brought a bucket of popcorn. I can't wait for them to reenact all those orgasms so I can watch.

For now, though, it's about me.

They've made that much clear.

I'm sitting on Max's lap on the sofa, in almost the exact place where he first bent me over and fucked me. His dick is swelling against my arse, his hands are all over my skin, rubbing and smoothing and admiring, and his mouth can't stay away from my shoulders, from kissing and licking and nipping them.

He gathers my hair back in a single handful and twists it into a rope, and I gaze dreamily up at Dex, who's standing in front of me. He's still in his shorts, that line of dark hair bisecting his olive abs, and the mere view of his body has me wanting his skin flush against mine.

'Have at her,' Max tells him, and he gets down on one knee. It's such a courtly, respectful gesture. A worshipful one, even. It's the pose of proposals, of genuflection, of receiving one's knighthood. And he looks like an angel, his dark hair falling over one eye. He's a storybook knight. He's every girl's Prince Charming, come to propose.

Which is why it's so ridiculously hot when he doesn't pop out a ring or make the sign of the cross but reaches behind my neck with a knowing smile and tugs hard at the silky tie so my halter tumbles down and my breasts are there for him to do with as he likes.

Max releases my hair and lays it over one shoulder in a rope. His hands slip under my arms and around my ribcage, cupping my breasts and supporting them, displaying them for Dex's gratification. I can't explain it, but the push-pull of having Max behind me and Dex in front of me, of Max's hands thrusting me forward, serving me up to Dex, is so erotic. I'm a plaything, a little doll for them to amuse themselves with.

Dex leans forward, all lashes and cheekbones and lips, kissing me slowly, self-indulgently, as Max's thumbs flicker over my nipples and his lips find my neck. I arch into Max's touch, into Dex's mouth. My pussy is already heating, dampening, at the intensity of it all, and we've barely begun.

Then Dex is bending and claiming my breasts for himself, his fingers brushing Max's as he takes over, his mouth latching on hard, and the otherworldly echo of his pulls somewhere deep in my core has me moaning a little, until Max slips a couple of fingers in my mouth.

'Suck,' he orders, and I do, using my tongue to show him

exactly what I'd do to his dick if I had the chance. It seems he gets my message, hardening further beneath me. I shift on him, seeking friction, my nerves from a few minutes ago forgotten, because the two of them already have me hot and bothered.

'Jesus fuck,' he groans, sliding his fingers in and out of my mouth. 'I can't wait to get inside that hot little arse.'

At that, Dex releases my breast. 'Help me get her dress off,' he tells Max. Between them, they hoist my bum up and manoeuvre my dress down my legs until it's a pool of fabric on the floor. I'm naked in Max's lap aside from my oversized gold hoop earrings, and that has the power dynamic shifting further.

I can tell Dex senses it too, because he gives my body a once-over that's filthy and proprietary and ominous in equal measure. I'm splayed back against Max now, my head on his shoulder, my legs dangling.

'Open her up for me,' he tells Max, and I inwardly rejoice. I love that Dex is such a natural switch; I love that he's Max's new little fuck toy but can join forces with him to overpower me.

'You heard the man,' Max says smoothly. 'Give him access to that pretty little cunt, sweetheart, or there'll be trouble. He needs to warm you up.' His dick is now fully erect and sticking into the small of my back. I widen my legs, and he reaches around, wrapping a hand around one knee and using it to hook my leg over his thigh so my foot is on the outside of his leg.

When he's done the same with the other and I feel stretched open, he collapses back into his semi-reclining position on the sofa, pulling me down with him.

'Relax,' he croons against my ear, tenderly brushing my hair away from my temple before bringing his hands to my breasts and fondling them. I'm locked into place, his legs as effective as gynaecological stirrups at holding me open, and fuck if it isn't incredibly arousing to have Max playing with me while I'm spread for Dex.

'God, that's more like it,' Dex says. He comes to kneel before me again, his knuckles brushing up the insides of my thighs, tantalisingly close to where I'm exposed and pulsing for him. 'Are you comfortable like this, angel?'

'Yes,' I say, and it sounds breathy, spaced out, because I swear the anticipation has me in a chemical haze already and Max's skilful fingers on my nipples are winding me higher.

'Good,' he says. His eyes look darker in this light, like he's some kind of fallen angel, always beautiful and newly depraved. 'Because you look like a goddess, all laid out for me like this. And I want to make you feel so amazing you'll never, ever forget it.'

With that oath, he bends his beautiful face to my pussy and I let my eyes drift closed.

63

DEX

Max is hard and lean and uncompromising. He's fucking relentless, and while this evening has confirmed for me just how much I love being on the receiving end of that relentlessness, I'm craving an antidote.

And that antidote is Darcy, with her soft curves and her easy smile and the sensual sway of her hips. She's a pre-Raphaelite painting come to life in the most contemporary, irreverent way, and my need to worship her is just as visceral as the need I feel to impose my authority on her.

I feel no vulnerability with Darcy. I don't feel flayed open by her the way I do when Max puts his eyes on me. Two people, both blue-eyed, both so vastly, vastly different. And they're both on the sofa in front of me, Darcy reclining in the cradle of Max's body, winched right open for me.

My performance, therefore, is as much for him as for her. Her eyes are closed; his are steadfastly on me. I want him to see my mouth on her pussy and wish it was on his dick. I want him to feel the aftershocks of her pleasure vibrate through his body as though they were his own.

I want this extraordinary, radical *thing* we're doing to bloom into something that's so much more than the sum of its parts.

Her body, though.

Satin skin, silken flesh. The way he has her trussed up, those long fingers that brought me such pleasure earlier toying so imperiously with her breasts. My tongue cuts through her core in a single exploratory sweep, and she arches into my touch with the breathiest, most blissed-out little moan.

'Look at your mouth on her,' Max says, his voice gravelly. 'Fuck, look at your perfect tongue on her pussy. Hold her open, why don't you, so she can feel every single lick you give her?'

A week ago, the sound of his entitled narration would have filled me with an emotion I'd probably have called irritation. I would have told myself it was bothersome, all the while allowing his voice to fuel that rush it gave me.

But now, I can't get enough. There's no conflict. Now, his filthy voiceover spurs me on, makes me more determined to reap unthinkable pleasure from Darcy's spectacular body. It's a golden thread, weaving itself into this rich, complex tapestry the three of us are creating together.

So I grunt my approval against her flesh, and I inhale the addictive essence of her, and I do as he says. I use my fingers to part her delicate lips, to pin them back like butterfly wings so I can sample her. Tease her. Drive her to distraction.

And it works. The sounds she's making are unabashed and wonderful. She writhes in Max's arms as he massages her breasts and tugs at her nipples and as I go to work on her.

I tongue-fuck her a couple of times, because the sensation of her wet heat gripping my tongue is out of this fucking world, and I lick along her delicate layers, and I roll her swelling clit around like it's a national sport, and all the time I'm growing impossibly harder, and Max's voice is growing more honeyed, more intoxicating, winding its tendrils around my consciousness.

Just like that, yes.

See what a slut she is? She fucking loves having one of us at each end like this.

I hope you're making that cunt nice and wet for your cock, because she's going to need it.

Drive her crazy. I want her begging. I want her fucking unhinged. Jesus, her nipples are so greedy.

Darcy's not the only one getting audibly more tightly wound in the face of my and Max's takes on lingual onslaughts. I'm devouring her more hungrily, more noisily, grunting against her as I slide my tongue inside her once more and rub my nose against her clit.

'She's going to come,' I mutter, coming up for air.

'Yes she is,' Max says. 'She's going to come because she loves having both of us working her, and because she knows in a few minutes she'll be lying between us, so full of dick she'll never be the same again. Do it.'

And I do. I drive two fingers inside her wet heat in the most vivid foreshadowing of where my dick will be shortly, and I lave at her clit like a starving man, and she pushes against my tongue and my fingers, practically sobbing with the need for release until Max turns her head and swallows her cries with frantic kisses.

And as she unravels, with full-body convulsions and kiss-strangled moans, I marvel at the extraordinary honour of undoing her.

I lick her until her shudders have subsided and she's

slumped in Max's arms, and then I press a kiss to her pelvic bone and straighten up. She turns her head and opens her eyes and sees me grinning at her. Watching her. I must look enraptured, because she strokes Max's arms and he helps her to sit up.

I lean forward on my knees and kiss her. I kiss her so she can taste her own perfection and so she can understand what she does to me. How new and mesmerising and transcendent it is for me to be a passenger on these inner journeys she takes.

Max *oofs* behind her, presumably because she's shifted on his dick. 'Let's move into the bedroom,' he says.

Yes.

I need to be on a bed, fully naked, with this man and this woman.

Finally.

His eyes meet mine as though he understands the significance for me, for Darcy, for all of us, of what he just said. As though he wants to make sure I'm still onboard.

'You want to go to the bedroom?' I ask Darcy, cupping her face and peppering it with kisses.

Her blue eyes meet mine, and she nods. She still looks spaced out, which I guess is a good thing. Because I know I want nothing more than for Max and I to be inside her body.

Together.

64

DARCY

Max carries me through to his bedroom, my arms and legs wrapped around him, and I smile at Dex over his shoulder, taking in the enormous tent in the front of his shorts that's all for me.

I'm little more than ether after that orgasm, and I'm definitely not confident of my emotions in this state, but the knowledge that they'll both be inside my body shortly has my heart swelling and my pussy aching and my stomach doing crazy flip-flops. However physically confronting it'll be, I don't think it would be possible to want anything more than these two men around me, above me, beneath me.

Inside me.

I know that fact like I know my own name. It's like my body understands it, craves it, without my brain having any part in it.

Like everything else in this ridiculous flat, Max's bed is completely over the top. It must be eight foot wide, with a ginormous cream leather headboard. I cling to his neck as he lays me down on his white sheets so gently, so tenderly, smiling down at me in awe like I'm something priceless and delicate and sacrosanct. The way he has of making me feel like that when I know damn well he intends to shatter me, to desecrate me in the filthiest manner I can think of, is gratifying beyond belief.

I suspect it is for them, too. Because where's the fun in claiming and profaning something unless it's special? Unless it's an irreplaceable treasure?

I shimmy up the bed a little, naked and wanton, and prop myself up on my elbows so I can eye up my delicious menfolk. Max is striding around the bed in his usual purposeful fashion, so I perv freely at Dex as he slides his shorts off. Flat stomach. The perfect smattering of soft, dark hair. Narrow hips with that vee-thingy going on: lines I want to get to know intimately with my tongue. His grin holds a hint of self-consciousness as he frees his dick, but then he's kicking his shorts off and stroking himself lightly, and I sigh with happiness at the sight of him.

'Get over here,' I tell him, stretching lazily, but Max stops him.

'Wait.'

He hands Dex a foil square and turns to me. 'Condoms tonight, okay? But going forward, I want to put some proper measures in place.'

How he can still sound like a CEO when he's stripping off his shorts and getting ready to sheath himself, I have no idea, but it's really fucking hot. I squirm on the bed. 'I'm on the pill.'

'Excellent. But I'm not going near you bare tonight. We get tested, and then we get to take you bare. Got it?'

'I haven't had sex since the last time I was tested,' I say.

'Me neither,' Dex says. 'I had a full checkup when I got here.'

'Fine,' Max says through gritted teeth. '*I'll* get tested, then. Satisfied?'

'Who's the little slut now?' Dex wonders aloud, and I giggle.

Max shoots a hand forward and grabs Dex's balls. 'I'd be very careful what you say, young man. Now get this on me.'

If I thought life's simple pleasures mainly consisted of sunshine and daffodils and oven-warmed white bread with salted butter, then I was wrong, because watching my men roll condoms on each other so they can take me is one of the most pleasurable moments of my life.

Move over, bread and butter.

This is the best porn ever.

Dex has his head bowed, teeth sinking into his full lower lip as he focuses on rolling what I hope is an XL condom over Max's cock. It seems Max can't handle it any better than I can, because he keeps one hand on Dex's cock and wraps the other around the back of his neck, drawing him in and taking that lip for himself.

Dex groans and releases Max's cock, at which point Max wraps his hand around both of them in what looks like a pretty vicious hold.

'Ready for this, sweetheart?' he asks against Dex's mouth.

God, yes.

'Come here,' I say, the pout evident in my voice, and Dex kisses Max once more before turning to me.

'We're coming, angel.'

'I'll be able to feel you through her walls,' Max tells him in an ominous tone before releasing their dicks. 'Get on that side of her.'

Then they're walking towards me, and climbing onto the bed, and this is so much better than the other night in the club, because Dex no longer looks like a terrified kitten and Max no longer looks like the cost of holding himself back from Dex may actually destroy him.

They collapse on either side of me in a tangle of muscle and hair and skin and heat, and it's not until this moment that I realise how worried I've been that this wouldn't happen. That we'd never get to this place.

'Fucking *finally*,' Max mutters, echoing my thoughts exactly, and Dex laughs sheepishly.

'Yeah. You two make sinning way too irresistible.'

'Stick with us, and we'll drag you all the way to Hell,' Max says, but he says it in such a sexy way that if this is Hell, and he's Lucifer himself, I'm doomed. Because there's nowhere I'd rather be.

65

DARCY

For a few minutes, we just kiss. Hug. Touch. Stroke. We're limbs and breath and sensation. Dex tugs me to one side so he can kiss me deeply, and the way Max's arm is banded around me from behind, I'm pretty sure he's having a good grope of Dex's outrageous bum.

Then I'm pulled onto my back, Max nipping at my lips and probing with his tongue before he raises his head and his mouth finds Dex over me. I watch the wet dance of their tongues, the slide of their stubbled jaws, as they kiss right above my face. It's the best show ever, and I have a front-row seat.

We can't get enough of exploring each other. I clamber up onto my knees and turn so I can simply take them in, sprawled out on the sheets with their legs akimbo and their hair mussed and their eyes watchful. Hungry. Max crosses his arms behind his head, and the heavy tufts of hair under his arms have me wanting to bury my face in them.

I reach out and stroke down their stomachs. Hard. So fucking hard. I skate my fingertips over their latex-covered erections and gently cup the darker, thinner skin of their balls. I'm a kid in a theme park who doesn't know what—or who—to ride first.

Dickneyland, I remember, and smile to myself.

'You look very smug,' Max observes, stretching out.

I shamelessly eye-fuck his naked body. 'I am indeed smug. Look at you both.'

He glances across at Dex. 'Time to see if she's all talk and no trousers,' he says with a mock-sigh, and I squeal as I'm tugged laughingly down to the bed and pounced upon.

'Right.' Max is the CEO again, or the conductor, maybe. I already know that the symphony he'll orchestrate for us tonight, in this huge, serene room with the summer dusk beyond the windows, will be magic. I know, whatever happens, its music will stay with me forever.

'Get on your back, sweetheart,' he tells me with a sweet brush of his lips over mine. I'm rolled onto my back, and Dex manoeuvres himself on top of me. The mood changes instantly. Less playful, darker. Anticipation hangs heavily in the air as I gaze up at him, Max stroking my hair off my face.

It's just me and them. No one else. Nothing to concern myself with except using my body as a channel for uniting the three of us in this most visceral way.

Then Dex is kissing me, and nudging at my entrance, and pushing inside me, and I'm gasping with how full I am, because this is how full should feel. Tight. Just the right side of overwhelm. He fits me perfectly, and when he drags his dick out of me and pushes back in it's so elemental I could weep.

Max mutters something to Dex that I don't catch, and then Dex is rolling onto his side and taking me with him. It's less overwhelming like this, I guess because he doesn't have as much leverage to thrust in this position, but it's still pretty intense, because having Dex gaze into your eyes while inside you in *any* position is going to send a girl crazy.

'I've been thinking about this every day since I got to be inside you last week,' he whispers. As I'm smiling back at him, there's a wet, squirting noise and then Max is sliding in behind me, smearing a *lot* of lube between my cheeks, and I stiffen.

'It's okay, angel,' Dex says, nodding reassuringly. 'Keep focusing on me.'

It's as if I'm at the doctor's surgery, on the cusp of getting some godawful injection, and Dex is the nurse tasked with distracting me. The difference is, he's way hotter than any nurse I've ever seen, and he's trembling with the effort of staying still inside me, and the things Max is doing with his lubed-up finger are incredibly, shamefully pleasurable.

He's stretched me like this before, a few times now, but never with the agenda that he has tonight. I remind myself that I can do this, that my body is fully capable of stretching to accommodate him if I can get out of my own head.

Thankfully, Max's particular formula for warming me up doesn't just include a lubricated finger but his own brand of prose so dirty it has my body melting, blooming, around him.

'She won't be content with just your cock,' he grunts in my ear. 'She wants to be sandwiched between us, wedged between two guys and impaled on two dicks like the dirty, incredible little whore that she is. Don't you, sweetheart?'

I moan something incoherently affirmative, because he, the consummate maximiser of every sliver of opportunity, takes the chance to slide another finger inside me, and all I can think is *burn. Burn.* Alarm bells are going off, my body is far too full, and the stretch down there between Dex's cock and Max's fingers is way, way too much.

'Breathe, angel,' Dex says, staring at me with desire and concern and wonder. I have a sudden, fleeting memory of a friend in Oz telling me how she felt like slapping her doula every time she told her to *just breathe* when in labour, and I feel exactly the same. I want to slap them both, tell them to fuck off, tell them I'm too hot and too impossibly tight and that I cannot fucking breathe, because there's no oxygen in the room.

'You're doing great, sweetheart,' Max says. 'I promise you it'll be worth it. And if you don't like it or it's too much, you say so and I'll take turns with Dex fucking your cunt. You'd like that too, wouldn't you?'

Yes. Yes I'd like that—I'd love being used by two men, one hole at a time. That sounds far more sensible. Why the ever-loving fuck I'm allowing Max to do this when I've never tried anal and I *have another man inside my body* is beyond me.

'Say your safe word, so we know you've got it to hand,' Dex says, running a featherlight palm over my nipple, and that feels good. That feels non-violating and very, very nice.

I close my eyes. 'Folklore,' I whisper, and it's amazing, the images that conjures up. Woodlands full of intricately furled ferns and low-lying mists. Cool streams. Smoking chimneys and swirling capes in plum-coloured velvet. It's so soothing, so mystical. A dreamy escape from the intensity of the here and now.

'Good girl,' Max tells me, withdrawing his fingers. 'I'm going in, okay sweetheart? Just bear down on me if you can.'

The initial pain is raw and intrusive and fucking awful. It hurts like a motherfucker, despite the lube. I pant hard, sweat slicking my body, Dex stroking my face and hair, the anguish on my face reflected in his.

'Fuck,' Max grunts. 'You're—it's so fucking tight back here. *Jesus*, sweetheart. You okay?'

'Yeah,' I shudder out. I'm okay except for being frozen and way too full. I'm terrified to move in case it hurts more.

'Try not to clench,' he says. 'Try to relax, baby.'

He's only called me *baby* once or twice, but I love it when he does, and my body softens around him in approval. Naturally, he presses his advantage, pushing forward, and it's deeper but not as awful than the initial pain of accommodating his crown.

I gaze at Dex while Max pauses, I take in his huge eyes and his stubble-dusted jaw and that lower lip, looking at him with genuine pleasure as he strokes my face.

'Can you feel him?' I whisper.

He smiles, and it's filled with awe. 'Yeah. I can feel him.'

'Good,' Max says behind me in a voice gruff with emotion, and beyond the pain there's a sense of wonder that these two men are meeting inside my body. It's unbelievable, and it's as close as we can physically get to each other. It's greater than just me and my physical discomfort.

I take a deep breath. 'Keep going,' I tell Max, and he presses a kiss to my hair and shunts forward once again.

66

MAX

I've done this before, with women whose bodies are much more used to taking multiple dicks than Darcy's is and with guys whose names and faces I can't remember. But I've never had the intensity of feeling I have now—I've never *respected* this act, and what it represents, and the human experience it allows us, until this moment.

Before, it's been about taking holes and claiming and dominating and kink for the sake of kink.

Tonight, it's about joining my body with those of two people who have me in their thrall. It's unity. Equality. Intensity.

But don't get me wrong, it's still fucking filthy, and to be inside Darcy's body with Dex, inside her tight, virgin space, his erection immovable against her front wall, fighting mine for jurisdiction, is physically and emotionally cataclysmic.

'I'm in,' I tell her gruffly, tugging at her hair so I can kiss her neck. I wrap my arm around her and Dex, marvelling at how the musculature of his back contracts under my touch. He responds in kind, snaking his arm over her waist to grab my arse, and I smile into Darcy's neck.

'I'm so proud of you, baby,' I tell her. 'So very proud of you for taking us both. I knew you could do it.'

I also knew it would be a lot, but her dancer's body, used to being commanded and pushed and abused in the name of aspiration, has risen to the challenge.

She's trembling between us, so strong and yet so vulnerable in this moment, and God knows it has some kind of unfamiliar emotional spin on elation coursing through me. I press my lips to her skin.

'I can't believe you're both in,' she says with a shuddery sigh. 'What now?'

'Now,' I say firmly, 'Dex moves. It won't be so deep at this angle, but it'll be very tight. And once you get used to that, I'll try moving. If it's too much, I'll wait till he's come before finishing the job. But I know you can do this. I know you can take two fat dicks pounding you at the same time.'

It strikes me that she doesn't know. She's in an unfamiliar—and supremely uncomfortable—position right now. So it's my job to know for her. It's my job to reassure her of her body's capabilities, even if I have no fucking clue how far we can push her beyond her limits.

Dex pulls out and pushes experimentally back in, and holy *fucking* Christ. The three of us make sounds of awe and disbelief as his dick drags against the fine web of tissue and muscle separating him from me.

'Fuck,' he says, his tone laced with astonishment. 'Holy shit. You okay, angel?' He squeezes my arse, and I have to stop myself from rutting into her.

'Yeah,' she manages.

'How does it feel?' I push, because I want more than a yes-no answer right now.

'It's... a lot.' She blows out a shuddery breath. 'But—I'm

not sure, but I think I can come like this. Maybe. It's like a really good kind of pain when Dex pushes in.'

'Of course you can come,' I croon in her ear. 'That body of yours can do anything you want it to. You've got two guys fucking you right now, and all we want to do is make you feel good. Got it?'

'Mmm, got it,' she moans dreamily.

Dex finds a rhythm, fucking her slowly, eliciting a little whimper of effort and, I think, arousal, from her each time he bottoms out and bringing me a little closer to the precipice, because Darcy's body has my dick in the most glorious chokehold, and Dex's dick is so close to mine. So fucking close.

I swear to God, I will get inside this guy's ass as soon as is humanly possible. The thought has my fingernails digging harder into Dex's back. It's a privilege to feel this man move deep within Darcy, to feel it from the inside and the outside. He's pushing and pulsing and thrumming with energy, with thinly-controlled desire, and it seems to me he's a miracle in human form.

I don't announce my intention to begin moving to either of them. I can't hold on like this much longer—it's a case of moving or pulling out and wanking myself off so furiously that I'm done in seconds. I release Dex from my grip and slide my arm between their bodies, my hand going to press down on Darcy's velvet-soft stomach. I edge out no more than an inch or so, and when Dex next thrusts, so do I.

Dex makes a sound of strangled incredulity, but it's Darcy's slow, guttural moan that's the real kicker. I bet she can feel us in her womb.

'Was that okay?' I ask her.

She laughs a little, like it's the stupidest question ever. 'God, yes.'

Okay, then. That's what I call a green fucking light.

'Go,' I tell Dex, and he does, and I do, and fuck. It's hot, and sweaty, and messy, and wet. The sounds of limbs slapping and of anguished, aroused breaths, and of Darcy's greedy, majestic, lubed-up body sucking us both in are as much of an impetus as the rhythmic shove of our dicks as we jostle for space in the very centre of her.

'How does she look?' I ask Dex, because while it's filthy back here, it's also a little isolating.

'So beautiful.' He pauses, and there's the sound of lips and tongues meeting. I wait. 'She's glowing, and she's gazing at me like...' His voice breaks a little. 'Like she feels how I feel, which is lit up from within. Her eyes are so incredible.'

'Every single part of her is incredible,' I say with a pant. 'You're both perfect. You're so *fucking* perfect I have no idea what do with you except fuck you both into oblivion and never let you leave my sight.'

I mean it. There—I can't even—I press down harder on her stomach. I want her to feel every fucking ridge, every drag of our dicks. She's thrashing around between the two of us, lost in some kind of haze, her cries the perfect metronome for our dicks, the fluttering of all those miraculous interior muscles intensifying.

'Fuck, I'm going to come,' Dex grits out. 'Jesus *fuck*, I—angel, I—'

The sensation of Darcy's orgasm detonating around my cock while Dex's dick stiffens and convulses so near mine is extraordinary beyond belief. His strangled shouts ring in my ear as fresh sweat breaks out on my temples, and I grind further inside her, further against him as I ride out their orgasms, holding her in place with my hand on her stomach as she convulses.

When her shuddering has subsided, I say with difficulty,

'Pull out,' and he does. I feel the loss of his dick, the instant drop in pressure, and I waste no time in flipping her onto her stomach and using my arm to hoist her upwards so she's on her knees.

Dex is lying on his side still, looking spent and stupefied and utterly lovely. He stares up at me as I crouch over her, my dick still in place. I give him a long, wild look.

'Watch this,' I tell him, before glancing down at where my body joins hers. Fuck, it's incredible from this angle, with the delicate, darker skin no longer puckered but stretched impossibly taut around my latex-covered dick, the fuck-tonne of lube I used making us both glossy.

This is it. I pull out and push back in to make sure she can take it from this angle. Her body is relaxed and orgasm-floppy; she can barely stay up like this. I marvel at the flawless skin of her back and the lustrous hair on my pillow and the impossible fragility of her spine, and then I let her fucking have it.

A few thrusts is all it takes, because my sanity and my physical control have been stretched far tonight, so far, and I'm a man barely capable of anything except rutting mindlessly into the most forbidden part of this woman until the white-hot ache in my dick is torched into something unimaginable.

When I detonate, it's violent and cataclysmic and exhaustive, my orgasm ripping through me and sparing no part of my body or soul until it's chewed up everything I know to be true about myself and spat me out at Darcy and Dex's feet.

67

DEX

I need to sleep.

I need to curl into Darcy and bury my head between her breasts and drift off into an exhausted, sated slumber while Max curls up behind me, the protective shell I didn't know I needed. He'll stand guard over us, even in his sleep.

But I'm not allowed to sleep, not yet, because Max is in aftercare mode. Besides, I don't want to sleep, because he's rolled Darcy onto her back so we can bracket her and pet her and stroke her and kiss her and admire her and tell her what a clever, beautiful, amazing, miraculous girl she is.

I've never seen anything like her: all post-orgasm bliss and shining eyes, her gorgeous body loose-limbed. And I've never felt anything like this: the three of us, drunk on each other and on the chemical highs we coaxed from each other's bodies.

Max and I are up on one elbow, grinning stupidly at each other. The vision of him fucking Darcy's arse like that will be forever seared onto my brain. I've seen him come before. I've *made* him come. And each time it's raw, animalistic. But the bunched muscles and clenched teeth and fierce eyes as he took her just now was another level, a side of him it was a privilege to see.

And it makes me brave.

'I want you to do that to me,' I tell him. 'What you just did.' I want him angry and deranged and all-powerful around me, behind me, inside me. I want him to consume me, to eradicate every other thing in the world so there's only him.

His face kind of collapses, like he can barely handle the idea of it, and he leans over Darcy and yanks me towards him by the scruff of my neck.

'Be very, very careful what you wish for, beautiful boy,' he tells me, and then he's biting down on my lip and kissing me, hard and without mercy, like I should take what he's capable of doing with his teeth and tongue as an ominous portent of the annihilation he's capable of wreaking on me with his dick.

'As long as I can watch with popcorn,' Darcy slurs from beneath us, and our kisses turn to snorts of laughter.

Max turns his head to look down at her, his expression amused and adoring. 'No popcorn for you. No view, either. He'll be inside your cunt when I take him.'

'That works,' she says airily, and he drops down to kiss her. I pause for a fraction of a second before joining them, so we're a lazy jumble of skin and breath.

Eventually, Max pulls himself away. 'You look after her —don't let her move. I'll run us all a bath. Darcy, I'm getting you some ibuprofen. *Don't move.*'

Our eyes follow him out of the room. His nakedness in no way detracts from that effortless aura of power he's cloaked in at all times. He's so… imposing. Imperial, even.

Also, he has a fine, fine arse.

I snuggle down with Darcy, nose to nose on our pillows, grinning conspiratorially at each other. 'How do you feel, really?' I ask her, sliding my hand around her neck and stroking my thumb along her jawline.

'Um.' She sighs. 'Physically a bit... violated. Like, tender. I'm kind of afraid to move. But really, I'm just knocked sideways. You know?' Her face softens. 'I'm so happy it's terrifying,' she whispers, and a wave of emotion hits me so hard it's like smacking into a cliff face.

'Yeah.' I move my hand over her shoulder and down her body so I can tug her as close to me as possible, and I throw a leg over her. 'I know exactly what you mean.'

I wish I could tell her it was just the post-multiple-orgasm endorphin rush, but I really don't think it is.

She's not the only one terrifyingly happy.

MAX RETURNS and insists on carrying Darcy into the bathroom like a bride over the threshold of her forever home. He's lit a multitude of candles on the marble surfaces, and the enormous oval bath is full and fragrant with bubbly water. There are three pint glasses of water on the vanity with electrolyte tablets fizzing in them and a box of Nurofen. He sits her on the side and has me hold her while he climbs in. When he's settled, I help her in, and she nestles between his legs.

She sucks in a breath through her teeth as her abused undercarriage hits the water. 'Ow. It stings.'

'Poor baby,' he purrs. The way he raises his knees and wraps his arms around her to cage her in has my heart hurting and an odd, unwelcome burst of something between FOMO and jealousy flaring, sharp and bright, inside my abdomen.

He jerks his head at me. 'Come on. Get in. Darcy and I want to enjoy the view. Don't we, sweetheart?'

I roll my eyes to conceal the pleased pang his words give me and clamber in, sitting so I'm at the far end, facing them. As soon as I'm down, Darcy stretches out her long legs and slides one between mine so we're alternating. Dark and hairy against slim and creamy.

The two of them, though. Fair and elegant and beautiful. I drink them in and wonder at this new me: the man who chooses his own pleasure, his own instincts, over everything he's ever been told he should want, or strive for. Who chooses the company and comfort of not one, but two extraordinary lovers.

I lie back against the generous lip of the huge marble bath and enjoy the view of Max soaping Darcy up, her head lolling against his chest. I take one of her feet in my hands—the one tantalisingly close to my dick—and use my thumbs to massage the arch of her foot until she's purring like a contented cat.

I smile at them, but I'm already grieving the bubble of wonderment we find ourselves in. Because bubbles are, by their very nature, beautiful, and fragile, and ephemeral as fuck.

And when their fleeting beauty bursts, they leave nothingness in their wake.

68

MAX

It turns out Dex is fucking useless in the kitchen.

'I finished uni and moved to Manhattan, where no one cooks at home,' he protests after I pry a massacred potato from his hand. 'I don't know what you expect. We can't all be Gordon Ramsey.'

I mock-glare at him. 'If you weren't so pretty, I'd toss you out onto the street.'

'I was doing fine. I'm peeling it, aren't I?'

'It's the *way* you're peeling it. It's offensive. I thought this peeler was fucking foolproof—until you proved me wrong.'

'You need to chill.' He wrangles the potato out of my grip. 'It's just a potato. Fuck's sake. No one's saving lives here.'

Despite the fact that it's the beginning of August and very warm, I've insisted on a full Sunday lunch. Dex mentioned yesterday that Sunday roasts were one of the things he missed most about living in the UK, and now that I understand how totally incompetent he is in the kitchen, I can see why. Clearly, the only roasts he has are the ones his doting mother cooks for him.

So no, I'm not chilling, because I want this lovely piece of sirloin with all the trimmings to be the best fucking Sunday roast he's ever put in that lovely mouth of his. And I know for sure the company will be far better than if he had to suffer through lunch with that bigoted bloody father of his.

'You turned down lunch with your family today,' is all I say. 'I want to make it worth your while.'

He puts the potato on the chopping board and sets down the peeler like he's laying down his weapons. His arms go around my neck, his head goes to my shoulder, and I enfold him in a hug.

'You could serve me up Pot Noodle,' he says against my neck, 'and it would still be worth my while.'

He is the sweetest, loveliest thing.

I hug him more tightly.

'Wow,' Darcy says from where she's doing a thoroughly decent job of julienning carrots in a palest pink terry-towelling romper so skimpy it should be illegal, 'that's really sweet. Never try to feed me Pot Noodle.'

I smile fondly at her over Dex's shoulder. 'I know your preferred currencies, sweetheart. Food and sex. Luckily for all of us, I'm highly skilled at both.'

'That you are,' she says, saluting me with a carrot stick. 'Dex, you need to know that cooking is Max's love language. That and shagging us senseless, obviously. So be a babe and just let him peel the fucking potatoes the way he likes them. He's making this entire meal because of you.'

I swear he stiffens a little in my arms at her casual use of the L-word before he kisses my cheek and releases me.

'I know. You're spoiling me. Just take the potatoes and give me something unskilled to do.'

'Peeling potatoes is literally as unskilled as labour gets,' I grumble, but I can't hide my smile, because standing in this vast kitchen with the two of them, assembling lunch, is pretty special.

I'm not sure how I've gone in the space of a few weeks from intentionally unfettered—*proudly* unfettered even—to playing house with not one but two lovers-slash-potential-partners.

Aside from our scorching hot night at Alchemy together, I haven't frequented the club since that first night I lured Darcy over here to dance for me, and my absence is less to do with my work commitments than my lack of desire to fuck anyone who isn't Darcy or Dex right now. I couldn't exactly tell you why, except that they... interest me, I suppose.

They're both hard to pin down in their own ways: she because she's a free spirit who, as far as I can tell, only does anything if it suits her, and he because he's at the very start of his journey to enlightenment, and it makes him quick to panic.

So yeah. I suppose you could say having them both here, where I can keep an eye on them, and feed them, and touch them whenever I want to is convenient. Or reassuring. Whatever you want to call it.

Let's just say it suits me. And let's also say I have my hands full with these two, so it's not like I feel the need to go sniffing around Alchemy in search of more mischief.

That's what I tell myself, anyway.

∽

IT'S EXCEEDINGLY PLEASANT, sitting on the terrace together and tucking into a full English roast along with some austere but excellent German pinot that's light enough for this weather. I haven't let the two of them out of my sight all weekend. Dex and I accompanied Darcy back to her sister's flat to grab her some clean clothes, and Dex is wearing my stuff. No reason for him to have traipsed across town when we take a similar size.

What is irksome is that tomorrow this little sex-bubble we're in will have burst, and Dex and I will have our pretty little noses to the grindstone with little hope of overlapping with Darcy, who dances most weeknights at the club.

I should be drinking in every single moment of this idyllic Sunday afternoon, then. But, being me, I'll always kick the tyres when I can. Which is why I bide my time as Dex experiences some minor orgasm over the quality of my roast potatoes. Of course they're excellent. I par-boiled them, roughed them up, rolled them in semolina and roasted them in a vat of goose fat.

'Big week this week,' I remark, watching him over the rim of my wineglass.

'Why?' Darcy asks, a forkful of sirloin and my excellent Yorkshire pudding halfway to her mouth.

'Because we're announcing which banks will run the Wolff IPO,' I explain for her benefit.

Dex glances at me like he's not sure what my point is. Obviously I'd never divulge privileged information outside of the office, but if he thinks he's going to slink out of here at the arse crack of dawn tomorrow without us having had a firm word, he obviously doesn't know me all that well yet.

'All I'm saying is that *if* Loeb is on the ticket, I expect you might want to consider having a conversation with your Compliance department and possibly Thum,' I say.

He seems genuinely confused. 'Meaning?'

Jesus Christ. I set my fork down. '*Meaning* if you're a division head of a bank who's involved with the deal and you're also fucking the CEO of the company you're taking public, I'd say that's a conflict that needs to be disclosed, don't you?'

I swear the guy goes pale.

'Come on. Surely you've thought about this?'

'I have,' he admits haltingly. 'I just—I didn't think it would get that far. With us, I mean.'

Darcy's gaze is darting between us like she's desperately trying to pick up subtext. Not that there's much to pick up. It's pretty straightforward, in my book.

'Well, it has,' I say shortly. 'So if you and I want to pursue this relationship and we find ourselves working together, then we need to make sure we follow procedure. I have no intention of letting my personal life jeopardise this deal for the thousands of people who are counting on it. I would absolutely alert Wolff's lawyers too, just so they have it on record.'

I'm coming on a little strong, perhaps, but if I hadn't given Dex the odd forceful nudge whenever he needed it, he'd still be pining for me and wanking off in the shower to memories of sucking my thumb instead of tucking into excellent roast potatoes and nursing his sex-chafed dick.

'I just—*fuck*. I thought I'd have more time to get this straight in my head.'

'I'm genuinely not trying to steamroll you,' I say more gently. 'This isn't about trying to get you to put labels on yourself or your feelings for me or Darcy before you're ready. But the IPO timetable isn't quite as forgiving.'

'You're right, obviously,' he says, pushing his plate away and reaching for his wine. 'I—the idea of sitting people down when I'm so new to the firm and telling them something this personal when it's only been days, really—it's horrifying.' His tone is as pleading as his expression, and a little sympathy finds its place alongside the frustration I'm feeling.

'Look.' I push my chair out and walk over to him so I can bend and wrap my arms around him. 'Nobody's asking you to wrap yourself in a rainbow flag and scale Nelson's Column and broadcast to the world that you now eat dick for breakfast, okay? It's one private, professional conversation—two, if you do Thum the courtesy of giving him a heads up, which I think is only fair given you're his newest, shiniest hire.

'Remember what I told you the night we met? You're a fucking partner there. You call the shots. You're not asking for their permission, or their fucking blessing—you're *telling* them. There is zero problem with you and I seeing each other. It's just something that needs to be recorded. It's a non-issue, believe me.'

I brush my nose along his cheekbone before bending to nip at his darkly stubbled jaw. 'Unless you don't want to do this again,' I murmur. 'In which case it's definitely a non-issue.'

It seems he likes my trump card very much, because he shivers in my arms.

'I think you know what the answer to that question is,' he mutters.

'That's my good boy.' I kiss his jaw and release him. 'Let's see what the deal announcement looks like, shall we?'

'If we're not on the ticket after all that, I'll be seriously fucked off.'

I laugh a little. 'Whatever. Now finish your roast, you ungrateful little shit.'

69

DEX

Loeb gets a spot on the ticket. Joint Bookrunner for the Wolff Holdings IPO. Which, given we're nowhere in the league tables the industry keeps for deal activity in each region, is a huge coup.

We, with several other banks, will be responsible for building the book of investors in the deal, ensuring the shareholder list is high quality—not too full of hedge funds who'll sell the stock to "flip" it as soon as it begins trading.

It's been a shitty few months for deal volume, so everyone is ecstatic, and I'm sure our Treasury department is upgrading its forecasts for Q4. Wolff will float on the London Stock Exchange in early November, giving the stock a solid month of trading before the Christmas festivities ramp up and trading volumes start to slide. If we do a good job on this landmark deal, it'll be a punchy way to begin my tenure as Head of Equities here, too.

It's only been a week and a day since Max waltzed in and demanded an off-the-cuff, cross-divisional pitch from us before proceeding to ruthlessly extract my soul through my dick in this very office.

He called me as soon as the news hit the wires this morning, both to give me his particularly harsh brand of pep talk and to demand I call him as soon as I've spoken to Thum. A part of me marvelled at the fact that Max Hunter now has me on speed dial. That he's grown familiar with the noises I make when I come, and that I know how satiny the underside of his dick feels against my tongue.

That I can kiss him whenever I want. Call him. Text him.

If the past week has been a crash course in yielding to desires I never allowed myself to acknowledge, let alone act on, then the weekend was full immersion into a cult whose god is Max Hunter. Our god is golden and dazzling and all-powerful, and he can be cruel, too. Merciless, even.

But when he shines that fulgent light on us mere mortals, we know in our hearts we'll do anything he asks. We'll do anything to serve him. We'll lay ourselves at his feet and offer up the sweetest sacrifices, it seems: our dignity; our most shameful, depraved desires; even our autonomy.

He's right about the labelling part. I chuckle to myself as the image of me, wrapped in a rainbow flag and trying desperately to climb Nelson's Column comes to mind. He's funny, too. But he doesn't mince his words, and he's equally correct that I need to disclose our "relationship", whatever that looks like, and that it doesn't follow that I'm putting a label on myself.

What he almost definitely fails to appreciate, or, if I'm being churlish, refuses to entertain, is that labels are important to me. After all, I've spent my entire life denying my feelings and depriving myself of my needs so I can fit the labels I've chosen for myself.

The concept of flipping that on its head, of cherry-picking labels that suit the man I am, rather than trying with every fibre of my being to conform to the labels deemed most "appropriate" by the privileged, bigoted bubble of my upbringing, is so weird as to be alien to me.

Thum wanders into my office midway through the morning, I assume to light a figurative cigar together and indulge in a little mutual back-slapping, because it's definitely a moment to pause. Celebrate.

He takes a seat at my desk and crosses one ankle over its opposite knee. His face is weathered from years of committed rock-climbing, and there's a huge grin across it.

'Well, how about that?' he asks. 'They must have been impressed with our research.'

'They should have been,' I say. 'It's really something. And I think everyone did a great job on the meeting, too.'

He chuckles. 'We certainly rallied. Not that they gave us much time to get our ducks in a row.'

It's now or never. I know that. My face heats preemptively; my palms prick with sweat. It's insane that my body acts as though making a standard disclosure is the professional and personal equivalent of voluntarily walking in front of a firing squad.

WWMD—What Would Max Do? He reminded me this morning to own it. Harness every ounce of my entitlement as a white male with an elite education and make my point without the merest hint of apology or attempt at justification.

I clear my throat. 'Actually, Jochen, there's a small matter I wanted to mention to you. Just so you're aware.'

'What is that?' He looks at me, his face open. Cheerful. Trusting.

'I'm in the, um, early stages of a personal relationship with someone on Wolff's management team. I'll let Compliance know shortly, but I wanted to do you the courtesy, too.'

He inclines his head. 'Not a problem. I'm grateful for the heads up. Anyone I know?'

A beat passes. I suck in a breath in a desperate attempt to stop myself from passing out.

'Max Hunter,' I say.

I wait as he visibly calibrates this information in his head. As he *recalibrates* what he thought he knew about me to date. And as I wait, I dig my fingernails into my palms and physically restrain myself from explaining or modifying.

Then that grin breaks out again, like he's tickled to death. 'Well, well, well,' he says with a chuckle. 'I have to admit, I did not see that coming. Wow. You got me on the back foot—I must apologise.'

'No apology necessary,' I say stiffly. I'm terrified to let my guard down, but he's shaking his head smilingly at me.

'You and Hunter. What a power couple. He's a most impressive guy.'

'We're not really a couple, yet,' I manage. 'It's very... new. But with the announcement... I thought you should know.' I trail off. Hearing the word *couple* from my lips is fantastical. Max Hunter and me. A power couple—with Darcy, obviously, because without her we're a two-legged stool.

But still.

Having this conversation with a man who paid seven figures to hire me and relocate me across the ocean and put his trust in me feels more portentous, somehow, than letting Max touch me. Because Max's flat is a bubble, a blessedly safe, private space for me to indulge in activities I never, ever thought I'd allow myself to experience.

But this is the real world, with its prejudices and cruelties, with its lack of empathy and its insistence on reducing our physical needs and our hearts' most elemental human desires to *labels*.

So it's only when Thum shakes my hand with genuine joy, and wishes me and Max all the luck in the world for our relationship, and promises to be the soul of discretion until I see fit to share the news more widely, that I realise I've been bracing this whole time for the emotional equivalent of a slap across the face.

A slap that hasn't come.

After all the fear, there's nothing. Nothing but simple goodwill from a man I look up to, whose respect carries so much weight for my career and my self-esteem.

And it's a gift. A gift so freely given it takes my breath away, although I'm acutely aware that my surprise at Thum's reaction is the only lamentable part of this entire interaction.

I feel weightless now. I feel absolved.

Perhaps I'll save the news that there's a third, wonderful, party in my and Max's relationship for another day.

70

MAX

When the Dangerous Ds, as I've privately christened them, stayed over on Friday night, we tried falling asleep with Darcy in the middle first. While three adults in a bed may be achievable, it's not necessarily comfortable, though my eight-footer helps.

But within a few minutes, she was complaining that she was overheating between the two of us, so I allowed her to swap places with Dex. I'd have tucked her in behind me, except Dex hadn't yet known the distinct pleasure of waking up next to Darcy, with her hair spilling over the pillow and her tits spilling over the sheets.

So he took the middle spot in my bed, which struck me as symbolic. After all, he'd allowed Darcy and me to tug him into the epicentre of our erotic entanglement.

Sleeping with him, though, felt like the right way to close the circle of our intimacy this evening—and I mean *right* less as *correct* and more as the most visceral kind of *righteous*: good and true and just. He submitted to me in my home. He let me unravel him—*willingly.* He helped me to fuck Darcy, the woman who's inveigled her way into my head with seemingly no effort on her part.

Really, he'd acquiesced so beautifully, so whole-heartedly all night, that it felt only natural that he should allow me to mould the full length of my body to his. To nestle my cock into the cleft of his arse, to bury my face in the crook of his neck. To feel the strength of his hamstrings against my quads, the firm, hairy shapeliness of his calves against my shins. To have his stomach rise and fall against the hollow of my palm.

That was the most perfect part, I think. Those quiet, even, somnolent breaths that filled his belly and warmed my hand. He even slept prettily. And I knew that, whatever demons and qualms still undoubtedly lingered in that intelligent, sensitive brain of his, sleep had allowed him to lay them aside, for a few hours, at least. His slumber was that of a man at peace with himself and his place in the world.

BUT THE PLACE of a queer person in the world isn't easy to find, even for someone like me who's accepted his queerness from the start. For a man like Dex, whose worldview has been warped rather than shaped by loathsome forces—bigotry and fear and shame—that place will be all the harder to find. I'm under no illusions that our orgasm count alone is enough to slay his demons.

That's why I've offered to go to his place this evening. Darcy's dancing tonight, and I don't want Dex having time alone to stew or spiral or spin himself any of the troublesome narratives I know he's more than capable of.

Far better for him to have company. Far better to remind him of all the excellent reasons he's taking these brave first steps.

His flat is on Poultry, which is an odd but historically relevant name for the wide, sweeping street that continues east from the former markets of Cheapside and which leads to the Bank of England. The flat itself is a smaller, less flashy version of mine, just as modern and soulless. That said, it has a decent view of Poultry, where modern buildings lie cheek by jowl with the kind of handsomely symmetrical sandstone constructions that always give the aesthete in me the best kind of ache.

At least my flat is in one of the best locations in London. Living in the heart of the financial district must be depressing during the week and downright eerie on the weekends. I privately resolve to employ my fine selection of carrots and sticks to induce him to spend more time on the west side of town from now on, either at mine or at Darcy's. Gen's former home is by far the most elegant and beautifully appointed of the three, but mine is currently the only one where three adults in one bed have a chance of a decent night's sleep.

Aside from my concerns for Dex's emotional and mental wellbeing, I couldn't give a fuck what his flat is like, because the man standing in the hallway as I stride in is my only focus. He's the kind of gently rumpled that twelve hours in the office will do for someone, his hair a little less perfect than it was this morning, his eyes screen-fatigued, his shirt rolled up at the sleeves and less creased than softened from its morning crispness.

Still, seeing him in his flat—or anywhere, in fact—is like chancing upon a Rodin sculpture in the middle of Ikea. He's as astonishing as he was the first time I saw his photo, the first time I had the distinct pleasure of laying eyes on him in person. Dexter Scott was most certainly crafted by the very best of God's celestial artisanal army. No attention, no expense was spared. His skin is lustrous; his bone structure suggests the angel in charge of his face was both a serious showoff and anal as fuck.

More than all that, more than the undeniable piece of angelic showmanship he represents, is the way he looks at me whenever he sees me. Like he's equal parts terrified and delirious with longing at the thought of what I might do to him. Of how—what—I might make him feel.

'So it went okay, then?' I demand, brushing my lips against his and wasting no time in tugging off my tie. I'm merely making myself comfortable on a horribly muggy day, but his eyes widen at my audacity. His French doors are open, the oppressive humidity so palpable in the room that surely it must break soon. I walk past him and chuck my tie on his sofa, noting the open laptop. He's been working since he got home. Tut tut. This boy needs to learn how to have fun.

'It was absolutely fine,' he says, which is precisely what he told me via text message earlier.

'Glad to hear it.' I help myself to one of the two open beer bottles on the island, their brown glass sweating temptingly. 'So Thum didn't threaten to stone you to death and bury you next to Oscar Wilde?'

His mouth drops open. 'You can't say things like that.'

'I just did.' I shrug and take my first sip of beer, the cold bubbles hitting the back of my throat like the most perfectly pitched song.

'If you think that's funny, it's not. It's incredibly distasteful.'

'I agree. I've been an openly queer man for two-and-a-half decades now. You think I don't rail every fucking day against the fact that people who've had the shitty luck of being born under the wrong regime face not only prejudice but persecution and the *fucking death penalty?*'

He's staring at me as though I'm such a loose cannon that he has no clue which way I'll go.

'I don't know,' is what he says, crossing to the island and grabbing the other beer. 'You always make it seem like you've had this charmed experience where you've glided through life, full of self-certainty and self-confidence and unwavering support, and everyone's just waved their rainbow flags and cheered you on as you forge a path as probably the most successful queer person in British industry.'

That gives me pause. I can see why he might feel blindsided by my apparently sudden giving of fucks.

The first truth is that, in my interactions with him, I've deliberately downplayed the abiding web of prejudice I've endured in all its vast array of forms, be they insidious or unthinking or fear-driven or verbal or physical or career-threatening or downright dangerous.

The second truth is that none of these moments or these people or these risks could ever, *ever* have scared me away from living a life where I'm true to myself and my desires or my feelings. On the contrary, succumbing to them would have felt like the worst, most hateful crime of all.

Which is why I've gone gung-ho with Dex. Painted a strictly rosy picture. Steamrolled him, even. Because fuck knows, the guy doesn't need a single additional datapoint for why he should subjugate his true self another day.

I set down my bottle and turn to face him. 'The self-certainty stuff is true,' I tell him, forcing my voice to sound more measured, less impassioned, than I feel, 'and I have my family to thank for that. I know you don't, and I know you haven't had sexual autonomy modelled for you, and I'm truly sorry for that.

'But none of the rest is true. I've had my fair share of support, but like most other queer people of my generation, I could write a book on all the fucking indignities and hatred and bullying and shitty, shitty stuff I've faced. And I've reacted to it as best I could, *but I have never, ever let it stop me from living my life.*'

I raise an eyebrow to underline that last message, and sure, it's harsher than it needs to be, but for fuck's sake. I'm far angrier on Dex's behalf that he's denied his reality and denied his needs for so long, and I *want* to provoke him. I want him to be pissed off at someone, even if that someone is me, because his being pissed off is far better than him taking it on the fucking chin and finding the world benign and blameless, like the good pseudo-Catholic boy he is.

'Wow,' he says. 'That was a lot of judgement from someone I thought was on my side.'

'I am on your side,' I say, and I take a step towards him, gripping the back of his neck so I can pierce him with the honesty in my eyes. I hope he can see it; I hope he can hear the sincerity ringing in my words. 'Honestly, sometimes it feels like Darcy and I are the only ones who are. But my form of being on your side isn't sitting with you and braiding your hair while you list all the ways you could get hurt by taking these steps. It's showing you that taking them, and allowing yourself to be with me, will be worth it. I *promise* it'll be worth it.'

He blinks. I know he wants reassurances and praise and back-slapping today, but he's come to the wrong person. That's not how I roll. What he'll realise in a few minutes is that the way I roll will feel so fucking otherworldly that it'll light a fire under that scared, tremulous, and sometimes pretty fucking hard to find backbone of his.

It will gird his loins far more effectively than any silly, patronising words of praise ever could.

71

DEX

Max's refusal to acknowledge how far I've come today stings, and quite honestly I resent it. God, I wish I had a fraction of his self-assurance.

'I took a big step today,' I argue. 'It might not seem like that to you, but for someone who's only just allowed himself to admit his queerness, let alone act on it, it's a big deal.'

'I'd argue you did that backwards,' he says with a little smirk. 'You acted on it before you admitted it, even to yourself.'

'Touché,' I mumble, because he's not wrong there.

'Look.' He strokes the back of my neck. 'I know you took a big step, and if you want me to say I'm proud of you, then I will. But I hope you did it for yourself. You should be proud of yourself. The point I'm trying to make, perhaps not as elegantly as I intended, is that I'm curious what you really thought could go wrong in there today with Thum.

'Worst case, he's a homophobe and you felt judged by him on a personal level. It's not a nice feeling, I know. But if you'd felt in the slightest bit shunned, I would have made you march straight into HR and tell them as well as Compliance. There's no *way* we'd let him get away with discriminating against an employee who's as senior and as high profile as you without it being escalated. Right? But it sounds like, in this case, he's given you his blessing?'

'Yeah,' I admit, deflating. There's nothing worse than patting yourself on the back, only to be told you didn't actually do anything impressive. 'He was lovely. I definitely took him by surprise, but once he'd recovered, he was super sweet and very supportive.' I give Max a wry smile, remembering how complimentary Thum was of him. 'I suspect he thought I'd done quite well for myself.'

'As you have,' he quips, and then pauses, his thumb stroking the skin of my neck. 'Can I tell you what I think is going on here?'

I roll my eyes, because of course Max has a view on what's going on.

'Of course,' I say, trying not to sound as churlish as I feel, though I'd gladly kick him in his self-satisfied shin right now, such are my levels of churlishness.

If he registers my eye-roll, he doesn't mention it. 'I think,' he says as though he's choosing his words carefully, 'that all the adults you were exposed to during your formative years crafted a very specific message, and that message is that you ought to behave and feel and love a certain way, and to err from that path would be sinful and unnatural and degenerate. Am I right?'

I nod, and he drops his forehead to mine. I yield to my supposedly sinful and unnatural and degenerate instincts and close my arms around his body, though if something that feels this beautiful is wrong, then I must have no moral compass whatsoever. I splay my palm over the small of his back, noting that his shirt sticks faintly to his skin, such is the humidity level in the air.

'Okay,' he whispers. His voice has lost its harsh edge; now it's tender and softly cajoling. 'And I think, thanks to a variety of circumstances and learnt behaviours that could probably buy your therapist a new yacht, you decided to conform to those totally fucking wacko moral codes. Very possibly, you didn't know not conforming was even an option.'

My eyes prick, not just at the gentleness, the kindness, in his tone but at the jolt of recognition. His theory reminds me of a conversation I had over FaceTime with my sister, shortly after our dad blew up at her and she had to have it out with him. I distinctly remember her words. *No one ever told me I was allowed to reject it all.*

So much doctrine.

So much dogma.

So many rules; so many lines of catechism and lists of sins, venial to mortal, catalogued so neatly for impressionable Catholic children with their relevant punishments indexed equally tightly. And right at the top of that list of mortal sins, up there with killing, were the depravities that caused a vengeful God to rain sulphur and hellfire down on the twin cities of Sodom and Gomorrah.

I've often wondered if the endless detail, the complex hierarchies of sin and the terrible, bloody Biblical examples, and the culture of fear and blame, and us-and-them mentality it all engendered, are a way for the Church to so overwhelm us with small print that it's easier to adopt a policy of blanket adherence.

Let's just stick to the contract, ordinary sinners like Belle and I say. *Let's just do what they say.* Nobody wants God's lawyers shaking paperwork at us at the gates of Heaven because we arbitrarily disregarded some clauses.

His lips are roaming over my face now, brushing along my jaw, trailing up my cheek, kissing the hollow of my temple, as if they've never kissed anything more precious than the skin of this exhausted, confused sinner who didn't get the fucking memo that nothing in the entire contract was legally binding in the first place.

That he could have just torn it up.

'The world is still a shitty place for people like us,' he whispers in my ear. 'It's still tough. Still dangerous—and far more so for people who don't look like you and me. Outside of places like Alchemy, even I still make judgement calls every day on what to disclose. What to hold safe. But it's getting less shitty, especially in parts of the world like this.

'And it makes me really fucking sad that you feel you can't walk into the office of a guy like Thum, as a member of his most valued senior management team, and maybe not *expect*, but at the very least not *hope for*, basic human decency in response to your disclosure.' He wraps his other arm around me tightly.

Just when I think he's finished, he adds: 'But I have a feeling that wasn't your greatest fear. I suspect you genuinely thought it was. But your greatest fear was having to speak those words out loud to someone in a professional setting. Having to tell someone you respect that you're in a queer relationship. Having to officially declare yourself as something—someone—that you've always been told is shameful, and unnatural, and unwholesome. The kind of person who probably seemed very much on the borderline of what you've been taught polite, civilised society is, hmm?

'I don't think it was about Thum, really. I think it was about finally having to give yourself permission to be that person and own it, because not only has no one ever given you permission before, but *they've never done you the courtesy of telling you you didn't need theirs in the first place.*

'So I won't say well done today, but I will say this. You can do whatever the fuck you want. You're a grown fucking man, and you have the right to march into anyone's office and tell them who you really are. Just promise me you won't ever, *ever* ask their permission.'

It's only after he's finished speaking, when my words fail me and I turn to find his mouth instead, to tell him with my lips and tongue how very wise, how disturbingly right, he is, that I hear the rain pelting down on the terrace outside, Heaven's downpour just as impassioned and aggrieved as my lover's unorthodox pep talk was.

72

DEX

The tattoo of rainfall in my bedroom becomes a roar of white noise as I pull the French doors open. The smell carries up from street level, too—that distinctive scent of oil deposits on long-parched roads being washed away. It's a smell that's objectively acrid, unpleasant, and yet always makes me happy, because of the associated relief it signifies, I suppose.

It's not unlike the relief I feel at this small, temporary break in my personal storm. I'm blindly feeling my way through this thing, acting mainly on instinct, keeping this fragile, secret side of me protected as I navigate such seismic shifts.

But Max is my very own deluge, merciless and corrosive and intoxicating, washing away all the layered bitterness that so many years of secrecy and lies and denial have created and leaving me clean. Renewed.

I tug him into my room, then, with a new sense of bravado, of ownership, because he's right about one thing. This man is a prize, a treasure, and God knows he'll make every one of my sacrifices worth it. Despite his brand of tough love just now, I know I did a good thing, a brave thing, today, and I'm damn well going to take my prize. I've earned it.

I've earned *him*.

And when I look into those striking eyes of his—eyes so clear and blue they could only belong to a man who doesn't guard the secrets of who he is, who doesn't shroud his authentic self in cloaks woven from shame or taint—I see the approval, the *permission* to be as bad, as depraved, a man as I possibly can.

He's totally egging me on with his gaze and his smirk as I paw at his shoulders and fumble with his belt buckle and shove his trousers down and wrench his shirt clumsily open. He undresses me at the same time, but his movements are elegant. Measured.

Of course they are.

And when we're both naked, he does that thing I love, taking my eager, straining cock and laying it against the impossibly hot hardness of his own in the palm of his hand.

'I brought lube,' he says. 'I figured you'd be far too proper to walk into a chemist and buy some for yourself.'

'I have lube,' I tell him archly. 'I got some in my online Waitrose shop last week.'

He grins, stroking his thumb over our cocks. It's a simple act, but it still feels like a miracle that I can even do this with him. 'You do Waitrose shops? I didn't think you knew how to cook.'

'It was beer, protein shakes and lube, I think. Oh, and some crisps.'

He laughs softly. 'Classy guy.'

'I try.' I tilt my head up for a kiss, but he dodges my mouth.

'I want to tell you something.'

I pout at his rejection. 'What?'

'You'll get your kiss in a second.' He squeezes us more tightly, and God, it feels so hot and so intense to have us pulsing together in his hand. 'But I want to tell you something.'

He looks at me with those clear blue eyes, and I almost forget how to breathe. His smile turns a little sheepish, I think, and something else. Self-conscious, maybe?

'The first time I saw you...' He trails off. 'I've wanted this from the very first second I saw you, basically.'

I think back to that moment at the club, where he was waiting for me with a G&T and an air of confidence I could never hope to emulate, and I recall how unsettled I was. I labelled the feeling hostility at the time, because he was with Darcy and I wasn't, and because he was obviously a smug bastard, but I'm well aware that was inaccurate at best.

'At the club,' I say.

'No. Well, yes, at the club. But before that, the night Darcy met you. She came home all giggly and confessed that there was a guy she'd met whom she was very attracted to. That was the night she pitched the threesome. And we found your photo on your sister's Instagram feed, and—'

He pauses, his hand flexing around our dicks. Desperate as I am to get off, I find myself more desperate to hear what he's going to say next.

'I took one look at your photo,' he says. His voice is so quiet now, his eyes on me so soft. 'You were laughing—you had your head thrown back, and—I was in freefall. As soon as I saw you, I was gone. You affected me so powerfully from that moment, and everything I've done since the second you walked into Alchemy that night has been to get you, and not just for Darcy. For myself, too.

'And I may have been heavy handed with you—I know I've pushed you hard, before you were ready for any of it—but I don't regret a thing. But I wanted you to know how I feel, because if you think I've come here this evening thinking with my dick alone, that couldn't be less true.'

His words, his amazing, potent, generous, raw words, hang in the air between us as the rain beats on and our dicks throb side by side. I'm used to Max being self-assured and cajoling and relentless; I'm used to him being in control. So vulnerable, heartfelt Max is a lot for my poor heart to contend with.

I resented his heavy-handedness at first, of course I did, because it forced me to do and feel all manner of things I absolutely wasn't ready for. But he knew I needed all those harsh, terrifying, mind-altering lessons more than I would ever let on to myself. From the moment we met, it's always felt like I'm utterly transparent to him, like he can see me more clearly than I can see myself.

We've come so far—he's led me so far—and I have no intention of meeting his honesty with anything less than my own truths.

'I think you affected me, too, from the second I met you,' I tell him now, 'and that's why I tried to run for the hills every time you pushed me. You scared the absolute shit out of me, because the reactions my body was having to you were everything I'd tried very hard not to acknowledge my whole life. And not just my body,' I add, because I don't want him thinking I'm leading with my dick, either. I couldn't bear it if he thought he didn't affect me the way he says I affect him.

When he kisses me, it's ardent and possessive, and the flames of new, astonishing emotions lick at my heart as fiercely as his tongue licks at my mouth. Our dicks are still in his hand, but I know I'll be able to hold off. I know I'll wait for whatever he deems it right to give me.

I know he'll make it worth my while.

He always does.

73

MAX

A minimalist bedroom. The wonderful roar of summer rain outside, the same rain diffusing the light in the room so it's soft and pearlescent.

And, best of all, a naked man lying on his stomach for me, his skin olive against the white sheets, his arse paler and so luscious-looking, dark head cradled in his arms and the most tantalising of shadows between his legs. His cock is out of sight, but I know better than anyone how hard it must be straining right now in its captivity between his stomach and his sheets.

The sight of him takes my breath away.

I kneel up on the bed and nudge his legs apart, taking in the delicate nodes of his spinal column, the curve of his lower back, the tautness of his hamstrings and the firm hairiness of his calves and the silken skin blanketing his shoulder blades. I take in the jut of his jaw, the fine lines of his nose in profile, the flickers of his eyelashes on his cheek as he awaits me, and I can scarcely breathe.

It's his first time doing this, so why in God's name I feel as awe-filled as a virgin, I do not know. It's the combination,

I think, of having wanted him so badly for what feels like far longer than it is and wanting so badly for it to be as transformative for him as he needs it to be. As *I* need it to be.

He's had all his firsts with me. First kiss from a man. First blowjob from a guy. First threesome. I've been attempting to crack this guy's brain open since the moment I met him with skills far closer to orthopaedics than neurosurgery in terms of their finesse level.

But this is the Big Leagues for him, this is serious stuff he's letting me do to him, and much as I want to rail the living daylights out of him, I want more fervently for him to rise from this bed a different man than the man who sank down onto it so willingly for me.

I pour myself on top of him, my body moulding to his, my dick finding the place between his legs like it's magnetised. Going gently with Dex has never been my MO. Pandering to his demons is out of the question. Taunting him with them, though, reminding him how fucking filthy and unleashed he really wants to be? Fuck, has that worked. That feeling of him grinding his cock against the heel of my palm as I baited him with how much he'd secretly loved our shower at Alchemy will be imprinted on my consciousness forever.

'Tell me something,' I murmur against the pretty shell of his ear. 'How many times over the years have you let yourself imagine that someone's big, fat cock was fucking this tight, shameful little hole?'

He groans against the pillow, and it's music. 'About three million.'

'Mmm-hmm. That's what I thought. And answer me this: have you ever let yourself enjoy it?' I already know the answer to this—we've had this conversation before—but I want to hear him admit it right before I breach him there, because it will make it all the sweeter for both of us.

'Not really. Only in—only when I'm about to come.'

'Exactly. And how does it feel to know I'll be pushing into you in a minute, and it'll feel every bit as filthy as you've ever dreamed, and you'll be harder than you've ever been in your life, and the feel of me fucking you will have you coming harder than you ever have, too?'

'Jesus, Max,' he moans.

'Answer my question.'

'Amazing, okay? It'll feel—just do it already, before I change my mind.'

I laugh a little at that, and at the ineffectual way he tries to arch that arse of his against my dick. He can't, of course, given how I've got him pinned down, but my dick appreciates the gesture all the same.

A moment later I'm rising to my knees again and popping the cap of the lube he bought. I dispense a generous amount and slather it between his cheeks. He shivers, and I suspect it's both the cold shock and my exploratory fingers that cause it. His entrance, his little virgin entrance, is tight and hot and clenched like a fist, and I laugh a little. 'Relax.'

He follows his grumble with several moans as I work for a few minutes on unclenching that ring of muscle with first one finger, then two, and an accompanying string of filth and praise. I get him up on his knees so I can fondle his sac and stroke his dick, reminding him that there's nothing to fear here. That I have only unthinkable pleasure in store for him.

When I curl my fingers down and press against his prostate, he nearly shoots off the bed. God bless him, he's so eager and so beautiful and I might lose my fucking mind when I get inside him, because the mere sight of my fingers disappearing into his shivering, gorgeous body is enough to have my own cock swelling impossibly harder.

I'm glad we waited for this. I'm glad I got my clean bill of health back, because I want nothing between us. The first time I take this arse, I'm taking it bare.

He's ready—or as ready as I can get him, anyhow. Another huge dollop of lube and my dick is slick and primed to replace my fingers. His entrance is glistening and prepped. I lie him back down on the sheets. Much as I want him on his hands and knees for me, it'll be too intense for his first time.

I notch my crown against his hole. 'Think about a time when you wanted a guy so badly, and you wouldn't let yourself make a move,' I tell him, my voice shaking with the exertion of self-control it takes not to wedge myself right in. I stroke him with my crown, wet, needy flesh sliding against wet, needy flesh. 'Think about all those filthy fantasies you had, and how incredible it will feel to finally get him.'

'No,' he protests gruffly. 'I've never wanted anyone like I want you. Ever.'

74

DEX

Max's hard body is on top of mine, his dick pressing at my entrance and his breath hot in my ear, and already tonight is perfect. Already, it's everything I could want.

His inhale, when I tell him I've never fantasised about anyone like I have with him, is sharp, almost as if I've surprised him. But he can't be surprised, can he? After all, he's the only guy who's ever spurred me into action. Though, if I'm honest with myself, it was all him. *Him* sticking his thumb in my mouth. *Him* kissing me in the shower, sucking me off in my office, of all places.

He's pushed and pushed, and I've acquiesced so begrudgingly I probably deserve a slap. Thank God he's him. Thank God he doesn't rest until he gets what he wants. Because any other man would have given up, called my bluff and left me to my bullshit and my sham heterosexuality.

'It's only you I fantasise about,' I tell him shakily.

'Oh, yeah?' He smears the lube wetly around my entrance once more and shunts forward, and *holy fucking shit*, he wedges his crown in and it's so intensely confronting and burning that I can't escape the low, anguished sound that escapes me or the instant, panicked coating of sweat that breaks out all over my body. 'It'll get better in a sec. Tell me what you fantasise about. Stuff we've done, or stuff you want me to do to you?'

'Both.' I grit my teeth, my entire body tensing as he presses forward a centimetre or two more, because it's so fucking huge, and, honestly, I'm scared. Maybe he should have worked me up to this a bit more.

'Jesus, sweetheart, you've got to relax,' he says, laughing a little, though his voice is strained. 'I promise, this is the worst bit. Now tell me what I do to you in your fantasies.'

I wish I could see him. I wish I could see *us*—me laid out on this bed, Max ranged over me, prodding me with his huge dick. I bet those arse muscles will really contract when he gives it to me properly. Just the thought of him moving over me like that, glutes tensing as he fucks me, is enough to cause a swell of desire within me, my cock jerking uselessly between my stomach and my sheets, and he, of course, takes the opportunity to press forward.

'The crown's in,' he says, the relief so palpable that I wonder if he doubted he'd get it in. 'Jesus fuck, you're so tight.'

Max's dick is partially inside my body. Oh my God. It's happening, and it's so carnal, so overwhelming, it almost steals my breath away.

'When you got me up against your fridge,' I manage, panting out the words. 'And you jerked me off and told me you were going to sodomise me every which way. That pretty much plays in my mind on a constant loop.'

'Huh,' he says, pleased. 'It does, does it? Even when you're in meetings?'

'Especially then,' I groan, and he laughs against my jaw.

'Good boy.'

'But when you put your thumb in my mouth in the shower and just stared at me?' I continue in my weak, shaky voice, because all the energy in my body is focused on this hot, monstrous invasion in my arse. 'I've never felt such a crazy maelstrom of emotions as I did then. I was so fucking horrified, but it was probably the sexiest moment of my life. I'll be thinking of that on my deathbed.'

'Oh, my sweet boy,' he mutters, rubbing his nose and mouth over my jaw, and he doesn't push in, but he does shift his hips a little, like he's preparing to do battle, preparing to forge ahead, no matter how much harder I'm making it for him with my clenching.

A surge of emotion comes, pricking at my eyes. 'You said I was perfect,' I murmur. 'You said something like *just as perfect as I thought*, and I couldn't believe a man like you was looking at me and pressing down on my lip and having that reaction.'

'You are perfect,' he whispers. 'Jesus Christ, you are so fucking perfect. Darcy and I didn't stand a chance. We both fell the moment we saw you, you perfect, perfect thing.'

And with that, he thrusts, and stops, and thrusts again, and the fucking size of him is so outrageous, so implausible, as is the feeling of having him inside my body that goes so far beyond *fullness*. I'm terrified to move, terrified he'll do what he promised and split me in two. But he's right—it's less brutal than the first couple of inches were.

'Sweet mother of God,' he groans against my cheek. 'I won't survive this.'

That makes two of us, pal.

'If you can,' he grits out, 'I want you up on your knees. If it's not too deep. Then I can play with your lovely, thick dick while I fuck you.'

He's already in so deep it feels like he's touching my lungs, but the greedy little slut in me, the part I've suppressed for so long and who loves nothing more than hearing words like that, is indecently, pathetically excited by the promises Max is making and the strain in his voice that tells me he's about to unleash himself on me.

With grunts from both of us, he hoists me up with an arm around my stomach and I get inelegantly, unsteadily, to my knees, my cock a stiff rod throbbing into nothingness and Max's sweat-slicked body heating me from behind. He kneels between my legs, the hair of his calves against mine, breaths coming harshly, and I wonder afresh at the fact that it's I who am undoing Max Hunter.

I've made him this hard.

I have his entire body straining with effort and need as it cradles mine like a protective outer shell.

It's *me* he thinks is perfect.

And then he begins to move, and I suspect he's trying to hold himself back for me, but each shunt is so impossibly, wonderfully invasive as his length drags against sensitive, unmapped parts of me, stretching me taut as he plunders and takes.

The sounds he's making each time he bottoms out are low and male and raw, and that's it, really. It's the rawness that gets me—of his noises, of mine, of the implausibly close fit between us, of the wet slurp of lube as my body sucks him in with reckless greed.

This is carnal and sweaty; he's fucking me properly now, with deliberate, thorough strokes, and my cock is jerking and weeping, and every time he bottoms out with that blunt, devastating crown of his, he feeds the delicious, staggering ache that's building and building.

I've wanked off as much as the next person. I've had as

much sex as the next person. But to imagine I thought Claudia's slim fingers back there were an indulgence—it's laughable. *This* is what my body was made for, and my body has always, always known that, always wanted it, yearned for it, dreamed of it, even when I was denying and repressing every urge.

This isn't just fullness—it's oneness and plentitude and holiness. And when he braces himself on one trembling arm and reaches around, wrapping his hand around my cock and giving it the home it's been craving, the heat inside my body finds its outlet and that oneness, impossibly, expands.

Max's dick inside my body and his hand on my dick is the best, most righteous, most powerful circuit I've ever experienced, and I let him know exactly that with my grunts and my full-body tremors and the shuddery gasps that get half swallowed up by the pounding of the rain on my concrete balcony.

Somewhere, I've stopped fearing these invasive thrusts and started demanding them, with greedy ruts against him every time he bottoms out. I'm a live wire, vibrating with need around him, splayed open and raw and wholly at his mercy for the orgasm that's shimmering so beautifully, so promisingly, on the horizon that I can scarcely believe I'll earn it.

So I do the only thing I'm capable of, the only thing I know he'll respond to.

I beg.

'Please.' I'm fevered, suspended somewhere between awestruck and broken. 'God, please.'

'He's praying. That seems like a good sign.' Max's voice may be jagged with effort, but it's still honeyed and superior and sardonic, and every submissive, eager-to-please part of my soul strains towards it.

'It's so good.' I can't. 'So good—*fuuuck*. So—'

I'm rocking on all fours, meeting him thrust for thrust, even though my wrists are burning and my biceps are quivering and my thighs are shaking. It's nothing compared to the slide of his body against mine, and the sweeping, glorious heat inside me as he works my cock with strokes that are deliberately way too shallow for what I need and his thick head shunts against the gland that has, until now, been so deeply buried I barely knew it existed.

But he found it.

He found me.

Of course he did.

'This is what I've wanted since I saw that fucking photo,' he grunts. 'I knew you'd be like this—I fucking *knew* I could get you to this state. I wish you could see what you look like, taking me. You could drive a man to do dangerous, dangerous things, sweetheart.'

I repeat what I told him in his flat when he had me up against his fridge, only now I say the words far more brokenly. 'I told you, I want you dangerous.'

More like I need him dangerous. In this moment, I want to be the sole outlet for the extraordinary power he wields. I want him to unleash every ounce of frustration and hunger and venom and might. I want him trigger-happy and sadistically omnipotent.

'And you'll get it,' he grits out. 'You have no idea, you perfect thing, how easy I'm going on you tonight.'

It seems the idea of abusing me more thoroughly sends him over the edge, his thrusts turning unfathomably more ferocious, his huge blunt instrument wreaking havoc on my body with the unlikely precision of a laser, the movements of his hand switching from teasing to purposeful as he prepares to milk my orgasm from me in every way he can.

The Max I first saw at Alchemy, with his perfectly long merino socks and knowing smile and incisive stare is now a grunting, sweating beast pumping into me from behind, and it's that as much as the riot of stimulation against my glands and along my shaft that has me hurtling towards orgasm like a skier who's gone right off the side of a mountain.

I submit to the feeling and the emotion and the raw, filthy exhilaration of being fucked in the arse and the rhythmic slap of his hips against my cheeks I fucking yield to it with every starved, deprived, denied atom in this miracle of nature we call the human body.

The swollen gland Max is hitting so mercilessly releases the most profound, violent climax imaginable, and I don't recognise myself in the guttural roar that bursts from my mouth as my cock surges in his fist and I come with violent convulsions, urgent spurts of ejaculate lashing the sheets.

The sound he makes at my orgasm is almost a laugh, a sound full of surprised delight. I thrash my head as I spend myself, but he's right behind me, rubbing his face in my hair and nipping at my earlobe as he fucks me through it, wringing me dry.

And then he's going rigid behind me, my clever, articulate Max a muddle of grunts and unintelligible curses as he swells and bucks and erupts hotly in the deep, marvellous nook of my body that now belongs irrevocably to him.

When he's eked out every drop of his own orgasm, I lower myself unsteadily to the bed. Before, I was afraid to move with him inside me in case it hurt or tore; now I'm afraid to move in case he slips out, because I'm not ready for that. I want us here, like this, with his dick plugging his cum inside me and his heaving, spent body a reassuring mass on top of me and my stomach plastered to the cooling, gluey wetness of my cum that now soils the crisp white sheets I purchased one recent Saturday at Peter Jones in Chelsea.

The Dex who stalked disinterestedly around that department store, beloved by middle-aged women and the epitome of all that is wholesome, who bought sensible, decent quality sheets and never for a moment imagined a dangerous, beautiful man would fuck the cum out of him and all over them, was a different man to the one who lies here, prostrate and immovable under Max like a flower to be pressed.

I never want to be that man again.

75

DARCY

Having two boyfriends is pretty cool. Not just for the sex, which is so incredible I'm not sure I could ever go back to only one guy, but for the variety. The fullness of experience. They're so similar in many ways: terrifyingly smart; ambitious; successful... but their energies are so different.

Max is all Daddy vibes and cutting jokes. He relishes being in control, and it definitely feels like he's the grownup in the relationship, whereas Dex is a lot softer, more easygoing, with his impeccable manners and far goofier sense of humour than I would have guessed at first glance. When he feels at ease, he's hilarious.

I'm getting the best of both worlds, no doubt about it. But if I had to sum up the difference between them both, Taylor Swift is it in a nutshell. They're both fascinated by the success of the Eras Tour. They can crunch those numbers together for hours and marvel at the tangible proof of her effect.

When it comes to her actual music, though, their reactions have been so different. They're well aware of my obsession with her—luckily they have no clue quite how many *1989* and *Midnights* rides I've done on Max's Peloton when they're at work.

But when I played *Champagne Problems* to Max and tried to explain why it was such an important song, he just laughed and asked why the fuck she mispronounced *Dom Perignon*. He said he couldn't un-hear it. *Rude.*

Whereas Dex not only listened the whole way through the ten-minute version of *All Too Well* with me, but he read the Genius lyrics while he listened *and* we had a heartfelt discussion afterwards about how the stuff with her dad and at her twenty-first felt like the biggest betrayal of all.

See what I mean???

The only downside to having two boyfriends, as far as I can see, is that trying to agree on what to watch on TV goes from painful to downright brutal.

Especially since I'm outnumbered.

Maybe I should have considered trading Dex in for another woman—at least we could have cast a majority vote and spent our evenings watching *The Eras Tour* or *Bridgerton* for the millionth time.

Instead, we've found ourselves in so many standoffs, these past couple of months. Max wants to watch thriller-y things like *Slow Horses* that honestly go over my head, even if the subtitles are on. Dex is happy with anything David Attenborough, which he says he finds "relaxing", but excuse me if I don't enjoy spending my evenings watching hundreds of teeny-tiny shivering baby flamingos perish in violent storms or giant, wobbly walruses plummeting off cliff edges to their messy deaths.

Happily, we've found a temporary compromise, and that compromise is *Shrinking*, even though the boys watch it purely for Harrison Ford and I watch it only for the female shrink, Gaby, and spend most of my time wishing she was real and lived in London and wanted to be my friend, because she might just be my all-time favourite TV character. (Though I will admit that the scene where Harrison Ford's character, Paul, gets stoned at Jimmy's party is Emmy-worthy.)

Fuck knows what we'll end up watching when we've got up to speed.

It's Friday night, and I've barely seen the boys all week. I'm not gonna lie—this *ships in the night* thing is taking its toll. They both get up at the crack of dawn to work out before hitting their day jobs, or to hit their day jobs before they work out, and I'm on stage at Alchemy at nine o'clock Monday to Thursday.

The lack of overlap in our workdays is shitty, though we do our best. I'll meet one or both of them in the City or in Mayfair for a quick lunch whenever they can get away from their desks, but Dex isn't yet publicly out of the closet, so we tend to keep our PDAs to a minimum when the boys are together.

In the evenings, we'll have a bite to eat at Max's when schedules allow. Dex can usually extricate himself from the office once the markets close, but Max is burning the candle as the IPO gathers pace. It's in a stage called, apparently, PDIE, or Pre Deal Investor Education, which is where the research analysts from the various banks go and see potential investors and teach them the ins and outs of the company.

Apparently, this stage triggers tonnes of extra work for Wolff's management team, as well as all its in-house analysts, because the investors invariably raise three million questions, from queries about forecasts for obscure parts of the business to bitching and moaning about the potential valuation of the shares. They're all doing their homework on their side, it seems, and every man and his dog has their own view on Wolff's future prospects, as well as how much a stake in those prospects is worth.

See? I'm practically a banker these days.

Anyway, it's all stressful and frantic and a mahoosive time and energy suck for Max. He's knackered, and he hasn't even been on the road yet. Dex and I stay here a couple of nights during the work week, but sometimes I race back from Alchemy, fresh off the stage, and slide into bed next to two adorable sleeping bodies.

Wafting around all day when they're hard at work feels a bit pointless. And when I'm actually on stage, I find I'm focused less on the thrill of having so many hungry eyes on my body and more focused on why I'm not at home with them. It seems, shockingly, that my inner attention whore is getting all her fixes from her two scarily gorgeous boyfriends and no longer feels the need to *Mirrorball* herself for strangers. Who'd have thought it?

It's all a bit shit, as I said, because the three of us are in our honeymoon period, yet our lack of spare time is ruining that. All of which explains why, instead of being out on the town on a Friday night, or at least hanging at Alchemy with our friends, we're on the sofa with a bottle of lovely white wine and bowls of Max's excellent Thai green curry in our hands while *Shrinking* plays.

And the weirdest part of all is that I fucking love it. I'm twenty-five. I should be out on the town, dancing my little socks off, but instead I'm vegging at Max's place, knowing full well that when the food and the wine and the downtime has restored my two gorgeous worker bees, we'll take each other to heights no cheering crowd could ever mimic.

'This is so fucking good,' Dex groans, shovelling more grub into his mouth.

'Isn't it? Max, you're so clever,' I say, nestling more closely against Dex. His hair is still damp from his post-gym shower, and he smells indecently good. Also, his t-shirt is the *softest*. I feel bad that Max cooked for us after the long week he's had, but he brushed off my concerns. His official line was that cooking is a way for him to unwind, but the unofficial line is that he's a major feeder. As I've told Dex before, feeding is his love language.

Yep. I've hit the jackpot.

Dex smiles down at me, resting his fork in his bowl so he can brush a stray strand of hair off my face. He looks relaxed and so very content. They both have my absolute favourite faces in the world. Truly *excellent* faces. I beam back at him.

'Fuck, you're beautiful,' he says, those big, expressive eyes of his so full of admiration. Affection. 'I love you so much.'

I don't freeze so much as gape at him, because I think he just said the L-word. And I'm pretty sure he didn't intend to.

On my other side, Max barks out a shocked laugh, but I keep on gaping at Dex, watching for him to react, to baulk or turn away or backtrack.

But he doesn't do any of those things. He widens his eyes and arches his eyebrows like *wow, what have I just said*, but he doesn't take it back. He just watches me and bites down on his lip, and I wait.

'Wow,' he says, leaning forward so he can set his bowl down on the table. 'Okay. I didn't—I planned for it to be a lot more romantic than that when I said it.'

'But did you mean it?' Max presses. He slides his arm around my shoulder, like he's showing me he has my back no matter what Dex says. I inwardly grimace a little, because

Max may push Dex all the time when it comes to their dynamic, but no girl wants a guy to double down on a spontaneous declaration of love under duress.

'It's okay,' I murmur, but Dex's gaze is flitting from me to Max, those long eyelashes fluttering.

'Of course I meant it, angel,' he says, a beautiful smile spreading across his face. 'How could I not? I'm surprised I haven't blurted it out before.'

My face is hot and my heart is racing and all these feelings are happening to me, swirling around me, enchanting me like a spell. *Dex loves me.* Oh my God. He *loves* me. This incredible, sensitive, stunning man loves me. I grip my bowl tightly with trembling hands as he leans in and kisses me slowly, worshipfully. This man and these kisses could melt me down until I'm nothing but a pile of bones.

He pulls away gently and looks over my shoulder, and I feel Max's arm tensing around me. Dex swallows, his Adam's apple bobbing, and there's no mistaking the quiet intensity in his gaze as he looks at Max. If what he said to me tumbled out easily, what he's about to say to Max strikes me as a truth it's far more terrifying for him to divulge.

In that split second where they hold each other's gaze, I find myself praying he says the same three words to Max. *Tell him you love him,* I urge him silently. *Tell him. You can't leave him hanging after saying that to me. It'll kill him. He's so crazy about you.*

'I love you, too,' he whispers to Max, and their mouths crash together over my shoulder. Max is holding me tightly to him, so we're in a kind of group hug as they kiss, but he breaks away after just a moment and stands up, pausing the TV. I look up to see what he's doing. He pushes his and Dex's half-empty bowls away from the edge of the coffee table and sits down on it so he can face us both.

'So we're doing this,' he says, and his voice sounds oddly stiff. I'd think it was dispassionate, too, if the tremor of emotion in it wasn't clearly audible. 'Because this is a big deal.'

It strikes me, then, that neither of us have said it back to Dex yet. He's given us these gifts, and we haven't reciprocated. The formal, uptight guy I met at Alchemy a couple of months ago has gone, and the Dex sitting next to me is open-hearted and so giddy with emotion that it just bursts out of him on a quiet Friday night together in front of the TV.

I smile a little self-consciously, because trust Max to decide we need some kind of board meeting—presided over by him, obviously—rather than letting the moment unfold organically. This is scary and grown-up as it is.

I know how I feel about them both—I've fallen so hard for them that it bloody terrifies me—but I wasn't planning on showing my cards yet. I've never told any guy I love him, and there's so much more at stake here. So many moving parts.

Three hearts instead of two.

I haven't just been trying to work out my dynamic with each of them, but the dynamic between them, too, because it all matters.

It matters if they fall so hard for each other that I get left behind.

It matters if our little trio, so explosive in the bedroom and so contented when we're alone together, is too radical, too unconventional, for Dex to ever get truly comfortable with.

It matters if Max, a guy who has a shitload on his plate and isn't used to sharing his life with anyone or making any sort of compromises, tires of his little playthings.

See what I mean? It has the potential to be a clusterfuck. But I don't think I've realised until this moment how much I've been taking it day by day, enjoying every time we steal an evening or a weekend together and refusing to let myself hope that there's any future for us, that our foundations go beyond the kinky to something that can sustain all three of our hearts. Our souls.

And it's only when Max steeples his fingers and brushes his lips against his fingertips that I feel the icy fingers of fear. Because I know he's about to say something I won't like.

76

MAX

I look from Darcy to Dex. My Dangerous Ds, both so young, so achingly beautiful. They were both supposed to be conquests—trophies I hankered after and then claimed, moving on when I'd had my fill.

What a fucking joke that was. They have me in a chokehold so strong that their power over me is complete. I'm a useless mess around them, but they don't seem to understand that.

Still, I haven't completely abandoned my self-respect, and while I can still cling to the vestiges of my agency, I should draw some lines in the sand. Starting with this.

I've grown greedier, you see. The goalposts keep shifting. Initially, I wanted to provoke a reaction in Dex. To make him admit he was queer, make him understand all the things about himself he'd previously denied. Then I wanted to unravel him. To take all his firsts. And I did, and it didn't help.

Because now I want him all.

I lean forward and take both their hands.

'This has come sooner than I expected,' I say, trying to

keep my voice even, 'but you're right, Dex. We should talk about our feelings and our hopes for this relationship, and it makes sense to do it now.' I drink them both in. They're wearing twin expressions of concern, doubt, and they crucify me, so my first priority is to assuage those doubts.

'I've fallen very deeply in love with both of you,' I tell them with foreign words that feel both revelatory and right. 'You're both very, very dear to me, and so is this. I can't quite articulate how special our relationship is, new though it may be.'

Their faces light up to such an extent that it's humbling.

'Oh, thank God,' Darcy says in a rush, grabbing at the back of my neck with her free hand and pulling me in so she can brush her mouth against mine. 'I thought you were going to dump us both for a second. Didn't you, Dex?'

He doesn't answer, because he's too busy gazing at me like he could stare at my face for all his tomorrows and never, ever grow tired of what he sees.

'I'm not finished,' I say. 'I know this is special. You know it, too.' I pause, my eyes fixed on Dex. I squeeze Darcy's hand more tightly to show her I've got her. And then I say, 'So it deserves more than sneaking around in the shadows and playing platonic friends at our City lunches and keeping these feelings to the privacy of our homes. It deserves oxygen and you damn well know it.'

Darcy lets out a little gasp, as if she can't believe I've called Dex out on this, but it's time. We've been sneaking around for two months now, and if there's one thing I don't do, it's sneak around like I've done something wrong. If I do something, I own it.

I stroke her knuckles, but my eyes are on Dex. It's been effortless with her since the start, but with him it's been a constant push-pull. Anyone who saw us together (if he ever fucking let anyone see us together, that is) would assume I'm the dominant one in the relationship. That's true in bed, at least.

But from where I'm standing, he's been in the driving seat from the word go, and every time I've pushed him, it's been as someone desperate to see him put his foot on the gas. Behind closed doors, our relationship is perfect. It's loving, it's exciting, it's intoxicating.

Something like that deserves to flourish out there in the world, no?

He is a deer caught in the fucking headlights, though he can't possibly have failed to see this coming. I refuse to look away from his ridiculous eyes, which right now reflect everything from adoration to terror.

Finally, he finds his words. 'You're right.' He falters, glancing at Darcy, who gives him a little nod of encouragement. Her lips are pressed together like she's trying not to cry. 'It's so special—it deserves everything.'

His concession makes me gentle. 'I know it must always feel like I'm railroading you, but that's not it. I love you. I want to be able to walk into any bar or restaurant with my arm around you. I'm so fucking proud and delighted to be with you—I want to shout it from the rooftops.' And if he doesn't feel the same way, that tells me everything I need to know.

He allows me a small, pleased smile then. 'I know. Me too.'

'Do you?' When Darcy meets him at work for a quick coffee, I know he kisses her in Loeb's lobby. I know he slings his arm around his ravishing, appropriate girlfriend as he saunters out into the sunshine with her. I know, because she's told me. And I can only imagine the looks they get—

looks of approval. Envy. Because they're a beautiful couple in the exact way that society expects.

Passersby will glance at the extraordinarily handsome, dark-haired guy in a suit, his arm around the gorgeous redhead. Her head is probably thrown back in laughter—it usually is—and he'll be smiling down at her adoringly. They make the kind of couple that you automatically look at and think *they should have babies together. They'd make such beautiful babies.*

I know this, because that's how I feel when I look at them, too. They're radiant. Darcy's so good for him. She nurtures him. Emboldens him. Her levity is the perfect counterbalance for his seriousness. And even if what he and I have is extraordinary, what they have is the culmination of everything he's been raised to aspire to.

Take me out of the equation, and you could argue that Darcy's an audacious choice for him. I can't see him telling his father his girlfriend dances naked at a sex club, although if his sister can hide the fact that her husband *owns* the club, I'm sure Dex could fudge the details of Darcy's job.

Still, you see what I mean. He's told me about his previous fuck buddies. Safe, over-achieving, impeccably groomed career women who want him for his patrician looks and job title and platinum Amex. Darcy's a breath of fucking fresh air compared to them. Thank fuck he's had the good sense to hitch his wagon to hers.

But that leaves me so far off left field on the spectrum of appropriate life choices for Dex that I'm pretty sure I'm sitting in the equivalent of a dung heap.

And I need him to choose me. Us. I need him to find his backbone, and make the conscious decision to fuck everyone who doesn't have his best interests at heart, and put on a giant pair of wellies, and take a flying leap into the dung heap with me.

So when I ask him if being public is something he really wants, I'm trying to dig under those layers of manners and work out *what the actual fuck he really wants.*

'I want it in that I fantasise about it, all the time,' he says, screwing his face up like he's articulating his thoughts in real time. 'I want to be that person, so badly I can't tell you. But then I imagine the steps I'd have to take to actually get there, and it's like asking me to jump out of a plane without a parachute. I totally freeze—it's completely terrifying.'

I have many, many things to say to this, but I force myself to be silent as he stumbles on.

'The idea of walking into, say, the Arts Club or Harry's Bar and having you stand up and cup my face in your hands and just *kiss* me in front of the entire place—I imagine it, and it makes me so proud and emotional that I could cry just thinking about it. I want that *so fucking much.*'

He reaches over now, cupping my face for a moment, and I wonder if he's even conscious he's doing it. But there's no doubting the sincerity in his devastating eyes.

'But it's also so horrifying it makes my balls shrivel up,' he confesses, and I spit out a shocked laugh. 'Not you—but all the judgement. Being looked at and talked about and called names. It would be exactly like standing up in the middle of one of those places and stripping naked while everyone watches.'

Darcy's rubbing his back, and she lays her head against his shoulder. 'That's so awful. I totally get it. And you're not the only one who's scared. It makes me feel a bit sick, too. I love you both so much, and I'd be so insanely proud to walk into a room with you two on my arms. I'd be like, *hi, bitches.* But the idea of having to explain to random fucking people every day that I'm with two guys, and knowing everyone's thinking, *wow, she must really like dick*, is completely mortifying. I'd argue the queer stuff is more normalised in society than the throuple stuff.'

I'm smiling at Darcy's humorous take on our situation, as well as her declaration of love, and so is Dex. But she's right, of course. There are two issues at stake here. Dex is queer and still in the closet. And the three of us are in the type of relationship that our society is not yet remotely equipped to handle.

'I love you, angel,' he tells her, brushing his lips over her temple. 'And I get that. It's scary for all of us.'

'You're right, both of you,' I interject. 'But you're wrong about one thing, Dex. You'd have a giant fucking parachute, and that's me and Darcy.'

He looks at me, and the emotion shining in his eyes has me pushing on.

'It's really quite straightforward,' I tell them. 'It comes down to choosing yourself, and choosing us, over everything else, plain and simple. Yes, it'll be shitty, especially for you'—I nod at Dex—'but what I've been telling you all along is that none of it—*none* of the bullshit or judgement or slurs—is more important than your happiness and your right to live your life as the person you are fucking supposed to be.'

I blink away the wetness in my eyes. It's so frustrating, this topic. Of course I can see how terrifying it is for him. Of *course*. But he's subjugated his desires for decades now, and I need him to be so fucking sick of it that he decides enough is enough. Only he can do that.

'There will be people who don't understand, and people who see your choices as sick or sinful or deviant. Whatever. I'm sure there'll be some heartbreaking choices for you to make, but I'm not asking you to choose me and Darcy over your parents or anyone else—I'm asking you to finally, for God's sake, choose your own fucking happiness.'

I squeeze Darcy's hand and release it before I reach over to Dex. It's my turn to take his face in my hands and I do, cradling his jaw, marvelling at the multitude of emotions warring in his eyes.

'I don't know how many times you need to hear this,' I tell him gruffly, 'but you are perfect. I've told you before, and I'll keep on telling you till you get it through that thick head of yours. You're perfect as you are. Your needs, your choices. You have a beautiful heart, and everyone who has you in their life is the better for it. And if they don't accept you for who you are, they don't deserve to be in your life.

'You get to exist in the world as yourself and not change a single fucking thing to accommodate anyone else. Understood? You're allowed to go out there, and take up space, and stand in the middle of a restaurant full of your industry peers and fucking *revel* in it when a man kisses you and tells you you're his favourite part of his day. You deserve all that. You deserve everything you've ever wanted, and I really, really wish you'd just *finally* make the decision to take it all. Because, God knows, it's overdue.'

77

DARCY

When the going gets tough, you know it's time to bring in the girls. Tonight's little rendezvous with Belle and Maddy has been in the diary for a couple of weeks, but it honestly couldn't have come at a better time.

We've even dragged Nat out. She and I don't need to be at Alchemy until eight, and Belle and Maddy are done for the day, which means we have a couple of hours to enjoy some food at Sexy Fish, an Asian restaurant in Mayfair that's totally up its own arse yet extremely fabulous.

Belle's a couple of months away from popping, but she's on good form, looking disgustingly glowy. Her bump is dinky and perky and ridiculously cute, and she even let me feel her baby kicking. The feel of that pressure against my hand did things to my ovaries that I don't remotely want to acknowledge.

Maddy's pregnant, too. Apparently she and Zach knew at their wedding that she was a few weeks along, but didn't make the news public until last month when they went for their twelve-week scan. They're finding out next month what they're having, unlike Belle and Rafe, who are keeping it a surprise. I'm so excited for both of them I can barely stand it, but to say I'm distracted tonight is an understatement.

'Ugh,' I say, slumping on the banquette. 'What a week.'

'Too much dick?' Maddy asks with phony sympathy, and we all cackle. The holy states of wedlock and pregnancy haven't changed her one iota, as far as I can tell, except for making her even happier than she was and even more gossip-hungry.

'That's the *least* of my problems, believe me.'

'Give one of them to Nat,' she says. 'It's plain rude, keeping both of them.'

'Nah.' I smile smugly. 'I'll keep them both.' Because they're both so fucking adorable. And *we love each other*. Even if we haven't yet worked out how that love will look.

'So *not* too much dick,' she presses.

Belle groans. 'Please stop referencing my brother's dick.'

'Not a chance. Darce? Details, babes.'

'Fine. I'm getting exactly the right amount of dick, but thank you for your concern. It's just... well, Max kind of threw down the gauntlet to Dex over the weekend.'

Belle's eyes grow wide with concern.

'Has anyone ever wondered what a gauntlet actually is, though?' Maddy muses aloud.

'It's a kind of fortified glove that medieval warriors wore in battle,' Nat offers.

We all swivel our heads so we can gape at her. She shrugs.

'What? My brother's a huge D&D fan.'

'I'm sorry, but can we go back to *my* brother?' Belle asks. 'What do you mean, exactly?'

I hesitate, because all of this is a major infringement of Dex's privacy, especially in front of Nat. But, honestly, this is my relationship too, and I desperately need advice. Anyway, Nat's already heard snippets about our little ménage.

'So, we had a big conversation on Friday night. Dex kind of blurted out that he loved me, and then we all said it.'

Maddy bounces up and down in her seat and squeals. Belle clamps her hand over her mouth. And Nat looks so genuinely delighted for me that I vow here and now to find her a good man. Because that's what people do when they're obnoxiously and smugly in love, right?

'Oh my God!' Belle says, removing her hand. 'You and my brother are in love!'

'Yep,' I say, and we share a moment of happy grinning, because this is big. 'He's so amazing.'

'He really is.'

'And the most gorgeous guy I've ever seen in my life.'

'I suppose so,' Belle grits out as Maddy raises her mocktail. 'Truth.'

'And he actually told Max he loved him?' Belle asks incredulously.

I nod. 'Yeah. He really did.'

'Holy crap,' she whispers. 'That's unbelievable.'

'So back to the gauntlet bit,' I say. 'Max basically went all funny. He told us he'd fallen very deeply in love with us both, or something just as romantic, but then he went full TED Talk on Dex. He gave him this heavy spiel about how special our relationship was, and how it deserved oxygen, and the bottom line was that he's not prepared to hide in the shadows forever if Dex can't get his arse in gear to come out of the closet.'

Belle puts her head in her hands. 'Oh my God.'

'It makes sense, right?' Maddy asks, putting her arm

around Belle. 'That's obviously going to be a source of tension between them.'

Belle looks up, her beautiful face stricken. 'Yeah. I mean, I agree. But poor Dex. God, I feel sick for him.'

'I know.' I reach over and squeeze her hand. 'But I'll say this. I think Max is kind of good for him. He definitely pushes him, but he never makes him feel alone. He actually said the most amazing stuff, all about how your brother is perfect just as he is, and he deserves to take up space in the world and have his needs met and do what he wants to do. It was really beautiful.'

Maddy presses her hand to her chest. 'Oh, my heart. That's so romantic.'

'It really was. I'm still worried for him, though.'

'How did he take it all?' Belle wants to know.

'He said he really wants it, he just doesn't know how to take the steps to get there. He cares so much about people's perceptions, and he didn't really go into it, but I think he's super worried about your dad.'

Belle's nodding slowly. 'I can only imagine. He's basically going to have to choose between Dad and you guys. I just don't see Dad being remotely willing to accept him as queer and in a poly relationship.' Her eyebrows rise at the thought of it. 'It's a bloody nightmare.'

'That was kind of the conclusion we reached, I think, though Max made it clear it was less about him choosing us and more about him choosing himself and his own happiness.'

'Sounds like the pep talk I had to give you when your dad went nuclear, babes,' Maddy says, nudging Belle with her elbow.

'Yeah, except this is a million times worse,' Belle says.

'That was sex before marriage, this is a whole other ballgame. You're right, Darce, I'm really glad he has you and Max. You'll look after him, won't you?'

'We'll smother him in love,' I say. 'He's not alone in this. So he's promised to give it serious thought, but he needs some time to process, I think. He knows what's at stake. Max is such a strong character—there's no way he'll keep sneaking around with Dex when he's always been so vocal about his own sexuality.'

'Have you thought about what would happen if Dex decided he couldn't do it?' Nat asks tentatively.

My eyes fill with tears. 'I can't. I can't even think about it. There's no way I could choose between them. We're so good together! You should see us. If I say so myself, we're adorable.'

'We want you all to be happy,' Belle says. 'We want this, too. We want you guys at Alchemy, having fun together, not feeling judged or constrained. Actually—'

Maddy looks up sharply. 'What?'

'If you think about it,' Belle says, 'Dex's life is pretty unbalanced. All his friends are getting married—to women. I can't imagine the City is the easiest place to build a queer community, even if all the banks say they're supporting diversity. All his life, his social circle has been seriously conservative. Think about it. And then he's got you guys, but that's all still behind closed doors. It's not a surprise that he can't imagine merging the two realities.

'I was like that, too, until I met Rafe and found a community that was way more open-minded and tolerant. I think he needs more exposure to that kind of vibe so he can normalise acting from the heart. He's never had it modelled for him, really.'

'What are you suggesting?' I ask. 'More time at Alchemy, maybe?'

Belle grins. 'I'm suggesting we get Rafe, Zach and Cal to give him a pep talk of their own.'

78

DARCY

We're all remarkably well behaved this evening. The pregnant ladies aren't drinking, obviously, and Nat and I are nursing our cocktails carefully, given neither of us can show up for work shitfaced. I'm in danger of making this evening all about me, but I have another question for the girls.

'Can I tell you something I'm thinking about and you tell me if I'm crazy?'

'Of course,' Nat says. 'What's up?'

'The difference between my and the boys' schedules is driving me crazy. They work all day, I dance all evening. I never get to see them. And I'm starting to get a bit icky about the naked dancing stuff.'

Maddy frowns. 'Are they making you feel bad about it?'

'God, no. Not in the slightest. They're really supportive. But I don't like it as much as when I was single. And also...' I trail off.

'What is it, hon?' Belle asks gently.

I sigh. 'I'm proud of my talents, but honestly, where do I

go from here? Dancing's my passion, but dancing in a club is hardly the stuff stellar careers are made of, is it?'

'Oh, I see what's happening,' Maddy says. 'You're dating two seriously ambitious guys, and you're feeling inadequate. That's it, isn't it?'

I consider. 'Not inadequate, because I'm not sure there's room in that relationship for three workaholics and I think my carefree vibe is good for them, but thoughtful, maybe. The dancing gig is great, and I've been sponging off my sister with a nice rent-free pad.

'But if Dex gets himself sorted out and we want to make this relationship work, then maybe it's time I start thinking a bit more about the future, you know? Like what I want to do longer term.'

'What are you thinking?' Belle asks.

'Well, I've always wanted to open a dance studio, especially one for kids. I love teaching them—remember how much fun I had with Zach's girls at the wedding?'

'You were amazing with them!' Maddy says. 'They're still doing that TikTok dance you taught them.'

I laugh. 'That makes me so happy. So yeah, that's what I'm thinking about at the moment. I ran it past the guys, and they both said they'd invest and help me get it off the ground, which is so generous. I'm not sure how I feel about it, but I'll see how things go between us.'

'Of course they'll invest,' Belle says. 'It'd be a shrewd business decision on their part. Don't feel like it's a favour.'

'I think it sounds amazing,' Nat chimes in. 'For what it's worth, running your own business, *especially* when it involves real-life stuff like staff and physical space, is a lot. The stuff that goes wrong—you can't make it up. I don't want to put you off, because I think it's a really cool idea, but if you have two men who love you and believe in you and want to be there to support you? Then honestly, don't think twice. Say yes. Because it'll make the world of difference.'

There's something in her voice that gives me pause. It's not bitter, but it's guarded. 'Do you have a business partner?' I ask. 'Or do you do it all yourself?'

She gives a self-deprecating laugh. 'I do it all myself. And it's ridiculous, and stressful, and lonely as hell.'

'You poor thing, babes,' Maddy says. 'Let me get this straight. You run your own fashion brand *by yourself* all day and then work in Alchemy at night?'

'I don't do it all myself,' Nat says. 'I have a team—they're amazing. But they're all seamstresses and pattern cutters. And we outsource some of the really labour-intensive stuff to specialist houses like Lésage and Lemarié.' At our blank looks, she clarifies, 'They're two of Chanel's specialist ateliers. Lemarié does feathers. They're fabulous.'

'It sounds dreamy,' Belle says.

Nat laughs again. 'Dreamy... yeah, sure. But also back-breaking work and stresses and logistics. I promise you, you can't make the shit that happens up. And the clients are... well, they're practically couture clients, so you can imagine how exacting they are.'

'How the hell do you do it all?' Maddy wants to know.

'Not much sleep. I try to stay very organised. And I don't even have one boyfriend, let alone two, so that helps free up my time.' She gives me a kind smile.

'There's so much more you can achieve when you're not getting dicked down by two guys every night,' Maddy muses, and I flick some of my cocktail at her.

'Fuck off.'

'Ooh, touchy.'

'So you run it all alone?' Belle asks, wide-eyed. 'That

makes me feel tired. I think you're amazing. You must have to be so resilient.'

'Yeah, well I had a tough time as a kid,' Nat says, 'and I think it's given me some perspective. At the end of the day, we're not saving lives. I'll do my absolute best, but I'm in the fashion industry. It's not life and death, and I have to remember that.'

'Are we allowed to ask why you had a tough childhood?' Maddy asks. Belle elbows her hard. 'Ouch!'

'We invited her out for some nice drinks,' Belle says, glaring at her, 'and she's already told us how short on time she is. So don't you think it would be nice if she could enjoy her cocktail without being interrogated?'

'It's okay,' Nat says shyly. 'I don't mind. And it wasn't that bad—I have an amazing family. We just went through some hard stuff, I suppose. My dad's company went bust when I was ten, and things were pretty awful. We lost our home and had to move into a council house, and I swear my mum cried for the first year.

'My brother and I got pulled out of our fancy schools and put in this really rough high school, and he got badly bullied for years. Like, really, really badly.'

'How badly?' Maddy asks, screwing up her face like she's scared to hear the answer.

Nat swallows, and we all stare at her. She's so lovely. So refined and impressive and hardworking. I bitch about my parents a lot, but God, my childhood was bliss compared to this shit.

'It was a gang,' she says. 'They really had it in for him—like I said, he's a D&D nerd. Really emo, and the sweetest guy on the planet. But they used to beat him up, and one day the gang leader attacked him with a broken bottle.'

She pauses, and we all stare at her in horror.

'Was he okay?' Belle asks in a tiny voice.

'He lost an eye,' Nat says, and we all gasp in unison. 'It was—it was so, so horrific. So now he has this glass eye, and he didn't finish his A-levels for years, because he was too traumatised to go back to school.'

'Oh my God,' I say, my hand clamped over my mouth. 'That is horrific. I'm so, so sorry. Please tell me they expelled the guy who did it.'

She laughs, and this time it's definitely bitter. 'Yeah. He got a couple of years in juvie, too. But you want to know the funny thing? He turned himself around, and I kid you not, the guy is a real, live billionaire. It was Adam Wright.'

Belle leans forward. 'Hang on a sec. Adam Wright as in *the* Adam Wright?'

Nat grimaces and nods. There's a stunned silence at the table, because Adam Wright is a household name, and he is *hot*. Like, mafia-book-boyfriend hot. And he definitely looks like a billionaire, not some cowardly thug who's done time behind bars.

She sighs. 'I know what you're thinking. You can say it.'

Maddy, obviously, is the first to voice what we're all thinking. 'But he's gorgeous. He's Max-level eligible and impressive.'

'Gorgeous people can have rotten cores too, Mads,' Nat says teasingly, but she's right, of course. 'It's not even a secret. He talks about it all the time in interviews. I swear he's made it part of his personal brand, like having this redemption arc will give him more authenticity.'

She slams her glass down on the table, and we all jump. 'And I'm sick of it. I'm so fucking sick of it. Because the untold part of his little *road to Damascus* story is that he ruined the lives of a whole family by being the disgusting, violent little shit that he was.'

Jesus Christ. I've never seen mild-mannered Nat so riled, but I can't blame her.

She inhales, her lips pressed in a firm line, and then takes a huge slug of her champagne. 'Anyway. Let's just say I hope our paths never cross, because I will bottle that man so hard he'll bleed out on the floor. He's a total fucking psycho. Leopards don't change their spots, you mark my words.'

79

DEX

Why the fuck I'm standing on Sunningdale's fifth tee on a cold, crisp Saturday morning with Rafe, Zach and Cal I have no clue.

All I know is this: I'm not here to play golf.

My game is pretty rusty. I've played here and there over the past decade, mainly in Connecticut at the invitation of generous colleagues, but I certainly wasn't a member of any club while I was stateside. These three aren't half bad at it, though.

Cal can drive the ball for miles, though his putting at the last few tees has been a bit hit and miss. Rafe's game is solid. Skilful. And Zach takes so long lining up his shot that he might want to think about switching to chess. I can see him mentally triangulating ground gradient and wind speed and distance for every shot, but it works for him, because most of them are bang-on.

Rafe and Cal are both members here, and it's a stunning course. Given our early tee time, there's no buildup of other players in front of us, though given Zach's constant prevaricating I suspect there'll soon be a line behind us. Forgoing my Saturday lie-in and extricating myself from between two warm bodies this morning was brutal, but Zach and Cal have kids to get back to, so it makes sense to do this early.

We talk about work, naturally, as we walk.

'How's the deal going?' Zach asks, his eyes on the distant green, where our balls lie.

'The interest level is insane,' I confess, 'and that's without Max having gone on the road yet. It's going to be a total fucking shit show, I can feel it.'

Banks always hope for a "hot" deal, which is industry speak for a deal whose shares are oversubscribed. But when there's as much demand as I suspect there will be for Wolff, it can turn into a giant headache. Every investor wants a decent allocation, and very few of them will get what they want.

If I had to guess at this moment, I'd say most people will end up getting ten percent of what they requested or less, which will make for some very unhappy clients.

'It's only going to get worse,' Rafe says sagely. 'He's bloody impressive.'

'Yeah,' I agree noncommittally.

'And how are you finding Loeb?' Cal asks.

I sigh. 'Lovely people. Great culture. It's no Goldman, that's for sure. The research is great, and Wolff was a win, but honestly, we have a mountain to climb to make our mark.'

'Not easy when there's so little business to go around,' Zach remarks, dropping his clubs next to his ball, which is the only one that actually made it onto the green, and retrieving his putter.

'Exactly,' I say, my gaze flickering between his face and his ball. It seems like a fairly straightforward shot on a flattish green, so what he's computing, I have no idea.

'Fuck's sake,' Cal groans. 'We'll be here all day.'

'You just want to get to the halfway house and stuff your face,' Zach retorts without taking his eye off his ball.

'Quite right. I won't play well until I have a bacon roll in my stomach,' Cal says.

'Thought you didn't do carbs,' Zach points out.

'Golf course carbs don't count. I'll do twenty thousand steps today.'

'Can't wait to see you smash the back nine, then,' Rafe says. 'You know,' he whispers to me, taking a step away from Mr Concentration, 'if the uphill battle ever gets too much, you can always join Cerulean. We're still tiny—it's mainly our money and our mates' funds, as you know—but we're seriously considering trying to grow this thing properly. Everyone wants to ramp up their family time these days, so bringing more hands on deck makes sense, and there's no better person I can think of than you to lead the charge.'

'Thanks, mate,' I say, genuinely touched. 'I'll bear that in mind.' True, Cerulean's assets under management are a drop in the ocean right now, but their performance across asset classes is fucking impressive, and it would be a fun challenge to see how much they could grow their assets without sacrificing performance.

It's definitely an option to tuck away for the future. It's hard enough seeing Darcy and Max as it is with all of our crazy schedules. I can barely allow myself to imagine a time when we might be fully committed to each other, practically as well as emotionally. I want it too badly, and it hurts too much given what I need to do to get us there.

'Of course,' he says. 'You're family now. Oh, Jesus *fuck*.'

The last is in response to Zach's eventual, perfectly executed putt. The ball rolls obediently into the hole, Zach punches the air, and the rest of us groan.

Cal steps up to his ball to forge bravely on with his putting despite his empty stomach. He hits it far too hard and it rolls straight past the hole.

'Fucking useless,' Zach crows.

'Speaking of family,' Rafe continues with a sideways glance at me as he lines up his shot, 'have you had any more thoughts on what you're going to do on that front?'

I understand him perfectly. I had a good chat with him and Belle about it a couple of weeks back when they kindly came over to the City for a midweek supper.

'I thought I might get you to fill Dad in,' I quip. 'You're far better with him than I am.'

'Happy to,' he replies, his tone smooth as he chips the ball onto the green, but it lands a couple of inches from the hole. 'Shite. But I don't think he'd appreciate my delivery.'

'I know,' I say in a small voice.

He nudges the ball into the hole, retrieves it, and walks with me to my ball. 'Is that your way of saying you've decided to come out with it all?'

I eye up my shot as I consider my response. I won't get it in one, but I should be able to make the next shot a dead cert.

'I know what I have to do,' I say as I take my shot. As I predicted, it lands a couple of feet from the hole.

'Yeah?' is all he says.

My situation has gone around and around and around in my head like clothes trapped in an endless washing cycle, and I'm so fucking exhausted. I pride myself on being a strategic thinker, a problem solver, but this one has me beaten.

'I'm not missing anything, am I?' I ask the guys now as we haul our golf bags onto our shoulders and trudge towards the next tee. 'This isn't a false binary?' I'm so well educated and intellectually superior that I loathe false binaries—situations where you think there are only two options and there's actually a third way.

'You know your parents far better than we do,' Zach says, 'except for maybe Rafe, so I don't want to speak out of line. But it seems to be this is a real dilemma, mate. The only compromises are so risky or so unsatisfactory that you're most likely better off taking charge of the situation yourself.'

'Talk me through them,' I say, and while a part of me despises myself for asking the advice of people I don't know all that well, I also know I'm far too close to this, and far too emotional over it, to turn down additional perspectives from these guys. They're smart, they're family, they care, and they understand these things.

Rafe's lived through it with my sister; they've all seen how Gen was apparently ostracised over the years, because she dared to run a sex club, and I know Zach has come a long way on his journey from grief and guilt to embracing a less orthodox lifestyle, largely thanks to Maddy.

If three guys educated at Loyola, a Catholic school even more conservative than my own school, Ampleforth, can untangle themselves from the bounded, doctrine-heavy form of love they were taught throughout their formative years and emerge whole and healed and happy, then so can I.

'The way I see it, coming out publicly and to your parents is the only viable option other than breaking things off with Max and risking losing Darcy, too,' Rafe says bluntly. 'The compromises Zach mentioned are inadequate. Come out and know that your dad will hear about it on the City grapevine?'

He sucks a sharp breath in through his teeth. 'Risky. Or fudge it for as long as you can and keep a low profile, but from what you've told me, Max won't go for that at all.' He stops walking and looks at me. 'But more importantly, mate, this is your fucking life. Forget what you owe Max and Darcy for a sec and think about what you owe yourself.'

It's so similar to what Max said about choosing myself that it gives me pause.

'It doesn't sound like a fair playing field,' Zach says. 'No offence, but your Dad's not a rational entity, so the game is rigged. From what I know, he won't be happy unless you marry a nice Catholic girl, produce lots of Catholic babies and spend every Sunday going to Mass. But even then he probably won't be happy, because you're not praying *enough* or being Catholic *enough*—he's a bottomless fucking pit, so *you* need to be the one to set rational, healthy boundaries that you can live with, because he sure as hell won't.'

'Been hanging with your wife much?' Rafe asks him, and Zach laughs. 'Seriously, that day when your dad kicked off at Belle and we got Maddy over—the boundary chat she gave Belle was un-fucking-believable. Sounds like you've learnt from the best.'

'That's my girl,' Zach says, his grin that of a man helplessly, hopelessly smitten. 'She's actually fucking good on boundaries. I'll send her your way if you need her.'

I imagine Maddy laying into me and laugh a little. 'I think Belle's passed most of it on to me. But what you said about Dad being irrational—that resonates, and it's what I keep coming back to. Because there's no doubt in my mind that I want to move forward with Max and Darcy. I really—I love them both so, so much.

'But I know I'll lose him as soon as I tell him. He'll probably kick me out, but even if he doesn't, I know I'll never be able to introduce the man and woman I love to him and have him give them the respect they deserve. So that's going to be it, pretty much.'

Cal groans. 'Shit, mate. It's so fucking tough.'

'Yeah.' We've reached the next tee, but none of us have made a move to play. I rake my hand through my hair. 'But, as you say, I'll never make him happy. That really helps. Nothing I do will make him happy unless I live a life that's one-hundred percent false to me, so when you put it like that, the only thing I can do is choose my own happiness. Any other outcome would be a fucking joke.'

'The thing I remember most about that afternoon,' Rafe says, 'is that Maddy told Belle she wasn't responsible for her father's reactions. He's a grown man, and he's chosen his own belief system, but you get to choose yours. You're responsible for your actions, and he's responsible for his.

'Don't even think about trying to take on the burden of whatever emotional reaction he has, whether it's grief or disgust or genuine fear for the damnation of your eternal soul—*that is not your burden to bear.* You hear me? I think that's been the biggest shift Belle's had to make, but absolving herself from that has allowed her to live for her own joy and not his approval.'

Fuck, that hits hard. And Rafe may actually be Yoda. How I ever suspected this guy may be morally questionable, I have no clue. Turns out I'm as bad as my father with all that insidious, hardwired Catholic judgement.

'You're totally right. And it's so easy to forget. I think I needed to hear that out loud. Thanks mate. It's just so fucking hard to walk into a room and know that you'll devastate the man who raised you, even if you wholeheartedly disagree with the basis of his devastation.'

'If it's any consolation,' Rafe says slowly, like he's choosing his words, 'I'm sure your dad loves you as much as he's capable. I really don't think he's had unconditional love modelled for him—he doesn't have that within himself to give. He's confused morals with love, and all that extremist shit in his head has made him fearful.

'But Darcy and Max love you unconditionally, and mate, you deserve that. You deserve to choose that for yourself— every single human deserves knowing how it feels to be loved wholly and unconditionally, no matter what filthy sinners the Church thinks we are. If people put conditions on their love, I'd argue it's not real love.'

Unconditional love.

God is love.

Love is love.

Jesus Christ, he's so fucking right.

80

DEX

Dad, I'm bisexual.
Dad, I'm dating a woman... and a man.
Dad, I tried so hard to tamp it down, but I couldn't. I'm in love with two people, and we're all together.

I can confidently say, after sleepless hours and worried weeks and uneasy years that there is no way to tell your religiously radicalised father that you are not only queer but in a happy, healthy relationship with two other people.

I know.

Believe me, I've employed every neuron in my usually dexterous brain to find that way.

The crux of the matter is that, as the boys agreed, this situation is binary. There is no possible way for me to live in the wonderful fullness of who I truly am with the people who make me truly happy and not break my father's heart.

That said heart resides in a dark place of false piousness and fear and fucked-upness is immaterial. I can condemn and despise my father's beliefs as much as I want. I can *know*, with unwavering certainty, that his worldview is wrong, that he's been barking up the wrong spiritual tree for decades now, but it doesn't stop the fact that his warped, bigoted version of the truth is just that.

His truth.

None of us humans can handle having our truth threatened, especially not by the people we've brought into the world—brought *up* in the world. And I wish it didn't have to be like this. I wish I didn't have to choose between my own happiness and self-actualisation and my father's love and respect for me.

As it is, I'm fairly sure I'll lose the former and I know with certainty I'll lose the latter.

All I can cling to is our conversation last weekend on the golf course. Telling my father is the respectful thing to do, no matter how unwelcome my message will be, and how he reacts to my life choices *is not my responsibility.*

I've picked Belle up from her home in Holland Park so we can go for dinner with our parents in Knightsbridge. A tiny, cowardly part of me flirted with the idea of going to a restaurant. If I told them in public, Dad couldn't make a scene, right?

But I've decided to be mature and rip off the bandaid. It's better to get it done. Max heads off on the IPO roadshow next week, and the idea of him jetting off to Europe without me having made the commitment to our future that he needs from me is unbearable. (I will admit, I also gave serious airtime to having Max here tonight to lambast Dad into acquiescence. Can you even imagine?!)

My only comforts right now are these:

One. My sister is here and has my back.

Two. Darcy and Max love me. *Unconditionally.*

And three. By the end of the evening, it'll be done, for better or for worse.

I just have to get the words out.

I saw something on Instagram the other day where a guy came out to his family and he said it had gone as badly as it could possibly have gone without physical violence occurring. I swear, when I read it I finally understood what it felt like to have your blood run cold.

My fears are pretty complex. They run somewhere between actually being scared of my father, who is a major believer in lashing out and whose fury is of the cold, poisonous sort, and knowing how much pain I'll cause him and Mum. A few years ago, I would have expected her to follow his lead and comply with any insistence he might have on cutting ties with me. But when she showed up to give my sister away at her wedding, it showed me that she's learned to stand up to him.

So I hope she can love me for who I am, and I hope I'll get a chance to introduce her to the two incredible people I love, too.

'Maddy told me,' my sister says, linking her arm with mine in the cab, 'that the most painful thing is when your family has never put boundaries in place, so you have to.'

I'm so fucking sick of hearing the B-word, but I know she's right.

'Yeah,' I say, rubbing the point of my shoe against the cab's scratchy carpeted floor. 'And honestly, it pisses me off that we have to do it.'

'It helped me to think about it visually,' she says. She lays her golden head on my shoulder. 'I imagined building this physical fort around myself where his toxicity couldn't get to me, you know? It made me feel protected.'

'I'm visualising it more as a full-on hazmat suit,' I deadpan, and she giggles.

'God, where's an emotional hazmat suit when you need it?'

'Seriously.' I sigh. 'But it's a good analogy. The major issue is that he's not rational, not from where I'm standing, and he's not stable, either, not in an emotionally healthy way. It makes trying to communicate with him on topics where we disagree really, really tough.'

'Maybe that's a comfort. If you know you're not dealing with a rational being, then you know he won't follow your logic. There's no point in trying to explain it, even. Why bother justifying yourself to someone who has no intention of meeting you halfway? When someone's as hardline as he is, you have to be equally hardline. Here's who I am. Here's where I stand. You can be in my life or not, but I won't have you disrespecting me, my lifestyle or my partners. *Boom.*'

'Yeah, you should definitely tell them for me,' I say, and she squeezes my arm more tightly.

'I would if I could.'

∼

WE HAVE SOME CHAMPAGNE.

We chat about the Wolff IPO in a way that's vague enough not to give away the fact that Wolff's much-lauded new CEO fucked me up the arse in his gigantic bed last night and made me come very, very hard.

We dine.

I've purposely shelved my bombshell for after dinner, so as not to disrespect or waste Mum's efforts in the kitchen. She's served up the most incredible supper—boeuf bourguignon and potato dauphinoise. Normally, I'd be shovelling it up like a student who's slunk home from uni for some home cooking, but it's an effort to get every mouthful down my constricted throat.

Perhaps it's a blessing. I absolutely do not need to be digesting a stomachful of beef if Max claims my arse later.

Happily, my angel of a sister holds most of the conversation, telling my parents about a swoon-worthy new artist her gallery, Liebermann's, has brought in and suggesting which pieces they should take a look at. Mum and Dad are major art whores, so this is their kryptonite, and the fact that I have nothing of value to add here gives me a little breathing space.

How the absolute fuck am I supposed to do this?

How to break news like this in a way that's forthright and respectful of who I am while also holding space and compassion for two people to whom my lifestyle will be incomprehensible at best and contemptible at worst?

There's a voice in my head, and it's Max's. I can almost feel his warm breath on my ear as he held me in his arms this morning and delivered his parting shot.

Who you are is nothing to be ashamed of. You're the most lovable man I've ever met. If they don't love you as you are, they don't deserve you.

Facts. Facts will be my friends here. I'll try to keep emotions out of it. I won't succumb to the temptation of preempting any issues they may have.

I'll tell my truth, and that'll be it.

It feels like I'm underwater. Everything is slower. Slightly more surreal. It's the nerves, I decide. That edge-of-the-precipice, *I can't believe I'm about to do this* feeling.

I meet my sister's gaze and take genuine comfort in the unconditional love I see there.

Then I clear my throat and raise my eyes to my father.

81

DEX

'There's, ah, something I wanted to talk to you about,' I say, hating how thin my voice sounds. My mum, who is a stunning woman, gives me a beatific smile and I return it gratefully.

I already hate this for her.

I hate that when Belle and I tear out of here like our arses are on fire, she'll be left to pick up the pieces.

I hate that, even though I'm slowly allowing myself to believe that I will have a beautiful family in the future, including plenty of babies, that picture won't look like what she thinks she wants for her firstborn.

They say kids teach their parents as much, if not more, than parents teach their kids. But the paradigm I'm introducing mine to is such a radical departure from the image of love and morals and family units they've been raised to want that I'm really not sure if even Mum can handle it.

And I know, just as I know the earth is round, that Dad will summarily condemn me with just as much moral indignation and just as little logical footing as the Inquisition condemned Galileo for his "ridiculous" theories of heliocentricity.

Somehow, that reminder of just how much the Catholic Church abhors a philosophical threat makes me feel a little better.

When I hesitate, Dad gives me a curt nod. 'Well, spit it out.'

You asked for it, mate.

I begin the coward's way. 'I've met a woman.'

(I know. Pathetic.)

Dad looks faintly, pleasantly surprised. Mum gives me an excited grin. And, in my periphery, I can see my sister trying her hardest not to react.

'That's wonderful!' Mum squeals. 'Do we know her?'

I glance at Belle, who's watching like she's waiting to see where I go with this.

'She's the sister of one of Rafe's... oldest friends. She's called Darcy and she's wonderful.'

'She's seriously amazing,' Belle says. Maybe if we pack as much positivity and glee into my Darcy news, no one will react when I tell them I've finally worked out I love dick as much as my sister does.

Ahhh. Wishful thinking, eh?

Before the gushing tangent derails us too far, though, I dig my fingernails into my thigh under the table and press on.

'That's not all. I've met a man, too.'

My parents give me what can only be described as blank looks. I notice in a haze that Belle's pressing her lips together and reach blindly for my wineglass. My fight-or-flight response has majorly kicked in, my throat is completely dry, and there's a very good chance I piss myself, such is the urgency with which my nervous system is responding to this perceived existential threat.

I force myself to clarify. 'I'm in a relationship with Darcy, and we're very happy, but the two of us are also in a relationship with a man, too. I realise it's unorthodox, but the three of us are very deeply in love.'

If I wasn't so bloody terrified, I'd laugh at my father's face right now. It's a purple-hued mask of stunned disbelief and horror, but I suspect his blood pressure has just ratcheted up so far that his eyeballs might actually pop out of their sockets.

This is a fucking nightmare, but the knowledge that I've done the worst bit, that *I've said it,* sends a rush of euphoria so strong I feel giddy. It's done, and everything else is on Dad now.

Move over Rafe and your butt-nakedness in Mum and Dad's kitchen.

I've just set our family on fire.

May as well toss another match onto the flames.

'And you do know the guy,' I say directly to Dad. 'He's Max Hunter.'

My father, one of the most articulate people I know, is completely mute, his mouth set in a grim line while those eyeballs of his wrestle against his blood pressure. I can't help but wonder if, deep down in a place he'd never admit even to himself, he's impressed that I landed Max.

Because I certainly fucking am, and Dad just spent a full fifteen minutes telling me what a high quality team Max is running. Whether he doesn't know or, for once, doesn't care that Max is queer, I'm unsure. Maybe astounding corporate success is cause to overlook loose morals in Dad's eyes.

Fuck knows.

Mum glances at him, probably looking for clarity as much as checking for possible cardiac arrest. She's always done this—always looked to him for guidance. It's a reflex so hardwired after thirty-something years of marriage that she can't help it, even when she knows he's full of shit.

When no clarity is forthcoming, she turns back to me.

'I don't understand,' she says like she's genuinely baffled. 'You say you're in a relationship with Max *and* with this girl, Darcy?'

'I am.' Maybe I'll just talk to her while we wait for the pressure cooker next to her to explode and give us all third-degree burns. 'Max and Darcy got together shortly before I met them. We all feel very strongly about each other, and we want to make a go of it. Max has always been openly queer, but I wanted to talk to you about it before we went public with our relationship.'

My father's jaw drops open. That's done it—if his horror at my moral transgressions wasn't enough to send him over the edge, the horrifying prospect of his son's queerness being muttered about all over the City is.

I wonder which he'll attack first—my polyamory or my queerness?

'The Bible is *very* clear on this,' he says, slamming his fork down with the weight of a judge passing judgement with his mallet.

I almost laugh. 'Yeah, the Bible's views on homosexuality tend not to be given much credence these days, Dad.'

Belle gives me a tiny, impressed smile, like *who is this badass and what have you done with my brother?*

'Not just—that. On all of these... practices you speak of. A man shall have one wife and a woman one husband. St. Paul is very, very clear. To allow a third party, or anyone else, into your relationship is to tempt Satan. These are the rules that Christianity is built on—not just Christianity, but the very basis of civilised society.'

When he starts quoting the Bible, the anger flares, licking at my soul with a wrathful tongue.

'That only matters if you care what the Bible says. What St. Paul says. I don't. It's not how I live my life. I rejected that framework a while ago, and I would have rejected it far earlier if I'd ever been given the option.'

He flinches. 'What the hell is that supposed to mean?'

'I never chose Catholicism. You chose it for me. And it was never, ever served up to me as an option, only as absolute truth. It's not for me—it's not the right framework.'

'This is not how we raised you,' Dad says with terrifying intensity, practically spitting the words out through gritted teeth. 'Just because you're a lapsed Catholic, it doesn't mean you can sink into moral corruption.'

Ah, here we go. Catholics love the word *lapsed*. It suggests that anyone who's abandoned their faith has done so out of laziness, or ethical apathy, or an inability to hack the uncompromising demands of this faith. Not because they've made a measured choice to walk away from a religious framework that doesn't serve them.

But I'm not here to eviscerate the man.

I'm here to tell my truth and set myself free.

'It's obviously very hurtful to me that you would condemn my relationship as morally corrupt before you've bothered to understand the slightest bit about it,' I tell him, 'but I'm afraid it's not surprising. And no, you certainly didn't raise me to find love outside of what the Church deems acceptable, but there comes a time when a man has to decide for himself what's right.'

Dad's face is twisted with disgust, and I suspect he's not even listening properly. Whatever I say, he'll tune out—he's retreating into himself before my eyes. The moral rectitude of what I've done is not up for discussion, because he's so certain of where God stands on this that he has no intention of entertaining my attempts at justification. The blinkers are well and truly on.

'No man decides what is right,' he snaps. 'The Church decides what is right, and we sinners plough on and try our very best, and we seek His mercy when we stumble. We do not throw away our values to embark on a relationship that is the epitome of wickedness. Because mark my words, whatever disgusting, unnatural activities you're indulging in are the epitome of wickedness. And your only option, my boy, is to walk away from this madness and repent and *throw yourself on God's mercy*, or you'll be lost. Utterly, utterly lost in the darkness.'

And there we have it. I stare at him, and God knows, my body and soul are churning with such a mix of disgust and hurt and pity, because only one person at this table is lost in the darkness, and it sure as fuck isn't me.

Everything he's said is an exact replica of what Belle and I anticipated. He's so predictable. So fearful, so closed-minded. He's on the verge of tearing our family apart, and it's entirely his choice—except it's not really a choice, if I think about it. There was never any choice. He'll always side with his beliefs. He did it with Belle, and he's doing it again now.

My sister is right.

Maddy is right.

This is all on him.

I'm not taking responsibility for any of his actions.

All I've done is tell him who I am.

Mum finally speaks up, sensing a natural break in this rant, I suppose. I hate having told her like this. I'd love to have given her advance warning, but I wouldn't have done that to her—she'd have stewed so badly over how Dad would take it when he finally found out. Best to have spared her the advance worry.

'Don't be so harsh, please, Ben,' she pleads, her eyes on her husband, and I wonder for the millionth time how she puts up with him and all his pious, religious bullshit. 'He's happy, and he's in love.'

'He's not in love,' my dad blurts out. 'He's in carnal lust, and I simply can't allow it. All I'm trying to do is convince him to save himself before he's damned forever.'

I roll my eyes. I thought I'd be more timid than this. I thought I'd cower before my father's fury, but he makes it easy to disrespect him when he offers so little respect—not to mention so little common sense and human decency—of his own. 'Don't tell me what I'm feeling,' I say. 'It's offensive. I've come to you as a grown man to do you the courtesy of sharing my news. Don't try to invalidate it.'

'I'm giving you the benefit of the doubt here, boy,' he spits out, and his *boy* has every bit of the patronising, patriarchal venom he intends. 'Because the alternative to you having lost your way is that you're a filthy, unrepentant sinner, and I simply cannot condone that.'

'Dad!' Belle cries in horror, but he rides roughshod over her protest.

'If you think your mother and I will engage with you or these people as long as you're with them, then you're very much mistaken. All I can say is I hope for the sake of your eternal soul that you come to your senses very soon, and the Good Lord will be waiting when you do.'

'Leave me out if it, please, Ben,' Mum says in a voice that's quiet but not to be messed with. She's sitting ramrod straight, as if she's worried one false move will have the rest of this dinner falling to pieces, but I'm afraid she's too late.

We're done here.

It's as shitty as it is predictable, and Dad's toxic bigotry rolls over me like a grimy film. I braced myself for abuse and for his revulsion, and I got both. No need to be the man's punching bag any longer.

I pull my napkin off my knees and lay it on the table before getting to my feet. 'You've got things completely the wrong way around, actually. If you think I'd let you go anywhere near Max and Darcy with this attitude, you're mistaken. I would never, ever give you a chance to disrespect them or tarnish them with your toxic energy.

'And good luck explaining yourself to your entire investment team when Max zeroes you guys in the IPO allocation. Mum, if you'd like to meet them, we'd all love that. You let me know when you're ready.'

I glance at Dad. I hate leaving her with him when he's like this. A black-tarred thundercloud of prejudice has settled on him. It'll be days before it lifts, and she'll have to stomach the brunt of it.

'Shall we go to Alchemy?' my sister asks, pushing back her chair and standing. She bends and gives Mum a hug, ignoring Dad, who's glowering at us from his seat, completely.

'Sounds good,' I say with genuine relief. Darcy's dancing there tonight. Max will be there too, waiting for me. Worrying about me. The thought of my favourite people in the world has my wounded, sickened heart soaring. Alchemy can't come quickly enough.

'What the hell is Alchemy?' my father barks.

Belle and I glance at each other, and I hesitate.
She turns to him. 'It's the sex club Rafe owns, actually.'
With that, we take our leave.

82

MAX

It's rare that the sight of my spectacular girlfriend dancing on stage at Alchemy doesn't raise a smile (and an erection) from me. But I've been so fucking worried for Dex that I'm barely registering her, even though the sight of her writhing in tonight's prop—a giant champagne coupe full of bubbly water—is gratifying in the extreme.

I can tell Dex he's perfect till I'm blue in the face.

I can tell him it'll all be worth it.

I can tell him that if his father's values are this warped, then his good opinion means less than nothing.

But none of it helps, because he's still the one who has to walk in there and confess to the man who raised him that he's queer and in love with two people. For all the tough love I spout at him, I'd love nothing more than to bear this cross for him. To go in there and tell Ben Scott, who is clearly a religious nut, that his son is a king among men and that loving him is the greatest honour of my life.

Thank fuck Belle's there with him.

I had a couple of drinks with Rafe earlier next door. The guy is a lost puppy when his wife's not around, and he hates the thought of her having to deal with her dad almost as much as I hate Dex having to do it, but he's opted to wait in the bar for her while I watch my girlfriend undulate in her bird bath, sending water and bubbles sloshing over the edge.

Then suddenly Dex is here, and all is good with the world, because I can take over now.

I can look after him.

He looks drained, but not as stricken as I'd feared he might. He's winding through the crowd, and I laugh when he gives a copulating couple on an ottoman a wide berth and a horrified look. My uptight little prince has come a long way, but he still has a way to go.

When he sees me, though, his entire demeanour changes. His face lifts, and he looks at me as though he's never truly seen me before. Like I'm some kind of mirage.

Perhaps, after what he's just endured, I am.

'Well?' I demand above the music as he closes the gap between us. I don't touch him. I've never touched him in public—not the way I want to. I wouldn't do that to him.

'It's done,' he says, and he shoots me a smile that's exhausted and seriously fucking triumphant, and then, for the first time in a public place, he tugs me into his arms and puts his mouth to mine.

DEX WON'T STOP KISSING me. He's devouring me like it's been twelve months and not twelve hours since we last saw each other. Like he needs the nerve endings of our lips and our tongues to explain viscerally to him that he has me.

'God, I love you so fucking much,' he mumbles when we finally come up for air.

I thread my fingers through his hair and hold his head in a firm cradle. 'I love you, too. What the hell happened with your dad? You okay?'

He laughs. 'Not remotely. But also—maybe?'

'Was it horrific?'

'He didn't let himself down. He was every bit as vile and judgemental as I knew he'd be, and he told me we were all damned and that he'd never condone our relationship. Oh, and he referenced St. Paul.'

I roll my eyes. 'Of course he did. And your mum?'

'She'd like to meet you guys, I think. I'll give her some processing time, though.'

'So it's done. This is it—you're going to come out now?'

He shrugs carelessly. 'Yup. I've done the hardest part, I guess. And you're too fucking gorgeous for me to stay away from you any longer.'

I squint at him. 'Are you drunk?'

'Not drunk enough.' He plants his palms flat on my chest and licks his lips. 'I'm shell-shocked, I think. That was the most brutal, surreal thing I've ever done. I feel kind of euphoric, weirdly. Like I don't care about anything anymore.'

I'm not surprised. I can't imagine the adrenalin that's flooding his veins right now. But this fevered, reeling version of Dex, with his glittering eyes and spontaneous public kissing, is a version I can very much get on board with.

'You'll be feeling a lot more euphoric by the end of the night,' I tell him darkly, and he smirks like all his survival instincts have left the building at the threat of a good fucking.

'Bring it.'

I jerk my head. 'Look at our girl.'

He turns then and takes Darcy in, and his entire

demeanour softens. 'Holy fuck,' he mutters, his fingers flexing over my heart. 'Do you think we can get one of those giant glasses for your flat?'

Darcy is balancing on the—hopefully reinforced—rim of the glass, creating pretty sprays of water across the stage with her kicks. The droplets glow pink under the lights. In keeping with tonight's retro, speakeasy theme, she's in a pale pink sequinned thong and matching nipple tassels, and she is so going to get it from us it's not funny.

'I'll get you anything you want,' I whisper in his ear. 'I'm so very, very proud of you.'

He turns his head sharply back to me. Our gazes hold, cutting through the music, the roomful of people dancing and fucking and fooling around, like lasers through fog. I turn us gently so he's facing Darcy.

'Really?' he asks.

I nod, sliding my hands down his arms before putting my fingers to the top of his zip. He's here, and he's a miracle, and he's set himself free, and he is ours now, mine and Darcy's. Fully, wonderfully ours.

To love and to cherish from this day forward.

'Will you let me show you how much?'

83

DEX

I stare into the beautiful face of the man I love. It's my favourite version of his face—the one he makes when he wants me so badly he's scarcely capable of knowing his own name. He's vibrating with it.

I want nothing more than to be alone with him and Darcy right now—to wrench her off the stage and wrap her in a fluffy towel and march them both to a private room. I ache for it, because this will, honest to God, be the first time we've been together with the golden light of benediction shining on us.

The benediction *I* bestowed upon us.

The benediction I didn't know I had the authority to give, when it turns out I was, all along, the *only* one who could give it.

And it terrifies me to think I may never have got that memo.

But Darcy has another few minutes before her set ends, and Max is looking at me with the whole world in those big blue eyes of his, and nobody can push me out of my comfort zone like him to heights I didn't know I needed, and I'm already hardening from his kisses, and the beat of Beyoncé's sultry, sexed-up version of *Back to Black* is coursing through my veins, and every hedge fund manager in Mayfair is probably here tonight, and if I'm going to be out, I may as well be fucking *out*.

So I kiss him, and I say yes.

The expression on his handsome face morphs instantly from need to satisfaction. If he wants to take this as a win, he should go for it, because of the two of us I'm the one getting blown.

The man at the helm of Europe's biggest IPO in half a decade is about to sink to his knees and suck me off in a sex club, before the great and good of the finance industry, and fuck my life in the best possible way, because if telling Dad to essentially go fuck himself felt surreal, this is on another level.

As if he can read my mind, he puts his mouth to my ear and whispers hotly, 'Everyone's going to know you're my absolute favourite little fuck toy now, and I want you to show them how much you fucking love it.'

He's right, of course. They will, and I will. Max holds the power here, whether he's on his knees or not.

And I fucking love it.

'I'll show them,' I say hoarsely, and he chuckles.

'I know you will, you little slut.'

I'm still laughing, my head thrown back, when he licks down my exposed throat and sinks to his knees with an elegance, a dignity, only Max can pull off.

I expect him to merely unzip me, but he unbuckles my belt and *then* unzips me, shoving my trousers and boxer briefs down with brutal efficiency until they're around my ankles and only my shirt tails preserve my modesty.

It's one way to ensure I don't do a runner, I suppose.

Then he licks the length of me, and I go from semi-hard to hard so fast the edges of my vision darken, while in the centre of it my beautiful girlfriend splashes around happily and shakes her fantastic, tassel-clad breasts at us.

If this is my new reality, I'll be the happiest sinner who ever sinned.

Alchemy:

Physical change.

A universal panacea.

Elaborate transformation.

The gold-embossed coasters in the bar next door inform us that alchemy is all this and more, an elixir of immortality, even. All I can say is that there's something in the water in this place.

The first time I came here, a woman bewitched me.

The second time, a man cast a spell on me from which I will never recover.

And now, all these times later, the timid, jumpy version of myself who first crossed this threshold is unrecognisable. I stand here, one lover blowing me, and as I cradle his head in my hands and bask in his onslaught while I watch the coquettish antics of my other lover on stage.

Just when I think my evening can't improve more from the very fucking low base of my father's reaction, Darcy spots me. Us. The two women who were blocking Max and me from her view move away, and I see the second she finds me before her gaze drops to Max's head and shoulders.

She gives me a wonderful Dita-Von-Teese-style smile, a curvature of her scarlet lips, before spotting what Max is doing and full-on breaking character for a second with an epic jaw-drop. She quickly recovers and blows us a saucy kiss before resuming a precarious crab-like pose, arched over the glass.

I drag my fingers through Max's hair in approval, because *fuck* is his mouth a wicked, wicked thing, and shudder with pleasure. It's only the second time he's done this to me, and I suspect the lessons he intends to impart is very different from the ones he taught me in my office.

You're mine now.
You made the right choice.
I promise it's worth it.
I've got you.

It's not romantic. It's not intended to be. He's devouring me, tongue swirling and cheeks hollowed as he caresses my balls and trails a decisive fingertip along my taint. As usual, he makes it feel like he's doing this for himself, that he's taking rather than giving, using me rather than indulging me.

It's as if, when he sees fit to milk me dry, it'll be imperiously, for his own pleasure, and I'll come on demand because he's declared it so, and that very arrogance, the entitlement with which he plays my body, knowing precisely how I'll respond, has my senses heightening and my inhibitions fading and that sublime heat in my dick building.

Darcy's torn down whatever veil she usually maintains between her and the audience, as her performance takes on a new edge. It's less playful, more hungry, as if she wants to contribute to my growing ecstasy, to feed my senses right alongside Max. As if my arousal is fuelling hers.

She faces the crowd and spreads her legs right there for us, her nipple tassels swaying, and God. I can't wait to lay her on a bed and feast on her and make those little pink nipples feel all better.

Keeping my eyes open is growing arduous, or it would be if my favourite little tease wasn't putting on one hell of a show for us. She bites down on her bottom lip and slides her hand under the front of her thong, which is taking things further than she usually does.

Everyone cheers her on.

But she doesn't take her eyes off me.

Max has ramped up his pace as if he can wait no longer for me to blow, as if my holding off any further is a personal affront. I groan aloud, the noise vibrating in my throat before being swallowed up by the music, and let him know with the dig of my fingertips into the base of his skull just how close I am.

When the intoxicating wetness and clever pulls of his perfect mouth tug me all the way under, I yield, head back, eyes squeezed shut, my body subsumed by wave after crashing wave of violent pleasure. He wrings every drop from me and I stand there, in the centre of a sex club, taking it all and wondering how an act that should apparently be a new moral low for me can be quite such a spectacular high.

I'm suddenly, horrifyingly aware of wolf-whistling and cat-calling around me and jerk my head upright and my eyes open. *Surely they're not applauding me and Max?*

But no. They're applauding a soaking wet and brightly smiling Darcy, who's leapt down from her kinky glass bath and is shimmying off the stage and forging a path straight to us.

84

DARCY

There is no way I'm letting my boys love each other like that and not muscling in on the action.

No way in hell.

Max is getting unsteadily to his feet when I reach them. The group of guys next to them is applauding me, and I see one of them do a double take when he gets a look at Max's face. Probably finance bros. But I'm not interested in random dudes, because tonight I've broken the house rules for *my* guys. I may be soaking wet and sudsy from the waist down, but that doesn't stop me from launching myself at them in front of the whole club.

Dex is all orgasm-flushed and dopily shellshocked—he's the guy who just woke up married in Vegas and is still too drunk to care how the fuck it happened. I throw my arms around his neck and jump on him, and he laughs out an *oof* as my cold, wet body collides with his softening dick. Max helps me get my legs around Dex so I'm wrapped around him like a koala and presses up behind me.

A Darcy sandwich. My favourite thing.

'Shit, you're soaking,' Max drawls, but he sounds amused.

'No change there,' I tell him, turning my head to accept his kiss before I bury my face in Dex's neck. 'So did you do it?'

He shifts, getting a better grip of my basically bare bottom. 'I did.'

'And?'

'And it was as awful as we thought it would be.'

'Ugh. Poor baby.' I squeeze him more tightly. Max gives my shoulder a little bite and gets to work behind me, stripping my hair of its pins. I had it up tonight in a chic starlet-style up-do, mainly to keep it out of the water, and once he gets it freed, he runs his fingers through it.

'It's okay,' Dex says. 'It's done. Now I get to be with you guys properly.'

I giggle. 'And I see you've begun the coming out process.' I kiss along his jaw, his laughter vibrating against my lips.

'You could say that.'

What a fucking relief. Waiting for Dex to get comfortable with the prospect of being official with me and Max has taken a greater toll on both of us than we'd ever have let him know. That's the weird, new, cool but also terrifying thing about this kind of relationship. A three-legged stool is pretty bloody useless if one of the legs gives out.

I nuzzle into him, playing with the ends of his hair. It's longer than Max's, and I love how it curls just a little at the nape of his neck. Just one of the zillion sexy things about him. 'Was it terrible?' I whisper. I swear he could have sent me and Max in his place, his very own pair of kinky Dobermans to tear strips off his father.

'It was shit,' he says, 'and I'm sure I'll feel completely devastated at some point, but right now I'm mainly pissed off at what a hateful twat my dad is and relieved that I got it over with. Belle was amazing. She told Dad Rafe owns a sex club—you should have seen his face. I'm not sure if it was her way of directing some of his anger away from me or she just hit zero tolerance, but it was bloody brilliant.'

I raise my head and grin at him as Max closes in behind me, pressing his dick against my thong's (very uncomfortable) sequinned strip. He wraps his arms around both of us, and it feels like the three of us are exactly where we should be.

'You're both bloody brilliant,' I tell him. 'And you're with us now. That's what matters. We love you.'

His eyes are dreamy wells of emotion as he glances from me to Max, whose chin is resting on my shoulder. 'I love you both so much I can't tell you.'

'We know exactly what you sacrificed for us today,' Max tells him gruffly. 'We know how hard it is, and we're so fucking relieved you chose us—and yourself, of course.'

'Yeah.' Dex's smile couldn't be wider, more loving. 'Me too.'

Max lets go of us and steps backwards. 'Come on. Put your dick away and come with us. Let us show you.'

85

DEX

Perhaps the sight of Darcy, naked and stretched out on this very same bed at Alchemy, should provoke some sort of déjà vu, but it doesn't, of course. Because, the room and the participants aside, nothing about tonight bears much resemblance to that fateful first evening here.

Max may be staring at me like he wants to fuck me all the way to Hell and back, but he's doing a far worse job of hiding it than he did last time. This time, I'll take anything he chooses to put in my mouth—tongue or fingers or thumb or dick—and I'll suck with the uncomplicated delight of a man who knows the pleasure it'll bring both of us.

Tonight, I'm not the interloper, the suspicious, judgemental guy who'll only admit to wanting one of them. I'm the conquering soldier returning from a front line rife with hatred and prejudice, and I'm damn well going to enjoy the spoils of the war I waged this evening.

Tonight, Darcy's not the only one getting fucked, and she's not the only one getting champagne sucked off her nipples, either. Nor will Max be left to get himself off with his fist. Because if I'm victorious, he's positively triumphant, and he isn't too shy to crow about it.

'Every single thing I've done since you walked in here that first time has been leading up to this moment,' he tells me, unearthing a bottle of Krug from the same cabinet he hid that initial stash in and making quick work of its foil and the little wire cage around the cork. 'So tonight I'm fucking celebrating.'

'Krug?' Darcy says, stretching luxuriously on the bed. 'Who smuggled that in for you?'

'Jesus Christ,' I say, catching a glimpse of the label. Krug Clos D'Ambonnay—1995, no less. 'That stuff must be three or four grand a bottle.'

'Your sister,' he tells Darcy, 'and the guys. This one is courtesy of your Alchemy family.'

He aims that last part at me, watching to see if it lands, and does it ever. That they've all been waiting in the wings for me to take this flying leap does something to my heart. The boys held space and compassion for me on the golf course the other day. I thought of their words all day, actually, while I was gearing up to talk to my parents.

Their incredibly generous gesture is a solid reminder that when your blood relations don't have it in them to love you in the way you need, there are friends standing in the wings, ready to accept you for who you are.

Max bestows a fleeting kiss to my lips before turning to Darcy and dribbling champagne all over her torso. She squeals and then lets out a volley of giggles, and this time I don't need him to spell out the invitation. I'm on that bed, catching the liquid with upward licks of her torso before taking as much of her breast in my mouth as I can.

'Mmm,' I mutter against her skin. 'So fucking delicious.'

'God, this is hot,' she says on a sigh.

'Good,' Max says. 'Dex. Feed her some champagne.'

He holds out the bottle to me. I grab it by the neck and take a swig before bending and kissing Darcy, letting the cool nectar drip through from my lips to hers, slowly, so she doesn't choke on it. She moans a little as she swallows it, her lips cool and slick, her tongue moving against mine as the bubbles fizz and pop, and I rub my hand over the back of Max's neck as he sucks on her champagne-soaked skin.

It's so decadent, doing this. The three of us, sharing a four-figure bottle of champagne off Darcy's tits, the rest of the evening stretching ahead, promising languid exploration and slow, sensual fucking. Nothing off the table. Knowing that everything we do will be filthy as fuck and most definitely not a sin.

I've finally given myself permission to revel in the sheer debauchery of it all without judging it as anything other than three consenting adults loving the fuck out of each other's bodies.

Maybe they should have named this place Hedonism.

WE PLAY. We play a *lot*. Tonight feels less about a race to the finish line and more about enjoying every second of the journey. Easy for me to say, perhaps, given I've already shot my load once. But Max and Darcy seem on board too. There's no rush. There's only time, and skin, and mouths, and hands.

I've ended up with a woman more sparkling, more carefree, more devoted than I could possibly have envisaged, and a man who—

What can I possibly say about Max? That I've ended up with a man at all still has the power to take my breath away.

That I've ended up with the most intelligent, driven, domineering, passionate, generous man I've ever met is a gift I'll never again allow myself to jeopardise.

They're both one in a million. I can't begin to calculate the odds of being loved by both of them.

My eyes meet Max's over Darcy's naked body. We have our beautiful girlfriend on her hands and knees for us, and she's teasing my cock with her tongue as she takes Max in her pussy. It should be nice and wet—he just made her come with his tongue.

I've got her long hair, curlier than usual from her up-do, wound softly around one fist to keep it off her face and the other wrapped around my cock so I can feed it to her. I shudder in deep bliss as she licks around my crown, and Max laughs, sliding his hands lovingly over her hips and arse as those blue, relentless eyes stay fixed on my face.

'Try not to do quite such a good job, sweetheart. He's already had one expert blowjob tonight. We want him to last.'

She giggles around my cock and dials her licking back a little, and I sigh.

'It's hard to last when you're so fucking beautiful. And I want to kiss you, too.' This is the problem. I want everything —I want her sinful little mouth everywhere. On my dick. On my mouth. All over my skin.

'Okay,' Max barks, releasing her hips and sliding out of her as she makes a disappointed little *mmph* around my dick. 'New position. Dex is going in the middle. Darce, baby, get on your back.'

86

DEX

Neither of us need to be told twice. We've done this a few times, and it's one of my absolute favourite things to do, because it's so intense and sweaty and elemental. Fucking my beautiful girlfriend, being face to face and able to kiss her, stare into her eyes, as my boyfriend pumps into me from behind, is circuitry so miraculous that I never knew to be able to imagine it, even in the filthiest of my right-before-orgasm fever dreams.

It feeds both sides of me, you see. It allows me to experience, in the most transcendent way possible, the fullest, most staggering potential of who I truly am, where men and women and submission and dominance all meld together into one astonishing expression of my every need. My diabolical, wonderful boyfriend knows this perfectly well and, I suspect, wants to give me this gift, tonight of all nights.

'Does that work for you?' I whisper to Darcy, loosening my grip on her hair. She slides off my dick. When she looks up at me, her mouth is wet, the saliva on it prettier, even, than dawn's dew on a flower petal.

'It more than works for me,' she says dreamily, bracing on one elbow so she can reach up and cup my face. 'You fuck me so hard when Max is fucking you.'

I clamp a hand over hers, holding her to me as I grin at her. 'Hard not to.'

'Hear, hear,' Max drawls. 'On your back, young lady.'

Darcy obliges, and I crawl over her. There's always something about this moment—about having her spread out for me, hair everywhere and mouth swollen and limbs loose as I loom over her, that has my throat tightening with the excitement of it.

I smile down at her as I push in, groaning with the outrageous wetness of her, the heat. 'Fuck, he kept you warm for me,' I tell her. If being inside Darcy isn't a homecoming, I don't know what is. Her body sucks me in and grips me tight, her eyelashes fluttering and back arching as she accommodates me.

'I love you,' is her response to that.

'And I love you. So much.' I bend to kiss her, rolling my hips a little as my dick adjusts from the delight of her mouth to the certain nirvana of her pussy.

'Don't move,' Max orders, climbing onto the bed behind me. The mattress sinks under the added weight as he pops the lid of a tube of lube. If Pavlov hadn't done his thing with his dogs, he could definitely have drawn some scientific conclusions about the reaction my body has to that sound—the most fucked-up, intoxicating mixture of fear and anticipation that roils in my stomach. Every. Single. Time. And it's definitely something unique to me that welcomes the sensation of him looming behind me just as fully as it welcomes having Darcy spread out beneath me.

I suck in a breath as Max strokes between my cheeks with two deft fingers, smearing the cold lube along my crack and massaging the improbably small, tight space where he expects me to yield and—oh, *fuck*.

'What's he doing?' Darcy asks, all big, curious eyes and flushed skin beneath me as she takes in my reaction

Max beats me to it. 'Prepping this fine little arse with a couple of fingers. He's getting so good at it.'

'I've always been a fast learner,' I say with a wince-slash-laugh as he twists his fingers.

'So advanced,' Max croons, pulling out and replacing his fingers with the obscene mass of his crown, which he drags slickly over my entrance. 'Don't worry, there's enough lube on it to run a brothel for a year.' He drops his head and whispers in my ear, breath warm on my neck and voice ominous enough to strike fear into my heart.

'But—stay still, dammit—remember when you're stuffed so full of me you think you might split open that this is what you chose tonight. You walked away from safe, and "normal", whatever the fuck that is, and vanilla. You chose this, my boy, and you'll take whatever I give you.'

My boy. Jesus. It's exactly the same turn of phrase Dad used, and I should be horrified by that in itself, just as I should be horrified by the memory of how scathing and contemptuous it felt earlier. Now, though, on Max's lips, as he rubs his grotesquely large dick against this most private, vulnerable part of me and prepares to commit an act I've been told is worthy of hellfire, *it really fucking works*, and I hope my groan tells him that. I'm so hard inside Darcy it's astounding.

'Give it to me,' Darcy says, her voice breathy, and I can tell she's in that same state of dizzying need that I'm in, where Max's words and this position have whipped her into something approaching delirium. 'Whatever he gives you, if it's too intense, give it to me. I'll be your outlet—I want it all.'

I stare down at her in wordless admiration. This cascade effect, this symbiosis between us, is everything to me. She'll take the pain, the physical intensity, the emotional overwhelm. She'll be my vessel; she'll let me pour into her body the same profound love and bottomless desire Max intends, I have no doubt, to pour into mine.

'Thank you,' I mouth, and she smiles beatifically.

'Jesus Christ,' Max grits out. 'My absolute favourite little sluts. Fuck, I love you. Hang on.'

He follows his *hang on* with a drive so aggressive that I make the kind of choked up grunt I'd make if he punched me in the stomach, and I shunt straight into Darcy, who moans far more prettily, her eyes wide with shock.

'Jesus Christ,' I tell Max.

Fuck me. He hasn't just notched his crown inside me—the whole bloody organ must be more than halfway in. This escapade is less like a game of dominos and more like operating heavy machinery, his dick being the cast-iron lever that, when engaged, wedges everything else into place. I'm pretty sure he could operate entire railway systems, shunting sidings and whatever the fuck else into place with that monster.

I'm burning, my flesh screaming where he's stretching me, but I'm so hard, too, and it's all some magical muddle of sensation that feels greater than the sum of its parts.

'Trust me,' he says, which I'm sure he means sincerely but is pretty fucking funny, if you consider what he's doing to me right now, and he goes one more time. He ruts into me, and another few key inches of prime digestive real estate burn like they'll never be the same again, and I inadvertently fuck Darcy harder.

Max's body is a furnace behind me, above me, radiating

heat, while beneath me Darcy's expressive face and beautiful body take our combined onslaught.

And then, finally and impossibly, he's in, and he slides his palm over my stomach and down to the place where Darcy and I are joined, his fingertips brushing the wet flesh there, and his *huh* tells us everything we need to know about how miraculous he, too, finds this.

'So shall I—' I start to ask, and he kisses across my shoulder.

'You worry about Darcy,' he says, 'and I'll worry about you. You won't have much choice, anyway.'

I won't, it turns out. When he starts moving properly, my body becomes a channel, taking his thrusts and harnessing that energy and delivering it to Darcy with brutal thrusts of my own. Max's moves become my moves; I'm effectively letting him fuck Darcy by proxy.

But if a channel sounds passive, my experience is anything but, because these two people who love me, who've waited for me to become a man who's free to love them in the way they deserve, are pouring their adoration into me and wringing it out of me.

Like every other fucking thing Max does, he's filling me up to the point of overwhelm and pushing me to the point of insanity, and it's so *much* I can barely breathe. Darcy was right. She's my outlet, she lets me drive that insupportable intensity into her body, and she takes it all.

We're a machine, the three of us, slick and oiled and rhythmic, a grouping that's as electric in practice as it is unlikely in theory. Our bodies work in sync, the air filled with Max's grunts and Darcy's moans and my own sounds of frantic, primal need.

Darcy comes first, thank fuck, because I'm seconds away from losing myself inside her. I fuck her through it, my movements rough, involuntary, thanks to the pounding I'm getting from behind. I now speak Darcy Orgasm like it's my mother tongue, and this one is special. Powerful.

Her eyes squeeze shut; her cries are raw, unfiltered, as she bucks beneath me, and when her inner muscles clench around mine I am a goner. Max is pounding me in a place so deep, so *good*, I can survive it no longer. I'm pure sensation, front and back, my body singing. And when I let go, emptying myself into Darcy, Max makes damn sure he fucks out every last drop before he lets himself go with a roar of triumph that sounds a lot, to my blissed-out ears, like *I told you so*.

After we've unplugged ourselves from each others' bodies, we lie in a hot, sticky, sated mess, arms and legs intertwined, Darcy's arms tightly around me and Max's heartbeat pulsing against my temple, both ways of reminding me they're here to stay.

The threads of that fucking cloak of shame have well and truly unravelled now in the hands of these two gorgeous, golden people. All that time, I thought I was adequately sewn together, but they found my loose ends.

They pulled, and they haven't stopped pulling. They've laid me bare now, and, miracle of miracles, they like what they've uncovered beneath all those impossibly neat seams of tightly stitched, repressed bullshit.

They tell me they love it, in fact.

EPILOGUE - DEX

On its first day of trading, Wolff Holdings traded up as much as twenty percent. No surprise given that the book—the list of investor requests for stock allocations—went from five times covered before Max went on the road to ten times covered by the time the corporate roadshow ended.

That shouldn't be much of a surprise either.

Think about it.

The guy got me, the most closeted, judgemental dick in the history of queerness, to kiss him within two hours of meeting him.

He was always going to charm the pants off every investor he met.

Bottom line: Max is now revoltingly rich—on paper, at least—and even more arrogant than he was when I met him, and I'm disgusted with myself at how much of a turn-on the latter is. Darcy and I are both total sluts for arrogant, power-hungry arseholes, it turns out.

And when said arsehole is, behind closed doors, the

most tender, passionate, relentlessly caring partner you could ever fathom, it's impossible to resist him.

In all seriousness, he's earned every ounce of his success and I burst with pride at every sight of him, which is a lot, because his handsome mug is everywhere. It turns out, this pride of ownership, this pure delight of hearing colleagues and clients and the press marvel at what a force of nature Max Hunter is and knowing he can't sleep at night unless he's curled up around you?

It's a feeling nothing could have prepared me for. And, as news of our relationship spreads across the City, I come in for my fair share of handshakes and back-slapping. It's so unexpected and so delightful that I suspect Max may have done the impossible: bubble-wrapped my coming out by folding it into the narrative of the IPO, so I'm automatically protected. I'm endorsed by association; I'm Max Hunter's guy, and he's the man who's made every institutional investor's Q4 performance numbers look pretty fucking stellar, and if the industry darling loves me, then I'm okay by everyone else.

I'd be naïve to think it will always be like this, or that there isn't nasty or homophobic or jealous vitriol doing the rounds, but I can't shake the idea that, however upsetting and difficult I found it to come out to my father, I've got away lightly.

I'll add it to the long list of things for which I'm indebted to Max, and, when the fear that I'll never be able to repay him and Darcy for saving me and loving me and accepting me and pushing me and every other fucking thing threatens to overwhelm me, I'll remind myself of my favourite truth: that they love me for me, and my very existence is repayment enough.

Unstitch

'Is it okay?' Max barks at Darcy for the tenth time. 'Are you happy with it?'

She laughs that gorgeous, tinkling laugh to which we're addicted and, to her credit, doesn't sigh at his repetition. 'It's the most stunning thing I've ever, ever seen in my life.'

He frowns down at her, and I can tell he's trying to hold in the emotion. 'You clearly haven't been looking in the mirror enough.'

'Oh my God, stop it!' she cries, turning to me in time to see me shake my head in quiet amusement, because he's *good*. 'How are Dex and I supposed to cope when you're *this* adorable? Right?'

'That was smooth, even for you,' I tell him, because someone's got to keep him humble. 'Must be the white tie, making those sweet nothings slip off the tongue like honey.'

'Fuck off,' he says, but he's grinning now, and Darcy's squishing his cheeks.

'It's incredible,' I tell him honestly. 'Even if it comes with, er, conditions. You did good.' I glance behind me at the brutish security guard standing outside the open door of our bedroom.

Max has twisted God knows how many arms tonight, in that way of his so charming that the poor jewellers weren't even aware of it, and borrowed an eight-figure diamond necklace from Chopard for Darcy to wear to the Wolff Holdings gala tonight. It's so valuable, it comes with its own ear-pieced guard.

It's his way of making up for the fact that she wouldn't let him buy her a new dress. He was all for Darcy showing up on our arms in couture, but she insisted on wearing her custom Givenchy number from Gen's wedding. Max wasn't impressed—he said the press would pick up on the fact that she'd worn the same dress at both events—and she argued that was precisely the point.

'You don't get chances more public than this to send the message that it's more than okay to rewear clothes, especially things this timeless,' she told him.

Even Max couldn't argue with that.

Hence the necklace, to "show the dress in a new light" (his turn of phrase).

Whatever. I didn't have the privilege of knowing Darcy then, or of dancing with her under a French sky while Santiago Vale crooned onstage. I didn't have the privilege Max had, but I still wonder that anyone could *ever* get enough of Darcy looking like this. She could wear it every day and still take my breath away each time.

Her hair is up in a chic, messy arrangement, piled on top of her head in russet coils with tendrils framing her face. Those huge blue eyes of hers look even more arresting than usual tonight, courtesy of the dark, smoky makeup ringing them. The hair and makeup team Gen recommended has certainly made the most of her devastating assets.

As for the dress itself, it's downright sinful, with all that sea foam silk adorning her breasts and arse and draping low at the back. It's simultaneously the classiest and sexiest thing I've ever seen, and I'm bursting with pride already.

THERE'S COMING out to your family, and there's disclosing your relationship to your boss and Compliance department, and there's getting slowly, awkwardly used to your private life being public knowledge across the City, and then there's *this*—walking the red carpet outside the Savoy Hotel before pausing with Max and Darcy to pose for photos in front of the backdrop featuring The Wolff Foundation's logo.

We arrive right behind Gen and Anton. Once they've cleared the photo area, we stand together, Darcy looking every inch a movie star, her looks eclipsing her pale green silk and diamonds. Max and I flank her, our arms around her waist. We're both in white tie tonight, in accordance with the dress code, only he's wearing custom Tom Ford and I'm in custom Lanvin.

It's not just the financial press here tonight. Every fucking society page in the UK, and plenty from across the pond, are represented here. The sea of lenses assembled in the quiet side street leading up to The Savoy is pretty fucking intimidating.

Within a few hours, anyone who cares will be able to take their pick of features about us, from the financially focused (the success of Wolff's IPO and Max's speculated net worth) to those celebrating the fact that there is finally an openly queer CEO at the helm of one of the UK's biggest companies and, inevitably, the snide right-wing commentaries questioning how the fuck we three deviants dare flaunt our perversions so brazenly and speculating on the moral demise of this once-great country.

I take a particular satisfaction from knowing that our smiling faces will greet my still-furious father from the neat stack of morning papers when he walks through the lobby of his investment firm tomorrow morning.

Max's arm rests just above mine along Darcy's back, and it strikes me how anchoring his touch is. How right this symmetry feels—Darcy in the middle, resplendent in her finery, and us guys flanking her in almost identical tuxedos, all three of us radiant with happiness.

The Rule of Three.

We understand its power from childhood, long before we're capable of analysing why it's so potent. Three is the magic number in storytelling. Oration. In any form of communication required to pack a punch. From Obama's rhetoric to the Three Little Pigs and the three-act story structure, the number three satisfies and regales and inspires.

So why the hell it's taken me this long to embrace, or even accept, the love the three of us share as the perfect foundation for a life built on happiness and truth, I have no fucking clue.

Max and I share a glance, a smile, over Darcy's head. It's fleeting, but in this moment, I understand everything he needs me to understand. How much he loves us both. How proud he is. How much it means to him to have Darcy and me here tonight to support him publicly.

It helps that he's told me all this over and over.

I have no way of knowing this right now, but these poses, offered up to the baying crowd of paparazzi, won't be the ones that make the majority of tomorrow's front pages.

Rather, the tabloids and broadsheets alike will pay up for a candid shot by one of Getty's photographers snapped during the champagne reception.

In it, Max has his arm tightly, possessively, around Darcy's shoulders. She's ravishing and directing her smile off camera while chatting animatedly to Gen and Anton.

But he's not looking at her.

He's leaning in towards me, brushing his lips lightly over my cheek. My eyes are closed in bliss. I must only have shut them for a second, but the photographer has captured that exact, flawless moment.

A moment that looks to this man like the most accurate depiction of perfect happiness he's ever seen.

It's a photo that will one day end up in pride of place, next to our favourite shots of our wedding day and our children, on the mantlepiece of the big white villa in Holland Park that Max will insist on buying. He'll insist later this evening, in fact, when we've all collapsed in our suite at the Savoy after too much dancing and he's pulled up the listing on his iPad.

He'll tell us that, as soon as he saw it, he knew it was the home the three of us would grow old in together.

THE END

Want to see Dex and Max proposing to Darcy in Lake Como? Me too! Download the swoony bonus epilogue here:
https://BookHip.com/MVMHWPG

What's hotter than the brother's best friend trope?
Brother's worst enemy.
That's right, Natalie is getting an enemies-to-lovers, billionaire romance with Adam in **Unbind**. Preorder here:
https://mybook.to/unbind_alchemy

A NOTE FROM ELODIE

Dex has been in the back of my mind as a character since I mentioned him fleetingly in *Unfurl*. Belle's hot, shadowy and probably fucked-up brother would make a fantastic MMC at some point, I mused.

Meanwhile, I fell pretty hard for Max from the moment he walked into Anton's office and begged Anton to let him help bang Anton's executive assistant (yes, I'm so predictable).

I planted Darcy in *Unveil*, and was idly considering making her and Dex an unlikely pair. But it wasn't until I was writing the *Unveil* epilogue that I realised the three of them needed to be together. It was one of my absolute favourite lightbulb moments when it went off in my head!

The person I am today is best described as a straight woman in a heteronormative marriage. Dex's journey of discovering his true sexuality is arguably not mine to tell.

But, if you've read *Unfurl*, you'll know that the journey through purity culture and religion at its most toxic and sickening absolutely *is* my story to tell, as is the journey of finding the courage to overturn everything you've been told is an absolute truth in favour of seizing on alternative truths.

There were times in my convent education that I had Big, Scary (and very fucking intense) Feelings for classmates I absolutely had no business having feelings for, feelings that caused me endless nights of worry over the years that I may not, in fact, be the straight little Catholic I was raised to be. That I may at some point face terrifying choices over living my truth and causing heartache and division.

I've made peace with a lot of this over the years. I hope that the messages we're imparting to our children come close to what Max told Dex:

> 'You get to exist in the world as yourself and not change a single fucking thing to accommodate anyone else. Understood? You're allowed to go out there, and take up space, and stand in the middle of a restaurant full of your industry peers and fucking *revel* in it when a man kisses you and tells you you're his favourite part of his day. You deserve all that. You deserve everything you've ever wanted.'

But I still ache for the conflicts I felt when I was younger, and believe me when I tell you it took no effort at all to step into Dex's shoes and feel every second of the intense turmoil he faced when he took the steps he needed to take to secure his own happiness.

I'm in love with Dex, Max and Darcy and their own beautiful manifestation of the magical Rule of Three. Thank you so much for reading their story!

Elodie xx

Come join the fun in my **FB reader group** - we'd love to have you.
https://www.facebook.com/groups/3060624120889625

ACKNOWLEDGMENTS

This is the fifth Alchemy book I've published in fifteen months, and it doesn't happen on its own. Far from it!

First, I'd like to thank my readers across the entire process:

My beta readers, Jennifer Brooks Brown and Lyndsey Gallagher, for their flexibility, wisdom and words of encouragement.

Jennifer also proof-read the book—your eagle eye is amazing. Thank you for always dropping everything for me, and please apologise to Bailey for her cancelled walks! I'm sure you'll make up for it when the audio comes out...

Thank you to my ARC readers, not only for reading and reviewing but for your lovely comments in my ARC reader Facebook group. You're the best people to unleash my precious book babies on. Thank you for loving my characters as much as I do and welcoming them into the world so enthusiastically.

A massive thank you to my Nerds—my Facebook group members—who show up for me very single day. You are my tribe and my favourite people. To all my readers—every time one of my books makes it through the crazy jungle of your TBR to your actual kindle it feels like a miracle.

THANK YOU FOR READING!

I have a very special thank you to say to Kathryn Nolan, who did a sensitivity read of this book and made suggestions with such wisdom and grace—thank you, my friend! I'm so grateful, and I'm so damn happy I flew across the Atlantic and met you!

I'd like to thank my fairy godfather, Bobby Kim. Running my ads is the least of the value you add—you're my Yoda and my business coach. You're one of the smartest, kindest and most hardworking people in the industry and I feel so grateful to call you a friend and mentor.

Thank you to Podium, who's taken a chance on this entire series. I cannot WAIT to hear what you guys do with Dex, Darcy and Max!

A huge thank you to Mitchell Wick and Michelle Lancaster for entrusting me with this stunning, stunning photo. Mitch-as-Dex inspired so much of the character of Dex for me as I was writing, and *that* facial expression inspired *that* office scene (oh yes).

To all the influencers who've supported me on my journey, I love you, and I feel honoured to work with you wonderful humans. A particularly big virtual hug to Tierney Page for supporting me so noisily and letting me steal her "wetter than a nun in a cucumber field" line for this book.

And finally, to all my author friends—Lyndsey, Rosa, Luna, Isa, Ryan and all the others with whom I FaceTime and WhatsApp and voice note—this is a tough industry. Working it all out together makes it so much more bearable, and even fun! I love you guys.

Elodie xx

ALSO BY ELODIE HART

All my books can be read as standalone.

ALCHEMY

Unfurl

Undulate

Unveil

Untether

Unstitch

Unbind

Always Alchemy

SERAPH

Audacity

By my real name, Sara Madderson:

LOVE IN LONDON

Parents and Teachers

A Fair Affair

A Very London Christmas

Falling Stars

Wilder at Heart

∼

SORREL FARM

Food for Thought

Heaven on Earth

Make Me Sweat (related material)

A Manny for Christmas

∼

STANDALONE

The Rest is History (coming to audio in July 2025)

Printed in Great Britain
by Amazon